Miss Percy's Pocket Guide

Miss Percy's Pocket Guide

to the Care and Feeding of British Dragons

Quenby Olson

World Tree Publishing

Miss Percy's Pocket Guide (to the Care and Feeding of British Dragons) is a work of fiction. Names, characters, places and incidents are products of the author's imagination or are used fictitiously. Any resemblance to actual events or locals or persons, living or dead, is entirely coincidental.

ISBN-10: 8-986224602

ISBN-13: 13: 979-8-9862246-0-2

Published in the United States of America by World Tree Publishing.

First Edition: June 2022

1 2 3 4 5 6 7 8 9 WTEP B2222

DEDICATION

To my cat, Dog (Nermal, Jerkface):
You peed on our things. You brought us mice and let them
loose in the house. We constantly had to trim your rear end
hair so you wouldn't get poop caught in it. And the hairballs,
oh my gosh.
But there would absolutely and 100% be no Fitz without
you.
I love you and I miss you.

Miss Percy's Pocket Guide

CHAPTER ONE

It was once a commonly-held belief that dragons were nothing more than creatures pocketed into the realm of myth and fairytale. But man also once believed the Earth to be flat, and that we sat with prim and unswerving confidence at the center of the universe.

Now it is merely man himself who believes himself to be seated at the center of everything. And - oh! - what a precarious position to maintain when that previously dismissed realm of myth and fairytale chooses to kick your chair out from under you.

-from the Prologue to Miss Percy's Pocket Guide (to the Care and Feeding of British Dragons)

Great Uncle Forthright was dead, and Mildred's toast had gone soggy on one side.

It wasn't the most pleasant of ways to begin one's day. The death more than the toast, of course, though Mildred had only spare memories of her Great Uncle Forthright and the soggy toast rushed into the lead as an immediate impediment to her current happiness.

But there was an edge to Diana's tone as she read over the letter—Mildred's letter, but her sister had plucked it up from the top of the pile and slit into it with her knife as if things like addresses and private communications were irrelevant—that had brought with it the news of Great Uncle Forthright's more-than-timely demise. Her words dropped like pebbles into still water, creating ripples that would no doubt have an effect on the rest of Mildred's day.

Ah, well. Perhaps the soggy toast would have to relinquish its early victory.

"Who is Great Uncle Forthright?" It was Belinda who asked, the only one of the Muncy children permitted to speak-without-being-spoken-to at the breakfast table.

(Belinda was seventeen years old and on her way towards being engaged to marry one Mr. Bertie Sampson. That is, if Mr. Sampson could be convinced that his own future happiness depended not on the liveliness of various Great Uncles or the humidity of his morning baked goods, but rather on being permanently attached to a woman who may or may not have "accidentally" set fire to Cynthia Bowlin's hair when the rumor went 'round that Mr. Bertie Sampson planned on asking Miss Bowlin to dance two country dances with him at Mr. and Mrs. Carvin's ball one month prior.)

"An eccentric," Diana said, her gaze still shifting from side to side as she read the second page of the letter. "Our mother's uncle, wasn't he?" She glanced up at Mildred, but her attention failed to linger long enough for Mildred to venture a reply. "Ghastly man. Never married, if I recall. Or if he did, there weren't any children." She turned over a page, her nose wrinkling. "Always in trouble for rambling about the countryside, spending all of his money on *artifacts*." That last word spoken in a voice reserved for mentions of indelicate body functions or something called 'the middle class.' "Mother loved him. Familial ties, I expect. But I always thought he—oh!" Her lips tightened into a rosebud. Her gaze returned to Mildred. "You're to receive an inheritance."

Mildred pushed her most recent bite of sausage from one

side of her mouth to the other. "Me?" she managed to say without spraying half-chewed meat over her corner of the table. "But I hardly remember him."

"I guess that doesn't matter to eccentric Great Uncles." She looked at the letter again. "Doesn't say what it's to be. Money? Oh, wouldn't that be a blessing. The girls could use some new gowns, and perhaps we could finally fix the remnants of that wall out past the east side of the garden."

"May I have a new fan if we're to have more money?" Belinda's dark eyebrows climbed high on her forehead. "Only Miss Lewis has an ivory one and mine's only painted wood."

"We'll see, we'll see." Diana's words sounded distracted. No doubt she was already performing a few feats of basic arithmetic in her head.

Mildred set down her knife and fork, wiped her mouth with her napkin, and drew in a deep breath. "May I see the letter, please?"

Diana stared at her from the other side of the table, her eyes wide and unblinking. "Why?" She shrugged. "I'm telling you everything it says."

"But I should like to read it for myself."

She clicked her tongue. "Oh, very well. But let me finish first, there's only a few more lines."

In her mind, Mildred reached across the table and snatched the two pages from her sister's hand. It was a lovely daydream, one that made her sit up a little taller in her seat, as if the mere power of her imagination was enough to fill her with a confidence she would never dare to put into practice. But the vision buoyed her through the rest of Diana's reading of the letter, so that Mildred was able to take it from her with a muttered "thank you" rather than a few choice words that remained locked up safe inside her head.

"I expect it's because you're the eldest," Diana said as she returned to her own breakfast, left to sit and congeal on her plate while she had been distracted by the letter. "Of course, if Great Uncle Forthright had given the matter the proper amount of thought, he would have left something directly to me or to the children. But you…"

Mildred swallowed. She swallowed because the words "Oh, shut up you stroppy cow" were balanced on the tip of her tongue, threatening to grab a hairpin and pick the very lock that held them back.

"This was dated three weeks ago." She looked at the direction on the front, written in a near unintelligible scrawl. Astonishment rippled through her that the thing had even managed to find its way to her at all.

"Hm. Well." That was it. Diana had lost all interest in the letter, though no doubt its contents were still plinking about inside her head like coins in a purse.

The letter was written in a neater hand than the direction on the front, but only by a little bit. Mildred couldn't tell if it meant the missive was composed in haste or if the writer was possessed of abominable handwriting skills.

There were several details stated in the letter that her sister had left out of the previous discussion. Apparently Great Uncle Forthright had lived to the ripe old age of ninety-four. He had died, not from some chronic malady or heart seizure, but from tripping over a tree root and falling into a hole he had dug in search of a lost Roman treasure supposedly hidden away by Boudica nearly two millennia before.

There was also a line dedicated to his love of mutton hand pies. Mildred read through the rest of the letter searching for any particular relevance to that reveal, but found nothing.

"It doesn't…" she began, but faltered into silence when she realized that everyone else was already excusing themselves from the table, leaving only Mr. Muncy behind. (Diana's husband, the sort who lived behind a newspaper or a book or any sort of reading wall that was meant to deter people from approaching in an oh-look-he's-reading-I'll-not-bother-him sort of way. This, of course, did not always work, as some people [re: Diana] took the presence of reading material to mean that the person reading was obviously bored and most likely pining away for the company of others [i.e., Diana when she was in need of a receptacle for her general complaints about life and motherhood] and would certainly have no compunction against setting aside their book with eagerness to listen.)

"It doesn't mention what the inheritance is," she went on, to herself, and the back of Mr. Muncy's newspaper. "Or why I'm to have it. Or how I'm to procure it."

She looked down at her plate. Her breakfast was only half-eaten. It was cold. Betsy had already scurried out from the kitchen to begin clearing the table. With a sigh that carried a lifetime's weight of disrespect and disregard and several other words beginning with a similar prefix, Mildred picked up the last of her drooping toast and pushed her chair back from the table.

She still held the letter as she walked up the stairs. The letter in one hand, the toast in the other. She munched on the toast as she returned to her room, that tiny little thing stuck under the eaves and where, after seventeen years of sleeping and dressing and bathing and hiding away, she still hit her head on the slanted ceiling and still bit out the same curse every time.

Her room was cold when she opened the door and slipped inside. She had to slip inside as the door wouldn't open fully because of the aforementioned ceiling. So she turned sideways and shimmied through the gap and breathed again once she was through. She then proceeded to stub her toe on the corner of the chest at the foot of her bed, and saved herself at the last minute from rearing up in pain and slamming the back of her head into the ceiling.

But at least no one bothered her here, tucked away as she was like an old mop and bucket. The children didn't play in this part of the house, and while the ceiling did leak in one corner, and while the view from the window was of a small compost heap beside the kitchen garden, it was still her own space.

Well, her own space in her brother-in-law's home. But it was better than nothing.

Wasn't it?

Of course it was. At least she had a bed and clothes and warm food and books to read. At the end of the day, she didn't really think she could give up a soft bed and a good book, even if her room did sometimes smell a bit mildewy on cloudy days.

She opened the letter again and read over the two pages of meandering scrawl. Her Great Uncle Forthright...

No, she didn't remember much of him. He'd been old, the last time she'd seen him. But she'd been a child at the time and almost everyone older than her would've fallen into the category of "decrepit figure about to crawl into their coffin" to her young, unsullied eyes. She recalled white hair worn much too long, and a wiry figure that never seemed to stop fidgeting about. And he'd given her a coin. A small thing, with a hole cut into the center and words in a language she didn't understand stamped around the edge.

And then Diana had taken the coin and tried to spend it on some ribbon for one of her dolls and Mildred had never seen it again.

She told herself she had forgotten that part of the story until just then. But she hadn't, really. Her vexation at losing her precious coin had remained with her, the kind of stalwart reaction that only the very young seem capable of achieving with such implacability. Little good her stubbornness had achieved, except to harden that initial vexation from its tiny crumb of coal into a glittering diamond that occasionally caused her to catch her breath at random moments. A feeling like missing a step on the stairs, like her throat closing around that last morsel of food she thought she had swallowed properly. A feeling like...

No, no. This was all silly. She folded up the letter and stuffed it into the top drawer of her dresser, tucked away with her stockings and gloves and other bits and pieces she had no place for. An inheritance from a Great Uncle she hardly remembered... Well, whatever it was, it wouldn't be much. The man had not been rich, had he? Most likely only comfortable enough to be permitted a place in society as an eccentric, rather than carted away as a loon if he'd had less than a few coins to rub together. But certainly not rich. At least not prosperous enough that Diana had taken any pains to ingratiate herself with him in the hopes of acquiring a large legacy in the event of his death. Her sister was not the sort to allow the opportunities connected with affluent and superannuated relatives to so easily slip through her fingers.

It was the thunder of footsteps that pulled her from these thoughts, as it so often was. The children had finished their breakfast and escaped the nursery again. Mildred gave herself one of those fortifying moments people often need before facing a task they know they will dislike but must endure anyway. Not really a girding of one's loins, but rather something equivalent to a slight shift of one's undergarments into a less chafing position.

It was the same routine, day after day, varying only according to changes in the weather or if someone was feeling poorly. (If Mildred was feeling poorly, she usually kept such information to herself. An admittance of illness tended to instigate an odd sort of one-upmanship with her sister where Diana would begin to complain about all of the ailments currently plaguing her until she had already described the details of her death some days before and yet was still managing to grouse from amid the folds of her winding sheet. If Mildred needed help of the medicinal variety, it was often safer to go to one of the servants or circumvent the household entirely and pay a visit to the doctor herself.)

First, she would herd the children back into the nursery.

Then she would run through their lessons with them. (Reading, writing, and arithmetic only. Such superfluous subjects as music and drawing and languages were deemed unnecessary by the fact that Diana had done very well without any talent beyond a self-aggrandized competency at composing poems about flowers and summer days.) If the weather was pretty enough—that was, if it wasn't storming in some Biblical fashion—then the children would be herded again outside to play. Somewhere in there a meal was acquired, usually eaten either in the aforementioned outside or in the kitchen. And then the day would unravel towards its inevitable end, Mildred feeling as if each minute was only crossed with the effort of pushing a boulder up the side of a mountain.

(There were two children in addition to Belinda, the eldest: Matthew and Nettie, close enough in age that the difference really doesn't bear mentioning. But the boy was short and quarrelsome and existed as little more than his mother's pet. Nettie, instead of taking after either parent, chose to inherit her personality from a pack of rangy wolves. Though Mildred wondered if that might be unkind to the generally accepted character of wolves at large.)

It was how this day passed, with its slow, steady ticking away of the hours. The cries and shouts of the children became inseparable from the soft ringing in Mildred's ears, and the sigh that slipped out of her as she returned to her tiny room to change for dinner carried the victorious relief of a champion standing over the fallen body of his foe.

She sat on her bed and stared at the wall for several minutes. Or perhaps it was an hour. It was often difficult to tell the passage of time without the wants and needs of children not her own pulling her from one end of the day to the other. Maybe, she thought, Diana could be convinced to hire a proper nurse or even a governess for the children should the inheritance from Great Uncle Forthright consist of something monetary in nature.

Mildred had already come to terms with the truth that if this promised inheritance was worth anything, Diana would claim it for herself. No, no. That wasn't quite true. No, she would claim it for the family. And didn't Mildred want to help the family? Wasn't she a part of the family, in her cupboard of a room and wearing the gowns her sister didn't want anymore? Hadn't they welcomed her into their home with open arms when she'd proven herself to be the spinster they always thought she'd be?

Mildred gripped the edge of the bed. Silly thoughts. That was what she told herself when they began to overwhelm her. Not that the thoughts themselves were silly, but that it was silly to waste time with them as long as her circumstances remained as they were.

And they would always remain this way, of course. She was forty years old. A difficult thing to believe most days, but she could not simply open the family Bible and shout at the date listed beneath her name and wait for the carefully calligraphed words there to rearrange themselves towards a more pleasing decade.

A deep breath, and she stood. She would dress for dinner, and she would eat with the family, and she would go to bed with a book and a candle and give a prayer of thanks for eyesight that hadn't failed her after all of these years of reading before bed with only a single flame to light the page.

Her progress towards her corner closet was interrupted by a knock on the door. It wasn't often that anyone bothered to knock on her door, both because she rarely had a moment of peace long enough for it to be interrupted, and because more often than not whoever was coming to interrupt that rare peace didn't bother to knock at all. But there was a knock, and Diana poked her head into the room before Mildred could give her leave to enter.

"Ah, I thought this was where you'd disappeared to." There was that tone again, the one that carried a light enough measure of scolding that she could never be accused of the offense directly. "Now, you do remember we're dining at the Lindons' tonight?"

No, she did not remember. Most likely it had never been mentioned to her, but it was simply easier to allow herself to be dismissed as forgetful so the others could plow forward with the conversation.

"We'll be taking Belinda with us tonight. She needs more practice in social settings, you know. The Lindons' son will be there, back from Cambridge, but I don't believe he did very well while he was there. Eustace? Or Eugene?" She waved a hand in front of her face, batting the disappointing Eustace/Eugene out of the conversation. "Either way, the children will be having their supper in the nursery, and if you could make certain they're in bed by eight o'clock?"

Mildred opened and closed her mouth several times while her mind pulled a few salient points from her sister's blather. First, that at no time had she been in consideration as a guest of the Lindons. Second: That the children would no doubt be on their very best (there was a great deal of sarcasm lacing these words as they skittered through Mildred's head) behavior with the knowledge that their parents and eldest sibling would be separated from them by several miles. And third: That Mildred no longer needed to change for dinner.

"Uh," she communicated, while a few of those points were still sorting themselves around behind her eyes. The single syllable was enough to act as acquiescence to Diana, who prattled on without the necessity of replies. In most situations, a mere object—preferably warm-blooded—was all that was needed to keep her tongue loosened.

Mildred saw the remainder of her evening sketched out before her. A small meal of cold, leftover things, probably eaten with the children or on her own in whichever room would cause the servants the least amount of trouble to prepare. (Her bedroom. It would be her bedroom.) But there was still the promise of the book and the candle and her bare toes wriggling between freshly laundered sheets once the rest of the house had gone quiet.

It really was the little things, she reminded herself, that raised each day to the level of something bearable.

And so Diana and Mr. Muncy and Belinda all packed themselves into the carriage and trundled off in the direction of the Lindons', leaving Mildred to chivvy the children into the nursery for their supper and chivvy them again into bed, the latter requiring over an hour of requests for numerous glasses of water and stories about dragons and then more water before Mildred finally put out the lights and shut the door on the beginnings of an argument on who had the flatter pillow.

She considered going to her room and making an early night of it, but a part of her couldn't resist the urge to spend some time in a house that didn't also contain her sister. There had been only a short period of time when they had not lived together, the first year of Diana's marriage. But then their father had breathed his last (their mother had died of consumption when they were eight and four, respectively), and so the house was passed on to a cousin and Mildred found herself without a place to live. Diana, having just given birth to Belinda, thought it the most prudent thing to have her sister come and stay with her until a regular nurse could be acquired.

Seventeen years later, and Mildred had just about given up hope that any sort of replacement would arrive.

She walked slowly through the house, admiring a few of the pieces that had come from their parents' home, including a miniature of their mother sitting on the mantel above the fireplace. Mildred remembered their mother. She wondered if Diana did, or if being the younger sister meant that she'd slowly lost all recollection of the former Mrs. Percy as the years had slipped away from them.

For a moment—well, for something longer than a moment, more along the lines of a solid quarter of an hour—Mildred wondered how things would've turned out if their places had been switched. If she, the elder sister, had been the one to marry and have a family, the one to offer a place to Diana when time would prove her incapable of finding a husband or a better situation for herself.

Funny enough, the imagery didn't please her as much as it had used to. A husband and children... Well, she lived with an example of that life every day, and now the question had become not how much she still wanted it, but instead how much longer it would be until the living diorama before her managed to snuff out the last cinder of desire she'd ever had for an existence mired in domesticity.

These were the thoughts that finally propelled her out of the drawing room and towards the stairs. Only a book and a good night's rest would clear her head, and she gazed up the length of the staircase with a yearning that—

There was a knock at the door.

Mildred paused, and removed her foot from the first step. And waited.

The knock came again.

So not her imagination then, and nothing she could blame on a wayward tree branch or a wayward cat or a wayward scrap of the house's outer shell banging against something else. The servants, she realized, had already found their way to their own beds, their own toes wriggling contentedly between freshly laundered—though lower quality—sheets.

Mildred hesitated. It was too late for any proper kind of caller. Several scenarios blossomed to life in her imagination while she crossed to the front door. Death was one of them. Robbers, another. Perhaps her sister and brother-in-law had been robbed on their way to the Larson's. Or maybe a group of robbers stood on the other side of the door, ready to strip the house bare of all its worthwhile trinkets and possessions.

Though she doubted that someone with larceny in their heart would go to the trouble of knocking on the front door.

She opened said door with a quick pull, fearful that at the last moment it would turn out to be a trick and there would be no one there at all. But all of her overimaginings were squashed at the appearance of Squire Manning on the front step. (Squire Manning was also rather squashed in appearance. This was through no fault or accident of his own, but simply that everything from his dress to the way he furrowed his brow to the curl of his hair made him look as if he were in a never ending process of being forced into a small canister. (Squire Manning also wasn't really a Squire, at least in any accepted definition of the word-he didn't own more than a few acres of land and there were no knights about for him to attend-but no one could remember a time when he did not call himself Squire Manning and apparently the constant insistence of an untruth proved to be more persuasive than the truth itself.))

"Miss Percy," Squire Manning ground out as soon as he was able, tipping forward from the waist in something that might have been a bow or might have been a momentary loss of equilibrium. "I didn't mean to startle you and all, but I was up and over at the Haversall's this afternoon, what with their great oak tree coming down and taking out the corner of their kitchen. You know we had some time trimming off all them branches, but they'll have a right good bit of firewood for next year once it's been stacked and seasoned for a turn, and they..."

The commentary continued for some time. More about the tree, the size of the stump still to be taken out, the work needed to repair the Haversall's kitchen, though the interior of the kitchen wasn't at all damaged and only one windowpane cracked by...

Mildred shifted her weight from foot to foot. She would have invited the poor man inside, but he didn't stop speaking long enough for her to do more than touch her tongue to the back of her teeth before he was off again.

"... and then I said I had to drive past your place anyway, or Mr. Muncy's place as I should pronounce it, but the letter and the trunk were addressed to you, so I said I'd drop it by on my way back to the farm rather than force anyone to go out of their way."

He stopped speaking. Mildred realized she'd let her mind begin to wander about four minutes before arrival at this portion of the speech and now had no idea what Squire Manning was referring to. "The trunk?"

"Aye, it's not a big thing, but heavy enough for its size. Should I take it 'round the back for you or haul it in here? As I said, it's not very large, nothing out of the ordinary, but I thought you might want it coming through the front as it's for you and looks to be a pretty kind of thing."

Mildred stepped back, opening the door fully. "Here is fine." She peered out into the dark, where she could just make out the shape of Squire Manning's horse and cart and the silhouette of one of his sons hunched over the reins. "Do you need any help?"

"Nah, I've got Roger here," he said as he traipsed back down the front steps and walked in his hobbling gait towards the back of his cart. Roger, hearing himself thus spoken of, leaped down from his seat, helped his father take down the trunk, and together they carried it into the house and set it against the wall.

"The Haversalls will be glad to know it's made it to its intended destination after all," Squire Manning said, a little breathily from the exertion of hoisting the trunk from cart to house. (It also turned out to be much larger than the "not a big thing" that was originally promised. It was nearly the size of a regular travelling trunk, but with large brass locks and latches that made it look more like a show piece than something functional. Mildred agreed that it was pretty in its way, though the great hulk of the thing clashed with the rest of the foyer and no doubt her sister would despise it on sight.)

"And here." Squire Manning fished around in the pocket of his coat and produced a letter, all folded corners and smudged ink on the outside of it. "The Haversalls send their apologies for having opened the letter already, but they had thought it was directed to them at the first. When they saw your name in the salutations and what it was about, they said they folded it back up directly and didn't dare have another peep."

She took the letter, tilting it towards the light long enough to recognize the writing on the front as penned by the same hand that had composed the letter read over breakfast that morning.

"I'll go on and see myself out. Bow to the woman, Roger!" Squire Manning nudged his son with his elbow until Roger thought to dip his chin and raise his fingers to the brim of his cap.

Mildred watched both men until they climbed back onto their cart and Roger set the horse into motion. As soon as they'd turned around and were heading back down the drive, she shut the door, bolted it, and stood with her back against the wood. The letter was still in her hand. She hadn't opened it yet, but her hand had begun to perspire around it.

It had all happened so quickly, Squire Manning appearing with the trunk and the letter and now the trunk was there, an oversized bit of bulk taking up too much space in the narrow, cluttered foyer. The letter was in her hand, hers to read at her leisure without Diana assuming ownership of it.

"Oh," she said, when the matter finally made an impression on her thoughts. And then, "Oh dear," once she looked at the chest, looked again at the letter, and realized that her inheritance from Great Uncle Forthright had arrived.

CHAPTER TWO

It is thought that dragon eggs closely resemble the average oblong rock or stone as a sort of camouflage to protect them from predators. Though there is another theory to explain the hardiness of their outward appearance, and that is the belief that dragon eggs can lie in a state of dormancy for months or even years...

-from Chapter Seven of Miss Percy's Pocket Guide (to the Care and Feeding of British Dragons)

Mildred did not travel.

When she was younger, she had not thought much beyond the borders of England as being the whole summation of all the world and everything in it. Her early education did little to expand her views beyond this point, all of her history and geography being of the various kings and queens who fought over the same island, as if there must be some great treasure or natural wealth harbored somewhere between its rocky shores.

When she was older—but still young in comparison to her current age—and her education pronounced as complete, she thought only of her father and her daily life taking care of him while her sister was courted by Mr. Muncy and then taken away from them by the vows of matrimony. (Her education had consisted of the usual subjects of music—she could play the piano very well and had a natural ear for it, which was most likely why Diana did not like to hear her practice since it only illuminated the fact that Diana's skills with any sort of musical instrument could most flatteringly be described as "sick cat caught inside [insert instrument of choice here]—language, and only enough mathematics as it would take to manage a simple household budget and various economies.)

And then Diana had married, Belinda had been born, and so life had gone along as it did.

So Mildred had never shown a need for a trunk or any of the other great pieces of luggage. As a child, she had lived at her childhood home, and as an adult, she had lived with her sister, the latter being positioned only eleven miles away from the former. This probably went some way towards explaining her fascination with the large trunk now before her, with all of its shining brass trappings and leather handles and a general appearance of having a bit of the entire world, thousands of miles beyond England's ragged edges, scuffed across its corners.

Her first instinct was to hesitate. Opening it seemed like an irrevocable action, like popping the lid off Pandora's box and then complaining once one couldn't force the horrors back inside. She still held the letter—composed, as the first one was, not by Great Uncle Forthright's solicitor as she would have assumed, but by a Mr. Richard Gorman who styled himself as her Great Uncle Forthright's assistant, companion, and heir. That much would explain the rambling nature of the letters (this one mentioned a predilection for wool socks worn inside out) and perhaps even the near-illegible quality of the handwriting—but folded it closed and tucked it into the collar of her gown in order to free her hands.

She wiggled her fingers. A breath slid out of her, and she licked her lips, wondering why they suddenly felt so dry. Quickly, she thought. Before her family returned. Before this precious pocket of solitude was revoked from her. Tugging at her skirts, she lowered herself down to her knees, and flipped open the first latch.

Nothing unusual occured. No gleam of gold from between the knife-thin seams. No puff of smoke or dust or odd smells wafting into the air. The anticlimactic nature of that first latch clinking open allowed her to tackle the rest without another pause.

She raised the lid.

Well, she made an attempt at raising the lid. The lid retaliated with a creaking sound, much like the breaking of a book's spine, and then silence.

"Oh." She dusted off her hands, altered her position to better attack the recalcitrant lid from a different angle, but still nothing. (Mildred knew she was not weak, as far as the strength of gentlewomen over the age of forty was generally measured. She spent her days carrying trays, chasing the children and hoisting them away from situations they were better kept apart from, helping the servants with the kitchen garden, etc. So a trunk lid should not have been such an impediment.) She considered giving the thing a few kicks with her heel, thought better of it, and instead fetched a pie server from the kitchen and wedged it into the gap to use as a lever.

Several minutes and a ruined pie server later (she would later consider confessing the loss of the pie server, then perhaps putting it back and pretending she knew nothing about its demise, but in the end it went into the depths of her top drawer behind her stockings) she had pried the lid open enough to slide her fingers beneath, shove it upwards, and finally see what was inside.

It took her a moment to understand what was before her. Not that any of the items packed into the trunk were unknown to her at first glance, but that there were so... many...things...that it was a similar feeling to dumping out the contents of a box of puzzle pieces and expecting one's mind to have it all assembled within the span of a few seconds.

There were books, she noticed. Stacks of books tucked into every available space. And rocks, and loose papers, and old coins, and a few bits that looked like bones, and all sorts of little sacks and bags and smaller boxes that would need to be sorted through over what would most likely take a considerable amount of time.

Diana would be disappointed. Mildred briefly considered slamming the lid shut and dragging the trunk to some hidden corner of the house where her sister wouldn't discover it, if only to delay the inevitable scene that would play out at the knowledge that there would be no great boon of a pecuniary nature gifted to the family in the wake of Great Uncle Forthright's death. Only the detritus of his life and interests, and as much as Midlred's curiosity tingled to life (a sadly ironic turnabout, that her own interest in Great Uncle Forthright's adventures would be fully piqued when he was no longer around to guide her through them) at the prospect of sifting through the eclectic collection of items, none of it would hold Diana in the same thrall.

The clock in the drawing room chimed out the hour, and Mildred waited until it was finished to make her decision.

No doubt her family wouldn't return for at least another hour or more. The distance between their home and the Lindons' meant that the evening would have to be drawn out enough to make it worth the journey, and if Diana was going to take the time to have her hair curled and makeup applied (in a way that was meant to convey that she did not wear makeup, as she was often heard to criticize others for succumbing to the weakness of using powders or rouge while her own was caked in the creases of her eyelids) then they would most certainly not be home again before midnight.

Mildred chewed on her bottom lip, wondered if she should slip off to the kitchen again for a fortifying spoonful of jam or some cold chicken, but decided against it in favor of the treasures before her. Because, to her, it was treasure. Merely looking over the surface of it all was enough to draw from her memories a fleeting hint of the child she had once been, the one who had climbed trees and attempted to make fossils of her own handprints in mud and built boats for insects out of woven blades of grass.

It struck her as fiercely as a physical blow, those memories. She didn't know which was more difficult to believe, that she had once been such an adventurous child, or that her transformation into the woman she'd become had happened without her even noticing.

She made a small sound, not quite a word, but enough to put an end to that particular line of thought and keep her attention focused on the work before her. She had to be pragmatic about this. If turned over to Diana's care, no doubt the trunk and most of its contents would be tipped out into a rubbish heap. Anything with an aura of value about it (monetary, of course) would be kept or sold. But these were Mildred's things. She placed her hand on one of the books, the dusty kind that always responded to a person's touch with soft crackling sounds and a flutter of debris from its pages like a puff of pollen from between the petals of a flower. She had so few things that were hers, that hadn't been given away when she'd left her childhood home, that hadn't been lost or broken over the years.

But this… She experienced a sudden urge to embrace it, to pull the trunk and all of its contents into her arms and somehow find a way to tuck it into her bodice like another woman would a handkerchief or a spare glove. As soon as the family returned, her claim on it would be lost. Diana would oversee its emptying, its cataloguing of contents. She would decide what was worth keeping and what wasn't. Mildred would lose another piece of herself, another bit of that little girl she had once been, cowed into quietude and compliance by her younger sister.

Quickly and with a care that came from living nearly twenty years with people she wished to be noticed by as little as her physicality would permit, she began to sort things. She took comfort in the act, stacking the books one by one, separating out the loose papers—some flat, some rolled up like scrolls, some even bearing great globs of sealing wax as if it were suddenly the fifteenth century and there were medieval secrets contained on all those pages—before she moved to sifting through the piles of drawstringed bags and little wooden boxes and handfuls of random objects that appeared to have been tossed into the depths of the trunk before the lid was latched shut.

At the very bottom, tucked in the center of the trunk and wrapped up in a mass of rags and linens and something that looked very much like a finer silk scarf than anything Diana had in her collection, was a stone larger than any of the others Mildred had already pulled out of its depths. This one was as big as a brick, though not quite as heavy as one. It had an almost rounded shape to its surface, not rough and jagged and yet not polished smooth either. She turned it around in her hands several times, wondering at the size of it, at the unusual iridescence on its surface if she tilted it towards the light just so.

The way it had been wrapped up with such care made Mildred suspect there was something special about it. She had seen a few of the other stones, or the pieces of stones, complete with little crystals inside, and she wondered if this was a much larger specimen of the same thing. "Goodness," she breathed, and gave the thing a little shake, as though it was a trinket box and she was listening for the rattle of seashells and a tarnished charm bracelet.

And there, the trunk was empty. Its contents sat in a sloping ring around her, filling up the entryway like a curving archipelago of books and too many things for her to count. So she set her hands on her thighs and she licked her lips and she told herself to begin somewhere. The books went upstairs first. Diana would loathe them, would complain about the extra dust they would bring into the house, the space they would usurp from other, more important (to her) things. Mildred filled her arms with them and lugged them to her room, stack by stack, until they were all tucked away beneath her bed. She wanted to search through all the pieces, to touch every coin and jar, to experience the exhilaration of discovery her Great Uncle Forthright must have experienced as he'd collected everything during his travels around the English countryside.

By the time she was finished, her room was stuffed to bursting. Her drawers, her closet, beneath the bed, beneath her pillow, hidden in every place that offered a share of space were all of the things from the trunk.

And then she was left with a very large, very empty trunk filling up the foyer.

She could pick it up, or at least drag it somewhere. But there was no place inside the house where it would be easily overlooked. Unless she were to drape a tablecloth over it, decorate it with some cushions, and see if she could fool the other members of the household into ignoring it as only another piece of furniture that did not need to be where it was. (This seemed to be the core tenet of Diana's decorating style, to continually stuff more and more items into a room until there was no longer enough space leftover for the people who wished to comfortably inhabit it.)

No, it would have to go outside somewhere. Mildred stood up, rubbing at an acute ache in her lower back. She considered the stables first, but they were too busy, the trunk too likely to be found. There was an old shed at the edge of the back garden, one with a bit of crumbling roof and enough of a look of dereliction about it that no one seemed keen on bothering with it, perhaps hoping that nature would take over the work of repair and simply reclaim it if given a few more seasons.

Mildred nodded to herself. She wasn't sure the trunk

would fit through the back door, though. Rather than risk wasting time pulling it through the house, she latched it closed, opened the front door, and dragged it towards the steps. Much tussling and indelicate grunting commenced, the trunk banging none-too-gently down the front steps and into the drive.

She wondered that the rest of the household didn't wake and come to see what she was about, but she supposed they were all enjoying the brief interlude of quiet afforded to them by the older half of the family's absence. Halfway around the house, a sound brought her up short. Of course, she was outside, so there were all manner of sounds to catch her attention. Insects and animals, the soft hooting of an owl or the softer whoosh of a bat's wings. But this was not the usual ambient noise that drifted in through her open window after ten o'clock in the evening.

Whistling. That was what it sounded like. And not the whistle of wind or nocturnal creature, but a definite melody produced by human lips.

She paused, her hands still gripping the leather strap on the side of the trunk. Someone was near the house. On the road? Cutting across one of the fields? Again, as before, she wondered if she was in any sort of danger. There she was, a solitary woman out of doors after dark, where anyone could come upon her. But the man—she was certain it was a man now, as the whistling had become interspersed with snatches of humming that denoted the voice as belonging to either a man or a woman with a severe cold, and she assumed the former was more likely than the latter—was whistling, which did not seem the mark of someone plotting something nefarious. Unless they were sort who looked forward to committing the nefarious deeds they were plotting, in which case—

She closed her eyes, as if with that small movement she could shutter her imagination. Diana had always accused her of thinking too much, of letting her fancies run away with her. And now she was nearly alone in the house with a trunkful of interesting artifacts stashed into every nook of her room and apparently that was all it took to set her mind towards chasing after windmills.

"Miss Percy?"

"Yes?" Her eyes snapped open again. She recognized the voice, though she couldn't connect it to the identity of the speaker until she squinted through the moonlit darkness. He was nothing more than a shape at first. As her vision cleared, more and more details sharpened into focus. A hat, of course, because what gentleman would be out and about without a hat on his head? Broad shoulders and broad…well, a lot of broad. He was not a small man, their vicar. Mr. Wiggan, she reminded herself. Not that she needed a tremendous amount of reminding. She saw him nearly every week at church, though little more than that. But she had always thought him to be a kind, affable sort of gentleman, and the fact that he had managed to avoid any matrimonial machinations from Diana in an effort to see Belinda wed to a kind, affable gentleman with a steady living only made him rise in Mildred's esteem.

That's not to say that she spent a lot of time measuring the amount of esteem set aside for country vicars with broad shoulders, but… well.

He walked up to the wall that separated them, one of those low, rough stone walls that seem to exist as a use for all of the rocks everywhere than for any actual means of barricading and marking off property. "Is everything well?"

She still held the trunk. The trunk he was looking at, the direction of his gaze picking out the light from the gibbous moon above them. She couldn't very well move to stand in front of it, first because he'd already spotted it, and second because once she'd pulled it down the front steps she realized it was comparable in size to a small sofa. "Everything, yes." She smiled, then didn't. The last thing she needed was to look crazed. "I'm just moving this"—she gestured towards the trunk behind her, as if he might not have already noticed the hulk of it taking up the entire width of the path that led around the house— "trunk to the shed over there. Before my sister and her husband return. From the Lindons'." The smile threatened to return, but she forced it away. If four decades of life had taught her anything, it was that a lack of emotion on one's face kept people from paying attention to the words that accompanied that void of expression.

Mr. Wiggan took another step closer to the wall. "I was actually on my way home from the Lindons' myself."

Panic. That was what Mildred felt, what made her glance up the road in the direction from where Mr. Wiggan had been walking, as if her brother-in-law's carriage would be racing down behind him, hard on his heels.

"Oh, I excused myself early," he explained, seeming to notice her distress.

"And you walked?" It was six miles to the Lindons', give or take. "Did you even have time to stay for dinner?"

He shook his head, gave a vague wave of his hand. "I wasn't invited to dine with them. I mean, I was, but I had no wish to stay. I was there to speak with Mrs. Lindon about the organ for the church. We're to have a few of the pipes replaced next month and I..." He cleared his throat and capped off the dwindling of his speech with a light sucking of his bottom teeth. "Do you need any help, Miss Percy?"

"Help?" She blinked quickly, released a slow breath, and tried her best to not resemble a foraging creature caught digging through someone's refuse.

He jutted his chin towards the spot just behind her. "With your trunk, there."

"Ah!" She turned around and looked at it, as if it had sprung out of a crevice in the ground, despite the fact she still held onto it with one hand. "No, no. Thank you, but you shouldn't trouble yourself. I've managed it this far. I'm perfectly capable of finishing the task."

"I've no doubt you are perfectly capable, Miss Percy. My offer of assistance was in no way meant to undermine those capabilities. I simply—" He shrugged. "I would like to help."

"As our vicar?" she asked, not knowing why she did. Nervous babble, perhaps? She always did poorly when speaking with others, what she wanted to say and what she actually said never matching up as well as she would have preferred. "Setting an example for your parishioners?"

"As a person," he corrected, but with a smile of his own. She recognized it as a smile even in the darkness, that narrow gleam of teeth that was there and then gone again. "Because I should."

"All right." Again, there went her mouth before she could stop it. But those two words were enough to trigger him into action. He walked towards the end of the wall (this was after he took a step towards the wall itself, his furrowed brow and courageous expression giving a hint that he might attempt to lever himself over the stones with a tip of his body and swing of his legs, but he appeared to think better of it and instead went in search of the path that connected with the road instead) and met up with her on the other side of it.

"Here, I'll…" He took hold of the strap on the other end of the trunk and hefted it up.

"Oh, it's empty," she remarked at his clear bafflement at how light it was. "That's why I'm taking it out to the shed. The one around the back there? So it's not in anyone's way."

"And this chore couldn't wait until… oh, a daylight hour?"

Both hands returned to her own strap as they began walking the trunk along the side of the house. "It's sometimes easier to accomplish a task when there is no one about. To interfere, I mean."

Mr. Wiggan replied with something like a sound of agreement from the back of his throat. "I had the pleasure of seeing your family on my way out from the Lindons'. Your sister is, ah…"

"Yes," Mildred agreed. "She is."

They made it easily to the shed, where Mildred had to beat on the door several times before it would open. With some careful maneuvering they were able to wedge the trunk inside along with all of the broken, rusted garden implements left to moulder there. She was brushing bits of dust and cobweb and torn, dried leaves from her skirt as they returned to the front of the house where the angle of the moon's light made it seem like their presence together was less clandestine than it could appear to a random onlooker. Though Mildred wondered how many onlookers there could be wandering along the road two miles from town. Well, apart from Mr. Wiggan.

"Should I invite you in?" she asked, just as he finished straightening his coat and said, "Well, I shouldn't keep you."

She laughed nervously. He didn't. "I'm sorry," she went on. "I suppose it would be awkward for me to invite you in for tea at…I don't know what time it is."

"Late," he put in. "But probably no more awkward than the two of us shifting an old trunk into an even older shed in the middle of the night."

"Yes, you're probably wondering about that." She dared a slight smile. Not one so large that he would think she made a habit of dragging large pieces of luggage across the garden beneath the moonlight, but enough that he wouldn't think she made a habit of dragging large pieces of luggage across the garden beneath the moonlight.

"I will say I'm rather curious." He took off his hat in order to wipe his hand across his brow. The aforementioned moonlight reflected off the parts of his head visible through his thinning hair (Mildred took this opportunity to note that Mr. Wiggan was not the sort of man who attempted to hide the slow loss of his hair by covering up the bare patches with other hair combed over from the sides or the back of his head, choosing rather to keep it trimmed neat and short in a kind of acceptance of how things—at least of a follicular nature—were now to be) and lit up the small smile he offered to match her own. "Though if you're about to confess to hiding away a deceased personage inside that trunk, I would prefer you had not made me an accomplice to your crime and allowed me to assist you."

She gaped at him. It was probably written down somewhere, in some massive tome dedicated to etiquette and manners and whether or not one could rest one's elbows on a flat surface also meant for the serving of food, that making facetious comments about casual murder was as impolite as speaking about finances or private health matters. But her gape turned into a snort and then a laugh that she covered with the back of her hand.

"It was my uncle's," she explained. "Not the body." She squeezed her eyes shut. "I mean, there is no body. Except my uncle's body, of course. But his is surely buried in some churchyard or another proper place. For bodies. But the trunk belonged to my Great Uncle Forthright. And he died, as I mentioned, and the trunk passed to me." Bodiless, she wanted to add, but held herself back before she could scoop out any more shovelfuls of dirt from the pit she now wanted to tip herself into.

"An empty trunk?"

"It wasn't empty when it arrived." She clasped and unclasped her hands, then crossed her arms over her chest, now aware of the night's chill as she was no longer occupied with lugging large items hither and thither. "He left me an inheritance, of a kind. All sorts of things, really. Books and interesting stones and so much I haven't even gone through most of it yet. I have it all hidden away in my room, and —"

He dipped his chin, as if trying to see into her face better from beneath the brim of his hat. "Hidden away? Is it a secret, then?"

Mildred opened her mouth to say something, but closed it again. And then she opened her mouth and said the exact thing she'd wanted to for the first time, but simply needed to work up the courage to speak it out loud. "My sister was hoping for something more pecuniary in nature."

"Ah," he said, in that way that expressed several paragraphs of thought on the matter in a single, succinct syllable. "Hence the stashing away of the trunk in the middle of the night."

Mildred nodded. She looked at Mr. Wiggan then, wondering why he didn't laugh at the situation, or at her. And she wondered why she couldn't stop speaking to him about it now that she'd gone and started. Before today, she'd only traded the most perfunctory of phrases with him, the usual repetitions of "how-do-you-do" and "I-hope-you-are-in-good-health" or "what-a-shame-about-Mrs. Piston's-rheumatism" that made the rounds every Sunday. Ten years, at least, she'd known him. And then it struck her that she did not really know him at all.

"It will take some time to sort through everything," she said, because she didn't want to stop speaking, because speaking to him felt right and freeing and a little bit like talking to herself when there was no one around to listen. "Perhaps once I have a better idea of what I've been given, once I've made some lists"—Mildred was a champion list-maker, and had accepted the knowledge years before that the only way she could successfully progress from one hour to the next was with a neatly-penned list of deeds and chores and activities carrying her along—"I can tell her about the inheritance. Perhaps by then her disappointment will not be quite as sharp."

Mr. Wiggan cleared his throat. He did not move any closer to her. In fact, he took a step back. But it had been that clearing of the throat, the presage to a change in tone, to something that might be a secret for only the two of them, that made it seem as if someone had pulled a cord and drawn the night sky closer about them. "If you would like," he said, his voice indeed softer than before, "I could help with some of the items. I don't claim to be a great historian, but I have always had a high regard for the natural history of the area, and if you would like…" he faltered at the repetition.

"Yes, of course. That would be…"

"You could even bring some things to the vicarage, if you're concerned about keeping them here. I have plenty of…"

"Oh, that would be such a great help."

"…space, as it's only myself and Mrs. Babbinton shuffling about the place."

She was still nodding. She couldn't help it. How long had it been since she had shared such a long conversation with someone who wasn't her sister or her family? (Seven years, three months, thirteen days. Mildred had spent half a luncheon caught at a table with a Miss Dimples (her name wasn't really Miss Dimples, but Mildred was terrible with names and all she could remember about the girl was the very deep dimples that appeared in her cheeks when she laughed…which she had a tendency to do…over everything) who would not cease talking about the width of her elbows (Miss Dimples' elbows, not Mildred's) and how the season's fashion of long sleeves would not suit her uncommonly substantial joints.) Suddenly, like a greedy child stuffing their face full of candies from a jar, she wanted to grab hold of him and make him talk to her all night. Even if his conversation consisted of nothing but comments on the weather, or politics, or elbows, she was desperate to speak with someone so wholly unconnected with herself or her family.

"Tomorrow, then?"

She stopped nodding. "Tomorrow?"

"Is that too soon? We could try for—"

"No, no. Tomorrow will be perfect."

He tilted his head from side to side, his brow furrowed in thought. "Around two o'clock, shall we say? You can bring some of the items rescued from your great uncle's trunk and we'll begin a catalog of them. Something detailed and proper. And perhaps if we uncover something of real interest, we can show it to some of the children who come to the vicarage for their lessons. I'm sure they would be more than keen to have a tangible thing to study, rather than mere notes and passages from dull history books."

"Two o'clock," she echoed, feeling as if she were still lagging a few paces behind him.

He smiled. A full smile that highlighted fine teeth and rounded cheeks and the shadow of a beard making its nighttime appearance at the edges of his jaw. "I'll have Mrs. Babbinton bake something special. No one can touch her for cardamom cakes."

They made their farewells and she watched him walk back into the night. By the time the heels of his boots struck the main road, he returned to his whistling, and Mildred lingered there, beneath the open sky, just listening to him.

CHAPTER THREE

Dragons are not solitary creatures, no matter the numerous tales about them withdrawing into caves with their piles of ill-gotten treasure. Instead, they seem to crave companionship. And if they cannot find it among their own kind (due either to animosity within their ranks or simply a lack of other dragons to be found) evidence shows they will look outside of their species for the fraternity they seek.

-from Chapter Thirteen of Miss Percy's Pocket Guide (to the Care and Feeding of British Dragons)

Mildred awoke with all of her things around her.

Her things. Hidden away as they were, tucked into drawers and shoved beneath the blankets at the foot of the bed, she was surrounded by this vast new accumulation of belongings that somehow managed to make her feel less solitary than usual. (And for once, Mildred's strange existence between the worlds of family and servitude were to her benefit. Betsy, the maid, rarely ventured into her room to clean. There was a scullery girl who came in to build fires and sweep out the day's ashes, but she scuttled along the edges of the house with the quickness of a mouse not wanting to be caught out by the family's cat. In other words, Mildred had little worry that the new fullness of her sleeping quarters would be noticed or summarily reported to Diana, seeing as how few people tended to seek out Diana for any reason. It almost always worked out the other way around.)

She wondered at how mere things could bring with them a sense of companionship, but when she threw back the covers and slid her feet down to the floor, she was almost struck with the desire to chat about her plans for the day, as if the objects possessed ears with which to hear.

The morning slipped away from her in a series of jarring fits and starts. By one o'clock, she had successfully wrangled the children into the kitchen, instructed cook to give them each a pile of potatoes, and told them that whoever peeled the most (to cook's specifications) would win a prize (to be determined by cook, who was also reminded that additional kitchen chores would not be accepted as a suitable prize). Once the children were settled, their eyes agleam with the promise of sibling competition and sharp knives, Mildred went up to her room and began filling a small basket with a random selection of items taken from the trunk the previous night.

A glance out the window told her the sky had that heaviness that promised rain, though whether it would only be a light drizzle or a deluge, she couldn't determine from the wisps of gray dragging their tendrils over the tops of the distant hills. With a shawl pinned around her shoulders and a sturdy bonnet on her head, she tucked a handkerchief over the top of her basket, walked down the back stairs, and—

"Where are you off to this afternoon?" Diana stood in the hall, looking as if she was about to take her embroidery and settle in the parlour until the call for dinner.

Mildred pulled up short. Her heart racing, she struggled for an instant to school her features into a look of bland innocence. "Town. There's a book Mr. Wiggan is going to lend me," she said, deciding to lace her excursion with enough truth so as not to risk being caught out on it later. "On the natural history of Wiltshire." And enough detail that her sister would most likely lose interest before Mildred had finished speaking.

"Oh, but it does look like it's going to rain. You're not taking the carriage, are you?"

"I had not planned on it."

"Good, I'd rather not trouble everyone getting it ready for you if you're only paying a call on the vicar. But, oh! Would you be willing to stop at Mrs. Debney's and pick up a length of pink ribbon for me? Only the one on my rose bonnet has begun to fray and I was planning on wearing it to church on Sunday." Diana walked past her towards the parlour. "And if you take an umbrella," she added over her shoulder, "leave the black one, the one with the tortoiseshell handle. It's my favorite and I may decide to take a walk around the garden later."

Mildred knew her sister was not going to take a walk around the garden later. Her sister never took walks, or excursions, or strolls. If she couldn't arrive at a place outside of her home without a vehicle consisting of a seat and wheels conveying her there, then it was deemed not worth journeying towards. But she left the black umbrella with the tortoiseshell handle, which was too large and too unwieldy anyway. Expensive, yes. Functional...not unless she was willing to hire a brawny servant to walk behind her holding it open over her head.

Instead, she picked up her usual umbrella. A short thing, with a battered handle and an odd slant to one of the panels that made it always look like it had weathered more storms than it had. She tucked it under her right arm, adjusted the basket hooked over her left, and set off towards town. And Mrs. Babbinton's cardamom cakes.

***

The vicarage was one of those old, stone buildings at the edge of the village that met every expectation of what a country vicarage should be. There were diamond-paned windows and vibrant green trim and a mass of climbing roses growing over every vertical surface. The windows, however, were currently shut against the chill in the air, and the roses were dormant for the season, but Mildred walked up to the front door as if it couldn't be anything but a bright spring day, rang the bell, and wrinkled her nose against the first light drops of rain to tap against the brim of her bonnet.

Mrs. Babbinton (gray haired, stout, kindly eyes but with a mouth that could curdle milk with a swift downturn of its corners) answered, her apron still displaying wet streaks from where she must have dried her hands moments before opening the door.

"Miss Percy, of course." She took a step back and gestured Mildred inside. "Mr. Wiggan mentioned that we should be expecting you this afternoon. Now, go straight down the hall there, last door on your left and you'll find him in his study. That's where he spends most of his day. Here, allow me to take that for you." Mrs. Babbinton divested Mildred of her shawl and her umbrella, though when she put out a hand as if to take the basket, Mildred held it close against her, her other arm curling around it protectively.

"These are for Mr. Wiggan, to study."

"Ah, right. He said something about that as well. Some sort of historical artifacts, they are? Very good, very good. He needs something to keep him occupied on these dreary days. Not a wedding or a funeral for months, you know. Such quiet times. But go on then, and I'll be right in with a tray."

Mildred went on then, down the narrow, cozy hall to the last door on the left. She knocked, waited for the anticipated "Come in," and entered.

The study—like the house, like the housekeeper, like the diamond-paned windows and the climbing roses and the vaguely Tudor-era shape to everything—was precisely as she had expected it to be. Warm, rich wood panelling (Oak?

Walnut? Mildred had often read books where the type of wood something was constructed from was mentioned, and she wondered how people could determine it on sight. At least it had certainly never been a requirement of her education) made up the walls and shelves; and there were shelves everywhere, stuffed with books in the kind of haphazard way that let her know they were the kind of books to be read and studied and enjoyed and not merely lined up by size or color to act as another accessory to the room.

Mr. Wiggan sat behind a large, cluttered desk, but he stood when he saw her and indicated an armchair (complete with faded, threadbare upholstery, also just as expected) on the other side of it for her to sit in.

But she didn't sit. Instead she walked forward and plunked the basket down on the clearest portion of his desk (careful not to knock over one of several ink pots, or tip over the precariously stacked pile of books onto the half-eaten plate of cold toast and jam that must have been his breakfast) before she lifted one corner of the handkerchief and waited for him to peer inside.

"I tried to pick out an interesting selection of things," she said, sweeping away the rest of the handkerchief and diving into the jumble of items with her bare hands. "Here," she gave him one of the little bags, tied up with a frayed drawstring. "I've not even had an opportunity to look inside any of these."

There was a palpable excitement in the air, as good as a holiday or birthday with treats and presents to pass around. At Mr. Wiggan's small gasp, Mildred looked up to see him holding an unusual rock up towards the window, the meager light from outside catching on the edges of something sparkling white and violet.

"Amethyst crystals," he said, a thread of wonder in his voice. "It is a geode," he told her, finally tearing his gaze away from the rock long enough to catch her eyes. "They form in pockets in the earth, like miniature caves with their awesome treasures inside."

Mildred took the rock from him, her thumb sliding over the dark outer shell before she turned it over and stared in wide-eyed wonder at the mass of brilliant crystals. "It's beautiful," she said, aware of how breathless she sounded. "I've never seen anything like it before."

"This must be another one," Mr. Wiggan said, pulling a dark stone from the depths of the basket, this one oblong in shape and perfectly intact. It was the last stone Mildred had pulled from the trunk when she had emptied it, the one so carefully swathed in fabric and set in the middle of everything else, as though it were an egg tucked in a nest. "If we were to crack this open, no doubt it would be just as filled with crystals, though there's no way to tell what color they would be until we look."

"Oh, leave it for the moment." She put her hand out as if to stop him, despite the fact he'd made no move to break the stone apart. She couldn't say what it was, but her breath caught at the thought of cracking it open then and there. Another part of her wanted to reach across the desk and snatch the stone out of Mr. Wiggan's hands entirely, but she shook the thought out of her head and cleared her throat instead. "Perhaps that could be an event for your pupils, center an entire lesson around it, allow them all a chance to participate."

He nodded, his fingers still gliding over the outer shell of the stone. "A wonderful idea," he said, a note in his voice telling her that he was no longer paying complete attention to her. "Amazing thing, how it almost feels warm to the touch. I wonder what sort of rock it is, that it can exude a feeling of heat?" He placed it on his desk, between a dish of unlit candles overflowing with wax and a cup filled with quills.

The quills reminded Mildred of their intention to record every item they studied, and so she begged for the necessary instruments and set to work putting down all the details of each piece pulled from the basket.

At some point Mrs. Babbinton came in with her tray piled high with tea and cardamom cakes and even an extra plate of sandwiches. "In case the rigors of their work gave them a greater appetite than intended," was how she put it, as she collected the other dishes (the plate of jam toast, several cups, and a saucer still bearing a few crumbs of cheese) and shuffled out of the room again, leaving the door partially open behind her. (For propriety's sake, of course. It wouldn't do for the decidedly unmarried town vicar and a decidedly unmarried woman of about the same age to have their heads bent together in the same room for hours on end with the door shut tight and no one to know if they were simply cataloguing an old man's collection of artifacts or if something more scandalous were transpiring between them. Mrs. Babbinton, having been housekeeper to Mr. Wiggan for nearly a decade, would not have suspected the vicar of harbouring scandalous feelings should even the most notorious of Salomes come traipsing through the cottage twirling her veils about the place. But despite Mr. Wiggan's seeming disinterest in the opposite sex—or any sex—thus far, he was still a man, and Miss Percy was a woman, and it would not do for word of them being shuttered together without any supervision to find its way into the gossip channels that ran like rivers through the village.)

It took them little time to eat all of the cakes, and the sandwiches, and for Mr. Wiggan to call for a second pot of tea. Mildred looked up at that, her gaze scanning the corners of the room for any kind of timepiece. "Oh. Oh! I should go." She collected her basket—now empty—and sorted the papers she'd filled with notes and various minutiae concerning the coins and rocks and the small skull they supposed had come from some kind of lizard or amphibious creature (most likely native to Britain considering that everything they'd seen thus far had connections to their native soil). "I was supposed to purchase a ribbon for my sister and now she'll wonder how I've gone and let an entire afternoon escape from me." She handed the papers to him, duly sorted and put in order, and hooked her basket over her arm. "Thank you for helping with this, and please offer my gratitude to Mrs. Babbinton for her delicious cakes."

"But you'll come again soon, won't you?" Mr. Wiggan stepped out from behind the desk, his fingers still wrapped around a handful of quartz. "Tomorrow, even?"

She glanced towards the windows and the darkening sky. "My sister—"

"Tell her you're assisting me with a project for my pupils. I'm already looking forward to showing them a few of these pieces tomorrow morning. That is, if you're still not averse to my sharing the knowledge of them with others."

Mildred bit at her lips. They still tasted of tea and cardamom, and that alone was enough to sway her towards agreeing to Mr. Wiggan's scheme. "Oh, no. Most certainly not. Anything your students might find of interest to them, I should love for them to see."

Mr. Wiggan set down the quartz and rubbed his palms together, eager as a child. "Then it's settled. Shall we make this a standing appointment, then? Every afternoon at two o'clock, until we've gone through all of your great uncle's things."

She grinned. Not a smile but a full grin, teeth and gums on display, her cheeks pushing upwards into her eyes. It shouldn't have thrilled her so much, she thought, to have something to do each day beyond the borders of her brother-in-law's home. To feel as if she had a purpose, even if it was really nothing more than going through a trunkful of assorted bits and pieces she'd inherited from a deceased relative who had an undeniable predilection for collecting every assorted bit and piece he came across.

"Yes." She said it without thinking—or wanting to think —about the repercussions of her agreement. Diana would certainly not like it, no matter if it was partially for the education of the local children. (Diana didn't give two figs for the fate or education of the local children, especially as her son would be going off to a proper public school in another year and not wasting his time picking up bad habits from the farmers' sons of the area or that portly vicar...is how she may have voiced her opinion on the matter, on more than one occasion.) But Mildred was feeling rebellious, an easy enough thing to do after spending an entire afternoon out of the shadow of the person she was feeling particularly rebellious against.

The feeling buoyed her out of the vicarage and carried her most of the way home. Even the rain coming down, forcing her to utilize her umbrella and keep to the edge of the road (and out of the ruts that turned to channels of mud with the addition of about as much moisture from a fellow pedestrian's sneeze) could not dampen her excitement about what the coming days might bring. And then her brother-in-law's house came into view, that bulky silhouette against the gray sky, made only grayer by the setting of the sun somewhere behind the layers of cloud cover.

Not her house, she was reminded as she stepped off the road and onto the lane that led to the front door. Seventeen years she'd lived beneath this roof, and yet she still felt as if she were a guest, a transient creature shunted up into the smallest available room, cursed to continually reside in some betwixt and between realm where she was neither family nor servant.

Like a fairy world from a book of children's tales. Only without the fairies. Or the magic.

So maybe more like a kind of purgatory, she mused, in a brief betrayal to her stolid Anglican roots.

Her earlier joy in rebellion continued to dwindle away as she veered off the lane and onto the path that took her around the side of the house and up to the rear entrance. No doubt her prolonged absence had already been noticed and become grist for the steady mill of complaints that Diana made about her. No doubt she would be scolded, as if she were a child, or a servant, and certainly not the eldest sister and the one who had chosen to remain at home and care for their father until age and ill health had claimed him.

Mildred shook out her umbrella and scraped her shoes on the rug. Her heart was beating faster than it should, faster than a quick walk from town would do. There was noise from the kitchen, the preparations for dinner well underway, the comforting clang of pots and the squeal of hinges from the oven door, Cook's voice scolding one of the maids a familiar enough sound to center Mildred's world for a moment, to release the breath she had been holding in her lungs and allow her to move further into the house.

None of the servants paid her any mind. She was not the mistress of the house, so they did not fully defer to her, though as she was not one of them either, they made no move to draw her into their orbit. She hurried up the back stairs to her room, her fingers trembling as she removed her bonnet and shawl and gown, all of them damp or splattered with mud. Into a clean gown for dinner, her hair unpinned, brushed, and pinned up again. By the time she arrived downstairs again, she hoped she looked like someone who had kept to their room for the past several hours instead of rushing home in the rain before the night fully descended over her head.

Her sister was in the drawing room. Belinda was there as well, slumped indecorously ("spilled" might have been a more accurate word, as she looked as if another tug of gravity on her skirts would have her cascading into a puddle on the floor) in an armchair beside the fire. The younger children sat on the floor playing a game that involved a deck of cards and grumbling in hushed voices over who was in possession of the greater amount of cards at any given moment.

"Where have you been?" Diana said, looking up from her embroidery—possibly the same embroidery she'd been working on earlier in the day. There was no scolding in her tone, only a distracted kind of curiosity, as if she weren't really paying attention to what she was saying.

"I was at the vicarage, with Mr. Wiggan, remember?"

"Oh, that. Yes." Diana sucked at the inside of her cheek while she untangled a strand of thread. "And were you able to get my ribbon?"

Of course her sister would not forget that. "Mmm, no." Mildred forced herself to breathe slowly, to keep her expression placid even though Diana hadn't bothered to look at her again since she'd first come into the room. "They were out of pink. There was only red and... ah, apricot."

Diana made a face, one that could best be described as "attempting to draw a hunk of mutton through her teeth." "I despise apricot," she said, and gave her head a minute shake. "It makes me look all sallow, don't you think?"

Mildred blinked. She viewed moments such as these as conversational traps, where there were many more wrong answers than right ones afforded to her. "I could not say," she dared, picking her words as carefully as choosing which rocks to step on while crossing a rapidly moving stream. "I think that perhaps we reserve our most critical opinions for ourselves. While you might believe that apricot does not suit you, someone else may believe it to be your best color." (Of course, after all of this, the truth of the matter remained that apricot did not suit Diana at all and tended to gift her complexion with a greenish undertone one should only sport when attempting rough nautical travel or after having consumed a bite of pork that had "turned.")

Her sister's eyes narrowed, only for a moment, in a way that caused Mildred to suspect Diana was searching for the slight in her words. When she couldn't find it on first examination, she returned her attention to her embroidery, which seemed to have transformed from a hobby with which to keep her hands occupied to a thing she could look at and thereby sever her attention from something she no longer wished to bother with.

"Um," Mildred said softly, and her sister's hands stilled.

"Tomorrow," Mildred went on, and her sister returned her embroidery to her lap.

"Well, the thing is…" Mildred paused, swallowed, nearly choked on the swallow, and with her hand at her throat began again. "The thing is, Mr. Wiggan requested that I return to the vicarage in order to help with his lessons for the local children. I do not know precisely how long he will rely on my assistance—perhaps for as long as a week or more—but I thought it right to tell you, so you do not wonder at my sudden absence most afternoons."

It startled her that she had managed to phrase it all as a declaration rather than a request. Through her stammered speech, she had removed Diana's ability to give or withhold permission. Mildred stood with her shoulders pushed back, her chin raised an inch higher than normal and her teeth locked together. Should her sister attempt to deny her now, to tell her she was instead to stay home for the children or the housekeeping or some other reason drawn from the empty air around her head, then it would be tantamount to admitting that she saw Mildred as a nurse for the children, an unpaid companion, or even as low as a housemaid.

"Well, the—" was as far as Diana went before her mouth snapped shut and her eyebrows formed that little furrow of tension between them. Her nostrils flared before she spoke again. "Perhaps you could take the children with you on one of your outings. I'm sure the walk and the fresh air would do them some good."

"What a fine idea," Mildred said, choosing to end the exchange with a balm to her sister's mood. "I would not have thought of that."

Diana smiled. Not a kind smile, not a sisterly smile that conveyed affection between the two of them (there had been affection between them at one time, and perhaps there still was—in its measure—but living together for the majority of their lives had not proven to endear them to one another, instead only serving to cast each other's foibles in an unattractive light) but a smile that seemed to draw a line on the floor between them.

"Of course. Which is why it falls to some of us to remember these things, when others cannot."

Mildred smiled in return, until the expression lost all meaning and she feared her teeth would grind down to dust inside her mouth. There had been no precise moment she could think of when Diana had succeeded in tipping the tables of their sororal relationship in her favor. They had been so different as children, so caught up in their own worlds of dolls (Diana) and mud puddles (Mildred) and wishing for marriage and children (both Diana and Mildred) that it had often seemed as though they had been raised in entirely separate households. But both of them had sat at their father's knee while he told them stories and helped them with their reading, both of them had shared the same nurse and the same governess and even the same bedroom for the first few years of their sisterhood.

And yet Mildred could think of so little they had in common with one another. Yes, they had both wanted marriage and children, but Diana's pursuit of it had been akin to the acquiring of a new bonnet or a fine gown, something to be flaunted and shown off at the season's next social event. Mildred had instead chosen to remain at home with their father, because...

Too many reasons, actually. The main one being that Mildred had not met a man she had cared to marry. Her sister's criteria for a potential husband had been that he was in possession of a reasonable fortune and a beating heart, but Mildred could not see herself merely settling for someone with whom she would be spending the rest of her life.

The second reason (or perhaps the third or the thirteenth, as they all became jumbled together after that first and most important one) was that Mildred had always assumed there was something that needed to be done before she could wed. When she was younger, it had been to have an adventure, because once she was married, what man would want a wife who would rather tramp through the woods and the mud than sit at home embroidering something onto a cushion? And when she was of an age to begin looking for a husband, her father's health—or loss of it—had taken priority. She would be with him first before settling down and shaping a life for herself. And by then she had been well into her twenties, and what man would want a wife who had been sitting on the shelf, collecting dust for so long? So she came to live with Diana, which had begun as a temporary thing. And once Diana found a nurse and a governess, and once everything at Ashby Lodge was taken care of, then Mildred could finally see to her own life and happiness.

A happy thought, seventeen years earlier.

Mildred looked at her sister, this person she would never have chosen as an acquaintance and yet knew better than anyone else in her life. "Thank you, Diana. I am not sure what I would do without you."

CHAPTER FOUR

I have yet to encounter any evidence of a child ever coming to harm at the hand (or claw) of a dragon.

-from Miss Mildred Percy's personal notes

Like the surety of time marching onwards, of the stars wheeling overhead, of buttered toast striking the floor butter-side-down, so were the children always better behaved once they were away from their mother.

They walked beside Mildred, Matthew to her left and Nettie to her right, full of the kind of comments and questions that children their age always ask, without any hint of disrespect or complaining. The sun was out, which helped matters. Yesterday's clouds and rain had been swept away by a chill breeze that still didn't diminish the brightness of the sky or the promise that winter would at some point finally have to release its hold on the countryside. That, and Mildred suspected the act of simply being outdoors and away from their father's property was enough to dredge up all of the various manners and rules of etiquette Mildred had been attempting to instill in them for the previous seven years.

The walk to the vicarage seemed to disappear behind them at a faster pace than it had for Mildred the previous afternoon. Her arm hadn't even begun to ache beneath the weight of her basket when the three of them all shuffled onto the front step of the vicar's home. She allowed both Matthew and Nettie to ring the bell in turn.

"And what is this?" came Mrs. Babbinton's greeting as

46

she opened the door to them.

Mildred held her breath. Not everyone liked children, especially when it came to other people's children. Mrs. Babbinton had spent the last decade of her life caring for only a single man whose greatest needs appeared to be being provided with enough cheese and an occasional reminder not to let his latest cup of tea go cold. Would the housekeeper balk at allowing two young children into her home (yes, it was called "the vicarage" which would make one believe that the vicar himself was the head of the household, but the most discerning and observant of individuals often knew the truth of such matters) to run amok through her daily routines and across her freshly scrubbed floors?

"I have my sister's children with me today," Mildred announced, hoping to infuse her words with enough cheer at the pronouncement that her feigned attitude would take on the qualities of an illness, something to be passed one to another. "I hope that is all right. They were eager to be out of the house today, to see a bit of the village—they've been at home quite a bit with their studies—and if you'd like, I can —"

But Mrs. Babbinton was already drawing the children inside like a pied piper with promises of delicacies in the kitchen and a romp in the back garden where they could help her to dig holes in the dirt in preparation for the early spring planting. "You'll find Mr. Wiggan in his study," she tossed over her shoulder. "I'll be in with your tea and things once the children are properly fed and watered."

The study appeared no different than it had the day before, except for a different scattering of empty dishes precariously balanced on the furniture. Mr. Wiggan sat behind his desk, studying the small skull she'd brought over on her previous trip with the aid of a magnifying glass. When he moved to stand as she entered the room, she waved for him to keep his seat and searched for a place to set her basket without knocking something else off balance and onto the floor.

"You know," he said, holding up the delicate cranium, "I've never seen the like of this before. When I was a boy— oh! The time I used to spend catching lizards and toads and finding ways to sneak them into my sister's bed or the pockets of her apron. But there's something in the design of this that makes it unusual."

Mildred uncovered her basket and began pulling out stacks of notebooks and journals two and three at a time. "A species not native to England, perhaps?"

There was a phrase Mildred had read, one that described someone as "pulling a face," and it had always sounded odd to her ears. But as she watched the parts of Mr. Wiggan's face droop one feature at a time—as if the corners of his mouth, his eyes, his brows, were all connected to a puppeteer's strings—she finally made sense of that written representation of the alteration in a person's expression.

"Possible," he said at length, though his words sounded heavy with doubt. "I don't know. I think I'm being fanciful today. Too much time spent indoors, is what Mrs. Babbinton would tell me." He smiled, more to himself than for his audience, Mildred thought, and returned the skull to the simple wooden box stuffed with cotton wool it had initially been transported in. "Now, what do you have for us this afternoon?"

"Books, mostly." Mildred finished emptying the contents of the basket and spread her hands apart, showing off the two stacks of volumes she'd smuggled out of her bedroom. "My great uncle kept a great many journals, it seems. Not diaries, from what I can tell, detailing the happenings of his daily life. These seem to be…" She picked up one from the top of the nearest pile, a thin book bound in soft calfskin, but the pages were so riddled with notes, with smears of ink and tea stains and countless other wrinkles and folds that it appeared twice as thick as it actually was. "Ramblings," she said, as she thumbed through the first few pages. "There's nothing connecting his thoughts, just hundreds of notes scrawled across every blank space. I don't know how he went back and found anything once it had been written down in here."

Mr. Wiggan picked up another book and began reading from page one. They were both silent for several minutes, Mildred turning her selection this way and that as she came across curious sketches of plants and wildlife and wide vistas of the countryside near where—Mildred assumed—Great Uncle Forthright had lived for the last five decades of his life.

"I'm willing to consider that these weren't made as the sort of journals to be kept as a reference for things," Mr. Wiggan said as he continued turning the pages of his book. "They appear to be more of an emptying of one's mind. A way to prevent his thoughts from becoming too cluttered, I imagine."

Mildred narrowed her eyes at a faint drawing done in pencil that resembled something like the clawed foot of a hawk or another type of predatory bird. "Do you find yourself suffering from a similar affliction, Mr. Wiggan?"

"Not so much during the day. But at night? All too often, I'm afraid."

She set down her book and picked up a rolled sheaf of papers that threatened to crumble at the edges as she untied the yellowed twine holding them together. "I wonder why that is? Why there are so many times throughout the day when we cannot seem to hold onto a thought or an idea, but then as soon as we lay down our heads in the hope of sleep, it becomes an inundation."

"We should keep journals such as these by our beds at night. Then, when we cannot find rest, try and empty our minds onto the page. We might sleep better for it."

The papers were thick and smelled of must and age. The ink on them had so faded that she could hardly make out any of the words. "Oh, it's in…" She pulled it closer to her face and then held it at arm's length. "Irish? No. What is this? I cannot make it out."

Mr. Wiggan took the papers from her and immediately picked up his magnifying glass. "Welsh," he said after only a few seconds of study. "I don't speak it, but I recognize it well enough." Carefully, he looked through the pages, paused at one in particular, and handed it across to her.

"Is that a...?" She tilted it towards the light streaming through the windows. "It looks like a bird?" (In her defense, the sketch—a curious amalgam of skeleton and tendons and muscle rendered in a mixture of pencil and ink—was not well done. Her Great Uncle Forthright may have had a talent for collecting interesting things and living a hearty life for an extraordinary number of years, but his drawings—while technically correct, for the most part—bore a childlike quality to them that made portions of them difficult to decipher.)

"Look at the head, the structure of it." He reached out and tapped a corner of the page she held, sending a small shower of dust and paper debris to float down through the air between them.

She did look. The head was drawn with part of the bone of jaw and cheek exposed, the rest covered in a smudged representation of musculature. "The skull," she said, and glanced back at the desk, at the wooden box that held an intricate construction of bone within. "But you said it resembled that of a lizard's?"

He shrugged. "Some birds and lizards share very similar qualities. And while I have an interest in natural history and animal biology, I am by no means an expert."

Mildred met his shrug with a head tilt of her own. "Or perhaps my Great Uncle Forthright is simply not very good at drawing."

Mrs. Babbinton bustled in at that moment, not bothering to knock first as the door to the study was already halfway open. "The children are in the kitchen helping shape the crusts for tonight's pork pies. If they come out more tough than usual, I'm absolving myself of blame here and now." She set down a tray with the usual accoutrements of cheese and sandwiches, cakes, tea with milk and sugar.

Mildred failed to notice how hungry she was until she saw all of the food laid out before her. She had always been blessed with a healthy appetite (as her father had been wont to put it, no matter how fashions could change from season to season as whether wispy bodies or plump ones were the preferred build, he was decided on the fact that he liked women who ate their fill) but living with her sister had made her much more aware of how much she consumed at each meal (mostly due to the fact that Diana had a tendency to bemoan the latest bill from the butcher, or the grocer, or the lack of leftovers for a cold supper every time Mildred made a move to help herself to a second portion).

But here in the vicarage, in the company of Mr. Wiggan and Mrs. Babbinton, she experienced no compunction against filling her plate and filling it then again. Mr. Wiggan certainly did not appear to have missed many meals and his housekeeper—at least from what Mildred had seen so far— made no move to check his appetite.

After their repast, Mildred and Mr. Wiggan set to work. Their task this afternoon was to sort as many of the journals and papers as they could into chronological order, but since her Great Uncle Forthright had a penchant for neglecting to leave a date on anything he wrote, they were left to make guesses as to age of things more by their state of deterioration rather than by their contents.

"Your great uncle was a thorough man," Mr. Wiggan said, heaving a sigh as he leaned back in his chair, their work for the day nearing its end.

Mildred rubbed her fingers together. There was dust everywhere—on her skin, on her clothes, gilding every surface in the room—and she wondered if it would be too much for her to request a bath to be brought to her bedroom when she returned home again. (Mildred was not one to give into such luxuries very often. First, her room was not large enough to conveniently fit the bathtub and the trooping of the servants in and out necessary to see it filled. Second, she disliked creating extra work for the servants when she could just as easily scrub herself down from her little basin of water on her dresser. Third, she had no wish to invite any commentary from her sister on the usage of hot water or the noise of having a tub carried upstairs or... Well, it was simply easier to bathe from her little basin and occasionally wash her hair by the warmth of the fire. That was all.)

But all thoughts of baths were knocked out of her head when the children came into the room, followed by Mrs. Babbinton. (Normally the children would have "scampered" or "darted" or "exploded" into any room they entered, but Mrs. Babbinton's influence apparently extended to reining in the walking speed of children under the age of ten years.) Both Matthew and Nettie carried a warm scent of apples and honey about their persons, and lit by the glow of waning sunlight from the windows, their aspects were lended a touch of the angelic.

"You may bring them along with you anytime you like," Mrs. Babbinton said, while bestowing such looks on the children as would make a stained glass saint appear less than virtuous. "I do miss the sound of children in a house, you know. I never had any of my own, but I was once housekeeper for a family with seven sons and four daughters, and there's something of a comfort in it, even if it's just to have something on which to blame all the odd noises of an old, drafty house."

Despite Mrs. Babbinton's control over them, Matthew and Nettie both began to wander about the room (as best as the clutter and overburdened shelves and furniture would allow). Nettie took a distinct interest in a case of butterflies pinned to a velvet backing, their bright wings gleaming like jeweled gossamer. Matthew's attention was riveted by the collection of objects scattered across the top of Mr. Wiggan's desk. It was the sort of collection that begged to be touched after one was vociferously instructed not to touch anything. Mildred could see his fingers twitching, wanting to poke, to prod, to grab, to wreak passive destruction over half of Mr. Wiggan's belongings in one fell swoop.

"What's this?" Nettie asked, now carefully stroking one corner of a page from a book filled with pressings of dried flowers and plants.

"Ah, well." Mr. Wiggan drifted off to tend to Nettie's curiosity, while Mildred finished putting her Great Uncle Forthright's notes into order. There was a soft clinking sound then, like a finger tapping against the edge of a cup. She looked over at Matthew, ready to remind him to keep his hands off of anything that looked breakable, but he stood out of arm's reach of the desk, his hands clasped behind his back.

"What are you doing?" she asked, doing everything in her power to not sound as if she were three ticks of the clock from scolding him.

"It moved," was all he said, and jutted out his chin towards the desk.

"What?" Mildred took a small step back, her hands still filled with paper and a stub of pencil, her fingers smudged with the evidence of her work. "What moved? The desk? Did you bump against it?"

Matthew shook his head. "No, that." He stretched out a hand, one finger with a ragged, bitten-down nail indicating the large, intact geode she had brought down to the vicarage the day before.

"The rock?" She placed her hand on its surface. It wasn't cool, as it should have been, as she assumed it would be. It reminded her of the sensation of slipping her fingers into a warm bath to test the temperature of the water, only when she pulled her hand away—and she did, rather quickly—they were still very much dry. "It probably rolled a little as I was gathering up my things. It should be all right."

"No, I saw it move, and no one else was near the desk," Matthew insisted. "It rolled all on its own, and it gave a little bit of a wobble."

"Mama says you're not to tell tales!" Nettie pushed back. "Stones cannot roll on their own and you know it!"

"But it did!" Matthew cried, as though his very honor were being impugned. "I saw it!"

"You did not!" Nettie shouted, and before Matthew could retaliate against this rebuttal with another cry or scream or some manner of elevated vocal activity, Mildred wedged herself in between them and placed a hand on the children's shoulders.

"Need I remind you that we are guests in Mr. Wiggan's home? I do not think we should be battling with one another after the vicar and Mrs. Babbinton have been so kind as to welcome us here. Now, if you can show yourself to behave very well over the next few weeks, perhaps I can bring the two of you along when Mr. Wiggan cracks open the stone for his pupils."

"What's inside of it?" Matthew scrunched up his face, dark eyes narrowed as if he could peer through the outer surface of the rock and see its interior without the help of a hammer or chisel.

"Crystals, we think. It may look like jewels inside, if we're fortunate."

The boy's eyes gleamed. "Oh, I'll be very good, Aunt Mildred. I will!"

Mildred grinned and reached out to give a playful tug to his ear. She had already decided that she would bring them to the lesson when Mr. Wiggan opened the stone, but she didn't have to let him know that. At least not yet. (The truth of the matter was, as much as Mildred was inclined to complain about the children, how exhausting, how exasperating, how exacting they could be with every hour of her day, she did care for them. She was also old enough now

54

to know that she most likely wouldn't be having any children of her own (a realization that did not cause her as much wailing or donning of sackcloth and ashes as she supposed was expected of her, being a reasonably healthy gentlewoman with a smidgen of childbearing years still left to her) and so she had learned to appreciate the time she had with her nieces and nephew... at least when they weren't being awful little terrors battling over who could do a more competent job of tearing the house down around their heads.)

"All right. We've imposed upon Mr. Wiggan and poor Mrs. Babbinton long enough." Mildred scooped up her empty basket and chivvied the children out of the study. Mr. Wiggan followed them to the door, while the housekeeper disappeared into the kitchen to fetch something edible for the children to take home with them.

"Will you come again tomorrow?" Mr. Wiggan asked as they stood on the front step of the vicarage, the children bolting towards the nearest tree with branches growing over the wall for them to clamber up and onto. "You do not have to if you have obligations elsewhere. I wouldn't wish to take up all of your free time if you'd rather..." He stopped himself, and swallowed, and tipped his head in a way Mildred had already begun to recognize as a precursor to a smile. "The invitation still stands, you know."

Mildred stood next to him. She was not particularly tall for a woman. Mr. Wiggan, on the other hand, was taller than most of the other men in the village. He was broader, as well, though no doubt he had all of Mrs. Babbinton's fine cooking to thank for that. But there was something about the way he stood, his posture, the slow and steady gestures that accompanied his words making him seem smaller in stature than he was. Not in a way that Mildred felt should draw criticism, but instead making him more approachable. More safe.

Her brow wrinkled at that. A fact that probably did her

expression no favors as she sniffed (the coolness of the air always gave her nose cause to dribble a bit) and fidgeted with her gloves (to better resist the urge to wipe at her nose in front of another person). "The day after tomorrow, I think. Friday, it would be?" She wanted a few hours to search through the hidden contents of her room, to find more of her Great Uncle Forthright's notes and journals she knew had been packed into the trunk. Better to have them all catalogued together at once than to make a harder task of it dragging things out one sketch or notebook at a time.

"Of course." He shuffled his feet and stepped back. "I wouldn't want to give your sister reason to think I'd gone and stolen you away from her. I'm sure she depends on you, on your time, your help to the household."

"Well, as long as I continue to take Matthew and Nettie out for daily exercise, I doubt she'll raise too many objections to my continued absences."

"Then you're welcome to bring them along with you," Mr. Wiggan said, that thread of hopefulness still limning all his words. He glanced back towards where Mrs. Babbinton came rushing up with a bundle of something tied up in a napkin. "As long as my housekeeper doesn't object."

"Here you are!" Mrs. Babbinton, seemingly oblivious to their conversation before she approached, plunked the bundle of baked goods (there was a definite scent of ginger that tickled Mildred's nose and set her mouth to watering, no matter how much food she had already eaten while toiling away in Mr. Wiggan's study) into Mildred's basket. "Now, don't let them be bolted down all at once. But I promise them some almond biscuits when they return. You will bring them again, won't you?"

Mildred looked at Mrs. Babbinton, then at the children still scampering about the branches of the tree in a manner that would put territorial squirrels to shame. A theory skirted at the edges of her mind, how the children were at their most... Well, she wanted to refrain from using the word "unlikable" in regards to them, but at the moment she couldn't come up with another that would suit—unlikable when they were somewhere in the vicinity of their mother. Was it Diana's mere presence alone that could cast such a shadow across them and how they were perceived? And if so, what else appeared worse than it was simply because it existed within her sister's sphere? Her own life, even?

Oh, but what dismal thoughts these could quickly become if she wasn't careful! Instead, she allowed herself an extra sniff of the ginger cakes in her basket, and she looked towards the west, allowing the lingering sunlight to spark in her eyes. It was a beautiful day. She had spent the majority of her afternoon occupied with a task wholly catered to her wants. Good food, good company, and the quiet employment that often came with the discovery of new things.

Bucolic. That was the word she wanted to use. It was all very bucolic in its way. And if she couldn't have the adventure she had so desired when she was a young girl, nursing her scraped knees and dirty fingernails and sun-bronzed cheeks, then perhaps a life that glimmered with an occasionally bucolic moment would be enough.

Well. It would have to be, wouldn't it?

CHAPTER FIVE

The hatching of a dragon is a unique experience, and no two hatchings are ever the same. The only constants from one instance to the next are that there will be a bit of a mess, someone will utter an exclamation most likely not fit for gentle ears, and all of the most delicate of one's appendages should be diligently protected.

-from Chapter Seven of Miss Percy's Pocket Guide (to the Care and Feeding of British Dragons)

Mildred was in her room when the letter came for her. She was still asleep, actually, and she suspected that the knocking on her door that finally woke her had begun as a gentle, polite tapping she had been too insensate to notice.

She struggled up to her feet, one eye still closed against the onslaught of another day, one hand scraping at the dried trail of drool on her chin before she opened the door and peered into the hall.

"Whatsit?" she slurred, then attempted sight with her other eye.

Her other eye refused to acknowledge such an early hour, so she closed it again.

"Here, Miss." Betsy, the maid, bobbed from foot to foot as if she were standing on hot coals. Or needed the water closet. But amid the bobbing, she held out a note, something small and square and, from what Mildred could determine with her one open eye, written in no small amount of haste.

"Who?" was all she said, and closed her mouth quickly once she caught a taste of her own breath in the back of her throat.

"Didn't say," Betsy pronounced in an exaggerated whisper. "But I was told I had to bring it straight up to you, no waitin' about for you to wake up or dress or anything."

Mildred unfolded it and read. Or tried to read. The light in the hall was dismal (the curtains hadn't even been opened yet) and her left eye was still refusing to cooperate. "Am I..." She cleared her throat and began again. "Am I to send a message in return?"

"Don't know."

Mildred turned away from the incredibly informative Betsy and shuffled back into her room. She batted at the drapes in front of the window, letting in enough light to see by. "Oh, it's from..." *Mr. Wiggan*, she was going to say. But failed to say as the confusion his note produced swept over her. Or dumped over her, like a bucket of tepid water first thing in the morning.

(*Dear Miss Percy*, the note began, for those who are curious.

I am loath to bother you at such an early hour, but something has happened with one of your Great Uncle Forthright's belongings.

I beg you to make haste and come at once, or as soon as certain familial obligations will allow.

Yours, etc.

Mr. Wiggan)

"What?" Mildred asked the note itself, as if that scrap of paper had the power to explain its intentions and fill in the gaps of information Mr. Wiggan had left vacant. Her head hurt. Not in the way a commonplace headache would cause her head to hurt, but in a way that felt like too many thoughts pushing their way through a space the size of a keyhole all at once. "This was just brought here?" She looked back over her shoulder at Betsy, who continued her bobbing in the doorway.

"Yes, Miss. Not five minutes before I knocked at your door."

Mildred forced both of her eyes to open at once. There. Nothing like proper peripheral vision to make one feel somewhat functional again. "Is anyone else awake yet? Mrs. Muncy or the children?"

"No, Miss. Only myself and Cook, so far."

"So." Mildred licked her lips. She needed tea or coffee or anything capable of helping her put together more than a half dozen words at a time. "I'm going to dress," she said slowly, trying out each word as they tripped off her tongue. "And then I will go for a walk. If anyone is to ask after my whereabouts, that is what you will tell them."

Betsy ceased her bobbing. Or at least she replaced it with a soft sway from side to side. "You're going out for a walk."

"Yes." Mildred nodded. "And I should be back before breakfast. Oh!" She held up one finger towards Betsy, and the maid suddenly stilled like a creature hypnotized. "And there was no note. Do you understand?"

"No note?" Betsy blinked at her from beneath the floppy brim of her cap.

"No note. I'm going out for a morning walk. That is all."

Betsy swallowed. "No note. Morning walk."

"Very good." Mildred smiled. The last smudge of drool she'd neglected to wipe away from her jaw stretched across her skin. "I should be down in a few minutes. Is there any coffee?"

"Oh, yes! Cook always has to have a cup before she'll even speak to anyone."

"Excellent!" Well, excellent for Mildred in that she would have a cup ready for her when she arrived downstairs, though not as excellent for the servants who had to deal with Cook before half past six in the morning.

Mildred dressed quickly. (She did not have a lady's maid nor had any use for one. Novels often had a way of making it seem that it was impossible to clothe oneself or do anything with one's own hair without the aid of a second pair of hands to button and brush and pin. But if that were truly the case, then the majority of England's population would be tottering around the countryside either shockingly half-appareled or wearing only shapeless sacks and trousers they could put on while stumbling around their hovels. Mildred preferred an adherence to fashion that did not make her into a doll needing to be daily dressed and undressed by its keeper.) She pulled on her spencer as she entered the kitchen, her bonnet and gloves crushed beneath her arm as she reached out a free hand for the cup Betsy handed to her.

"Mm, thank you." She took a sip of coffee, grimaced, then downed half the cup in the next swallow. (She did not care for coffee, really. No amount of cream or sugar made it more than half-palatable to her. But she couldn't argue with its efficacy in putting her thoughts in order and transforming her into a more companionable person overall. Lord bless that vile, bitter liquid.)

"Heated it up for you," Cook said as she held out a fresh buttered roll, wrapped up in a crisp napkin. "It's chilly out there. You'll need it to warm you up on your way."

"My walk," Mildred corrected, with a long look in Cook's direction. "Not my way, my walk. Only a walk."

"Of course, Miss." And Cook winked. Mildred took this to mean that she had already finished with her second cup of vile, bitter liquid to earn such a spark of mischief so early in the morning.

The sun, thankfully, was out again in full force. Not a single cloud hovered in any portion of the sky that Mildred could see from beneath the edge of her bonnet, causing her to contemplate if she was even still in England or if this was all a dream of a fantastical place where the sun shone down from a clear firmament two days in a row.

The village was a different place this early in the morning, not merely because of the altered angle of the light from which she usually saw it as it cut around buildings and cast new shadows on everything. There was a purpose the place conveyed, maids and mothers out sweeping and scrubbing their front steps, farmers driving their carts over the rutted lanes, children carrying freshly collected eggs in their aprons, and further along were the shopkeepers refreshing their window displays or knocking abandoned bird's nests from the top of their signs.

She arrived at the vicarage without trading more than a nod in greeting with any of the other townspeople. If anyone followed her progress towards Mr. Wiggan's home, or wondered why she was calling at such an early hour, she paid no heed as she rang the bell and bounced on the balls of her feet until Mrs. Babbinton opened the door.

"Ah, goodness. You're here." Mrs. Babbinton nearly grabbed at her arm and hauled her inside like a piece of baggage. "He's been in a state all night. Refuses to tell me what is happening and could hardly wait until daylight to see a note sent off to you."

Mildred didn't even have time to remove her bonnet or gloves before she was being unceremoniously steered towards not the study this time, but rather the sitting room at the front of the house. "Why is it so—" *warm in here?* was what she tried to say as Mr. Wiggan leapt to his feet from his place in front of the fire, as Mrs. Babbinton backed out of the room before Mr. Wiggan could rush over and slam the door in her face, and as Mildred blinked at the darkness of the room she'd just been pushed into.

Mr. Wiggan turned around, his back pressed against the now firmly-shut door. On the other side of it came an audible huff of frustration before the quick retreat of Mrs. Babbinton's footsteps marked her departure for the sanctuary of the kitchen.

"What—" Mildred tried again, but Mr. Wiggan raised

one finger to his lips.

"Miss Percy," he said, his voice a rough whisper. And then he paused, the fingers of the hand in front of his mouth unfurling as he held it towards her, imploring her with that movement to remain where she was. "Something extraordinary has occurred."

She studied his face. He did not look well. There were shadows beneath his eyes, eyes that were rimmed with red and decorated with an assortment of tiny red veins creeping their way across the whites. "Are you...?" She glanced around the room, searching specifically for any bottles or decanters or flasks that would denote a night spent imbibing too many spirits, and not of a variety associated with the Holy Trinity. "Have you slept at all?" she amended when there was nothing obvious to be found.

"No, of course not," he replied, flicking her query away with a wave of his hand. He then smoothed his fingers over his head, an action that only served to show how many times he must have repeated the movement over the last several hours. (Though Mr. Wiggan was not in possession of much hair worth boasting about, the tonsure he did have was alternately sticking out from his head or laying flat, as if greased in place, without any pretension towards neatness or style.) "Come here," he said finally, and grasping her gloved hands, pulled her further into the room and towards the fire.

The fire, Mildred noted, had been built up to a raging blaze. With the drapes drawn tight it gave the room the feel of a cocoon. Already there was perspiration gathering beneath her arms and along her upper lip, enough that she tugged one of her hands free from Mr. Wiggan's grip and fought with the tie of her bonnet beneath her chin, before her entire scalp turned into an itchy, sweating mess beneath the straw. "What—?" she said, fully aware that she hadn't managed more than one complete sentence since arriving at the vicarage, but this time, instead of someone else interrupting her, it was the sight that met her as she neared the fireplace that halted her speech.

There was a nest. On the floor. In front of the fire.

Well, not a nest as one would expect to find in a tree, constructed of leaves and twigs, daubed together with mud or other pieces of refuse birds tended to pluck from all over the place. This nest (and she recognized it as a nest immediately, seeing as how there was an egg tucked in the middle of a mess of sheets and blankets all twisted into the best approximation of a nest one could create from a haphazard collection of bed linens) sat against the bricks at the edge of the hearth, the light from the flames flashing across it's uneven surface.

"Look," he instructed.

She looked. In the center of the nest was a rock. Well, not *a* rock, but rather *the* rock. The rock from her Great Uncle Forthright's trunk. The gorgeously large rock that Matthew had argued he had witnessed roll and wobble on Mr. Wiggan's desk. And now a crack ran down one side of the rock, the simple stone they had assumed—oh, surely they would be able to laugh about that at some point in the future?—was nothing more than a geode, a geological specimen with which to teach the village children about the formation of various minerals and crystals over time. One segment appeared to have already broken away, leaving a small hole in its upper half. "Is it…?"

"An egg," he finished for her, his voice still low, for her ears alone. Though 'egg' was the last word she would have come up with on her own. "It began twitching last night, while I worked at my desk. Sunday's sermon, you know. I always put it off for too long." He swept the back of his hand across his brow. "But anyway, it moved. And not a small vibration from my jostling the thing." He licked his lips. "There was something inside it. There *is* something inside it. If you listen closely, you might hear it, a kind of scratching, chirruping sound."

Mildred finished removing her bonnet. Then she pulled

off her gloves, tugging at one finger at a time. And her spencer, she tackled that as well, her hands turning into thick, stupid sausages that seemed to have forgotten how things like buttons generally worked. But it gave her a minute to think, while she tended to the normalcy of removing her outer garments and pretending as if this were a charming social call and Mrs. Babbinton would barge in at any moment with her overladen tray of tea and other comestibles. "It's rather large, for an egg."

Without heeding ceremony, he dropped down to his knees and gestured for her to join him on the floor. "There are some birds, not native to England of course..." He shook his head. "But I do not believe..." Again, he paused, long enough to draw a breath that seemed weighted with something Mildred could not identify. A gravity, of sorts. A kind of weight being affixed to his next words. "I do not believe this is a bird."

She went down onto her knees beside him. On closer inspection, she could clearly see the break in the surface of the egg's shell. A few pieces of that outer layer lay amid the folds of the twisted-up blankets and she picked up one of them, surprised at the thickness of it, the weight of that tiny sliver between her fingers.

"Miss Percy!" Mr. Wiggan suddenly cried out, and the both of them put their heads together as the egg jolted in the middle of its wrappings, the dark shadow of some creature shifting within.

"I think I see an eye?" Mildred wanted to open the curtains, wanted the additional light of a lamp or even a candle to better illuminate what was happening in front of them. "It doesn't look like a bird," she said, her own voice dropping to the level of the vicar's rough whispers. The egg rocked lightly from side to side, while the head of the animal inside jerked and beat away at the shell with a determined vehemence that made her lean back an inch. "Perhaps it is a —"

And then the egg burst apart, spattering them with flecks of shell and some wet, sticky substance. Mr. Wiggan might have sworn. Mildred did, the oaths tumbling out before she could recall to herself any kind of preventative measures against barking curses in front of the local vicar. (As a rule, Mildred rarely swore. She was aware that her knowledge of improper words was limited, that there likely existed a vast panoply of curious and colorful language she would most likely never live to hear or speak, but what words she did know she tended to keep to herself, or to the walls of her bedroom whenever she happened to strike her head on the ceiling or mutter a few chosen phrases in imaginary conversations with Diana.)

"Damn!" she said. One look at the creature spilled across the blankets, and she said it again. "Damn!"

Mr. Wiggan's mouth moved but without anything audible coming out of it.

"It's not a bird." Mildred breathed. She knew that she breathed because she had to take the trouble of reminding herself to do so. "It's some kind of…"

"Bat?" The vicar extended one hand towards the not-bird/bat as it writhed around on the damp, shell-laden blankets. And throughout all of that writhing, the thing… Well, Mildred couldn't think of any better way to describe the noise it made than as a screech. Not a chirp or a peep or any other sound one would expect from a winged animal. But a cry that dug into her ears like metal scraped across a slate.

And, yes. There were wings. Muddy brown stretches of nearly translucent skin that shuddered and crinkled in on themselves as the pitiful thing struggled to right itself.

"Bats don't hatch from eggs," Mildred said, her eyes still on the not-bird/not-bat. If anything, it most resembled a lizard. But with larger feet. And strange bumps running across the top of its narrow, pointed head.

"Well, I *know* that." Mr. Wiggan sounded exasperated.

And eager. He still had not touched the creature, the fingers of his left hand poised only a few inches away from the animal's nose. "I wonder if he will let me—"

The creature twisted its neck around and snapped at Mr. Wiggan's finger, one wing stretching taut as if the thing wanted to leap up from its makeshift nest and fly at the man's head.

Mildred bit back a sound that might have been the beginning of a laugh or the first syllable of another swear. "No. I do not believe he will let you," she finally managed, with a quaver in her voice.

Mr. Wiggan sat back on his heels, taking the time to inspect his—uninjured—finger while the hatchling (Mildred paused at that, and realized she preferred that word for it above all others she'd considered thus far) screeched and snorted and flailed like a staggering drunk every time it attempted to climb onto its feet. (Four feet, she noticed. Four clawed feet, not including the wings. So not like a bird, it seemed. Nor like a bat. More like a cranky hairless kitten. With wings.)

"It's probably hungry, poor thing." She looked around the room from where she sat, still down on the floor, her skirt twisted and tucked around her legs. "Goodness, what do you think it eats?"

"Fingers, I would wager." Mr. Wiggan glared at the hatchling as if the thing were salivating at the thought of fitting its tiny jaws around one of his knuckles. "But most birds feed on insects and worms. Larger birds will make a feast of a mouse or other such animal, but as this one is still so small…"

His use of the word 'small' seemed to be open for further discussion. It was difficult to gain an accurate measure of size from merely observing the hatchling in all of its damp, shrieking, wobbling glory, but even a cursory estimation of its length from nose to stubby tail placed it in the range of "large as a dinner plate."

"I'll fetch Mrs. Babbinton," Mildred said, and wrestled with the hem of her skirt until her legs were unencumbered enough to allow her to stand without immediately tripping over herself again.

"Wait, no!" Mr. Wiggan struggled to his own feet, his attention snapping back and forth between Mildred's progress towards the door and the hatchling behind him. He compromised by holding himself in a low crouch, one hand within arm's reach of the squalling creature, his other held out to Mildred, his palm held upwards in a gesture no doubt meant to halt her progress. "She cannot know!"

His appearance served as a tableau depiction of burgeoning madness. The mess of his hair, the exhausted wildness of his eyes, and then the sheen of perspiration across his face and staining the parts of his shirt that were still visible beneath the coat he had not thought to remove under the onslaught of the room's unbearable warmth. And his hands trembled, an extension of the penned-up energy that vibrated through his figure.

Mildred turned up her own hands, her shoulders lifting in a shrug. "Why not?"

He hesitated. For several seconds, his eyes darted around, his gaze settling on nothing while his mouth worked over words that would not pass the barrier of his lips. "I-I don't know."

"But surely she can help!" She placed one hand on the doorknob. Mr. Wiggan lurched forward, stopping himself from physically hindering her movement, though his hands twitched as if with some reined in urge to grab at her arm.

"It's a secret." Those three words, pushed out on a rush of breath without sound.

Mildred swallowed. "It's a secret?" she repeated, careful to give her version that upwards climb on the last word. "Whatever for?"

Mr. Wiggan turned around himself, the span of his arms taking in the hatchling, the mess of its shell, the curtains, the fire, the entirety of the universe with that sweep of his upper body. "Miss Percy," he said, his voice returning to normal volume after all of his rasping whispers. "Surely you see the gravity of this situation? We've just witnessed the birth of a..." He pointed at the creature, whose screeches were climbing to a feverish pitch. "It has wings! It is a dark thing with wings! And a tail!"

It took a moment for his implications to dawn on her. When they did, she wasn't sure if she was in need of a laugh or if he was in need of a slap. "Are you laboring under the belief you've just hatched out a demon on your drawing room floor?" (There were a fair number of things Mildred had gone through her life assuming she would never have to say. Not until that moment did she realize that this one had failed to make the list because of its obvious aspirations towards utter preposterousness.)

"No, I—" His words were cut off by a choking catch in his throat. A sob? Mildred would not have thought worse of him if it was. "I know it's not a demon," he continued, his hands going to his temples in a way that made her wonder if he was attempting to keep his head firmly attached to the rest of his body. "Of course it's not. Demons don't exist." His gaze shot to her, his eyes widening in horror. "I mean, they do! I'm a vicar! I know they do! But I doubt they hatch from eggs. On the floor of my house. In Wiltshire."

There were times when Mildred very much felt the weight of having been born the eldest sibling in her family, the one who had remained behind with her father and taken care of him as age and illness had overwhelmed him, the one left to shoulder so many of those unseen responsibilities that made up the foundation of a household, everything else resting on those sprawling, stable roots. Releasing the doorknob, she took Mr. Wiggan's arm and led him—he moved with an almost feeble gait, as if he had aged several decades overnight—to one of the armchairs set at a remove from the fireplace and the worst of its heat.

"Where do you keep your spirits?" she asked herself as she left him long enough to search the shelves and one or two cabinets for a small collection of crystal bottles. Most of them bore a fine layer of dust, including the accompanying glasses. She snatched up one of the glasses, wiped it off on her skirt, and filled it halfway with brandy. "Take this," she told him, and pressed the drink into his hand.

He behaved as if he would protest, but he finally accepted the drink and downed half of it in the first swallow. With Mr. Wiggan seated and out of the way, she again went to the door, opened it, and called for Mrs. Babbinton. The good lady must have known an eventual summons was inevitable, as she popped out from the direction of the kitchen with the asperity of a freshly oiled jack-in-the-box.

"I need your help," Mildred said as the housekeeper approached. No doubt it was best to prostrate herself at Mrs. Babbinton's feet if she wanted everything to be seen to as it should be.

"It's Mr. Wiggan, isn't it?" Mrs. Babbinton buried her hands in her apron, then smoothed the fabric down again. "Is it an attack of some sort? I never thought he would be the kind to succumb to weak nerves, but—"

Mildred pushed open the door, giving the housekeeper a full view of the sitting room and all of its inhabitants. "Mr. Wiggan is as well as can be expected," she said as Mrs. Babbinton stepped past her and into the room. "But it seems we have an unexpected arrival this morning."

"Heavens." Mrs. Babbinton stopped halfway across the room, both of her work-raw hands flying to her chest. "It looks like a broiled pheasant."

Mr. Wiggan drained the last of his brandy and rested the empty glass on his knee. "It must be an exotic species," he said, and Mildred was glad to see some of the wildness had already faded from his eyes. "Can't think where your great uncle must have found it."

"It needs to eat, I imagine," Mildred said, drawing Mrs.

Babbinton's attention again. "It's newly born and it's hungry. Can you fetch a few things it might like to eat?"

"U-Um," came the housekeeper's steady and not at all baffled reply.

"Any kind of soft, boiled meat you might have? I do not know if it has any teeth—"

A snort from Mr. Wiggan, who was still slowly twirling his glass on his knee.

"—but if you could arrange a selection of things, to see what it might prefer?"

Mrs. Babbinton's hands drifted away from the vicinity of her chest as her shoulders pushed back, a measure of steel reinvigorating her spine now that she'd been given a task to complete. "Yes, yes. I'll see what I have set aside. And maybe some fruit? Do you think it would like a few berries or an apple?"

"Birds like berries," Mr. Wiggan announced, looking at no one in particular. "And some bats eat fruit."

"It's not a bat," Mildred reminded him, her words balanced on a fraying thread of patience. "Unfortunately, we don't know what it is," she said to Mrs. Babbinton. "So until we do, I'm afraid there is going to be quite a bit of trial and error ahead of us."

Mildred thought she heard another snort from the vicar, but when she glanced towards where he sat, it was to see that he had slumped down into his chair, his head lolling against his shoulder as he snored himself into a deeper slumber.

"I'll return in a few minutes with some food for the..." the housekeeper's gaze flicked to the hatchling—now half tangled in a sheet and furiously gnawing at the end of its own tail—"Well, just give me a few minutes. Oh, and don't worry about him," she added as she headed towards the door, nudging her elbow in the direction of Mr. Wiggan's unconscious form. "Just toss a blanket over him and he'll be fine until it's time for tea!"

CHAPTER SIX

The familial patterns followed by dragons in the raising of their young is an intriguing one. They are not like some lizards, laying their eggs and then leaving them to fare for themselves. Neither are they like many birds, building a nest and with the male or female sharing responsibility for the eggs and the chicks to hatch from them. Instead, the care of a young dragon appears to fall to whichever senior member of the group is most willing to take on the task. And while it may seem an unconventional arrangement to some observers, it has shown nothing but success among their own ranks.

-from Chapter Eight of Miss Percy's Pocket Guide (to the Care and Feeding of British Dragons)

The hatchling did not seem to care for the fruit Mrs. Babbinton offered. Two sniffs at a sliver of rapidly browning pear, a lick at a dollop of blackberry preserves, and the creature's slitted nostrils flared as it whipped its head away.

Chicken, however, proved itself a clear favorite. And ham. And even a few cold, roasted potatoes edged with a congealed layer of the fat they had been cooked in.

"Well, he's a hungry thing, make no mistake." Mrs.

Babbinton dried the last of the dishes and stacked them neatly on the shelf. The hatchling, his small belly swollen from his inaugural feast, now dozed ("dozed" being the polite word choice for "tipped over unconscious after devouring a third helping of ham and not bothering to budge since") on a bed of old sheets tucked into one of the housekeeper's laundry baskets.

The basket sat near the fire, and Mildred sat on a stiff-backed chair beside the basket, a hot cup of tea held between her hands. Her own stomach was filled with the breakfast Mrs. Babbinton had prepared for her, a larger plate that had mirrored the hatchling's own selections. But now she wanted nothing more than to sit, and to warm her hands with the cup of tea and think about everything that wasn't connected with leaving the vicarage kitchen and returning home again.

It was still early. She had consulted the clock a few minutes ago and found that not two hours had passed since Betsy had first knocked on her door and delivered Mr. Wiggan's confounding note to her. Diana would most likely still be asleep, the younger children perhaps only just waking for the day. Another hour was most likely all she had left to her before her absence would be noted and made into a possible cause for—

Not alarm. No, Mildred did not flatter herself enough to believe her family would go out of their way to worry about her should she suddenly stumble beyond the boundaries of things they considered fully deserving of their care and attention. Now, inconvenience…yes, that would be a more apt reaction from them, she decided. Like waking to find that a favorite shawl or a most comfortable pair of shoes had been misplaced. Nothing so life-altering that one could not soldier on with only a slight hiccough marring their day.

Mildred tapped her fingers on the side of her cup and took another sip. Her fingers were cold, even with the heat of the tea held against them. Cold fingers and cold feet and her heart jolting about in her chest at a more rapid pace than sitting in a chair by the fire sipping tea and digesting ham and potatoes should have warranted. A mild sort of shock, she assumed it was, and touched the tip of her shoe to the edge of the basket in front of her.

Now that the creature was asleep, she was at liberty to study it more closely. The first thing she had noticed, once they had carried the sleeping thing out of the darkened sitting room and into the brilliant, open light of the kitchen, was its color. In the golden glow of the sun from the windows, its skin carried a bronze sheen to it over the dark, muddy brown of its hide. There was something almost pearlescent to it, noticeable in the slight shifting of colors as it breathed.

"It's beautiful," she admitted, unaware she'd spoken the words out loud until Mrs. Babbinton came up to stand beside her.

"Like nothing else I've ever set my eyes on," the housekeeper said, drying her hands on her apron. "You'll have a chore ahead of you, you know. Figuring out what to do with it, who it belongs to."

"Oh." Mildred hadn't dared to push her thoughts that far ahead. For now, it was this small, sleeping animal, curled up and seemingly harmless in its bed. But surely the thing would grow. Already half the size of a fully matured house cat, her imagination balked at attempting to draw a picture of how large an adult of its species could become.

And then there was the matter of its wings…

Her grip on her cup tightened, her knuckles turning from pink to white. "I suppose that means it's my responsibility. At least, until we can find someone more knowledgeable on the subject of…" She bit at the inside of her bottom lip. She didn't want to say "winged lizards." In fact, the hatchling's wings were what she suspected had sent her into her current state of bewilderment. She knew of the existence of creatures like crocodiles and alligators, those monstrous animals with their jaws full of teeth and whip-like tails and...

Oh, but they didn't have wings.

Mildred closed her eyes. Sipped her tea. Listened to that eerie, whistling hum that emanated from the hatchling's tiny lungs on its every exhalation.

"But I cannot take it home with me." She looked up at Mrs. Babbinton, and all of a sudden she felt like a small child, her heart in her throat, her expression imploring. "My sister, her children... Do you think, for a little while, it could stay here? At least until we discover what it is and how to better care for it. And I'm sure if we write to my great uncle's assistant, he might know the name of someone who could help us, someone in the scientific community, perhaps."

"I'm sure it would be happier here for the time being, without having to worry about being poked and teased by your niece and nephew. And as we don't yet know how this poor mite would tolerate children, it might be the safest choice."

The last of her tea slid down her throat with all the ease of a large pineapple. The hatchling had burst out of its egg ready to snip at Mr. Wiggan's hands as if his fingers were sausages, so the thought of keeping it in a home that included young, curious children—each with their own set of young, curious fingers—seemed like a traumatic bodily injury bouncing eagerly in the wings for its turn onstage.

"Not well," Mildred said, her voice calm and steady and utterly unlike the chaos whirling around in her head. "I don't think it would tolerate children well at all. Though perhaps when it is..." Older? Larger? Possessed of teeth?

Mrs. Babbinton placed her hand on Mildred's shoulder. "I'll speak with Mr. Wiggan about it, but I'm sure he'll agree to it." *Once he wakes up*, was the unspoken part of that sentence. Once the initial shock wore off and he was no longer raving about demons spitting out puffs of hellfire onto his sitting room carpet.

She looked at the hatchling—Had she really ceased to look at it since helping Mrs. Babbinton settle it into its makeshift bed by the fire?—and a strange thought assailed her. Well, more of a picture really. From one of the books she often read to the children in an effort to help them calm down before bed each night, an illustration all done in vivid colors, faded only from years of busy hands sliding over the pages.

"St. George," Mildred muttered, and snapped her mouth shut again before the thought could progress any further.

"What was that, dear?" Mrs. Babbinton had already taken her empty cup and was rinsing the tea leaves from the bottom.

"Oh, nothing." She shook her head, and with it shook off a momentary sensation of dizziness. "I believe I was up too early, is all." A reassuring smile for Mrs. Babbinton and she rose from her chair. "You will let me know if you need anything?" Her gaze darted to the basket and back again.

"No worries, dear. I've enough food here to see us through a siege! Now, let me fetch your things and I've another basket of cakes for the children."

She didn't want to return home. It was a realization that nipped at her heels all the way from the vicarage, through town, and around to the back door of the house where she let herself in through the kitchen. The final tumult of preparations for breakfast were underway, so she set her basket down from Mrs. Babbinton (though not before reaching inside and tearing off a chunk of spiced pear cake that clung deliciously to her fingers) and did her best to stay out of the way as she slipped out of her spencer and bonnet, shoving them under the nearest side table until she could fetch them later.

"Is everyone at home?" she asked Betsy, who was filling a platter with strips of bacon.

"The family is in the dining room," the maid said with only a quick glance from beneath a furrowed, perspiring brow. "I told Mrs. Muncy you were out for an early walk around the house when she asked after you."

A weight dropped into her stomach, along with her last bite of cake. "She asked after me?"

"Master Matthew and Miss Nettie were up early," was all Patsy would divulge. But it acted as a kind of coded message, and Mildred managed a quick check of her hair (two pins out of place, one lock of hair sticking out from her temple like a pennant) and her hem (damp and bearing a few streaks of mud, but nothing overly offensive) before she swiped her mouth free of crumbs and walked through to join the rest of the family in the dining room.

At first, no one seemed to take notice of her entrance. Mr. Muncy sat behind his fortification of newsprint and steaming eggs, while Diana continued buttering a slice of toast for Matthew without even a twitch of an eyebrow shifting the placidity of her expression. Belinda was engrossed with the distorted reflection of herself in the back of her spoon, one eye narrowed in survey of a large spot on the left side of her chin. Nettie was the only one who smiled at her arrival, even going so far as to nudge the empty chair beside her with the side of her foot.

"You were awake very early this morning," Diana said, after she'd finished buttering the toast and turned her attention back to her own plate. She did not look at Mildred, behaving as if her food was the most engrossing thing in the room.

The silence following this stretched on. It wasn't until Mildred had filled her own plate (it did not signify that she had already consumed coffee and a bun and breakfast at the vicarage and a stolen chunk of pear cake before coming into the dining room, because when something had her all in a panic, she often found the most successful way of pushing the panic aside was to continually nibble on things until there was simply no more room in her physical body for anything like worry or fear to take up residence) that she realized her sister wasn't intending to speak again and had instead swatted the conversational shuttlecock towards her side of the table.

"Oh, um. Yes? I was?" She was flustered. She hated when she was flustered, when her cheeks warmed and her mouth stuttered over words and everything she said came out in the tone of a question, as if she were seeking approval for each phrase.

"If you're going to traipse about the garden before the grass has fully dried, perhaps consider changing into another gown before you join us at the table, hmm?" Diana did look up then, her words delivered on the curve of a smile that made them more severe than if her features had been cast in a censorious light.

"Ah." Mildred spared a glance for her arms, her sleeves still displaying minute spatters from the hatchling's shattered egg. "I am sorry." She took an extra slice of bacon for her plate, then changed her mind and began to push her chair back from the table.

Diana waved a hand, compelling her back to her seat. "No need to fret about it now. What's done is done. But from here forward, you know what I would prefer."

From here forward, yes. She knew. Those three words had so often been the preface to Diana's unsolicited swathes of advice, cutting through all other dialogue with the neat, precise swing of a farmer's scythe. So often that her sister no longer had need of continuing on with the delivery of the advice itself, only that passive addition of "from here forward" to subtly shift the receiver of the unspoken advice into place.

The stains on her gown were not so bad, Mildred thought, studying her own sleeves and the front of her bodice where some of the spray from the hatchling's introduction to the world had struck her. Like a fine scattering of light raindrops, is how it appeared on the fabric. Nothing, thankfully, that would serve to betray where she had been or what she had been involved in only a short while before.

"Aunt Mildred," Nettie piped up from her seat beside her, her mouth still half-filled with egg. "When are we going to visit the vicarage again?"

The tines of Mildred's fork scratched against the edge of her plate. She cleared her throat as if the sound had been a fumble of words from her own mouth. Then she put down her fork, then picked it up again. "Oh, that. Well." She had told her sister that she had planned on visiting the vicarage regularly to help Mr. Wiggan with the lessons for his students. The children, plied into satiety with the aid of Mrs. Babbinton's cakes, would voice every wish to return. Mildred's tongue dug into her back teeth as she attempted to concoct a reply that wouldn't begin a scattering of pebbles down a hill which would become a tumble of boulders which would become an avalanche which would all culminate with two young children learning of the existence of a...

"I want to see the rock again," Matthew said, speaking around a bite of sausage pushed into his cheek. "I want to see if it will roll the entire way across a table!"

Her mind skittered to a halt, just as it had done before. A veritable portcullis dropping in place, and she struggled for a moment to find her way back to the original conversation. "The rock." She glanced towards her sister, though seeing as how they were not speaking of matters fashionable or financial, Diana's attention had already drifted back towards the contents of her plate. "Yes, that. Well, there are some other curious things in Mr. Wiggan's keeping I'm sure you would be interested in."

"Where did the rock come from?" Nettie asked, and Mildred briefly nursed a wish to be close enough to kick the girl under the table. Because she couldn't say that it had come in a trunk from her Great Uncle Forthright. A trunk that she had yet to confess to Diana had ever been delivered. A trunk containing a rock that had hatched some sort of creature that wasn't a chicken or a lizard or a bat or anything else regularly occurring in nature.

"You would have to ask Mr. Wiggan about that." Mildred wiped her mouth with her napkin and thought about excusing herself from the table before her heart bounded out of her throat like a regurgitated fish bone. "And I'm sure Mrs. Babbinton would enjoy seeing you again, but you must understand that we cannot take up all of her time. She has much to do," she added, her voice tightening as she pulled things out of the air to say. "Seeing to the vicarage and all of the little tasks that go along with being so closely connected to the church."

"But Mr. Wiggan is a single gentleman," Diana said, and her gaze flicked towards where Belinda sat—still attempting to make out her reflection in the silverware, this time drawing in her cheeks until little hollows appeared beneath her cheekbones. "I cannot imagine his housekeeper must have much to do, without even the addition of a wife to cook for or clean up after. I wonder, you know, why he has not married."

"Perhaps he has yet to be tempted by any of the local ladies." Belinda wrinkled her nose as she put down her spoon. "If I were a gentleman, and I was forced to choose a wife from our village, I might decide to remain unmarried as well. And I wager I would be happier for it."

Diana rolled her eyes heavenward, a silent prayer for guidance in that glance. "Don't you realize that you insult yourself by saying such things?" *Stupid girl*, was the unspoken cap to that sentence, though it still managed to echo across the table as if it had been rung out with a gong. "But I cannot understand why he doesn't marry. He's been here almost ten years, and I've not heard a single rumor connecting him with anyone he might have had his eye on for a wife."

"He might have other matters on his mind," Mildred said, thinking of his cluttered study, his insects and butterflies, the unknown creature nestled in a basket by the kitchen fire.

"Well, I hope he's not one of those who styles himself along the lines of the Roman Catholics, thinking they must dedicate themselves wholly to the church. His living is nothing to turn up one's nose at, and I've heard tell there's a baronetcy somewhere in his family line. A waste for all of that to be gifted on a man who shows no interest in the matrimonial state." Diana forked a piece of bacon with a grand display of vehemence, Mr. Wiggan's decision to keep himself unmarried into his fifth decade apparently taken by her as a personal affront.

The meal faltered along, Mildred steadily eating and avoiding speaking as much as she could while she calculated how long before she could escape from the table and not be accused of harboring a lack of manners. Belinda was the first to leave (Mildred would add a special mention of her and her spotty chin in her evening prayers), allowing everyone else to drift away as they would. Diana needed to pay a visit to Mrs. Haverstick (for tea and gossip and to bask in the mutual loathing that only two married women with unmarried daughters could hold for one another) and Mr. Muncy needed to go over the accounts (an accepted way of admitting that he wanted to sit in his study and stuff the bowl of his pipe with tobacco without his wife raising a complaint about the smell).

"Come along upstairs," Mildred instructed the children as she pushed back her chair and stood. "Nettie, wipe your face first, please. No, Matthew, you cannot take the pot of honey with you. Leave it. Leave it!"

Upstairs, upstairs. It was all she could think about. Corralling the children into the nursery, setting them up with their primers and their slates, sinking comfortably into the monotony that threaded through her day, a pastoral suite of soft strings and predictable woodwinds. They would read and do their sums and she would take them out into the garden, perhaps even let them go down to the stream and search beneath the rocks on the shore for the little grubs and worms keeping themselves warm just beneath the ground's surface. The entire day rolled out before her, a play of her own composition. And even while she added small details to the scenes—mending a hole in her sleeve after dinner, seeking out a new book to take to bed with her—her steps took her over to the shelf of books along the wall, filled mostly with toys but boasting a few volumes of stories and histories she'd read to the children over and again.

There, she plucked one particular book from the shelf. There, her fingers danced quickly through to the correct page. There, there, there. The man on the horse, St. George, clad in his armor, wielding his sword and his spear. And there, on the opposite page, the illustration done in broad strokes of brown and gold, the dragon with his nostrils flared, his jaws wide open, his teeth, his claws, his wide, wide wings…

"Aunt Mildred, I cannot figure out what's become of my seven! Every time I add up all the numbers, the seven disappears!"

She closed the book with a snap. Silly, silly, silly. Her imagination was running away from her again. To think that the hatchling could in any way resemble…that she could ever entertain the notion, even in jest…

Her fingers felt chilled again. She thought she might have to sit down. Would she need smelling salts? She had never needed them before in all her life, but then there was always a first instance for everything. (It would come to her later that perhaps there should be a type of measurement scale devised in the usage of smelling salts as an indication of how desperate and debilitating a situation was. The bottom of the scale could begin with a minor family drama, then sliding up towards unanticipated pieces of scandalous gossip before it finally levered its way to unidentified creatures that resemble demons, or possibly dragons, hatching out of large rocks in one's presence.)

Dragon. Ah, there it was. The very word she'd been

avoiding all of this time. After helping Matthew with his missing seven, she opened the book again, her thumb having been tucked inside, marking the page she wanted.

She knew, of course, that the hatchling couldn't be a dragon. Not in the way they were depicted in fairy tale stories, as massive creatures stealing away princesses and breathing fire and wheeling over the ramparts of crumbling castles as they tilted their massive wings to catch an updraft of warm air. But she also knew that myths often came with their roots embedded in truth. Perhaps there had once existed a type of animal, one with wings or claws, something placed away from the ordinary enough that it managed to plant the seed capable of growing into an altogether new kind of something. The kind that gilded reality with the fanciful aspect of make-believe.

Or perhaps the hatchling currently residing in Mr. Wiggan's kitchen was simply an unidentified species of lizard or a crocodilian cousin with a penchant for biting things and over-indulging on cold chicken. The wings would most likely turn out to be useless. And all of her imaginings would serve little more than to cause her undue worry and an unhealthful appetite for baked things.

"Now," Mildred said, setting down the book and giving it an extra push away from her. "Let us see how we are with our reading today, hmm?"

The reading, however, did not distract her from her thoughts. Halfway through the lesson and Matthew's monotonous recitations had left her mind with nothing more to do than sketch out a picture of a knight in full armor tramping towards the vicarage with his sword and shield raised against the mewling onslaught of a chicken-sized dragon shrieking from his perch on the roof for want of more ham and gravy.

"What do you think of dragons?" She asked the question out loud, though it had been playing inside her head much like the first few notes of a tune Belinda could never master on the pianoforte.

Matthew's head popped up first, as though he had been waiting for any sort of interruption to pull him away from the morals and drudgery (and moral drudgery) of his primer. "Like a real dragon?"

"Well—" Mildred began, before Nettie interjected with:

"What do you mean, a real dragon? Dragons aren't real!" She looked at Mildred, eyes wide with a need for confirmation of her rightness. "Aunt Mildred, tell him they're not real."

She had lied to the children before, of course. Those little white lies one tells to make the day progress with fewer bumps and tantrums, such as letting them believe that if they failed to clean their teeth before bed, ants would come in and carry their teeth away crumb by crumb (which began as a story Matthew told to horrify his sister but Mildred was too busy trying not to laugh that she could neither confirm nor deny its veracity, and so it was left to take on an edge of truth). But she found she could not open her mouth and say the words—or any words that could be construed as negating the existence of dragons—'No, they are not real.'

"I believe many myths have an element of truth to them, some bit of history mingled with the fantastical. So even though it is quite easy to say that dragons do not exist simply because we are not tripping over them like cats in the street, that doesn't mean there might not have possibly been some creature, at some point in time, that might have resembled a dragon. Or even have been one. Possibly, of course." And she cleared her throat. And she sniffed. And she glanced from Matthew to Nettie and back again.

"Aunt Mildred," Nettie began, sitting up straight and setting her hands on her on the edge of the little school table in front of her. "You cannot believe in dragons. That's all fairy stuff! Like princesses falling under magic spells and knights having to battle ogres and trolls in order to rescue them!"

"I believe in dragons." Matthew's tone bordered on mulish, his jaw set in a way meant to demonstrate he would not be bullied from his faith. And then he looked at his sister and stuck his tongue out at her.

"Now, that's enough," Mildred said, and tapped the corner of Matthew's primer. "Back to your lesson. We've strayed far enough from your work for one day."

"But what about you?" Matthew looked up at her, his eyes wide as saucers, his expression as open as a window looking out onto an entirely new world. "You never said. Do you believe dragons exist?"

Oh, but it was like taking a step off the edge of a cliff and hoping the wind itself would rush over to catch her. "Yes," she said. Such a small word, and yet bearing all of her courage on it. "Yes, I rather think they do."

CHAPTER SEVEN

Dragons are known for their hoarding, a trait often presented as singular to species classed lower than human in the kingdom Animalia. And yet, after more than four decades of observing people ambling about in their daily lives, it leaves one to wonder if it is not merely dragons and magpies who should be acknowledged for delighting in taking and keeping things for themselves...

-from the first draft of Miss Percy's Pocket Guide (to the Care and Feeding of British Dragons), an excerpt later deleted

If Reginald Hawthorne had known he was going to be the villain of the piece, he might have made a greater effort to dress the part.

Instead, he wore what he always wore, the same brown coat and brown trousers and one of three linen shirts that he owned (this one with the small patch in the sleeve he'd had to mend himself because what else was he to do without a valet or a maid at his disposal?) and all on a foundation of top boots in dire need of a polish. (He was perfectly capable of polishing his own boots, but the boots bore enough scuffs and scratches that even a good buffing couldn't clear away. Better to leave them looking a bit shabby on purpose and allow people to believe they would be in fine condition again if only he would look after them better.)

There was no looking glass in his room with which to judge his appearance. So he brushed his hair and shaved his chin (hardly something he needed to do every day, as he was young and he was fair and the hair that occasionally chose to decorate the lower half of his face preferred to grow as intemperate patches of pale fuzz) and did the best he could with an unstarched, unlaundered neckcloth.

It was not a fine day, he realized, when he stepped outside and squinted up at the sky (the sky choosing to practice its own brand of intemperance with a drizzly sort of precipitation that was too light to necessitate an umbrella but too heavy to be ignored.) It didn't matter that this was the same day and the same sky beneath which one Miss Mildred Percy was currently contemplating and frantically dismissing the notion of dragons as a veritable part of England's history. London was two counties away from Wiltshire, and if England was known for anything, it was that one region often had no desire to share its weather with any other place.

So he scrunched up his shoulders, pulled his head down until his neck disappeared into his collar, and surrendered to feeling very much like an upright turtle making its way along the pavement. There were no friendly glances exchanged with passersby. Head down, hands pushed into his pockets, he completed the transformation from terrapin to surly schoolboy.

By jove, he hated the rain. Hated how it leaked through the thin soles of his boots and left his socks damp, his toes cold and rubbed raw. The first thing he would do when he succeeded in recovering his father's legacy—well, *his* legacy, now that his father was dead and summarily buried —was to purchase himself a new pair of boots. And more than three shirts. And possibly even hire someone to give his laundry a proper cleaning and starching.

Reginald was tired of wandering about through his life bearing a patina of poverty. Not so poor that he was dependent on charity or burning peat for warmth or begging for his next meal, but poor enough that no one who was capable of boosting him up another rung or two of life's fiscal ladder would reach a hand down to help him.

He wasn't greedy. He told himself this again and again, and again as he adjusted his hat in the hope the brim would prevent a few drops of rain from landing on the back of his neck. He simply wanted enough to no longer have to worry from day to day about the basic necessities that so many were privileged enough to take for granted.

And, to be perfectly honest, he wanted a wife. And a family. And he didn't want to risk bringing either of those things under his care when he couldn't afford better lodgings than an attic room at the top of Mrs. Tadcaster's Lodging House for Gentlemen of Quality. (Mrs. Tadcaster's Lodging House for Gentlemen of Quality had only ever housed one Gentleman of Quality (capital letters, of course) though it was questionable if having a down-on-his-luck Marquess pass out on the doorstep for three hours one April morning when George III was still in full possession of his wits fell under the definition of "housed.")

Which was why he was striding down a narrow avenue, cursing every time his foot slipped and landed in the gutter or some unseen hole in the pavement, all while keeping one eye open for the entrance to The Bull and Horns.

A bell jangled when he opened the door and stepped inside, though no one turned to look his way. The Bull and Horns did a middling sort of business, never full enough to make one think it was someplace to be, and never so deserted that one worried what was so reprehensible as to keep the custom away. Reginald shut the door behind him and stood on the scrap of straw mat set out for visitors to drip onto, his gaze struggling to permeate the haze of smoke from pipes and cigarettes and the smoke from a large, hissing fireplace and the smoke from candles that dribbled greasily onto the various tables scattered about the room.

He found who he was looking for near the rear of the

room, as all persons in want of being sought out by another person tended to be. Reginald made his way through the maze of men who gave all the appearance of existing in a state of partial inebriation, his boots slipping slightly on the combination of wet from his own boots mingled with the grease and grit (one hoped that was all it was) decorating the floor.

"Mr. Purvis?"

Mr. Purvis looked up from his previous task of staring blankly at some point off in the middle distance. "Mr. Hawthorne? Ah, yes. There you are."

Reginald kept his face clear of distaste. It wasn't that he didn't like Mr. Purvis. Perhaps Mr. Purvis was a fine, magnanimous fellow with a beloved family at home, the type of man who bounced his children on his knees and emptied his own pockets of spare coins whenever he saw someone in need. But Mr. Purvis was also afflicted with the unfortunate trait of being perpetually moist.

Mr. Purvis held out his hand—his bare hand—to shake.

Reginald took it, gritting his teeth at the dampness that clung to the other man's palm. "Do you have any news?" he asked, using the question to end the handshake as quickly as possible. He pulled out a chair at the other side of the small table and sat down, using a feigned obsession with the seat's placement adjacent to the table as a shield behind which he could wipe his hand down the length of his thigh.

"Oh, yes. Do not trouble yourself to think that I am the sort of man who doesn't work for his income." Mr. Purvis opened up a small valise he'd been holding on his lap, pulled out a sheaf of papers, and thumbed through them, the tip of his tongue poking out from the corner of his mouth with the effort. "First, I was able to ascertain that the gentleman you inquired of, a Mr. Charles Forthright?"

Reginald nodded. How that name had haunted him for the last decade of his life, lurking like a red-eyed devil behind every spot of bad luck to come his way.

"Well, yes." Another shuffle of a few more papers. "He's dead."

"He's...?" Reginald closed his mouth. He hadn't been expecting that. "Oh. So—"

"His house and lands have gone to his former assistant." Red-rimmed eyes, as if the man were always on the verge of betraying some intense feeling, peered at him from over the edge of his wilting papers. "But you're not interested in any of that, I gather."

"I want the stone." It came out, an almost childish demand in its clarity and single-mindedness.

"Well, yes. And thankfully, a few coins in the right hands..." Mr. Purvis made a gesture towards Reginald, one that etched a figure in the air between them, of pounds and pence, of so much—too much—of Reginald's pathetic savings given over to this Mr. Purvis in order that he might track the whereabouts of the stone.

His inward self rolled his eyes at his choice of wording. He knew it wasn't a bloody stone. As if it were a fancy pebble his father had uncovered and applied some drink-induced worth to over a dozen years ago. But, no. He knew the truth of it. He'd seen the truth of it. The stone wasn't a stone but a beginning. A renaissance. Ah, yes. He liked that word. A new age in England's story, one that would carve its place in the long memories of men, one in which he would play a substantial part.

This was the grandiose version of the dream, of course. A fellow couldn't avoid having multiple versions of the same dream, the more probable version often kicked to the bottom of the stack in favor of ones involving names etched on plaques and heads recreated on sizable chunks of marble. The attainable version of events, the one that came to him most often at night when all the usual anxieties and fears preferred to creep onto his pillow and settle there like little lozenges of botheration, promised a bit of security. Perhaps a tentative foothold in the next level of society. And, if he was fortunate enough in the pecuniary way of things, enough money to support a wife and family and all of the expenses that came with it.

What he would *not* do was follow in the same path as his father. He would not drink. He would not gamble away things like family fortunes (well, it hadn't exactly been a fortune as people often defined the word, but it would have been enough to see Reginald through the rest of his years at Oxford and given him a tidy sum with which to maybe head to London and begin an apprenticeship with someone, anyone.) And he would not meet his fate by tripping and falling into a freshly dug grave (thankfully empty of the person it had been dug for), thereby chiseling his own name into the same local tales and ale-marinated jokes his father's now circulated within.

"...and I was able to view a copy of Mr. Charles Forthright's last will and testament," Mr. Purvis finished, broad lips glistening as they stretched into a humble smile.

"Yes? And?" Reginald had told himself he did not wish to appear too eager. Don't allow Mr. Purvis to see how very much this meant to him. Let the man think this entire matter was constructed on the shifting foundations of a young gentleman's whims (and yes, he would refer to himself as a gentleman, in total disregard of the state of his boots.)

Mr. Purvis's shining eyes picked up the light from the fire, from the candles set on nearby tables, giving them a jaundiced sheen. "I've made some notes here and there"—a shake of the pages in his hands—"and I believe I have ascertained the disposal of all of Mr. Charles Forthrights earthly belongings."

Reginald's fingers twitched with the urge to grab at the damp pages, but instead he curled his hands into fists on the tabletop, bitten-down nails scratching at the skin of his palms.

"The majority of his belongings—house and property and such—have all been given away to the former assistant, a

Mr. Richard Gorman. The rest has gone to the usual sprinkling of male relatives, the usual sort of thing." A flick of his fingers, a click of his tongue against his teeth, and all of the laws of primogeniture echoed in that sucking sound from his mouth. "However, there was a mention of Miss Mildred Percy—a great niece, if my search of their family tree has not turned up rotten fruit." He flashed another dewy smile at his own wit, cleared his throat at Reginald's lack of appreciation of said wit, and returned his gaze to the papers before him. "She was listed as inheriting a 'great many of Mr. Charles Forthright's personal items of historical import and interest, to be chosen by Mr. Charles Forthright himself.'" He looked up at Reginald. "There you have it!"

Reginald breathed, that light, quick exhalation one often does before bathing with cold water or speaking with a person to whom one nurtures a serious attraction. "Miss Mildred Percy?"

"She has inherited most of his personal papers, artifacts, all of the little things on which no one else has attempted to stake a claim."

"Miss Mildred Percy," he said her name again. And he did not doubt he would say it another hundred times, until it no longer sounded like a name or anything that even consisted of English letters and sounds. "And did you discover where she lives?"

Mr. Purvis held up a finger, his skin as smooth and soft as an infant's. "Wiltshire. She lives with her sister and brother-in-law, Mr. Muncy. Oh, just outside of Upper Plimpton."

"Upper Plimpton. Wiltshire." Not as far as he feared, then. He could be there in a day or two, which would keep the cost of travel lower than anticipated. "I think I will write to her, this Miss Percy."

Mr. Purvis nodded, sniffing. "Ah, that would be the best way to go about all this, I'm sure. Introduce yourself, let her know of your interest in this stone of yours—of your father's —and see if things can be managed from there. You'll most likely find that it holds no value to her at all and you'll have it returned to your care with minimal difficulty."

They were the sort of words that begged the accompaniment of music in a minor key, words to make a more astute person experience a shiver of fear at the premonition of irony contained in those syllables, words to cause the author of them to laugh softly in a manner composed of both fiendishness and glee at the future already planned several chapters ahead.

Words that Reginald heartily clung to with an uncharacteristic measure of optimism. His penchant for cynicism had been battered into the corner by those daydreams of comfort and family and financial security. His toes wiggled inside his boots, a soft squelch of wet skin and wet socks and wet soles working like waterlogged flint and steel to begin a smolder of anticipation beneath his feet.

He would go to Wiltshire at once. No, not at once. He couldn't very well show up on this Miss Mildred Percy's doorstep and demand the return of the stone to his possession looking like some bedraggled thing living off a pittance and the fading wisps of good favor. He would have to look the part. He wasn't absolutely certain what part he was supposed to resemble, but he knew that 'Ragged Desperation' was not a role that would win him a great deal of sympathy with the average person.

Numbers ricocheted off the inside of his skull. To be fair, the numbers did not add up to a grand total, but with a few economies (he would have to give up his room at Mrs. Tadcaster's Lodging House for Gentlemen of Quality, and whittle himself down from three meals per day to two, and if he sold what was left of his books, and his watch...) he could just afford to style himself into a person with at least a few gildings of respectability.

And perhaps that would be enough to win Miss Mildred Percy to his cause. If she proved susceptible enough to his pleas, that is.

Damn his father, he thought, and immediately regretted the traitorous outburst. But Reginald would fix everything. He would win back the esteem his family had once courted. He would erase the mockery that now clanged along with the stories of his father's death. And he would have the stone again, the one promised to him by his father.

He would have his fortune.

CHAPTER EIGHT

Not all dragons are possessed of the capacity to breathe fire. This is considered advantageous for many reasons, the foremost of them being that a mass of creatures roaming about the countryside with an ability to incinerate objects at their choosing

Not all dragons are possessed of the capacity to breathe fire. The mechanics of this ability are still shrouded in some mystery, despite multiple examinations of gifted specimens - following their natural demise, of course. But from the scant evidence uncovered, it appears that fire-breathing is akin to the production of venom or a poison sting to ward off enemies, and not an attribute to instill unwarranted amounts of fear in a sensible person.

-from Chapter Four of Miss Percy's Pocket Guide (to the Care and Feeding of British Dragons)

Mornings were never welcome. Mildred understood their place in the world; everything must have a beginning of some sort, and things like days and weeks and years and even time could not be exempt from that. But mornings weighed on her like a burden, like a trial to be endured before she could arrive at the legitimate part of the day, with the sun fully risen and the birds already digesting their ill-gotten worms.

And yet she was often awake before the rest of the household, her body behaving in the most traitorous manner to a mind determined to huddle beneath the covers and not come out until such things as bread and chocolate and afternoons were on offer. "Often" being the operative word, as on this morning—a day after being woken early and summoned to the vicarage by Mr. Wiggan to watch the hatching of a...thing, and a late night spent rummaging through all of her Great Uncle Forthright's papers (the ones not already taken over to the vicarage) in search of any note or mention of winged lizards hatching from large stone eggs —she didn't believe she could muster herself into movement even if Bonaparte himself rolled up a cannon to the side of the house and took aim for the attic windows.

She rallied as best she could. She dressed (a clean but slightly rumpled gown), did something or other with her hair (pins might have been involved?), remembered to don footwear (shoes, matching), and walked downstairs to breakfast.

Except that she had missed breakfast.

She looked around the empty dining room, blinking as if she had the power to bring her family to their seats with a few flutters of her puffy eyelids. "Oh," she said. She looked at the angle of the sunlight coming through the windows, then realized she hadn't bothered to glance at a clock since battling her way out of her bed. "Oh," came again, this time with a wince.

The kitchen, then. She made her way there, hearing voices before she arrived at the door. The younger children sat on low stools, kicking their heels against the rungs while they peeled last season's wrinkled apples and stole more bites than what went into the bowl before them.

96

"I see you're up at last!" Cook glanced up from her work, trimming the fat from a dauntingly sized wedge of ham. "Mrs. Muncy was looking for you, and as I hadn't seen you, I took the liberty of telling her that I thought you looked a touch unwell last night." Her gray eyebrows did a little kick on her forehead. "And I thought you would be tired, after all that running about yesterday."

"Thank you." Mildred said it without thinking if she should be offended by Cook's mention of her less-than-lustrous appearance the evening before. She knew she had looked unwell. Stress did not suit her, no matter how many people throughout her life had referred to her ability to remain calm in a crisis as something to be complimented. But then, how were others to know that beneath her cloak of adept composure there existed a panicked thing, alternately crying and screaming and longing for a nap and all while craving something glazed in sugar? "I suppose I will have to seek her out at some point, let her know that I am well."

"No worries about that!" Betsy said, sailing into the room with a basket of laundry clutched beneath one arm. "Mrs. Muncy has already gone out for the morning, making her calls."

Mildred rubbed the back of her hand over the bridge of her nose. "Is it that late?"

Cook herded her towards the other side of the small wooden table where the children sat, still munching on rapidly browning slices of apple with all the furtiveness that would accompany nipping forbidden candies from a jar. "I'll bring you something to eat," she told her, after plunking her onto a hard chair.

A plate soon made an appearance in front of her, quickly filled with re-warmed potatoes and fresh eggs and mushrooms dripping with butter. She ate while the children pinched and kicked at one another, in between making a game of spinning apple cores across the table like tops.

"Are we going to the vicarage today?" Nettie asked

suddenly after her apple core had tumbled over the edge and onto the floor.

Mildred had learned quite early on with her sister's children (a fact she then later applied to all children, regardless of parentage) that they rarely built up towards anything by small degrees. At some point, she knew she would have to relinquish her mental usage of the word "suddenly" as a descriptor of their behavior, since it had been rendered utterly superfluous years before.

She picked up her tea (extra sugar, God bless Cook) and washed down her bite of potatoes with a healthy sip. "Well, I'm not certain—"

"Can we?" Matthew, then. His face sticky from the apples and his words lisping a bit over a recently lost tooth. "I want to go see Mrs. Babbinton! She makes the best cakes in all the world!"

A clatter of dishes and a grumble was heard from the other side of the kitchen. Mildred made a note to do something kind for Cook later on, to soothe her wounded pride.

"Well, perhaps—" she began again, but couldn't seem to make it past the first few words. Every time she attempted to speak, to come up with an excuse for why the children shouldn't visit the vicarage, she saw bronze, leathery scales and translucent wings and tiny, flaring nostrils that twitched with a desire to shoot out crackling sparks of fire. "Um."

"Oh, please! Please, Aunt Mildred!" And on it went, a chorus of pleading that Mildred determined to harden herself against, despite knowing she would eventually crumble like the walls of Jericho to the Israelites trumpeting.

"Very well, very well!" She held up her hands. "We'll go once you've finished your lessons, all right?"

A cheer went up, followed by the scrape of stool legs on the floor as the children scrambled to rush upstairs and fetch their books and slates.

Mildred looked down at her plate. She'd gone and eaten

everything without even realizing it, without feeling a whit more satisfied than when she'd raised the first bite to her mouth. If she wasn't careful she would have to let out her dresses soon. Not that she minded the change in her figure, but the effort involved to make everything else in her life accommodate that change was more work than she wished to tackle.

And here she was, thinking about eating and alterations and the span of her thighs instead of...

She swallowed down the last of her tea, the dregs so sweet her teeth ached. No, she had a plan in mind. Well, not precisely a plan, as far as strict adherence to definitions went, but she would take the children to the vicarage, and she would show them the hatchling, and surely they would treat it no different than if they'd discovered a local toad or turtle or dark featherless chicken with heightened carnivorous instincts.

Yes, that would work. And then she and Mr. Wiggan would have a good search through the rest of her Great Uncle Forthright's papers and find out that the hatchling came from some far off place and perhaps they could even have it returned to said far off place. At least before it ate up everything in Mrs. Babbinton's larder.

Several hours later and they were at the vicarage again, Mrs. Babbinton letting them in and Mildred trying to smile while entertaining the thought of being sick in the azaleas planted on either side of the front door.

"Shall I?" Mrs. Babbinton paused and looked at Mildred over the children's heads, her hands resting on their shoulders before she allowed them through to the kitchen.

"It's fine," Mildred assured her. "It's not some great secret." Of course not. Not a secret at all. Why would it be? "And I am sure they'll find it fascinating."

"Right." Mrs. Babbinton lowered her chin and looked at both Matthew and Nettie in turn. "Now, I have milk and I have scones and I have a surprise. Which would you like first? Or shall we take them all together?"

Mildred made her way towards the study, where she expected Mr. Wiggan to be, but Mrs. Babbinton called out to her before she disappeared around the corner with the children. "He's not in there today, Miss Percy. You'll find him in the kitchen, along with everything else."

Her feet moved with all the ready lightness of lead. In her mind, surely, she had made the hatchling out to be more fantastic than it really was. She blamed her imagination, the stories she read to the children, her own residual desires from her formative years to stumble upon an adventure that would lift her up and away from the doldrums of the life around her. When surely—*surely!* (she would repeat the word until she had herself convinced)—there was nothing remarkable about the hatchling or the egg it had come from or—

She walked into the kitchen. And stopped.

There sat Mr. Wiggan, cross-legged on the floor, one knee tipped against the edge of the basket. A table nearby was buried beneath papers and books and all of it topped with plates of half-eaten slices of bread and cheese and forgotten cups of tea until the entire structure resembled the sketches of some ancient Sumerian city.

The children were already flanking him, one positioned at each shoulder, peering into the basket with their hands clasped tight behind their backs, as if they had already been warned to keep their fingers to themselves before Mildred had even entered the room. But she held herself back, a new wariness overtaking her. She was reluctant to step up and to see the thing that had so embedded itself on her thoughts over the last day, as if by keeping it at the edges of her vision she could continue to believe it as a commonplace creature.

Curiosity, of course, won out. She walked forward, her own hands flexing and curling inside her gloves until she saw the little thing in the basket, on its back, wings oddly splayed as it let out a series of chirruping screeches and batted at a piece of string dangling from the end of a stick.

The stick was wielded by Mr. Wiggan, who had apparently lost all of his own panic from the previous day, his eyes bright as a child's as he teased the hatchling with the string and laughed heartily when the claws caught on the twisted wool and the wings tensed in anticipation of a full tantrum.

"Ah, Miss Percy!" Mr. Wiggan passed the stick to Nettie and after a few moments in which he struggled to summon the right measure of coordination needed to unfold himself to his feet, he stood and brushed the dust of the floor from the seat of his trousers. (This being a pointless gesture, as Mrs. Babbinton's floors were kept as clean as her plates in a clear demonstration that neither dirt nor sin should cling to any one of the vicarage's more impermeable surfaces.) "How are you today?"

His joviality left her baffled. Overall, the man looked rested and well and completely unconcerned about the squawking contents of the basket over which her niece and nephew were currently huddled. For a little while, she allowed herself to entertain a sliver of...well, not hatred towards him, but jealousy that he could greet her with such energetic, pink-cheeked happiness when she felt as if she had aged a decade since the first crack of the hatchling's shell.

"I am—"

"Did you bring something else for us today?" Mr. Wiggan's gaze dropped to the basket hooked over her forearm. "No more eggs, I hope!" And he laughed, and Mildred thought she caught a touch of hysteria in that ruffle of sound from his throat. And perhaps that was the thing; while she stressed and fretted and permitted the unbelievability of it all to fester away inside of her, she wondered if Mr. Wiggan was of the temperament to hide his own unease behind a shell—well, of course she would use that turn of phrase, since she couldn't seem to shake all thoughts of shells and eggs and every word that wasn't dragon but clearly implied dragon from her mind—of giddy effervescence.

She slid the basket from her arm and held it out to him. "More of my Great Uncle Forthright's notes and things. I went through more of his papers last night, searching for anything that might help us to identify our new arrival." She swallowed and looked at the hatchling and swallowed again.

"Excellent!" He took the basket, hooked his foot around the leg of a chair beside the table, and sat down. Along with the previous day's panic, he seemed to have also lost a hold on most of his manners. Mildred pulled out her own chair and lowered herself into it, careful not to jostle any of the stacks or towers that wobbled precariously from their places on the table beside her.

"Have you discovered anything?" she pressed when a full minute passed during which Mr. Wiggan did nothing but study the papers in his hands.

"Hmm, what?" His brow furrowed, then cleared, then settled into an entirely new expression of perplexity. "Oh, about the—" And he cut himself off, just as she had been interrupting herself for the last night and a day. "Mrs. Babbinton?" he raised his voice to be heard clear to the other side of the house, no matter that the housekeeper stood less than ten feet away from him, busily chopping up pieces of… meat, was all Mildred could tell from where she sat. "Mrs. Babbinton," he said again. "Where are the…?" He snapped his fingers like one who believed themselves possessed of the ability to conjure desired nouns from thin air. "You know, I showed them to you this morning?"

His ramblings continued until Mrs. Babbinton appeared at his side, her hands freshly washed and holding onto a neat stack of papers.

"Ah, yes." He smiled, all childlike and toothy again, and nodded towards Mildred. "I set aside everything that appeared to hold a connection with our winged friend. I'm honestly surprised at the dearth of information on the matter. It makes one wonder if indeed your relative was even aware of what he had."

Mildred took the papers and began to rifle through them, waiting for her eyes to pick out anything of interest. "Maybe he didn't. Everything he sent to me was in such a muddle, nothing documented properly or catalogued in any way. As if it had all been thrown together in haste and the trunk shoved onto the first available coach to Wiltshire."

"You believe if he'd known what the stone was, he wouldn't have sent it on?"

"If he'd known *that*"—she gestured towards the basket with a handful of papers— "was going to produce a living thing, I doubt he'd have tossed it into the bottom of some old luggage and buried it with so much junk."

Mr. Wiggan shook his head. At first, Mildred assumed it meant he was disagreeing with her assessment of her Great Uncle Forthright's intentions, but once he spoke again, she understood it was rather that he expressed his confusion at the entire situation. "But he had to have known *something*. The sketches." He reached across and flicked through several of the pages she held, all of them decorated at the corners, in the margins, between the lines with quick, amateur drawings of the same figure, or variations of the same creature, the underlying structure of a bird-like lizard-thing with wings and claws and more teeth than Mildred thought were necessary.

"They're all…" She stopped, and sighed, leaning back until her shoulders settled against the hard, unforgiving back of her chair. "They're all incomplete. And mostly skeletal in nature. I don't think he ever saw one alive."

As if in reaction to her movement backwards, Mr. Wiggan tilted forward until his elbows rested on his knees. Not the most gentlemanly of poses, though it acted as a suitable accompaniment to her unladylike slump. It seemed all that was needed to breach the walls of strict etiquette between two people was to throw a newborn animal among them.

"It also means this one isn't the first." He ran a hand over his bare head and raised his eyes to her face. "There are others."

A bracing thought. Mildred looked towards the basket. Both children sat on the floor, alternately teasing the hatchling and giggling over the creature's antics from the depths of his makeshift nest. "But what do we do with it? I cannot prey upon your hospitality and allow you to bear the burden of keeping it in your kitchen forever." A new idea entered her head, one that had her sitting up as straight as if she'd been given a prod from her governess's ruler. "How large do you think it will become? It's not a tiny thing now, as far as comparing it to other animals that typically hatch from eggs." Indeed, her mind seemed to have settled on "scrawny chicken" as its nearest compatriot in the "feisty/nippy/bird-ish thing" genus of animals.

"As much as it eats," Mrs. Babbinton said from her side of the kitchen, breaking into their discussion, "I can't see it staying as small as it is for long."

Mr. Wiggan sat with his tongue pushed into his cheek. He chuckled softly to himself, but Mildred saw the cracks creeping in at the edges of his convivial facade, his own shield of optimism breaking down before her eyes. "In Egypt, in the Nile, they've discovered alligators exceeding eighteen feet in length, longer than three grown men laid end to end." He swallowed. His smile brightened, his eyes gleaming with a touch of the maniacal. "And their eggs are not half so large."

Mildred swallowed. (Nervous people tend to do a great deal of swallowing at key moments, so this is simply a brief note from the author reminding you, the reader, of this fact rather than leave you to exist under the misapprehension that I, the author, cannot think of another action to give my characters in order to show how difficult a time this is for them. I am quite sure they would rather swallow more than usual than give way to the ascending dread caused by having a bitey winged crocodile with chicken-legs nestled in a basket only a few feet away from them. Thank you.) "So you think…"

Mr. Wiggan nodded. "I think, yes."

Mrs. Babbinton brought tea to Mildred. Mildred didn't know if it was time for tea, could not remember if she was even thirsty, but she took the tea (milky and sweet; the housekeeper proved herself a keen scholar in the art of her guests' tea preferences) and the cream biscuits that came with it. She ate, because it gave her something to do, something to occupy her mouth and hands and a small segment of her thoughts as she considered the buttery-ness of the biscuits and that latent bitterness of the tea that clung to the back of her tongue after every sip. She ate and she drank and when she was finished she added her empty cup to the tottering structure on the tabletop and brushed the crumbs from her hands and her skirt and asked the same question she had asked only a few minutes before. "But what do we do with it?"

It was a question deserving of repetition. (Quite honestly, it was a question deserving of being painted across the walls, carved into the foundations of the vicarage, stamped across their foreheads in ink so it would dog them throughout every conversation with one another. But for the moment, a second mention of it would have to suffice.) Mildred let it hover in the air between them, while Mr. Wiggan's face burrowed into its wardrobe of expressions for an appropriate reaction.

"I've given it some thought," he said, in a way that told Mildred he had given it an incredible amount of thought, to the point that he had really thought about little else over the previous twenty-odd hours. "And I believe we would be served best by contacting that assistant chap of your Great Uncle's, um…" he snapped his fingers again while one of his eyes squeezed shut in thought.

"Mr. Richard Gorman," Mildred provided, not even trying for the briefest of moments to pretend that she had not read all of the correspondence (yes, only two letters, but…) associated with the inheritance from her Great Uncle Forthright and memorized them to the point of being able to recite them on command (along with several of Shakespeare's sonnets, five Psalms, and possibly one or two limericks of questionable content she had learned from her father (on the rare occasions he imbibed enough to become more jolly than usual.))

"Gorman, yes. We'll write to him and see if he knows of any colleagues of your great uncle's—did your Great Uncle Forthright have any colleagues, do you think?"

"Uh," and then a shake of her head. Again, she disliked how little she knew of her Great Uncle Forthright, especially when she had been so singled out as to receive an inheritance from the man (unless he made a habit of foisting oversized eggs on unsuspecting individuals of tenuous acquaintance).

It illuminated how small, how undiverse her circle of friends and company really was. There was her family and the members of the household staff, and there were a few ladies who occasionally invited her to tea, along with the people she nodded to and exchanged harmless pleasantries with at church. But she often had to decline what few invitations she did receive (and most of those were for all of the ladies of the Muncy household, and not only Mildred herself) and then Diana would usually say that she (Mildred, of course) must stay home with the children or that she (Mildred, of course) must run an errand for her that could not be postponed until later.

"Well, we'll begin with this Gorman fellow," Mr. Wiggan went on, as if Mildred had not experienced a quiet crisis of identity right there in the kitchen with him. "And until then, I fear we'll have no choice but to forge ahead as best we can."

"We could make a place for him outside, behind the

house," Mrs. Babbinton said as she began clearing the towers on the table of their empty plates and cups and spoons. "If we put him far enough away from the chickens, I doubt there will be a problem."

Mildred tried to picture the scene in her mind. All she could come up with was an image of the hatchling pecking along Mrs. Babbinton's rows of vegetables with the rest of the chickens for company.

"I'll hire Mr. Clemson's oldest boy. He built the first chicken house for us two years ago and it still looks as good as the day he hammered the last nail in place." Mrs. Babbinton smiled at them both before she called the children over to her, beckoning them with promises of milk and biscuits for dunking.

"That seems to be settled." Mildred watched Mr. Wiggan for any sign that he was displeased with his housekeeper making such a grand decision without waiting for either of their opinions on the matter, but he appeared to take the older woman's leadership as an expected event. "Hopefully it should only be for a few weeks. Maybe a month, at the longest. And I thank you," she added quickly, when she realized she couldn't remember if she had made an offer of gratitude yet for all of the trouble she seemed to have brought to his doorstep. "For all of this. I don't think... Well, my sister wouldn't have... I mean." She cleared her throat once it became clear that she could not finish her sentence in a manner that would not cast her sister in a less than advantageous light.

"No, no." Mr. Wiggan smiled, and not the shaky grin meant to hide a panoply of fear and panic and trepidation, but a true smile that helped to ease Mildred's next breath from her lungs. "I should be thanking *you*. This is turning out to be quite the little adventure, don't you think? And here when I thought I would be spending all of this week preparing new lessons for the schoolchildren and deciding which letter from the Apostle Paul to study for the sermon on Sunday."

Mildred stood. A restlessness had come over her legs, and she could not yet tell if it was fueled by an urge to move towards their "little adventure" or run away from it.

"Here, now," Mrs. Babbinton returned with a dish of chopped meat and a few other scraps that appeared to be leftovers from breakfast. "The poor thing's going to need feeding again," she nodded towards the basket, where the hatchling's screeches had begun to rise in strength with no one paying attention to him. "The children begged to do it, but I'm not fully confident in how careful they'll be with their fingers. Would you like a turn, Miss Percy?"

"Yes." She said it so quickly it surprised even herself. So she took the plate and she knelt down beside the basket, only giving Mr. Wiggan the briefest of acknowledgements as he settled on the floor beside her.

She began with a shred of chicken, pinching it between two fingers, then bringing it slowly towards the hatchling's nose, waiting for him to catch the scent. His eyes opened as his nostrils flared, and then his head lifted from the sheet. His eyes were clearer today, she noticed. She wondered how much of anything he could see, or if he was dependent on smell and taste and temperature to place himself in his surroundings.

The hatchling's head jutted forward on its neck just as Mildred released the chicken. He snapped it up before it even touched the sheet beneath him, gobbling it down with such vehemence one could believe the creature had never been fed before this moment.

"I fear he will grow large," Mr. Wiggan said in a low voice.

Mildred glanced over at him after giving the hatchling his second bite of food. No trace of a smile on his face anymore. But neither did he appear fearful or vexed, merely resigned. And—if she pretended she could read further into the lines and shadows and the cut of his eyebrows, as if his face were made of tea leaves—a touch curious.

"How large?" she wanted to ask, her own interest piqued. As large as an alligator? As an elephant? And with great, leathery wings that could cover a half dozen men in their shadow from tip to tip?

A breath slid out, almost a laugh. "Well, I'm sure he'll be gone from here before he becomes too troublesome." A skip of her heart brought to her attention how tempting to fate those words could be, so she fed the hatchling three more pieces of chicken and a fatty bit of bacon before she decided to attach a codicil to that statement. "And if not, we'll manage."

And there. That brought back his smile. His entire face softened along with it, and Mildred had to fight off the urge to look towards the windows behind her and see if a shaft of sunlight had broken through to illuminate his face. "And if we don't," he said, still smiling, his voice still low, still conspiratorial, "I'm sure Mrs. Babbinton will have everything in hand before our own failures have struck the ground."

The sequence of events that followed these lines of conversation would repeat themselves in Mildred's mind for days, weeks afterwards, like a melody one hears only once but cannot forget for some time.

Mildred picked up another piece of meat. She did not know if her movements were too slow or if she failed to pay enough attention to the hatchling, but as she reached to feed him and as he shot his pointed head forward to nip the meat from her fingers, she accidentally butted his nose with her knuckles—quite hard, so much that she gasped and snatched her hand back again for fear that she'd harmed him.

The hatchling blinked, his head twitching, his nostrils letting out little snuffles of sound until he sneezed, and there was a spark of something. Light, flame, Mildred almost missed it, so rapidly was it there and gone again. But the remnants of it lingered, a sharp smell of heat and burning, along with the specks of black ash that peppered the pale sheet on which the hatchling lounged. And drifting up from its nostrils, a thread of smoke, curling through the sunlit air of the kitchen with all the laziness of a puff of cloud floating across a summer sky.

"What?" Mildred managed. Or maybe she did not manage it at all and only a burp of astonishment fell out of her mouth.

"Did you...?" Mr. Wiggan seemed momentarily unable to tear his gaze away from the creature.

"Ah," Mildred had another go at speaking, and finished it with a swallow. And then she swallowed again and again until she thought she would never stop swallowing and the rest of her life would be spent swallowing and fighting for breath and wondering how it could feel like her heart was beating in every part of her body at once.

"So." Mr. Wiggan looked at her. But, oh, the amount of words, the pages of description and venting of thoughts and feelings and sympathies in that single syllable.

Mildred flexed her fingers around the edge of the plate. From the basket, the hatchling started up his plaintive screeching again, scrambling impatiently for his next bite of food. "Yes," she said, proud of her return to coherency. "Yes, I did."

CHAPTER NINE

As has been noted previously, female dragons tend to be slightly larger and more powerful than their male counterparts.

-from Chapter Fourteen of Miss Percy's Pocket Guide (to the Care and Feeding of British Dragons)

Upper Plimpton was a pleasant sort of village. (It should be noted that sometimes its occupants referred to it as a town when they were feeling more aspirational than usual, but then the next day it could shrink back to the status of village if comparisons with larger, more bustling centers of population—London, usually—showed Upper Plimpton in a less than satisfactory light. Some had even learned to use Upper Plimpton's current claims of status as a barometer for the general feelings towards cities and their inhabitants—London, usually—on any particular day. Not always a precise measurement, but it often did the job.)

Now, as the charms of the place have already been described elsewhere in the story, the author will refrain from repeating those sentiments here. But the farms were still quaint and the sheep were still safely grazing and the stone walls were still creating their patchwork of untouched trees and plowed fields as Reginald Hawthorne's coach rolled up the main street and halted in the center of town (or village, depending).

The words "Reginald's coach" are used, but it was not, in fact, Reginald's coach. He'd purchased a seat on the coach (managing to afford one inside and away from the worst of the dirt and weather) and had spent the last two days wedged in between two other gentlemen and across from four ladies. He didn't know the names of either the two other gentlemen or the four ladies. Introductions had been attempted and he'd wasted no time in flinging the information out of his head before it took up the space of something more important in need of remembering. What he did recall is how flatulent one of the ladies had been and how the gentleman to his left had made a habit of falling asleep with his hand on his (Reginald's) knee.

There was nothing auspicious about his departure from the coach, his boots crunching on the mix of stones and dirt that made up the main thoroughfare of Upper Plimpton. If it had been a stage play, surely there would have been a change in the lighting, the orchestra's incidental accompaniment might have added a dramatic flourish to the proceedings, marking this moment as Important (capital "I", of course.) But the sky remained cloudy, threatening a light drizzle at most. No ominous thunder, nor a beam of sunlight piercing through the clouds to illuminate his position at the edge of the street. A horse stamped his hooves and a distant shop bell jingled and a raindrop landed on his shoulder as his bags were deposited on the ground at his feet. Nothing significantly memorable, as far as inciting incidents went.

Reginald needed a place to stay, first of all. He located the nearest inn easily enough, and after paying for the cheapest room available, ordering the cheapest meal available, and changing out of his travel-rumpled clothes into something a bit smarter, went in search of Miss Mildred Percy. The only difficulty being that he didn't know exactly where Miss Mildred Percy lived (in Upper Plimpton and with a sister by the name of Muncy, were all the details Mr. Purvis had been able to ascertain).

But as mentioned earlier, Upper Plimpton treaded that fine line between a village and a town, which meant that nearly every person living within the confines of the village/town was well versed in all of the pertinent bits of information that made up the daily lives of their neighbors.

A few questions asked—and without even a coin needing to change hands!—and Reginald knew exactly where Miss Percy lived and how long of a walk it would take for him to arrive there.

He would go at once. He was both exhausted and strangely jittery from his journey, but the sooner he could get this business with the stone and his father and that thrice-damned Mr. Charles Forthright out of the way, the sooner he could be back in London and looking for a wife and having his feet measured for a new pair of boots. All good things, and all worth a few more hours of trouble before he could crawl into his narrow, lumpy bed at the inn and find some rest.

It was a two mile walk to Ashby Lodge (where he was told the Muncy family resided, and where he hoped to find genteel people of good sense and of a class high enough to live in a house bearing a name). Dressed in his new coat (new to him, at least, as "previously owned" was all he could afford from the sale of his watch and several of his books) and with his neckcloth tied and folded and tweaked to perfection, he set off down the road.

The rain held off, if indeed there was rain in the clouds above him and they weren't merely sweeping overhead for the sole purpose of blotting out the sun and lending a chill to the spring air. He found his way to the house (two miles of not-terrible road and a lane edged by a stone wall that guided him up to the front door of a building that was neither too large nor too small, and so aggressively Jacobean in style he wondered if the door would be opened to him by someone wearing a doublet and hose).

It wasn't until he rang the bell that he realized he should have taken Mr. Purvis's advice and written first. He had not taken the time to introduce himself to the family, and here he stood, scuffing his heels on the front step like some common tradesman come to sell brushes or a cure-all tonic. He was about to turn around and race back towards Upper Plimpton when the door opened and a maid stood there, her tongue pushed into her cheek as she surveyed him.

"So," Reginald began, for no other reason than it was the first word to come out of his mouth. "I am Mr. Hawthorne?" He hadn't intended it to sound like a question, as if he was unaware of his own name. But once it was out, he understood how it might come across to another person, the implication that a man by the name of 'Mr. Hawthorne' had been expected. And so he raised his eyebrows a little, gave his head a bit of a tilt, and attempted a smile that was not so much of a smile as to make him appear unsettled.

The maid's own eyebrows rose up until they nearly disappeared beneath the flopping edge of her white cap.

"Oh, this is the seventh of April, isn't it?" He put his hands on his coat as if he were checking for a watch (sold) or a calendar to tell him the day. "I had mentioned in my letter that I hoped to arrive by the afternoon of the seventh. Perhaps there has been some confusion? Though, I am sure if there has been any mistake, it is mine." The lies were easy enough to construct once he gave them a start. And all throughout he continued to smile and to break eye contact often enough so as to look embarrassed rather than untrustworthy.

The maid still said nothing. Reginald resisted the urge to tug at his neckcloth like a man under suspicion of murder. "Of course," he went on, chuckling to himself. "I've gone about this all wrong. I'm here to see Miss Percy? I believe she lives here, with her sister's family? I was an old friend of her uncle's—her great uncle, I mean—a Mr. Charles Forthright? I've a letter from him..." Here he dug into the inner pocket of his coat and produced the letter in question (forged from documents Mr. Purvis had provided, giving Reginald a foundation from which to copy Mr. Charles

Forthright's penmanship) holding it up as if it were an invitation to the premiere event of the season. "...though I do not know what good this will do my if my own missive has failed to arrive?"

It was such a barrage of questions and statements delivered in a questioning tone that the maid reeled a bit from her place stopping up the gap in the open doorway. "Well, Miss Percy?" She glanced back over her shoulder, to some interior space Reginald could not make out from where he stood. "She's not at home at the moment. Did you want to wait for her?"

No, he didn't. But he also didn't want to walk the two miles back to Upper Plimpton so he could scuff his heels there for an evening and a morning before walking back to Ashby Lodge (two miles, again) in order to try his luck a second time. "I will wait, yes."

He followed the maid inside. The house, what he could see of it from the foyer, was a fine, unassuming place. This Miss Percy was comfortable, then. Or at least better off than he had been for quite some time. He was shown into a sitting room (or parlour, or drawing room, he really didn't know what the precise qualifications were for each) where there was a cheerful fire burning and too many porcelain figurines staring at him from spindle-legged tables and dainty shelves built into the walls. He sat once the maid had left him alone, then stood and paced as best he could among all of the furniture cluttering every corner and available space, then sat again. The fire snapped and a clock ticked and he thought he heard the step of children on one of the floors above him. And then the door swung open and a vision of loveliness stepped into the room.

Reginald was not the sort to be distracted from his purpose. And his purpose was to come here and finagle the return of his father's—now his—stone from Miss Mildred Percy's possession and thereby set himself up for a more stable—financially, anyway—future life. Or that *had* been his purpose, before an angel walked into the room and took away both his breath and his brains with the dimpling of her cheek.

"Hello," she said, in a voice that might have been a human voice or it might have been the crystalline chime of angels singing. "I'm Miss Muncy. I've been told you're here to see my aunt?"

Miss Muncy. Reginald couldn't tell if it was relief or frustration that coursed through him at the knowledge that this was not the sought-after Miss Percy. "Your aunt, yes. She's not here?" A stupid thing to ask. He already knew Miss Percy wasn't there. But he wanted to keep the conversation moving forward. He wanted to sit in this drawing room/parlour/sitting room for the next three hours and drink tea and eat tiny sandwiches stuffed with smoked meats and watercress and whatever else they smeared across miniature triangles of white bread and offered to guests in houses that bore names and dainty shelves and Jacobean crenellations. And he wanted to speak with this Miss Muncy. Or hear her speak. Or gaze at her as one would a piece of art put up for display on a museum wall.

"She went into town, some"—she waved her hand—"charitable work at the vicarage, I believe. But she should return shortly. And my mother is off on one of her errands, I'm afraid." After calling for the maid and requesting refreshments for their guest, she sat down in a chair and gestured for Reginald to take the seat opposite. "And you are...?" she went on, then cut off the question with, "You'll have to forgive me. Betsy mentioned your name but I've always suffered with a terrible memory when it comes to them."

"U-um, Mr. Hawthorne," he stammered, and sat, and shifted forward to the edge of his seat. "Reginald Hawthorne. I'm just lately come from London."

"London!" Miss Muncy clapped her hands together, eyes sparking with delight. "You must tell me all about it! I've never been, no matter that Mama has promised to take me more than a dozen times. But then there is always some reason we cannot go and I find myself being disappointed all over again."

Her mouth shaped into a perfect pout, not so much that it seemed affected, but enough that Reginald was struck with the immediate and irrepressible urge to take Miss Muncy to London and show her all of the delights it had to offer. (It did not matter that he could not afford such a scheme nor had he any claim on Miss Muncy to even escort her as far as the front door. Less than two minutes in her company and he was completely under her sway. (This was a gift Belinda possessed, one she often made no choice to employ. When amongst others—in other words, people to whom she was not related—she was all that was charming, vivacious, sweet, and knowledgeable without being so knowledgeable as to make others aware of their deficits. Her power was made doubly potent by its ability to shape itself to those around her, so if she found herself in the company of someone who was in need of a quiet and concerned ear, Belinda was able to provide it. If the person was of a variety who needed to be petted and complimented, she could provide that as well. Fortunately for the world at large, she was not yet fully aware of the strength of this gift, or else she could have set herself up as a rival to any of the leaders of men who had recently battled their way across Europe.))

"I hope you will have the pleasure of visiting there, one day." Reginald smiled. He felt like a fool to be smiling. It wouldn't have been a wonder if this Miss Muncy had dozens of eligible gentlemen sending her flowers and poems and declarations of love every single day. And he sat there with his scuffed boots and second-hand coat and a forged letter in his pocket.

The letter. Right. That's why he was there, at Ashby Lodge. For Miss Percy and his father and new boots and…

Right.

He blinked and wiped his hand across his brow, as if clearing away a glamour from his vision. "Your aunt," he began, and said it again with greater strength, as his first attempt had been a touch warbly. "Your aunt, Miss Percy. Has she been staying with you long?"

"Staying with us?" Her brow knitted in confusion. "Oh! Well, I cannot recall a time when she wasn't with us. She was my nurse, you know. And then my governess, in a way. Why, she's just always been here. I have no memory of her not being a fixture of the household."

The maid returned with a tray, upon which was arranged tea and a plate of little tarts filled with jam and cream. Reginald's mouth watered, the insides of his cheeks aching as his fingers twitched with a need to gather up a half dozen of those flaky comestibles and cram them into his mouth before they disappeared from sight.

He had no love of London's culinary offerings, or better stated, he had no love of the culinary offerings available to a young man existing on harsh budgetary restraints. Of late, food had become something he experienced only because it was common knowledge that the alternative to eating was a death of the slow and miserable variety. At least if he ate (even if what he was eating might not always fall under the category of "fit for human consumption") it meant he was staving off his inevitable demise for a little while longer. (And if, on the off chance, something he ate was responsible for his death, he assumed it would come more swiftly than one carried on the wings of hunger.)

He waited for Miss Muncy to pour the tea, to sort out the delicate plates and offer several of the tarts to him. He silently applauded himself for the small sip and the careful nip of buttery crust with which he began his repast. "You must allow me to offer my condolences," he said, after dabbing at the corners of his mouth with the provided napkin.

"Condolences?" Her eyes darted from one corner of the

room to the other, as if there might be a corpse stashed away in the nearest cupboard. "Has someone died?"

Reginald set down his cup. "Your uncle? I mean, Mr. Charles Forthright, if I'm not mistaken. So he would be your..." He counted out the branches on the family tree with the tips of his fingers. "Great great uncle, I suppose."

"Oh, him!" Belinda smiled, then blushed, then seemed to chide herself with a click of her tongue and a shake of her head. "You must think so ill of me, to not know to whom you were alluding. But I must confess that I never had the opportunity to meet the poor man. I think it was my aunt who knew him best, being the eldest. But I'm afraid Mama never had much interaction with him."

He took another bite of tart. Then another, before venturing to speak again. "Your aunt, though, Miss Percy? She shared a close relationship with him? Being the eldest, as you mentioned?"

But Miss Muncy was already shaking her head. "Why, I never heard her speak of him until several weeks ago, when the letter arrived. Before then, I wouldn't have even known he existed." She paused to take a sip of her own tea. Reginald watched the performance, riveted and a bit envious of the cup. "I take it you were well acquainted with him?"

"I worked with him, yes." He hoped his hesitation would be counted as a sign of his grief at the loss of a colleague rather than evidence of a hastily cobbled-together falsehood. "He was a great motivator, I would say. Never have I made the acquaintance of someone who inspired me to do such tremendous things."

Belinda smiled. (Reginald took it as the kind of smile he could crawl into with all the comfort and leisure of resting on a hammock.) "He sounds like quite the gentleman! Now I wish I *had* known him."

"Yes, he was." Reginald swallowed down the last bite of the last tart on his plate. "Quite."

"We were supposed to hear from him again," Belinda

went on, reaching for Reginald's plate and filling it with another helping of tarts as if she could read his mind. "Or some associate of his, I should say. Something about an inheritance for my aunt? But it's been weeks and weeks and now not a word. Probably tied up in all sorts of legalities, I assume."

"Oh, I had thought—" Reginald stopped himself. The information he'd received from Mr. Purvis had made it clear that Miss Percy's inheritance—stone included—from her Great Uncle Forthright had already been packed up and dispatched. But perhaps its arrival in the household had been an unremarked upon event, which might lead Miss Muncy to know nothing about it. "What I mean to say is, I am interested in hearing any stories your aunt might have to share with me about her Great Uncle Forthright. He was a fascinating man, and I feel my time with him was cut regretfully short."

"Well." Belinda took a bite of tart and licked a flake of crust from the corner of her mouth. (Reginald shifted in his seat and wondered if it would be considered too forward for him to drop onto one knee and propose marriage then and there.) "As I said, I hope she will return soon. She has been so busy at the vicarage lately, helping with the school? Or the church? One of the two, I'm sure. But would you prefer to stay and wait for her—"

"I would not wish to be a nuisance," Reginald interrupted.

"—or you could come again tomorrow? If I tell my aunt of your impending visit beforehand, then we can assure her presence."

Reginald considered both plans of action. The one would allow him to continue in Miss Muncy's presence until Miss Percy arrived. The second might permit him another chance to see Miss Muncy and a guarantee of an audience with Miss Percy, which was what had brought him all the way from London in the first place.

"As I would not wish to make a burden of myself," he began slowly, as if he could draw out the time left to him on this visit with Miss Muncy. "I think I will call again tomorrow, since it seems the letter I had sent—I did send a letter, you know, announcing my coming to Upper Plimpton? But I fear it must have gone astray. But, yes. Tomorrow would be better, I think."

Belinda stood, a susurration of skirts mingled with a soft scent of perfume (Lilac? It had to be lilac, Reginald thought, trying hard not to make a great demonstration of sniffing the air around her) marking her movement. "Then I look forward to seeing you again tomorrow, Mr. Hawthorne."

She held out her hand. Reginald took it, his imagination supplying a small spark leaping from one set of fingertips to the other. Should he kiss her hand? No, that would be too forward. Wouldn't it? Bloody hell, he knew nothing about how to interact with the opposite sex, or more accurately, how to interact with the opposite sex when they were so clearly from a higher class, one he had spent his entire life aspiring to reach, like a child clambering among the bottom branches of an apple tree, fingers stretching, grasping for that perfect fruit.

"Tomorrow, Miss Muncy." And he kissed her hand. And did not at all regret it.

CHAPTER TEN

The arrival of a stranger in their midst will, of course, ignite a dragon's defensive instincts. But there is always a period of investigation before the proverbial (or not proverbial, in the case of the Pritchard's Frill-Necked) hackles are raised. In most cases, several dragons will join together to greet the newcomer and judge whether or not they are a threat. And in most cases, this meeting proceeds with little to no violence incurred against either party*.

-From Chapter Eleven of Miss Percy's Pocket Guide (to the Care and Feeding of British Dragons)

*For a more detailed example of when this was not the case, please turn to Appendix B, Note IV: iii or The Evisceration Incident

---

The children decided to call him Fitzwilliam. Fitz for short.

Mildred took care to remind them that the hatchling was not a pet, that it was likely (please, let it be likely) it would not be with them for very long. (Mr. Wiggan had gladly taken on the task of writing to Mr. Gorman in order to inquire about a way to contact some of Charles Forthright's colleagues and peers. The hope being that one of them would be knowledgeable enough about the situation to offer advice pertaining to a three-week old winged lizard that occasionally snuffled sparks and smoke when he sneezed.) But the children still begged to trail along with her to the vicarage at every opportunity, fighting over who should be allowed to feed Fitz or help him to toddle across the garden or generally treat the creature as if it were a mewling kitten or puppy they should take home and allow to sleep at the foot of their bed.

Though Mildred couldn't imagine how such a thing would ever be possible, especially when one took into account that the hatchling had already begun to outgrow his fire-side basket.

As much as the thing ate, she shouldn't have been surprised at its penchant for growth. But it had doubled in size at only two weeks of age and only continued to look larger every time she saw it.

"Look, Aunt Mildred! Look what he can do!" Matthew stood near the garden wall, holding out a piece of meat at arm's length. Beneath his hand, the hatchling squawked and struggled to rise onto his hind legs, his wings (Mildred's heart fluttered every time she saw those wings stretched out, every time she saw the potential for flight and freedom and so many other frightening things in those burgeoning muscles) flapping madly as if it was a moment—a breath, a blink—away from leaping off the ground and snatching the food directly from her nephew's fingers.

"Please, be careful!" she reminded him. It had become a chant of late, every time the children came too close, every time the hatchling spun around and snapped at something other than the end of his own tail. But so far, no one had been bitten, no one even suffering more than a faint scratch from the hatchling's claws.

An easy thing to crow about, when the hatchling was still small enough to be picked up and held upside down like an unruly chicken. (Mildred had not attempted to hold the hatchling in such a manner, but the thought had occurred to her more times than it probably should have.) But what would happen when it grew even larger? There was no denying it would prove to be a beast of monstrous proportions. Mildred thought of all the illustrations and stories she'd read of elephants and alligators and the massive creatures that populated the seas. And this one had wings. Along with an unnerving tendency to send up a curl of smoke from its nostrils when it was particularly riled.

"Have you had any news?" Mildred asked Mr. Wiggan, her attention still fixed on her niece and nephew, playing with the hatchling at the other end of the garden. It was the same question she asked at every visit to the vicarage, if he had yet to receive a response from Mr. Gorman. And then the answer would be in the negative, and then Mildred's imagination would skip ahead to some vague future several months forward, with their attempting to transport a creature —one the size of a small horse and bearing a resemblance to something inked on the pages of a collection of mythological tales—by one of the main roads to London and some expert or scientist there.

"No, nothing." Mr. Wiggan reached out to the nearest tree branch, from which he pulled a soft, green spring leaf that he immediately tore to bits. "If I've not had a response within the next two weeks, I'm going to leap over this Mr. Gorman's head and contact a few naturalists and scientists directly. I've been compiling a list of candidates, and also determining the best way to introduce the subject of our Fitz to them without inciting their ridicule."

"Our Fitz? Oh, not you as well."

Mr. Wiggan ducked his head, as if embarrassed, but Mildred saw his small smile peeking through. "Miss Percy, he's such a clever creature. Have you noticed? Why, the other day, Mrs. Babbinton could not discover why the basket was being continually nudged closer to the fire, when she was being so careful not to leave it near enough to risk it burning. And then only this morning she caught him tumbling out of his basket, pushing it towards the warmth with his nose, and then clambering back inside again."

"He can climb in and out of his basket?" She should not have been shocked. After the first day or so of displaying more newborn tendencies, the hatchling seemed intent on acquiring as many skills in as short a span of time as his rapidly growing body would permit. "Oh, he'll need to be kept outside sooner than we had anticipated."

"We've someone coming to build a pen for him tomorrow. I had wanted to wait until the evenings were warm enough that he would not be too chilled outside and away from the heat of the kitchen. And I'm sure if we line it with enough rags and leaves and other such things, he'll be able to burrow himself down into a comfortable sort of nest."

Mildred looked at Mr. Wiggan, waiting to speak until he met her gaze. "And what about when he grows beyond the confines of the pen? Or when he learns how to free himself from it without any help from either of us?"

"Miss Percy."

"You cannot deny it." (An exercise in hypocrisy, as she had done nothing but deny to herself what she was about to say to him.) "Look at it. Him. Fitz."

And he did. But there was no great revelation expressed in his eyes, the panic that had nearly debilitated him weeks before gone as instead a faint look of yearning settled into the lines of his face. "What did you believe in, Miss Percy? When you were a girl?"

What do you mean? is what she almost asked. It was also what she did not ask, because she feared she already knew what he meant, what mysteries his own question intended to probe.

"I believe in God," Mr. Wiggan continued, still watching the hatchling, still watching the children as they settled on the ground with him, urging him to pick up small twigs in his delicate claws and carry them back and forth from one lap to the other. "I believe in miracles that every logical part of my mind says I should not give credit to. I pray, every day, to an unseen spirit I believe—I truly believe—guides each and every part of our lives. And yet, through everything, I am told that a creature such as that—" a nod in the direction of the scene before them, "—should be an impossibility. Something from a fairy tale, a made up story. I am going to write to these learned gentlemen, who claim to believe in God and floods and fish that can swallow men and spit them back out again after three days, and I am going to tell them that I watched as a dragon," and then a small exhalation, almost a laugh at the admittance of that word, "burst free of its shell and tried to bite off the edge of my thumb only three weeks ago. And yet, I'm hesitant. Because I fear they will not believe me, that they will claim what I stand here and see with my own two eyes is a thing that cannot exist."

Mildred let his words roll around her, envelop her for a moment before they were borne away on the breeze that pushed through the leaves he'd just plucked from the trembling branches above. "When I was a girl," and she paused, and licked her lips, and tried not to dwell on just how long ago the time was to which she referred. "About Nettie's age, I believed in the fantastic. I believed I would grow up and have a great adventure." She raised her eyebrows and let them fall again, a shrug acted out upon her face.

"There's still time, you know." He said it so quickly and so simply she might have thought he had not said it at all. She glanced at him, but he was not looking at her anymore, instead knocking the side of his foot against a loose brick that edged a bed of lavender. "For your adventure."

She laughed outright. "Ladies of my age do not have adventures." She wasn't sure if ladies were meant to have adventures at any age, but most certainly not ladies who had already begun to find strands of gray in their hair or who knew when it was going to rain by the strength of the ache in their knees and lower back.

"But what are you going to do?" Mr. Wiggan appeared genuinely nonplussed by her statement. "You care for your sister's children, I know. But…" His eyes strayed again towards the hatchling (now curled up in a bed of warm compost and snuffling into the dark soil for leftover scraps that had not yet broken down) and then the children, sitting at the edge of a freshly tilled bed and feasting on baked potatoes Mrs. Babbinton had brought out for them.

"Nettie will not be grown for another ten years," Mildred pointed out. "I'll be…" she balked at saying it out loud, but pressed on regardless. "I'll be over fifty years old by that time. Long past the age of marriage and children and…" The final 'and' seemed superfluous. What more could there be for her, aside from those two things? And once she was into her sixth decade, both of those ways would be shut. Even now, she knew she would be lucky to snag even a widower, if she had been inclined to search for one.

Mr. Wiggan shifted his weight forward, something he did when he was about to add another observation to the conversation, but then Mrs. Babbinton approached with the promise of food and drink, and Mr. Wiggan recalled that he needed to plant a few more rows of carrots before the rain started in earnest. It wasn't long then until the hatchling was seen back to his basket (Mildred had begun to carry him, having learned that she could scoop him up from underneath like one would a cat, his belly so smooth and warm against her fingers, a juxtaposition to the rougher scales and small nub-like protuberances that ran along the length of his spine from his nose to his tail) and the farewells were made and another parcel of cakes and other good things was given to the children to take home with them.

Mildred chivvied them along swiftly, as a few raindrops struck her bonnet and she had neglected to bring an umbrella before leaving the house. They arrived home before the worst of the deluge began, the children struggling out of their wet outer garments and wiping crumbs from their mouths (they had insisted on 'rescuing' Mrs. Babbinton's cakes from the rain by eating them all on the way home (Mildred helped them on their self-appointed mission by devouring two cakes and a lemon biscuit)) and Mildred pushing damp curls of hair from the back of her neck as Belinda walked out of the drawing room.

"Oh, you've returned already! Did you pass Mr. Hawthorne on your way?"

"Mr. Hawthorne?" Mildred asked. "But is my sister back from town yet?"

"Mm, no. She'll probably try and contrive an invitation to supper and avoid coming home in the rain. She went to visit Mrs. Greyling," she added with a knowing glance.

"Ah," was all Mildred said, or needed to say. (Mrs. Greyling, for those who are curious, was an old widow of some means who claimed a friendship with a Lady Peavley, the daughter of a Marquess. This meant that at least half of Upper Plimpton's inhabitants wished to be on good terms with Mrs. Greyling in order to then claim a connection— albeit an indirect one—with Lady Peavley, daughter of a Marquess. Unfortunately for those hoping for a stepping stone into the aristocracy, Mrs. Greyling's entire history with Lady Peavley consisted of the former once treading on the hem of the latter's gown and spilling a glass of punch down her front. Colorful words were used (by the latter) which led Mrs. Greyling to add "passionate and opinionated" to her description of her great friend and daughter of a Marquess, Lady Peavley.) "Wait, Mr. Hawthorne? Who is he?"

Belinda wrinkled her nose, then scratched at a spot behind her ear. (With only her aunt as an audience, her powers of charm and finesse had dwindled down from their previous raging fire in Mr. Hawthorne's presence to a mere smoking pile of embers.) "He called while you were out. Said he was a friend of your uncle's? Forsythe?"

"Forthright," Mildred corrected, all while knowing Belinda wouldn't take the time to remember it. "He said he knew my uncle? Did he work with him on his studies?" A flare of hope lit inside of her. Would they not have to depend on hearing back from Mr. Gorman after all? Had their salvation decided instead to come to them?

"I believe he did," Belinda went on grudgingly, already bored with the conversation as it no longer pertained to herself. "He spoke as if he held your uncle in high esteem."

"But where is he? Will he come again?"

"He said something about calling again tomorrow?" She had already drifted towards the front of the clock in the hall, where her eyes narrowed at her own reflection in the glass. "I liked him," she said, as if she were defending him from criticism. "He had lovely eyelashes."

Well, Mildred thought, and blew out a breath. With any luck, she would be able to form her own opinion of Mr. Hawthorne's eyelashes very soon.

***

Mr. Hawthorne, along with his eyelashes, arrived not long after breakfast the next day. Diana took it as a sign of poor manners, as no one should have the effrontery to call on others while those others were still digesting their previous meal. But Belinda pointed out that he was from London (as in "Mama, he is from *London*," with enough emphasis on the final word to transform it into a decree absolving all natives from that place of their crimes) and Mildred was too eager to meet him to voice any sort of complaint (not that she would have voiced much of a complaint in her sister's presence anyway). So there they sat, all three ladies assembled in the drawing room when young Mr. Hawthorne was announced.

And he *was* young. Mildred noticed that first of all. Not that she had expected someone older (Belinda wouldn't have paid attention to his eyelashes even if they were made of gold or if they had been trained to sing compliments to her if the man had been aged more than thirty-five years (possibly forty if his air could be described as "distinguished")) but he strode into the drawing room looking so bright and so vital. And he was handsome. Not in a way that affected her (she enjoyed a handsome young man about as well as she enjoyed studying a fine piece of art) but she noticed Belinda straighten in her seat, and she thought she heard a small, sharp intake of breath from Diana, as well.

"Mr. Hawthorne," Diana said, rising from her seat. She held out her hand. Mr. Hathorne took it and bowed over it. His gaze met Belinda's over her mother's knuckles, and he smiled. And then the smile dimmed and his attention found its way towards Mildred.

Mildred took no offence. Most men didn't bother to waste their smiles on her. But she realized that his smile gave way to an earnest expression of sympathy, and once the exchange of introductions was made, it was to her side that he came first.

"I was very sorry to hear about your uncle, Miss Percy. May I?" He gestured towards the chair nearest to hers.

"Of course. And thank you. I will admit the news was a bit of a shock." She neglected to add the majority of the shock had come from everything that had occurred since hearing of his demise, and not the death of her Great Uncle Forthright in and of itself. But all of that seemed too much to pour into the man's ear so early on in an acquaintance. "He was in good health, I understand?"

"The best of health." He shook his head. "Such a vibrant man. Such a vibrant mind!"

"Yes," Diana chimed in, having already returned to her seat. "We did have a great deal of respect for *our* Uncle Forthright." Lest their guest forget that Mildred was not the only one to claim him as an antecedent. "We shared such a special relationship with him that he even thought to leave Mildred something in his will, though..." She cleared her throat. Talking about wills and inheritances was almost as impolite as talking about fortunes and budgets, but she shaped her mouth into a polite pout, a show that she would press on with the difficult subject regardless. "We've not heard anything more about it yet. I wonder if you might have a theory as to what has become of the inheritance? Does it usually take so long for such things to be organized?"

Mr. Hawthorne looked genuinely concerned. "You have not received anything yet? That is most peculiar. I clearly recall your uncle mentioning something—"

"He spoke about me?" Mildred moved forward in her seat. "Why, I'd not seen him since I was a girl. I have to say, I'm astonished he remembered me at all."

"Are you?" His eyebrows pulled downward. The back of his hand stroked along the side of his jaw. "I mean, you were not a constant topic of conversation, but I suspect that as he aged, as he felt the weight of his years upon his shoulders, he began to think more and more about those things that were important to him. Such as family," he said, nodding to each of the three women in turn.

Diana nodded. "I always say, family is more important than anything. Because if you do not have your family…" She spread her hands wide. Belinda looked away and began picking bits of imaginary lint from the arm of her chair. Mildred counted to five, the amount of time it usually took until she could introduce a new subject without it seeming as if she had interrupted her sister's turn in the dialogue.

"Belinda tells me you are from London," Mildred said. "Is your own family there?"

His expression tightened, the angles of his youthful face honing their edges to a blade's sharpness. "I am an only child," he said. Or admitted. It felt much more like an admittance, than anything. "My parents, well. My mother died when I was young, and I lost my father last year."

"I am sorry," Belinda put in, leaning forward, hands clasping her knees. "I cannot imagine what it must be like to lose someone so close to you." She tilted her head, one curl sliding attractively across her cheek, as if she could control the hairs on her head with a mere thought. "You were close to him? Your father? Oh, but I can tell by your face that you were."

"We were close, yes," Mr. Hawthorne nodded, eager to switch his attention over to Belinda. "Of course, there were the usual disagreements and difficulties that exist between parent and child—"

A slight hiss of sound from Diana's mouth interrupted that statement, though she covered it quickly with a light cough.

"—and I wish that we had parted on better terms. Though I would not doubt there are many who admit as much after losing someone. But I have resolved to do better, because of him. To do better for him, I should amend."

"A parent could not wish for a greater sentiment from their child," Diana said, her eyes closed as she seemed to savor Mr. Hawthorne's words. (It did help that Mr. Hawthorne was in possession of a lovely voice to go along with his sculpted face, deep and rich enough to lend needed years to his countenance. Mildred could also appreciate a lovely male voice, though it struck her how much she preferred Mr. Wiggan's voice; its timbre and gravity, the weight of years and wisdom contained in its tones. (Here Mildred continued to rhapsodize to herself about Mr. Wiggan's voice for several more minutes while her sister went on about the pleasure incurred by being a mother and the bond with one's children, etc. So to sum up: Mildred liked Mr. Wiggan's voice better than Mr. Hawthorne's and Diana wouldn't stop talking.))

"Mama," Belinda began, pouncing on the moment following her mother's speech to ask for something. (Mildred always knew when Belinda was about to ask for something. But much like a rumble of thunder in the distance or a cow raising its tail behind him, it often prefaced trouble ahead.) "You should ask Mr. Hawthorne to join us for lunch."

Diana's lips thinned. "What a charming idea, child. And how clever of you to think of it. But I'm sure Mr. Hawthorne has many demands on his time, and I wouldn't presume to —"

"Oh, not at all." Mr. Hawthorne smiled, his gaze darting from Mildred to Belinda and back again. "I would consider it a privilege to dine with you. That is, only if it is all right with you, Mrs. Muncy?" He cast the full glow of his loveliness on Diana, and though she did not approve of the man, or more specifically, the glances he continued to cast in Belinda's direction (no doubt she had noticed the state of his boots as well as Mildred had) it was a punishing thing to attempt a slight on such a handsome face.

"Yes, lunch. Please stay, Mr. Hawthorne." The request was spoken with a rictus grin. "I'll tell Cook to expect a guest, and then perhaps you can regale us all with your tales of London in these last few months, hmm?"

"I am honored," he said, bowing his head to her. "Thank you, Mrs. Muncy. I will do my best not to disappoint."

"I'm sure you will not," Belinda said, just as something that sounded like thunder to Mildred's keen ears rolled towards them from the distant hills.

CHAPTER ELEVEN

Because of their keen senses, it is nigh impossible to conceal something from a young dragon.

-From Chapter Seventeen of Miss Percy's Pocket Guide (to the Care and Feeding of British Dragons)

Diana prided herself on the arrangement of her table whenever the opportunity to entertain arose. For her better visitors, her finest plates were brought out, flowers—when in season—were carefully arranged, their colors chosen to complement the decorations of the dining room or perhaps even to set off the shade of her gown that day. Cook would prepare something remarkable and Diana would then offer profuse apologies for the poor quality of her menu ("If I'd only had more time to prepare…") in order to promote the belief that this was how they dined at every meal, every day. Fresh fruit was often offered. Dessert, as well. And all for her best, most esteemed guests.

Mr. Hawthorne, in contrast, received a selection of cold salads and various pickled things retrieved from the back of the larder. There were no flowers, and the good plates were kept locked away with the silver and the cut crystal glassware. Their guest, however, showed no sign that he recognized this slight. In fact, he ate with such gusto and such obvious appreciation of the meal before him that Mildred wondered if the chiseled angles of his face were not entirely due to his youth but perhaps also the product of an unsatisfied appetite.

"How did you meet my great uncle?" Mildred asked, offering him another helping of chicken.

"Through correspondence, at first." He took another bite and hastily wiped at his mouth with a napkin. "I was an eager follower of his work throughout my youth, and so I gathered up my courage and wrote a letter to him. I was barely sixteen," he said, smiling at the memory. "I feared he would think me nothing more than a foolish child and dismiss my untried thoughts and theories entirely. But then I received a reply. He was kind and courteous, answered all of my questions and posed several in return. Of course, he already knew the answers, but I believe he wanted to stimulate my education by sending me off to research those things for myself."

Mildred sighed, and scratched her nose. The nose-scratching would not have been remarkable except that it was needed to cover a strange pressure behind her eyes and in her sinuses, an itching feeling that often presaged a desire to cry. She didn't understand it at first, how her physical body could react to a word or an event before her mind had even fully processed the thing causing the reaction in the first place. But she sniffed, and she breathed slowly until the hot, red feeling abated from the most promontory parts of her face, and she tried not to think any more about it.

She thought more about it.

While Mr. Hawthorne waxed on about his relationship with her great uncle—the knowledge imparted, the ideas exchanged—she felt the lack of such a relationship in her own life, almost like... Well, she couldn't determine if the absence was more akin to something having been taken away from her, like a gift meant for her and delivered to another person, or if she simply mourned the privation because it had never been intended for her at all.

"How wonderful for you!" Belinda said, dabbing at her own lips with her napkin. (Not that Belinda's lips were in need of wiping, but it was an unconscious way of drawing attention to her mouth.) "To have a mentor, a person to guide you in such a way."

"Yes," Mildred agreed, trusting her voice for the first time in several minutes. "You are very fortunate. You make me wish I had known him better." Another pang, this one less severe, more of guilt than of any specific hurt. That she should have done more, should have striven to become better acquainted with her Great Uncle Forthright, this man who had left to her so many of his personal and private things, and who she could only remember from her childhood, the glint of pleasure in his eye when her childlike interests and curiosity had aligned with his own.

"I believe so much of my sadness at his loss stems from what more he had to offer the world," Mr. Hawthorne said, clearing the second helping from his plate and eyeing the dishes in front of him, clearly debating if reaching for thirds would be equivalent to setting fire to his manners and stamping them out on Diana's best carpet. "He was old, yes. But not in body nor in spirit." He exhaled. Not quite a sigh, nothing so unguarded as that. But his feelings were there, just beneath the surface, ready to reveal themselves at the slightest provocation. "I had so much still to learn from him. It is a grief I believe I will feel acutely for some time."

Mildred set down her fork. Normally she could have kept pace with even the most voracious of eaters without a problem (and she often took advantage of the situation when guests were present and Diana's comments on her eating habits were shuttered) but her appetite had diminished slowly throughout today's meal. It would have been an easy thing to attribute the unusual smothering of her hunger to the current track of her thoughts concerning her Great Uncle Forthright. Unfortunately, and true to character, her mind rarely followed the easiest route.

It was something in Mr. Hawthorne's manner. She couldn't find any fault in his face or expression. Goodness, he had the sort of face that could inspire a thousand cantos written in his honor. But there was such a lack of artifice in all he said and did that it seemed to swing the pendulum back towards his every blink and breath seeming as carefully curated as a performance.

Or perhaps she was nursing a jealous edge towards him because of the relationship he had shared with her Great Uncle Forthright, one she had never even known might have been hers if she'd made an attempt for it. (Later, she would blame Great Uncle Forthright for not putting enough effort into keeping in contact with her, but the fact that he was dead and had left her a trunkful of amazing things (including something she still had trouble admitting to herself may, or may not be a dragon) made it more difficult to keep her ire focused in that direction for long.)

"And how long do you plan to stay in Wiltshire?" Diana asked this while toying with the last few bites of food on her plate.

Mildred had noticed that her sister's initial and brief liking towards Mr. Hawthorne had faded quickly, probably to do with his impertinence at showing up on their doorstep without either a respectable fortune or a respectable name. (The glances he continued to trade with Belinda across the dining table also did him nary a favor. Diana had plans for Belinda. Though it had never been spoken out loud what those plans entailed, Mildred suspected they involved a suitable marriage (to Mr. Bertie Sampson) to a suitable gentleman (Mr. Bertie Sampson) with a suitable fortune of no less than a thousand pounds a year (like Mr. Bertie Sampson's).)

Mr. Hawthorne smiled at Diana, an expression so full of winsome charm Mildred felt the force of it like a sudden wash of heat from a fireplace after the logs had sparked and shifted. "I had no initial intentions of staying for very long, maybe not more than a few days at the most. But if things were to take a turn, and I found myself compelled to make a longer sojourn of it…" He glanced at Belinda. Her cheeks turned rosy and she picked up her glass to take a drink. "– well, I would not complain."

"Hmm," Diana said, her fork stabbing at her food with unchecked ferocity. (Once, in a fit of unchecked ferocity provoked by her husband informing her that their annual budget would not accommodate the rental of a three-storey house in Brighton near where the Prince Regent was known to occasionally stroll (Mr. Muncy's first argument against the scheme being that if one were to judge by the Prince Regent's current state of health, it was doubtful the man had taken a proper stroll in over a decade) Diana had managed to cut through her plate, the tablecloth, and left a significant gouge in the wood of the tabletop underneath). "You do not have some work that will speed your return to town?"

Mildred sucked in a breath. It was an ingenious question from her sister, and laden with traps. If Mr. Hawthorne said that work would take him back to London, then he would be decried as a person low enough to seek regular employment for his wages. And if he declared that he could remain in Wiltshire for an unspecified amount of time, then Diana would dismiss him as a wastrel who had no care for his work or future.

"Some of my work is here, actually." Mr. Hawthorne turned the full strength of his gaze on Mildred. "Though the depth of it will depend on Miss Percy, I believe."

"Me?" Mildred glanced first left then right, as if there might be a full row of Miss Percys lined up behind her.

"Mildred?" Diana's astonishment had overtaken her urge to continue her interrogation of their guest. "Why is everyone so interested in Mildred all of a sudden?"

"I do not understand, Mr. Hawthorne." She ignored her sister's attention (she had spent a great many years trying to ignore many of the things Diana said and did, as it made her life—if not easier, than at least easier to bear) and focused on their guest's interest in her (a baffling thing in and of itself, what with Belinda seated so near). "As I stated before, I was not very well acquainted with my uncle. I had not even seen him or corresponded with him in…oh, thirty years. I have no great intelligence of him to give to you. If that is what you were seeking."

Her own thoughts hovered over that last word, one she had chosen to use without any particular motive. But it was what fed her wariness about him, despite his charm and openness and the pleasing lines of his face. When he looked at her, it was not in appreciation of who she was, but rather as if he were trying to see into her—no, through her—for something he wanted, something that had nothing to do with her at all.

"I will confess," he said, blushing slightly, glancing down at his plate, a pained smile bringing out a dimple in his cheek. "I had received a letter from your uncle's assistant and heir, Mr. Gorman? Do you know of him?" A flick of his eyes away from the plate to meet hers before they returned to the table. "Well, I am unsure if it was a breach of some trust, or if he was not at liberty to tell me, and I apologize for being too forward if indeed it was, but he mentioned that you had received something from your uncle, the inheritance that was mentioned. Mr. Gorman implied that it was a collection of some personal belongings from his studies and research over the years?"

Mildred opened her mouth and closed it again. She had never revealed to her sister that anything of their Great Uncle Forthright's had arrived at the house. Her hands flexed and relaxed, her thoughts straying back to the effort of dragging the empty trunk out the front door and around to the abandoned shed. "I…" she began.

"But we've not heard anything about this inheritance of hers," Diana interrupted. "As we explained to you already, it's been weeks! And all without even a single letter about when it should arrive or what we should expect or–"

Mildred cleared her throat. "There was a small thing. I

nearly forgot about it until now. Just a parcel of books and other objects," she said, her gaze darting from Mr. Hawthorne's face to her sister's. "It came one day while you were out. I failed to mention it because there was nothing I saw that would have been of interest to you," she added to Diana. "Only papers and notebooks and other research things. A motley collection of items, really."

"Oh." Diana visibly deflated. "Oh, was that all? Well, I had at least hoped for... Well." She balled up her napkin and made an effort not to throw it down on her plate in a fit of pique, all while muttering something that sounded suspiciously like "books and things" on a sibilant breath.

"You're welcome to take a look at what I have," she told Mr. Hawthorne, hoping that a small offering might be enough to distract him from the large selection of her Uncle Forthright's belongings—her own belongings now, she reminded herself, which went far towards explaining her inclination to be careful with them—she had taken such pains to conceal. And she also worried that if she did not make this small concession, Mr. Hawthorne might take it into his head to linger in Upper Plimpton long enough to stumble on evidence of a creature that may or may not resemble a dragon stashed away within the confines of the vicarage. "It's not much, but there might be something relevant to your interests."

"If it would not be too much trouble," he said, as if he would say more, but no other words were spoken.

Mildred did everything she could not to swallow, or fidget, or make a display of how much more there was she had neglected to mention. The trunk, the crystals, the bones, the egg...

... the hatchling, perhaps even now cavorting around the back garden at the vicarage, screeching at birds and terrorizing Mrs. Babbinton's chickens through the barrier of their pen. And for a moment—oh, not even for as long as it took her to form the thought, she saw something pass across his face, like the shadow of a cloud sweeping over the landscape.

He knew.

Not about the hatchling. No, she didn't think he could have known about that. She suspected even her uncle had not fully realized what the thing was, what it was capable of becoming. But Mr. Hawthorne wanted something she had, and she very much doubted that thing would be found in a stack of loose papers or mouldering books.

"Let me have a look through some of the things and I can have them sent on to…" Mildred forced a small smile, though her teeth felt like they wanted to knock together. "Where are you staying?"

"At the inn, in town."

"Ah, right. Of course. I can put together a few items and —"

"Or you could just come back here!" Belinda said, so full of helpful good cheer that Mildred wondered how much force would be necessary to hook her foot around the leg of Belinda's chair and send it all—chair and niece—toppling backwards onto the rug. "It would save so much running about with packages and books and we could even send the carriage for you, on the days when the weather is not as cooperative."

"Well," Diana began. And stopped. As everyone proceeded to talk over her.

"Tomorrow?" Belinda continued, oblivious—or rather, completely livious of the glances sent her way by her mother and her aunt, but not caring a whit what either of them thought as she sorted out an itinerary for Mr. Hawthorne. "If you've only come here to see my aunt, then the time should not matter. You can come early, and Aunt Mildred can bring everything down to the drawing room and once you've had your look, you can join us for another lunch. Hmm?" She raised her eyes, bright as jewels, to meet her mother's lightning hot gaze blazing out from the other side of the table. "And if it is fair, perhaps even a picnic!"

Diana laughed. At least, on the surface it could have earned the dictionary's definition of a laugh. It possessed all of the outward signs of mirth and happiness: teeth glinting, eyes crinkling ever-so-slightly at the corners, chin tilted upwards just an inch or so. "I do not think Mr. Hawthorne came all the way to Upper Plimpton in order to have picnics with young..." and here her gaze cut its way towards Mildred, "... and other unmarried ladies. He wants to see Mildred's *books and things*, so we'll do as she suggested and have them sent on to the inn. I see no reason to have the carriage dragged back and forth when all of this might be solved with a small measure of efficiency and forethought."

Diana could not have made her meaning more clear if she'd clambered over the chairs and written "Get out of my house!" in pickle relish across the white of the tablecloth.

And Mildred sat in the middle of everything, wishing for a sudden shout of "Fire!" from the kitchen or a flash flood (despite the current lack of precipitation) or one of the children to sneak out of the nursery and shatter something in a loud and irreplaceable manner. Anything, she thought, to interrupt this scene and prevent her from having to continue as one of its participants.

She drew in a deep breath. And swallowed. And gripped the edge of the table as if the strength of her hands alone would prevent her from being violently sick all over the remains of their lunch. "I like the idea of the picnic." She looked at her sister, not in challenge but–

No, it was clearly a challenge.

Mildred knew she had little on which to stand. This was not her home. For the last seventeen years, she had resided there solely on the whims of her sister's grace and favor (and laziness, as her presence there had saved Diana the trouble and cost of seeking out the various parade of nurses and governesses she might have had to otherwise). But still the possibility always remained, that at any point she could have been turned out without ceremony, left to rely on the benevolence of distant cousins residing counties away and unknown to her. Mildred had nothing (well, she had fifty pounds a year, but fifty pounds a year in the hands of a woman without the support of a husband or family could be counted as equal to nothing) and her sister was well aware of it.

"This is no insult to you," she said, turning her attention towards Mr. Hawthorne. "But I would prefer to keep my uncle's things here with me rather than have them carted about the countryside. I've only just acquired them, and I haven't even had a chance to look through everything as much as I would like. So yes, if it would not be too much trouble to return here, as my guest, then I will bring down what I have of my uncle's things that might be of interest to you."

As my guest.

It had taken all of her courage to state her intention to make regular visits to the vicarage, but that had been accepted as a harmless bit of charity (Diana still believed Mildred was helping with Mr. Wiggan's students and other tasks related to the church, and Mildred was not about to relieve her of that misapprehension) and not something that affected her directly. But this second act of independence dragged Belinda and a handsome young gentleman into the fray, and also brought to light the revelation that Mildred had received her inheritance from their Great Uncle Forthright and not told anyone about it. So many acts of independence within such a short span of time made Mildred feel about as safe as sailing off into waters marked on the map with *'Here there be monsters.'*

"Thank you, Miss Percy." Mr. Hawthorne gifted her with an easy grin. "That is most obliging. And very intelligent, I must add. No, I do not feel any slight at your wish to keep your things close around you. Very intelligent, indeed, and it shows that your uncle was right to trust you with the care of them in the first place."

It would have been easy to feel elation at so much praise, and in sight and hearing of her sister, too. Mildred even made every show of shyly enjoying his approbation, dipping her chin and looking away as if she did not quite know how to take the kindness of his words, while allowing her cheeks to color with pleasure.

The color was managed by sheer panic over all the things she would have to conceal, how best to satiate Mr. Hawthorne's curiosity with a few papers sketched with some vague notes and send him back to London before he could discover what a terrible liar she tended to be.

Of course, she shouldn't have to lie at all. If she hadn't spent all her courage on her sister, on hiding the presence of the hatchling at the vicarage, she would find the words to tell Mr. Hawthorne to stuff his compliments and his enviable relationship with her Great Uncle Forthright and—

"We shall see you tomorrow, then." Belinda said, all soft looks and pink-tinged skin, as light and fresh as an apple blossom.

"I look forward to it, Miss Muncy." He nodded to Diana. "Mrs. Muncy." His attention arced its way back towards Mildred. "Miss Percy."

And there it was again, just beneath the shine on the surface of his eyes, behind the gleam of his teeth. He wanted something. Not papers. Not books. Not to share stories of London or her uncle or even to bask in the radiance Belinda chose to light like a firework for the entertainment of strangers.

No, he wanted...

The egg? The egg that was no longer an egg but now a squawking terror in the vicar's garden? What else would possess a strong enough pull to drag a young man all the way from London to call on an aging spinster in order to share stories of an old man she could hardly remember?

"Mr. Hawthorne," she said, and returned his smile. "Until

tomorrow."

CHAPTER TWELVE

Dragons are equipped with a vast array of tools for communication. Depending on the type of dragon, sounds as varied as chirps, clicks, whistles, growls, hums, and purrs have all been recorded as being used for one seeking to deliver information to another. Some have even been known to use a 'preening' language with each other, though this has only been witnessed between two or three dragons already in possession of a close bond.

-From Chapter Eleven of Miss Percy's Pocket Guide (to the Care and Feeding of British Dragons)

She was lying.

Reginald knew she was lying because he had already seen a copy of the will (thanks to Mr. Purvis) and learned that the items meant for her had already been sent to Wiltshire several weeks before (thanks again to Mr. Purvis). But he had certainly not sold half his belongings and squeezed himself into a carriage that reeked of body odor and mildew in order to spend two days trundling all the way to Wiltshire for a brief chat and a glance at an old man's journals.

The difficulty of the situation was that he could not be certain if she was lying because she knew about the stone—about what it was and its worth (doubtful, seeing as how she had the look of every other tightly-wound spinster he'd ever had the misfortune to encounter, the sort whose education failed to extend beyond the boundaries of knitting and gossip and eating too much cake) or if she was nothing more than a possessive ninny determined to grasp onto her things like a child unwilling to share her toys.

He had seen the tension between the sisters, Mrs. Muncy and Miss Percy. Or rather, he'd felt it, as thick as the heat before a summer storm. And the married one hadn't even known the inheritance had already been delivered, that Miss Percy had hidden it all away right beneath her nose.

And these were the people he had to deal with, a harridan and a spinster and a—

Ah, but then there was Miss Muncy. Like an angel, like a dream. She was feminine perfection, her voice, her face, even the slight curl at the ends of her hair everything he could have wanted in a woman, everything he hadn't even been aware he had wanted until she had walked into the drawing room—no, glided. Like a swan. Like a…

Miss Muncy. He would move heaven and earth for her. He would shower her in riches, drape her in silks, see her settled on the largest estate money could buy. But he could not do that until he had what he'd come to Wiltshire for.

He walked back to the inn, up to his room, and sat, thinking. Dinner, sleep, and then breakfast yet to be got through, before he could have another opportunity to discover where Miss Percy was keeping the stone. He did not doubt she had it, but he feared she would not give it up without a great amount of reluctance on her part. On his journey from London (and as a way to distract himself from his company), he had drawn up a scenario inside his mind about how all of it would go: He imagined going to the house, finding Miss Percy (his thoughts had rendered her thin, nervous, but agreeable) and relating just enough of his life story (one where his father wasn't a gambling drunkard and Mr. Charles Forthright played a more influential part) to draw on her sympathetic and biddable nature and thereby win the stone from her.

Unfortunately, the reality of the situation was a stark contrast to the one his fancy had created. The first obstacle was that Miss Percy did not trust him. He had sorted through a dozen reasons why: Because he was young, because he smiled too much, because he did not smile enough, because he did not pay her enough attention, because she was simply the sort of person who did not give her trust away easily. But whatever the reason, he did not have the time nor the money (a pocket watch and a few old books were not worth much) to spend days—perhaps weeks—winning his way into her confidence.

So he would have to make an attempt at things from a different direction. Because what none of his fanciful imaginings had succeeded in conjuring was Miss Muncy, she of the voice and the face and the perfectly curled hair.

And with the image of Miss Muncy (voice, face, hair) burning bright as a star in his thoughts, he returned to Ashby Lodge, a plan beginning to form in his mind.

The maid greeted him at the door. He was shown through the house and into the garden behind, where there was a table and chairs on a small terrace along with a blanket spread out on the grass for the children (there were two of them—children, that is—both of them small and probably sticky as most children tended to be) and where the three ladies (Mrs. Muncy, Miss Muncy, and Miss Percy) had already congregated.

He hesitated then, his mind tripping over that number. Auguries often came in threes, did they not? And then there were the three fates, the three witches in Macbeth (or were the three witches meant to represent the three fates? He should have paid more attention to his studies...) and there stood three ladies, the sun shining down upon their heads, the light breeze (tinged with a mingling of lilac and manure) stirring the hems of their gowns and the lace at their sleeves and collars.

"Good afternoon," he said, finally dipping into his courage and walking towards them. Mrs. Muncy saw him first. Though, judging by the pinched look on her face, he assumed she had heard every sound of his entrance to her home, all the way from the first step he had taken outside of the inn in Upper Plimpton nearly a half an hour before.

"Mr. Hawthorne." Her smile greeted him with all the joy of a dying wheeze from a set of ragged bagpipes. "You came. Of course."

Miss Muncy was the next one to give him her attention, and he nearly reeled backwards from the force of it. Her eyes lit up with a warmth of feeling at the sight of him, making him believe that no other man, woman, or beast could elicit such a reaction from her. "Miss Muncy," he said, his voice higher than normal, and bowed over her outstretched hand. "And Miss Percy."

She looked over at him at the sound of her name. She had been keeping an eye on the children (the both of them following a trail of ants through a small patch of clover, probably anticipating some cataclysmic murder of their entire colony beneath their small, devilish hands) but dragged her gaze to his face as her own expression adjusted its features into something tolerable. (Tolerable both for him to look at (Miss Percy was not a beauty, though he could not determine if his opinion of her attractiveness was due to her age, his antipathy towards her, or merely her proximity to Miss Muncy) and tolerable in how she seemed to accept his presence there rather than enjoy it.)

No, there would be no success if he depended on her opinion of him alone.

***

The picnic was interminable, as picnics are wont to be. Reginald could never decipher the reasons for the general adoration of them. Why eat outside where there were insects and birds and the sun beating down on the back of one's neck when there were perfectly good rooms specifically designed for dining (hence their title of 'dining rooms') only a few yards away? But he ate and he smiled and he pretended not to notice the ants crawling along the edge of the blanket and the tree root digging into his thigh and the children (... Lord, the children) screeching and bouncing and somehow making a mess of their food despite the fact they were gifted with the same hands and arms and mouths as everyone else.

The conversation that accompanied the food was stilted and awkward. Mrs. Muncy spoke only in subtle scathes and inferred criticisms, while Belinda flitted and sparkled with all the energy of a bird shaking the morning dew from its wings before catching the first waft of dawn-lit air over the grass. Miss Percy hardly spoke at all, unless it was to reprimand the children or ask for more ham. (The ham was delicious, he had to admit, though he still did not trust his own palate to discern whether the food was of truly excellent quality or if he was still half-starved from his years of scraping by, eating London's offerings of "could it be mutton or could it be horse?" too many days of the week.)

Before everyone had finished eating, Miss Percy excused herself and went inside the house. She came back quickly, as if what she had gone inside to retrieve had only been just inside the door.

"Here," she said, placing a large stack of notebooks, books, papers, all sorts of things containing a large quantity of writing and scribbled notes and minute printing on the blanket before him. "This is the bulk of what my Great Uncle Forthright sent to me. There are a few more books upstairs, but they did not seem unique or interesting enough to be of any import."

He watched as she fiddled with her hands in her lap, as her teeth scraped across her bottom lip.

"Goodness, so much!" He picked up the first item—a small journal—and began leafing through it. His eyes saw nothing. Unless the stone was somehow magicked down to the size of a seed and tucked between the pages, it wasn't there. "You must be an uncommon reader, to find your way through all of this."

"I am not an uncommon reader," she said. "I do not even know what you mean by that. But I have read all of what you see there. Twice over."

While the children played and a maid came to clear away their dishes, Reginald made a great show of going through the books and the papers, scanning the nearly indecipherable lines of a letter, nodding over the passage in a journal that he could not have cared less about if it had been written in another language. "This is all fascinating," he said, and met Miss Percy's gaze over the pile.

She did not believe him. It was writ across her face as clear as the lines fanning out from the corners of her eyes, squinted against the afternoon sunlight. "It is, isn't it? If there is something there that interests you, I do believe I would be willing to part with a few small items. Considering your close acquaintance with my uncle, that is. I would not wish for you to feel you had come all this way for nothing."

Dear God, was she onto him? Her words had struck the ground between them with the force of a gauntlet. She had to have known why he was there, why he had sought her out, some aging spinster mouldering away in the middle of bloody Wiltshire. What other reason would he have to waste so much of his time and scant resources? Certainly not for a bloody pile of bloody books. "How generous of you!" he exclaimed. "For you to practice such magnanimity, and to a near stranger…" A smile, he thought, would be too much. He aimed for an expression of wistfulness. Not quite sad, but with a touch of something earnest gilding its edges.

They could go back and forth like this for some time, a performance dragging on for hours, neither of them willing to fully accede to the other. And then Belinda held out her hand towards him and made a waving gesture with her other until he understood that he was supposed to stand up. "Take a turn about the garden with me, Mr. Hawthorne? I find I have quite eaten my fill and I need to walk or I will never be able to rise to my feet again."

Of course he would oblige. He nearly tripped over his own feet in his haste to take her hand and help her up from her seat on the blanket. She moved beside him and tucked her hand within the crook of his arm. Her face was shaded by the brim of her bonnet (her mother had made a loud pronouncement insisting she wear a hat to prevent her face breaking out in—the shudder here had been enough to send vibrations through the air—freckles) and she used it as another lady would use a fan to practice coquettish arts. A tip of her head to peer up at him from beneath the brim. Another tilt and the scent of her hair swept towards him. Or she would hide her face away entirely, leaving him to wonder what secret smile she was keeping from his sight.

They walked towards the edge of the garden, where it spread out into a plain bit of lawn spotted with some trees before frittering down to a low stone wall and a few outbuildings in need of restoration. Miss Muncy looked back over her shoulder and made a small 'hmmph' of satisfaction.

"There now. We shall be able to speak to one another without being overheard. And they can still see us so there cannot be anything inappropriate about our being together." She turned her head so that she faced him completely, the brim of her bonnet forming a halo of straw and lace around her.

"Miss Muncy," he said. His mouth had gone dry. His throat was tight. There was something he had wanted to say to her since he had arrived at Ashby Lodge, something that had to do with the stone and his plan and something that all floated away from him as she blinked and smiled and gave his forearm a bit of a squeeze. "Miss Muncy," he said again, his voice cracking as if he were a mere lad of thirteen again. "I find myself facing a predicament, of sorts."

"Oh?" Fine eyebrows curved upwards. "Are you going to confide in me? I assure you, I am quite trustworthy." Spoken with a smile, with a hint of teasing underlying her words.

He latched onto that lightness, allowing it to carry him upwards as if he were dangling from the tail of a kite. "Oh, I'm not even sure how best to begin. It's a curious situation, and with the death of your Uncle Forthright still so recent, I find it difficult to mention to your aunt, lest I bring up some unwanted grief."

She patted his arm. He could have died happily beneath the weight of that additional touch. "I would not worry about that. I will confess, I do not think either my Aunt Mildred or my Mama are truly grieved at all about it. They hardly knew him. I had never been introduced to him, hardly even knew he existed before we received the letter announcing that he was gone."

"Well," Reginald paused long enough to draw in a fortifying breath. This much was not an act. He needed a moment to think, to arrange the words he wanted to say in their proper order so as to ensure they worked the way he wished them to. Practicing legerdemain, he thought, could not be so hard as this. "That is, I'm afraid, what leads me to the very predicament of which I spoke. You see, I was rather close with your—with *their* great uncle, and there were a few items which I believe he intended to leave in my care." He shook his head. "I shouldn't demur so much. I *know* he wanted me to have them. We talked about it. Unfortunately, I fear none of those particular wishes were put in writing. He was strong and healthy, none of us could have anticipated the accident that would so suddenly snuff out his life."

Miss Muncy had drawn her lips in between her teeth while her gaze took on a pensive sheen. She tipped her head, an unspoken invitation for him to continue.

"How do I approach such a subject with your aunt? To

ask her if she is now in possession of the items in question?" He lowered his voice, turned the direction of their walk so that their backs were towards the members of the family still gathered around the blanket. "Oh, it is indelicate of me to even entertain such a notion, but I think she may be hiding a portion of her inheritance."

At the crinkle in Miss Muncy's forehead, he pressed on. "I mean, she did not even tell you or your mother that anything from your great uncle's estate had arrived. Only when pressed did she finally admit it. For some reason, one I cannot possibly fathom, she is hiding away what should… well, what should be mine."

Miss Muncy looked back towards the house, towards Miss Percy. There was puzzlement on her face, but she did not appear as if she were preparing for battle, to stand up for her aunt's good name and reputation. "But why would she behave so? What is it that Great Uncle Forthright wanted you to have, that she would keep it from you?"

A point! He had scored a point! Already her speech was framed in his defense. "Without delving too deeply into specifics, one of the things… Well, I believe—your great uncle never intimated as much, but I suspect it might be worth a significant amount of money."

Her eyes widened. "Oh."

"Which is why he wanted me to have it. My father was not a rich man. He tried his best, but circumstances always seemed to be against him." A propensity for drink and cards always seemed to be against him, as well, but he neglected to mention that portion of the narrative. "But Mr. Forthright wanted to ensure my needs were met, that I would not encounter any difficulty acquiring a home and…" He looked at Miss Muncy, his gaze steady. "A wife."

"I see," she said. Her grip on his arm tightened.

Reginald pushed on, realizing he was so close to completely winning her over to his side. "Your aunt has so much already. What does she want for? She lives in this beautiful home, she is well clothed and fed. She has everything a woman of her age and status should desire! Whereas I—"

Miss Muncy stopped walking. She moved until she almost faced him, but not so much that they would appear to be standing too close to one another. "If my aunt is keeping these things from you, then we will have them from her. It is despicable behavior, and I will not tolerate it. As you said, what more could she want? My family has welcomed her into our home, provided for her in every possible way. And for her to practice such subterfuge? No," she shook her head, ribbons and lace and curls of hair set fluttering. "We will fix this."

We will fix this.

He would cling to that use of the word 'we.' Like a benediction, like a dove alighting, like the pledging of a troth, he thought—he knew—his life would change. It was no longer him alone, struggling to find purchase on the shore against the waning tide of his life before this moment. Now he had Miss Muncy by his side, and with her hand on his arm, her fingers just grazing the fold of his sleeve, he felt transformed into something unstoppable.

"Thank you, Miss Muncy." If her mother were not watching them, eyes trained like a hawk's following the trail of a mouse through a deserted field, he would have kissed her hand. (He would have kissed any part of her available to him to kiss, though even daring to press his lips to her knuckles would most likely bring down all the ire of Mrs. Muncy upon them in an instant.) "I must say, it feels very encouraging to have an ally in you."

She turned them around and started their walk again, a leisurely stroll that began to circle them around again to the blanket and where several pairs of ears would be able to overhear them. "And I will admit that I have thought very well of you since I first saw you in our drawing room. It is in your eyes, I think. Something that just wills a person to trust you."

"And you do trust me?" He sounded desperate, but he didn't care. He would make an utter fool of himself if it meant another minute by Miss Muncy's side.

She leaned into him slightly, a brief push of her figure against his. "Implicitly," she said, honesty in every syllable.

"Well, then." He glanced up at the sky above them. An almost impossible blue, streaked with clouds as softly edged as feathers. "I hope you have a rather large capacity for belief, Miss Muncy. Because I have a great deal more to tell you."

CHAPTER THIRTEEN

*It may not come as a surprise, but dragons
are territorial creatures.*

*-From Chapter Two of Miss Percy's Pocket
Guide (to the Care and Feeding of British
Dragons)*

"We have a problem."

It was not the most auspicious way to begin a conversation. Mildred spoke those four words before she had even removed her gloves or her bonnet, before Mrs. Babbinton had closed the door behind her.

Mr. Wiggan stood in the front hall, his hair disheveled from having passed his hand over the top of his head, down to the nape of his neck, and back again. "A problem?"

Mildred finished fighting with the buttons of her spencer and shrugged out of it, one sleeve turning itself inside out as it clung to her arm like seaweed wrapping around her ankles (a thing she had experienced first-hand, the one—and only—time she had ever dared to wade into the edge of the ocean on a trip to the beach when Belinda was small). "Mr. Hawthorne," she panted, still struggling with the sleeve. Mrs. Babbinton gentled her with a hand on her arm before she gave the offending article a final tug to set Mildred free. "Has any mention of him reached you? Has he made any attempt to speak to you? To come here?"

Mr. Wiggan blinked at her dumbly. "Hawthorne, you say?"

"Good." Mildred smoothed her perspiring palms down the front of her skirt. "Right." She looked at Mr. Wiggan and dread filled her at the conversation that lay ahead. "Where is Fitz?"

A funny thing how she had previously refused to refer to the hatchling by the name the children bestowed upon him until there existed a threat to his safekeeping. And yes, she viewed Mr. Hawthorne as a threat. In the vicarage kitchen, her tongue and her worries shaken loose by tea (with extra milk and sugar) and one of Mrs. Babbinton's baked creations (moist wedges of spiced plum cake) she untangled everything she knew of Mr. Hawthorne and his arrival in Upper Plimpton.

It was not until she reached the end of her narrative that she began to enumerate her suspicions about him. That Mr. Hawthorne was acquainted with her Great Uncle Forthright in some fashion, she did not doubt. (How else would he have come to know about the egg? she asked herself. Of course, he had not made any mention of the egg or that he was aware of its existence, but what else would have brought him all the way to Wiltshire? Surely not to pay his condolences to a niece who hadn't seen the uncle in question in nearly three decades. And she coupled that with the avaricious gleam in his eye (and not only when Belinda happened to cross his line of vision) flickering in and out of sight as quick as a piece of dust floating through a shaft of sunlight. Certainly not the sort of gleam a few faded journals and dry books had the power to elicit from most young men.) But every other part of his story seemed crafted especially to manipulate, to win himself favor from his listeners.

When she had finished (her tale taking her up to the events of the picnic the previous afternoon) a ripple of unease passed through her, that perhaps she was being unkind to Mr. Hawthorne, allowing her first impressions of him to taint her overall opinion of his character. Perhaps he was too handsome (not that beautiful people should have ranked as particularly untrustworthy, but she was disinclined to fall into the trap of lending her unerring confidence towards individuals who may only give the appearance of sincerity rather than allowing their character the opportunity to mature and prove itself over time) and too easy with his smiles. But then, she realized, if he had shown himself to be more reserved, would she not have criticised him for a lack of feeling?

No, no. It was more than all of that. She simply didn't like him. Every time she looked at him, every time she heard his voice, something small and aching twisted in her gut, like an alarm bell sounding, like the flicker of a lamp from a lighthouse warning of rocks in the shallows.

"So." Mr. Wiggan leaned back in his chair, his gaze scraping the rafters above his head. "You believe he knows about Fitz?"

Mildred glanced at the basket, where the hatchling had been snoring (Purring? Was something with wings and scales capable of purring?) soundly since her arrival. Had he grown larger again since she had last seen him two days before? With one wing open and draped over the edge of the basket, he looked ready to snort and snuffle himself awake and take off through the kitchen window. "I don't think he knows about Fitz." She flicked a hand towards the basket. "But I think Mr. Hawthorne knows—or at least greatly suspects—that my Great Uncle Forthright left something of great value and import to me."

Mr. Wiggan leaned forward in his chair, elbows bracing themselves on his knees. "The egg?"

She blew out a breath. "The egg."

"But what would he want with it?" Mr. Wiggan, while having shown no additional sign of his first panic the day the hatchling had come out of his shell, looked tired. Harried. Like the parent of a newborn child, Mildred thought, and was wracked with guilt that he and Mrs. Babbinton had taken so much upon themselves—so much that she was responsible for bringing upon them—and all without a single noise of complaint.

"It may have escaped your notice," Mildred said, twisting around in her chair to reach for another slice of cake. "But that's not a basket of kittens over there by the fire. If Mr. Hawthorne knew of the egg, or even suspected its existence, I do not doubt he believes it to be worth something. A rare creature such as that? Here on England's shores?"

Mr. Wiggan ran a finger beneath the wilting folds of his neckcloth. Had he shaved yet today? Mildred studied the lines of his throat, visible to her where he had worked the fabric loose. When he spoke again, she swallowed quickly and looked away. "Does this Mr. Hawthorne seem a greedy, grasping type of person?"

What could she say? Didn't every person want something for themselves? "He is poor, I think." She placed her plate on her lap and held up her hands as soon as the words were out, aware how Mr. Wiggan could interpret them. "Not that his fortune, or lack thereof, should immediately paint him as a blackguard. If fortune were the only factor to decide a person's goodness, I should be as guilty as him. If not for my sister—" She closed her mouth, shook her head, took another large bite of cake before more words she did not want to say came spilling out of her.

"He wants for money, you mean."

Mildred nodded, still eating.

"And you think, in desperation, he might have come here, hoping to obtain the egg and exchange it for something more in the pecuniary way of things?"

Another nod. A sip of lukewarm tea and she rendered herself able to speak again. "I cannot blame him for it, if that is his reason for coming to Wiltshire. And it's plain he is doing everything in his power to hide it." Such as wearing a new coat over a threadbare shirt, the scuffs on his boots buffed away until she was surprised they even succeeded in keeping his feet dry. "He is proud, and—as you said— possibly desperate. If he was as close to my uncle as he says, perhaps he expected something to be left to him in the will, but was disappointed."

"What will happen when he discovers..." Mr. Wiggan raised his eyebrows and jerked his chin towards the basket.

"Oh, he won't. If it's an egg he's looking for," Mildred spread her hands. "There's none to be found. As long as he doesn't come here, I cannot think how he should learn of Fitz's existence."

"But the children?"

Mildred shook her head. "They won't speak of it. It's been weeks and they've not said a word to anyone. I think they're too afraid of losing their access to Mrs. Babbinton's kitchen should they say too much about what happens when they come here."

"So you're saying I should be on my guard while Mr. Hawthorne continues his stay in Upper Plimpton?"

"Yes, I suppose." She stopped speaking, wishing that she was still young enough to fall into a fit of dramatics. Why should an overabundance of emotions only be allowed to those who had not the years to appreciate them? "I am so sorry for bringing all of this on you, on Mrs. Babbinton. Perhaps things would have been better if you had never offered to help me move my uncle's trunk."

One corner of his mouth quirked upwards. "Allow me to say here and now, Miss Percy, that I do not regret a single action I have taken since that day."

"Well, then." She finished her cake, eyed a third slice, but set her plate aside instead. "All we can do is hope Mr. Hawthorne tires of country life and returns to London as soon as possible. Unfortunately, I think he is beginning to form an alliance with my niece. And she seems to be more than welcoming of the attention."

"Do you think she is in any danger from him?"

Mildred tried to stifle her laughter, but ended up snorting behind her hand. "You do not know Belinda very well, do you? She is..." A chameleon, a shapeshifter, a siren luring sailors to their deaths. "... incomparably talented at making people love her or loathe her as she will. Thankfully for us, she seems to thrive well enough on our collective indifference towards her."

But what if…

No, she would not allow her thoughts to go in that direction.

But what if Belinda and Mr. Hawthorne…

No, surely Diana would step in and prevent anything from happening in that quarter. But then again, Belinda was Belinda, and if Diana made a great performance of not wanting her eldest daughter to have something, it only followed—judging by every day of the last seventeen years that Mildred had witnessed of her niece's life—that Belinda would shake the very foundations of the earth in order to acquire that certain something being held out of her reach.

"More cake?" Mrs. Babbinton stood beside the table, a small streak of flour on her jaw, though every other part of her was as neat as the proverbial pin.

Mildred knew that she shouldn't. Surely too much cake, even cake as fine as Mrs. Babbinton's, had to be detrimental to her health when taken in too large a quantity. But then Fitz snuffled from his basket, not quite a sneeze, but enough of something to send out a spark and fizzle of smoke curling upwards through the air.

"Yes, please," Mildred said, and held out her plate.

***

She wanted the day to be over, and yet it felt as if it had only begun an hour or so before. She had awoken, eaten breakfast, tended to the children's studies, visited the vicarage, and now the minutes were rapidly carrying her along towards dinner and that would be the end of it. It did not help that her thoughts were mired in the day previous to this one, the day of the picnic and Mr. Hawthorne's pathetic attempt to be engrossed in the sampling of her great uncle's things she'd shown to him. Her mind struggled to move forward from that point, each attempt to step further into the present like drawing her feet out from the thick, sucking mud of the past.

As soon as she was home again from the vicarage, the children begged to be taken into the garden. Diana had not been in the best of moods since Mr. Hawthorne's shadow had first darkened their doorstep (an understatement of such grand proportions that Mildred wondered if the word 'understatement' should feel slighted at its misuse), and so she obliged by taking them out and away from the tense (another understatement, as 'histrionic' or 'directing one's prayers towards the Lord above for a quick and painless end to things' seemed a bit overdone) atmosphere that had settled over every room of the house.

She sat with a book taken from the study. She didn't much care for many of the books in the study. Neither her sister nor her brother-in-law were great readers, and so the volumes stored there served more as accessories to the room rather than how Mildred believed a personal library should exist: as pieces of the curator's character, bound and shelved but available to be read again and again, like memories brought out and pored over until they were rounded down as smooth as pebbles.

She held this one in her lap, turning over the pages mindlessly, their sliding sound like waves lapping upon the shore. She would not be at ease again, she knew, until Mr. Hawthorne was safely (she was not sure why she insisted on using that word, as if some quiet, unconscious part of herself would wish him harm if given the opportunity) removed from Upper Plimpton. And there would only be Fitz to worry about. Fitz outgrowing his basket. Fitz learning to toddle across the garden without tripping over his own claws and landing on his snout. Fitz flapping his prodigious wings and

—

"Aunt Mildred! Aunt Mildred!" Nettie ran up to her, her

hair wild, eyes bright and shining, hands and skirt streaked with rich, dark mud. "When can we go to the vicarage again?" She spoke the question—a question oft-repeated, as previous scenes with the children will attest—as if it was a great secret, a pleasure shared between only Mildred, her brother, and herself. "I've a new trick I want to teach Fitz, and—"

Mildred held up her hand. "Nettie, can you make a promise to me?"

The girl clasped her hands in front of her and bounced on the balls of her feet. "Yes, yes. What is it?"

"As long as Mr. Hawthorne is in town, could you do your best to avoid speaking of Fitz and your trips to the vicarage? Even with Matthew? Now, I give my word I will still take you, the both of you," she assured her as Nettie's face began to crumple. "But I think we should be careful. Fitz is special. And I believe the fewer people who know about him, the better. For now, at least."

Nettie nodded, a picture of compliance. Mildred would wonder at that, at how much the children's behavior had altered with the addition of cakes and a dragon to their lives. But what more could a child want?

Mildred sank back into her seat, closing the unread book on her lap. What more could anyone want, really?

She dragged the children inside (not an exaggeration, as she had to hook her finger beneath Matthew's collar and pull him away from a pot overflowing with earthworms he had dug up from beneath the rose bushes (though Mildred was careful to return the worms to the earth before the birds found them like a selection of meats left out on a platter)), saw them up to the nursery to be washed and changed into clothing that did not carry half the garden in their threads, and finally made her way back to her own room for the first time since she had left it before going to see Mr. Wiggan and Mrs. Babbinton at the vicarage.

She opened her door. Something, she noticed right away,

was different.

She stood in the doorway, her hand still curled around the doorknob. Everything looked just as it should, just as she had left it hours before. The servants, she knew, rarely came in to clean. She made her own bed, swept her own floor, even rolled up her own small rug and carried it downstairs to be beaten. Her laundry, once washed, was set beside the door in a basket and she took on the responsibility of seeing everything sorted into the appropriate drawers and the wardrobe. She was even careful to leave a few spiders in the corners, to help with the insects when the warmer weather came around.

It was her space, the one pocket of solitude allowed to her in all of the house. And someone had been in it.

It was subtle, almost infinitesimal things that caught her eye. Her slippers were gone from their place on the rug, instead sticking halfway out from under the bed. The books on her nightstand were no longer stacked haphazardly, but arranged in a neat pile, the corners aligned. An edge of something—a stocking, a handkerchief, she could not tell from where she stood—poked out from above her topmost drawer, a sliver of white standing out like a wound against the dark wood. And there was a smell…

She closed her eyes, inhaled deeply. It smelled of a garden. To be specific, it smelled of lilacs.

"Belinda," she muttered, as muttering was the only correct way of pronouncing such a name at such a time and in the stultifying quiet of her freshly invaded room.

Mildred stepped inside and shut the door behind her. Not once, in seventeen years, had Belinda ever set foot in her bedroom. If the children were sick, if they were in need of her, she went to them, even going so far as to sleep on the nursery floor when their symptoms required constant observation (or cleaning, as a difficult night after a two-year-old Matthew had eaten several bites of soap had shown). But they did not come into her room without permission. An unspoken rule, and yet the entire household adhered to it. (Though Mildred suspected it was not a burdensome concession, as she doubted anyone was pining away to infiltrate her tiny, musty space for some trifling need of their own.)

She dropped onto her knees, heedless of any dust her skirt might sweep up from the floor. Beneath her bed were stacks of books, of papers, piles of little boxes and containers she had yet to take to the vicarage for a more thorough sorting. And every single thing, every one of those books and papers and boxes and bags had been moved.

If someone had begged her to explain how she knew, she was not sure she would be able to provide them with a clear, succinct line of reasoning. But everything had been touched, had been shifted slightly, as if the person responsible (Belinda, she knew it was Belinda) had taken tremendous pains to drag out the items and then return them as close as possible to their original positions. Except it had not been done with a deft hand. Either that, or Belinda thought so little of Mildred's sensibility towards her own belongings that she (the former) had not worried that she (the latter) would notice any discrepancies.

She searched through everything. She was not aware of how long it took her. A few minutes? An hour? But every book was thumbed through, every letter, every rock turned over in the palm of her hand. She closed her bottom drawer —the last drawer she had gone through (yes, all the items were present and accounted for... yes, she was slightly mortified that someone had borne witness to the state and quality of her underthings) and sat on the edge of her bed.

There was no point in dwelling on the question of what Belinda had been searching for. At the moment, the 'why' of it seemed a trivial thing. The fact that it had happened at all, on the other hand, that someone—no, not merely 'someone', but a member of her family, a person she had helped to raise from infancy—had come into her room while she was out, had made a sham of her privacy, of her place in the household was insupportable. (Here, 'insupportable' stands in for 'enough to make one quake with a fiery hot rage, the type that could set one of weaker character on a path of destruction and desolation.')

Mildred gripped the edge of the bed. She wanted to grip Belinda's pretty little shoulders and shake some measure of sense into the girl. Of course, she had seen the various looks shared between her niece and Mr. Hawthorne, had taken note of their little tete-a-tete at the end of the garden the previous day. But their acquaintance had been one of such short duration that Mildred had gone and underestimated how quickly a young person's passions could be ignited.

She bit her lip. Apparently passions could catch on fire at the same speed necessary for Mildred to take Mr. Hawthorne into dislike.

So.

Nothing had been taken, at least not as far as Mildred could tell. That much was important. All of the journals and papers that had contained any allusion to the egg or the hatchling had already been transported to the vicarage, along with all of the fragments of bone and bits of fossilized shell she had mistaken for mere stones. And there should have been safety in that realization, that there was no evidence of Fitz's existence in her room, anywhere in the house for that matter. But her thoughts, as they had an irritating tendency to do, spiralled outward and away from her, creating new thoughts and worries of their own, until she had sketched out enough worrisome possibilities to fill up a dozen lifetimes.

She should change for dinner. That was the current thought in her head, the one that reminded her of the grass and mud stains on her hem, the streaks of dust on her skirt and sleeves, the wrinkles and folds that made no secret of her time spent crawling about on the floor of her bedroom.

Except it did not feel like her bedroom anymore. It had been infiltrated, this tiny space, the one at the back of the house given to her out of the kindness of her sister's heart. The place where she had spent nearly half of her life—too much of her life—feeling as worthy to those around her as a forgotten pair of slippers with a hole in one toe.

She stood. She undressed. She washed herself with tepid water left standing in the pitcher on her dresser. Her hands shook as she fastened the buttons on her clean gown, fingers trembling with the force of an internal earthquake as she brushed out her hair and pinned it up again. A brief glance in her looking glass, and she stilled. She was pale. She had known it without having to see the fish-belly pallor of her cheeks for herself, but the smudges of shadow beneath her eyes surprised her, like prints left behind by thumbs stained with newspaper ink.

Poor Aunt Mildred. Silly Aunt Mildred. Aunt Mildred who slept in her box of a room beneath the attic, stalking about the house like a shadow, waiting for someone else's sun to give her definition. Miss Mildred Percy, who rarely said what she wanted to or did what she wanted to. Who had given herself over for her family, and in return was given...

And then her sister's voice poured into her ear, as if she were standing there beside her. "We've taken you in, you know, and at no small expense to ourselves. You do not know what economies we have made in order to accomodate you. Of course, you do not have a family of your own, so you would not have any idea how much–"

Mildred turned away from her reflection, cutting off her sister's voice as neatly as if it were a thread to be severed. (If this were a different sort of story or if Mildred were a different sort of heroine, this moment would be marked as something of a turning point. Mildred would square her shoulders and shake off the mantle of meek submissiveness she had worn for so long. She would march downstairs (heroines, especially ones made newly aware of their self-worth, often marched around to various places as if each successive encounter were now a battle to be fought) and assert herself whenever the opportunity to be assertive arose. She would speak her thoughts aloud without regard for such frivolities as consequences or etiquette. She would go where she wished to go and do what she wished to do and eat as much cake as the seams of her gowns would permit. But this is not that sort of story and Mildred is not that sort of heroine. However, even though a drastic and sudden change to her behavior may never occur on future pages, it is good to keep in mind that even the smallest trickle of water has the power to alter the very foundations of the earth.)

"I am tired of this." Not her sister's voice, but her own. And not words that heralded a surrender, but ones that served to shake her loose of her thoughts and the room and the pain of the privacy she had lost. Down the stairs she would go, into the dining room where her family was no doubt already waiting. Diana would comment on her tardiness, the children—if permitted to have their meal downstairs this evening—would twitch and misbehave as they always did when both of their parents were in attendance, and Belinda...

Mildred paused in the corridor outside her room. She tried to consider the sort of questions she thought she should worry over, whether Belinda would show any signs of guilt (most likely not) or if her gaze would appear scheming (possible) or watchful (not as possible). But the exhaustion she felt about... well, everything worked its way through her limbs until she thought she was dragging chains behind her in her wake. And by the time she arrived at the door to the drawing room (Diana often liked to make a show of moving from the drawing room to the dining room before dinner, as if they resided in some great house, the kind that necessitated a progress of sorts from one room to the next), she realized that what she thought of most of all, what made her shut her eyes in a moment of blissful want, was nothing more than a bit of Mrs. Babbinton's cake, a bit of good conversation with Mr. Wiggan, and the quiet thrill she had experienced at seeing the hatchling break free of its shell.

Such minor things, weren't they? But oh, how she clung to them as she opened the drawing room door and stepped inside.

CHAPTER FOURTEEN

The more time one spends in the presence of dragons, the more one learns they are rather quiet, contemplative creatures. The loud moments, the moments of fire and flight, of shining teeth and sharpened claws are remarkably rare. Much like a summer storm, it is the quick flash of lightning one remembers, but it is the slow roll of thunder across the sky that remains.

-from Chapter Nineteen of Miss Percy's Pocket Guide (to the Care and Feeding of British Dragons)

Mr. Wiggan did not teach his pupils in the vicarage. As much as Mrs. Babbinton might have enjoyed the mayhem of a dozen or more local boys tearing through the dark-panelled rooms and corridors of the house in her care, the truth of the matter was that the vicarage was small, Mr. Wiggan was possessed of a great many items he did not wish to see trampled and prodded by scuff-knuckled fingers, and the church itself (where he chose to conduct their lessons) lended an austerity to the affair. Or at least, to put it bluntly, a fear of the good Lord and His watchful eye.

Mildred found them there, thirteen boys scuffing their feet beneath the pews, their heads bent over slates or books or whatever other work Mr. Wiggan had dealt to them that morning. At a small table near the front, a rickety wooden thing dragged out from the shadows and put away again at the beginning and end of every school session, Mr. Wiggan was bent over a collection of rocks and other miscellania that Mildred assumed had been a part of the day's lesson.

She shuffled sideways and sat down on a pew near the very back of the church. The wood let out an almighty creak —as wood always did when one most wanted it to stay quiet —and Mr. Wiggan looked up, his eyes narrowing until he found her.

He almost always smiled when he saw her. If she had been in a different mood, she might have worried such a frequency of emotion would cheapen it, make it meaningless. But she was in just the right sort of mood, her worries about Mr. Hawthorne and Belinda dampened down by her walk into Upper Plimpton, by the angle and the warmth of the light piercing through the stained glass windows that lined the church in which she now sat. That same light hit Mr. Wiggan, catching a few threads of bronze in the otherwise plain brown of his hair.

"Now, Peter," he said, his gaze switching towards the young boy nearest to him. "Allow me to check your declensions. You've been having some trouble with those of late."

Mildred was happy to sit and wait. The church was quiet in the way that all large, old buildings were, as if the length of their existence imbued them with a particular variety of sentience known only to roughly-hewn stones and beams. Mildred had sat in this church hundreds of times, attended weddings and funerals, had listened to Mr. Wiggan—and before him, a Mr. Paucy, who had died as he lived, napping peacefully through the third hymn of the Sunday service— deliver countless sermons on life and death and charity and hellfire.

Strange, she thought, how a building constructed with the purpose of welcoming as many people as possible through its doors could seem more beautiful, more holy without so many of those people inside of it.

At the end of their lessons, the boys bolted out of their seats as if shot from a line of cannon, only called back long enough to stack their slates and their books before they made another attempt towards the door, elbows and shoulders used like battering rams against one another to see who could break out and into the blessed late morning sunlight first.

Mildred waited until their shouts had died down before she stood again and walked forward, the strike of her heels on the floor of the main aisle sounding strangely profane in the renewed silence of the place.

"They seem a boisterous group," Mildred said by way of greeting. "I do not recall Mr. Paucy educating any of the local children in such a way."

Mr. Wiggan shook his head as he wiped the slates clean one by one with a ragged cloth, already streaked with chalk. "That would be because he did not. Mr. Paucy, God rest his... well. He was one of the old sorts, you know."

Mildred blinked. If by 'old sort' he meant that no one actually knew how old Mr. Paucy had been at the time of his death (which meant that the birth date etched onto his gravestone was merely a 'best guess', and that most in the town believed that keeping his age at one year before a century was a conservative estimate) then she agreed with that assessment.

"He did not believe in education for the masses," Mr. Wiggan went on. "Whether because he thought the average layman did not have the time for education or because it would distract them from more important things..." He shrugged. "But I am happy with how things are progressing now. They are a fine collection of young men, and I hope that at least a few of them will grow to be even finer adults."

"I notice, though..." Mildred swallowed and tapped the toe of her right foot on the uneven stone of the floor. "No girls."

Mr. Wiggan sighed, his hands pausing over the rocks he

was clearing off the table. "I have tried."

"I do not doubt it."

"But the families that wish their daughters to be taught can more often than not afford a nurse or governess to teach them, and the others say they cannot spare the girls from their home and chores. Believe me, it was difficult enough convincing some of the families to allow their sons to attend at least a few mornings out of the week. Yet change is not often wrought by great revolutions, no matter what history would attempt to teach us," he finished, and with a small sound of effort, or frustration, hefted up the wooden table and carried it to the side of the nave, tucking it into the shadows there.

"Though I doubt those great writers of history care to waste their time cataloguing all of the little progresses forward, the ones hardly noticed until years later."

Another smile from him. "Too true. Who wants to read about Stephen the Steady or Richard the Reliable when there are a bevy of Conquerors and Lionhearts to keep us entertained? So," he said, wiping the dust from his hands onto the front of his waistcoat.

"So," Mildred echoed, and breathed in the warm, beeswax smell of the polished wood around her.

"I take it you're not here to discuss your requirements for a successful revolution? Though if you wish to test your plans for a girls' school, you may find that Upper Plimpton would be more amenable to the hammering plowshares into swords idea than the one that involves teaching their daughters how to read."

Mildred had not been there to discuss revolutions of either the political or educational variety, though the latter idea planted itself in her head like a small seed, only waiting for a measure of sun and water and fertile soil to bring it to life. (The aforementioned planting was accompanied by irritation at herself for never before noticing the dearth of proper education for young girls in the town which she had inhabited for nearly two decades. Had she been so wrapped up in her existence caring for her sister's children—a rather comfortable and privileged existence, now that she considered it—and living a life according to the one Diana had sketched out for her that she had failed to notice anything beyond the walls of Ashby Lodge?

The brief answer, and the one that cut her to the quick, was 'yes'.)

"I came to ask about Fitz," she said, her voice suddenly timorous as her thoughts struggled to return to the subject that had brought her to the church in the first place. "I was going to stop in at the vicarage, but then remembered that you had your school today."

"His pen is finished." Mr. Wiggan put on his hat and waited for her to begin walking towards the door before he fell in a half a step behind her. "Mrs. Babbinton has already lamented the loss of the creature in her kitchen. But he seems happier with more room in which to move around and has made himself a marvelous nest out of the straw put down for him."

The vicarage was only across the lane from the church, but Mildred's heart began to pound faster as they stepped onto the property. Instead of passing through the house, they instead walked around to the back garden, mostly hidden as it was by various trees and trellises and climbing vegetation already thickening back to life for the season. Mr. Wiggan opened the gate, one of those quaint pieces of hardware that gives the appearance of being rickety, but could most likely hold back a line of invading hordes if put to the test. (The invaders would then be faced with the daunting visage of Mrs. Babbinton standing her ground, heavy kitchen implement in hand. If one were to dig back into history far enough, it is fair to assume that the Romans finally gave up on keeping a toe in England because there were simply too many of Mrs. Babbinton's stalwart ancestors treading its shores, brandishing a set of fire tongs or a sturdy rolling pin.)

"Oh, I see," Mildred said, and she did. The pen was complete, its unfinished wood pale and bright against the backdrop of an aged garden wall and the shadows cast by the trees arching over it. A combination of narrow slats and wire mesh kept the hatchling safely inside (though Mildred didn't want to think how little effort it would take for the creature to tear through the barrier like wet paper). And there, half-burrowed into the straw, sat the hatchling itself, his head and front legs visible while the rest of him twitched and scraped himself deeper into his bed.

Mildred knelt down on the grass, the fingers of her left hand hooked into the wire. It took a moment, and then the hatchling's nostrils flared, his head lifting from the straw before he struggled up onto all four legs, his back arching like a feline's as he stretched out his wings. Mildred caught her breath, unable to even think as the sunlight illuminated the membrane. But the warmth of the light, the beauty of it was so like the light that had shone through the stained glass windows of the church that she could not ignore the similarities.

"Well, hello." She smiled. She could not help it. Fitz walked towards her in his lumbering way, navigating the uneven ground with claws gripping the straw beneath him. He folded up his wings—How quickly he managed it! Faster than even the most practiced seamen could trim a sail—and rose onto his hind legs, his front claws climbing onto the mesh and towards her fingers.

"Oh, no!" she said, still playful, and pulled her hand back. He squawked at her in dismay, then shook his head and snorted. No sparks, thankfully. No ribbon of smoke to give evidence to the quiet fire that somehow burned inside him. Mildred looked back at Mr. Wiggan, who had dropped down to his haunches behind her. "Isn't there a danger of him setting the straw alight?"

"He's done very well with it so far. And we must keep in mind that he slept on a lot of old blankets and rags in the kitchen for weeks without singeing a single thread." He shrugged. "Or we've just been singularly fortunate and he'll burn the whole thing down around him before the day is out."

She reached for the latch that held the little wooden door shut. "May I?"

"Go ahead."

A flick of her thumb and the latch opened. She did not think Fitz would notice right away, that some manner of coaxing would be necessary to draw him towards the opening, but his head cocked to the side with focused immediacy, eyes glinting like the edge of a well-honed blade. He stumbled forward, tripping only once. He righted himself, edged towards the door, and stretched out his neck as if first testing the quality of the world outside his cage.

"He is grown. Again." He looked to be about the size of a healthy chicken, though longer than that from nose to tail. There were still a few bits of straw clinging to the protuberances that decorated his back, and without thinking she reached out and picked them off, one by one. She did not expect him to twist around and snap at her. He seemed to have already matured beyond the point of wanting to bite every finger-like thing to come within a yard of him. But she certainly did not anticipate the soft rumble of sound that vibrated from his throat at her touch.

She had heard it before—when he slept, when he was full of Mrs. Babbinton's good food, when he had been curled up in his basket, tail flicking lazily towards the ashes that had spilled out of the fire—but now he turned his head and nosed into her palm, his scales warm as they scratched against her skin.

Without being bidden, he made to climb into her lap. She obliged him by settling more comfortably on the grass, spreading out her skirt and making a hollow there for him to curl into. His claws poked through the fabric of her gown and stabbed her legs, but she only winced slightly as he turned around himself and—still vibrating, his nose still burrowed into her palm—laid down.

Beside her, Mr. Wiggan chuckled. "Shall I fetch you some tea, since it seems you will not be moving again for some time?"

Mildred placed her hand lightly on Fitz's back. It struck her how hard, how tough his hide was along his spine, as if he were armoured for a battle yet to be fought. But the skin along his neck, under his jaw, down to his belly was as smooth and supple as her sister's finest pair of kid gloves. (The comparison of Fitz's abdominal area to the leather of Diana's most expensive pair of gloves sent a shiver through Mildred, but the fact that her own thoughts had so easily tripped in that direction brought back all of the fear for the hatchling's safety that Mr. Hawthorne's arrival had first brought to life.)

"Nothing from Mr. Gorman yet, I fear?"

Still balanced on the balls of his feet, Mr. Wiggan plucked up a few blades of grass and began weaving them together between his fingers. "Absolute silence from that end. I already have a few drafts of letters sitting on my desk, ready to be sent to several naturalists and heads of scientific communities in London, Paris, Vienna." He spoke the names of the cities with a kind of reverence, as if he believed their reputation multiplied by their distance from Upper Plimpton would result in a greater chance of finding help there. "But I do not anticipate a hasty reply from any of them, especially as I have gone to great pains to word my inquiries in a manner that will not have me dismissed as a raving madman before they've read down to the end of the third paragraph. So to them, it will appear that there is no urgency to the matter."

Mildred trailed her fingertip over Fitz's back, still mesmerized by the dips and curves of the ridges there. The sound of his purring increased, and he nipped at the base of her thumb, gumming it lightly before settling back into a deeper state of relaxation.

"Well, at least he seems to be happy enough here for the moment." Indeed, she wondered if she would even be able to return him again to his pen when the time came for her to leave.

"I believe I would be at the height of contentment as well, if I were to find myself in a similar position."

Mildred looked over at Mr. Wiggan just as a rise of color appeared in his face. He coughed into his shoulder and quickly looked away, as though anything and everything on the ground was of greater interest than the lady and dragon less than three feet away.

Embarrassment, she had always thought, was a kingdom ruled by people much younger than she and Mr. Wiggan. Furtive glances and warm blushes were for couples only just out of the schoolroom, not for a lady and gentleman with over eighty years between them. But she turned her attention away from Mr. Wiggan, which was easy enough to do with Fitz nestled snugly against her. Mr. Wiggan then took that opportunity to lean slightly towards Mildred, his balance wavering enough that he had to place a hand on the ground to steady himself. And then Mildred began to speak, and Mr. Wiggan started to say something as well, and they both apologized and stumbled over their words and faltered back into an awkward silence.

"I wanted to thank you," Mildred began again. She found she could speak more easily if she pretended as though Mr. Wiggan was not actually there, and it was only herself, alone in the vicarage garden with a dozing dragon humming against her bosom. "I do not want to imagine how things would be if I had kept the egg at home with me, if it had hatched and I'd found myself with such a creature stashed away in my tiny bedroom, with my family clamoring their way through the halls."

"You do not need to thank me, Miss Percy."

"Oh, but I do!" She raised her head, meeting Mr.

Wiggan's gaze across that scant few feet between them. "I detest when people say they do not want to be thanked or congratulated or consoled. It may sound selfish, but it is as much for me as it is for you. To let you know how much of a help you have been, and to remind myself that there are a few things in this life I simply cannot manage on my own."

He reached over as if to touch the curl of Fitz's tail around her wrist, but instead his hand bumped against hers, his fingers warm as they brushed across her skin. "It is not always good to be on one's own," he said. "At least, that's what I'm beginning to discover for myself."

She laughed. She did not know why. Or she did know why and she was reluctant to admit that it was a nervous reaction to a touch that might have meant nothing or might have been the beginning of something that had been frustratingly stubborn in finding its way forward for far too long. "Well, you do have Mrs. Babbinton," she said, and wanted to reel the words back into her mouth the moment they burst forth.

"Mrs. Babbinton, yes." And he smiled, and she tried not to notice the poignancy edging it. That, perhaps, she had even been the one to put it there. "Speaking of, I'm sure she has some tea and a little something else waiting inside for us. If you would care to stay for a bit," he added, in case she was inclined to run off like a shot after the awkwardness of only a moment before.

"Thank you, that would be lovely." She managed to slide Fitz out of her arms and place him back in the pen, nestling him down into a bed of straw and rags he burrowed into sleepily as she latched the door behind him. Tea with the vicar and Mrs. Babbinton, and then an easy walk home again to look after the children until it was time for dinner. A funny thing, she thought, how life with a dragon seemed hardly altered from the one she had led before. And a funny thing, how the realization of it made her a little sad.

CHAPTER FIFTEEN

*To take on the care of a young dragon… oh,
woe to anyone who treats it as nothing more
than a transient fancy.*

-from Miss Mildred Percy's personal journal

Mildred had a bit of a routine she preferred to follow as she prepared for bed every evening. Once the children were tucked into their own beds—a process that usually required multiple stories and multiple cups of water and multiple checks of the wardrobe to make certain there was nothing monstrous lurking among the shadows and the little balls of dust—she retired to her own room, where she practiced the usual ablutions (teeth cleaning and washing pertinent portions of her body and changing into her nightgown) and slipped into bed with a book and a large enough stub of candle to see her through at least an hour's reading. There were, of course, the occasional evenings that failed to follow this pattern, such as when unusual trunks were delivered late in the day. But more often than not, Mildred could be found in bed well before nine o'clock, a pair of wool socks on her feet—depending on the weather—and a book balanced on her bosom while her candle flickered its way down to a shining puddle of wax.

That was the usual routine. Tonight, however, Mildred had only reached the teeth cleaning portion of the evening when there was a raised voice from one of the rooms below her (her sister's, as the vibration it carried through the walls was as distinct as a fingerprint or the six points of a snowflake) and then the rapid thump of running footsteps (not her sister's, as Diana would never ascend or descend from one floor to the other in a manner that would necessitate the use of the word 'thump') followed by—

"Miss Percy? Miss Percy!"

The repetition of her name was accompanied by a staccato knocking on her door, as though whoever was on the other side was too distracted to deliver a steady, rhythmic pounding.

Mildred wiped her mouth and opened the door. Betsy stood there, shifting from foot to foot and looking very much like a person who wanted to run away and yet could not do so until she had delivered the message burning like a hot coal on the tip of her tongue.

"Betsy?"

"Fire!" Betsy said, spitting out the word like it was carried on smoke and flames itself. "There is a fire!"

Mildred glanced around the room, hoping nothing had taken to incinerating itself while her back was turned. "Where?" she finally asked when the maid did not prove herself to be more forthcoming.

"At the Old Gables, where the Miss Primroses have been staying."

The Old Gables was not as ancient as the title might suggest. It was rather a newer cottage, built within the last ten years but fitted out with some of those architectural touches (gables, diamond-paned windows, low ceilings and narrow doorways) meant to convey a quaint and comforting sense of age, but without all the inconveniences of rotted timbers or squirrel-infested attics that often plagued houses with a greater collection of years under their leaking roofs.

"But that's out by the vicarage," Mildred remarked, and somewhat stupidly, she would later admit to herself. As if fires were incapable of burning in the eastern half of Upper Plimpton. And then something caught in her throat, a bit of fear wrapped around a lozenge of prescience and all of it coated in an acrid sauce of anxiety. "Why are you telling me this?"

Betsy's eyes looked very much like a startled cow's, in that moment, all white around the edges and preternaturally large. Boggled was the word that came to Mildred's mind, and she took a small step back in case the maid's boggling eyes decided to leap from their sockets entirely and roll like marbles across the bedroom floor. "There was also a message," she said, in a whisper that somehow managed to also fashion itself as a shout. "From Mr. Wiggan."

She held out a folded slip of paper. It wasn't sealed, and Mildred could not bring herself to care whether or not it had already been opened and read by any other eyes than her own. So she unfolded it and read it and gulped audibly (at least it reached the heights of audibility to her own ears, though whether anyone could hear it beyond the boundaries of her skull, she would never know) at the three words written there.

Fitz has escaped.

Mildred did not consider herself to be in possession of the quickest of minds. If asked to place herself on a scale measuring deductive abilities, she would most likely plonk herself somewhere round and about the lower end of things, and that was being most generous. But the fact that there was now a fire near the vicarage and a note in her hand announcing a spark-sneezing dragon's expatriation from his newly-built pen was an equation as easy to figure as someone holding up one finger of each hand and asking how many fingers it made in total.

"Right," Mildred said, surprised she was able to speak at all around the gulping and the anxiety and the realization that she would not be able to slip into bed with her book and her wool socks at any point in the immediate future. "I need my shoes."

Her shoes were still on her feet—as already mentioned she had not progressed beyond cleaning her teeth for the evening—but she did collect her shawl and a pair of gloves and the first bonnet she could find, a plain straw thing she yanked down onto her head without even bothering to tie the ribbons before she scuttled down the servants' stairs with Betsy hurrying along in her wake.

"What is going on?"

Diana, unfortunately (for Mildred, for the fire, though perhaps not for the extra dose of tension and conflict needed to keep the scene moving along at a brisk and interesting pace) had situated herself in the rear of the house, perhaps even in anticipation of Mildred's flight down the back staircase. She stood with her hands clasped before her, her head tipped at a slight angle, a question mark drawn with that slope of her neck. She also stood between Mildred and the kitchen, which led to the back door, which was the route Mildred had planned to take in order to leave the house without enduring the confrontation she had just stumbled into.

Diana's question still hung in the air. Mildred was afraid to speak, afraid to stammer or offer little more than brief bursts of monosyllabic speech that would fall like a poorly-nocked arrow landing well short of its target. "There's a fire," she managed to say, and tightened her shawl around her shoulders.

"I'm well aware of this supposed fire Betsy was going on about," Diana remarked, punctuating her words with a quick glance at the maid as she slipped out from behind Mildred and escaped to the kitchen. "I have already scolded the girl for trying to set the house in a needless uproar. But what I am not convinced of is why you feel the need to go running off in the middle of the night—"

"It's a quarter to nine!"

"—while the entire household descends into chaos over something that has nothing whatsoever to do with any of us."

Mildred straightened her spine, which was rendered more difficult by the fact that she was already standing as straight as a broomhandle due to the tension rippling through her.

"The fire is quite near to the vicarage. And the Misses Primrose... Well, someone could be hurt, and I am going to see if they need any help."

"And what would the addition of your presence possibly achieve?"

It was in that moment that Mildred wished she could somehow snip herself out of her sister's life, as though she were nothing more than a few tangled threads in an abandoned piece of embroidery. Would her absence act as proof enough that she could leave an impact on another's life? What of the children and the running of the household in general? How many things would change if Mildred simply... wasn't there?

Oh, but that was a fancy suited for another time, one designed for long, quiet bouts of contemplation. Fires, on the other hand, did not do well when left with long bouts of contemplation at their disposal (or rather, they did very well with long bouts of contemplation at their disposal, which was why Mildred began to inch her way forward and around the blockade that was her younger sister). "I am sure someone will find a use for me," she said, and finally pushed past Diana without looking back.

Once she was outside, she allowed herself the luxury of glancing behind her at the house without any fear that her sister's power extended far enough to transform her into a pillar of salt or something else equally devastating and Biblical. It was absurd to feel like she was running away, as though she was a child and breaking a rule delivered by her parents. But still she looked up towards the window of her little bedroom, a faint glow visible through the curtains from her fire and the candle still flickering away on the nightstand. And a tremble of fear vibrated through her, at the thought of having to return and face her sister again. And she hated that her life had reached such a point. Or rather, that she had so easily allowed it to.

She tore her gaze from the house and looked up at the

sky, seeing nothing but the dark of clouds. The clouds, at least, kept it from being too cold, and the brisk pace she set for herself once she stepped out onto the road meant her shawl, gloves, and bonnet were enough to keep her from feeling chilled. In fact, by the time the lights of Upper Plimpton came into view she had worked up a healthy amount of perspiration ('healthy' being a more palatable word choice than 'dank' or 'water-logged') and was ready to rip off her bonnet in order to give her hair a chance to dry. And she would have done it, if there had not been the social impediment of a rather large crowd gathered around the Old Gables (large for what Upper Plimpton was capable of producing from its meager population), half of which (the cottage, not the crowd) was currently up in flames.

There were no expletives to spare, no ejaculations along the tenor of "Oh!" or "Ahh!" or "There is a decidedly large conflagration just over there!" to mark her arrival at the rear of the crowd. Only her eyes open wide and her mouth open wider and her hands clutched tight to her chest as though her fingers were imbued with the power to keep her heart from leaping out beyond the confines of her rib cage.

"Miss Percy?"

Mildred jumped. Mrs. Babbinton stood beside her, one hand hovering over her arm as though to calm her should she feel a sudden urge to bolt like an unruly horse. "Where is Mr. Wiggan?" she asked, and with such haste it all tumbled out as one garbled word. "Where is Fitz?" she asked, this question coming out with only a slight improvement in enunciation. "Where are the Misses Primrose?" came the third question, this last one garnering a near frantic edge.

Mrs. Babbinton placed both of her hands on Mildred's forearm. "Mr. Wiggan is helping to fight the blaze. Fitz is asleep in the kitchen. I may or may not have added a dollop of the vicar's whisky to his water dish in order to ensure he would sleep heavily enough to dare leave him alone again. And the Misses Primrose were removed from the house before any injury could befall them. They are... well." She gestured towards the front of the line where two older ladies — Miss Margaret and Miss Jessica Primrose, respectively — stood huddled together, crying into matching handkerchiefs while they each kept hold of their pets also rescued from the fire (Miss Margaret, a ginger cat and Miss Jessica, a parakeet in a small cage). "Come along," she said, and gave Mildred's arm a gentle tug. "It will do you no good to stand out here breathing in all manner of smoke and fumes. A nice cup of tea will suit you, and perhaps—"

"No." Mildred gently pulled her arm from the housekeeper's grasp. "Not until I'm certain Mr. Wiggan is safe."

She pushed her way through the assembled ring of onlookers, placing herself near enough that she could see the individual flames through the windows of the upper floors. Men raced in and out of the cottage, armed with buckets of water, pails of dirt, and all while the way was cleared for some sort of contraption made up of a tank and a levered sort of pump and a long hose that was pushed through a broken window.

Mr. Wiggan was there, her gaze fixing on him the moment she caught sight of the broad line of his shoulders. He wore neither hat nor coat, his shirtsleeves rolled up as he helped to feed the hose through the window before rushing back to work one of the handles that would pump water into the cottage.

He appeared unharmed, which gave her comfort. She did not know what she would have done if he had managed to hurt himself because of some trouble Fitz had caused. She had been the one to bring the egg to the vicarage, and so she held herself responsible for any and all events that spiraled out from that single, seemingly innocent action.

It took too long to bring the fire under control, or at least it seemed as though they would never extinguish the flames before they could gnaw their way through the entirety of the village and all of its most flammable parts. But at last a cheer went up and the men emerged from the smoking shell of the cottage, all streaked with soot and ready to assure the the Misses Primrose that there was very little damage to the structure itself, mostly smoke and water and nothing that an industrious group of volunteers could not come in and fix for them with a few days of steady work.

"Oh, but what happened?" someone asked the Misses Primrose, while another person queried, "How did the fire start?"

"It was all so strange," Miss Margaret Primrose said, her voice a reedy quaver of fear and relief and more decades of existence than most people wished to acknowledge (since acknowledging how many years the Misses Primrose carried between them might succeed in drawing attention to the fact that perhaps they had stymied the natural order of things and the universe would need to swoop in and correct its negligence). "We were in the parlor, and Jessica said she heard a noise in the kitchen. At first I thought perhaps Pilchard—" (the parakeet, for those curious) "—had escaped from his cage. He does like to try and unlatch his little door, you know." A moment here, for an indulgent smile towards the bird as it fluttered around in its cage. "But I went in—"

"No, I went in first," Jessica interrupted, in a more stentorian tone than her sister. "You stood behind me, crying about the bat fluttering around the kitchen."

"Well, I thought it was a bat—"

"I've never seen a bat that large—"

"But when I was a girl—"

"We were girls together, if I remember correctly—"

A bit of a hubbub occurred suddenly, the crowd shifting as the tank with the hose was taken away and someone brought over a few blankets with which to wrap the Misses Primrose in case they should go into shock over seeing their home go up in flames. Mildred was pushed to the rear of the group for a minute, left to watch the gray heads of the elderly sisters bob and sway as they were drawn away from the cottage and towards the inn where they were most likely going to spend the night. By the time Mildred caught up with them again, the conversation had reached a point of:

"—and it's tongue was made of fire!"

"—utter nonsense!"

"But I saw it! It screeched and then it set the curtains alight!"

A cannonball lobbed into the middle of the street could not have distracted Mildred from the Misses Primrose and their retelling of how their cottage had caught on fire. She wanted to chase them down, to shake them (well, perhaps only a gentle rocking as a good shake might too easily see the sisters' bones rattled to dust inside their unfashionable gowns), to force them to relay every detail of the mysterious fire-breathing bat (according to them, and about as accurate as Mildred hoped it would remain) that had found its way into their kitchen. But to accost them with a barrage of questions would also mean to draw attention to the "bat" and to lend credence to their tale with the force of her interest in it.

As it currently stood, the Misses Primrose were old and feeble enough (Mildred wasn't entirely certain where the line was drawn, and how near to it she might have happened to be) to have their story of a winged intruder coughing sparks onto their window dressings dismissed as mere incoherent ravings. Mildred, more than aware that the descriptors "old" and "feeble" would very likely be applied to herself at some point in a future that was hurtling towards her at a faster pace than she cared to admit, had little desire to count herself among the throng of people willing to listen to them with a tight expression of forbearance before shunting the aging sisters off to bed as though they were a pair of children attempting to tell their parents of a monster sighted in the shadows of the closet.

Because she knew they were not incoherent ramblings.

Because she knew Old Gables had been infiltrated by a curious (she hoped it was only curiosity that had drawn Fitz from his pen and prompted him to toddle over to a neighboring house and set it on fire rather than because of any kind of malice directing his actions) dragon that would most likely not be viewed by the rest of the village's inhabitants as a mere peculiarity deserving of boiled meat and chin scratches and a comfortable basket by the fireplace.

Mildred bit her lip. It was nicer to say that she 'bit her lip' rather than 'she chewed on her lip as though it were a sausage after she had gone without a proper meal for two full days,' but she bit her lip, and she took a step back from the Misses Primrose and the villagers gathered around them, and she turned around to look for Mrs. Babbinton.

… who was not there. Instead, Mr. Wiggan stood at the edge of the street, still without his coat and with his shirtsleeves rolled up, his hair sticking out from his head while streaks of soot decorated his face and forearms like a scattering of bruises. She rushed over to him, hands reaching out as though to grasp him and pull him towards her, to make certain all of his limbs were still properly attached to his body and no part of him had been singed by the flames. But she stopped herself before she touched him, the fingers of her right hand just brushing over a damp wrinkle of his shirt before she drew her arms back and clasped her hands in front of her.

"You're not hurt?"

He shook his head. "I am well." He did not sound well. His voice had a rasp to it (an attractive rasp, Mildred would later admit to herself, though she could do without it if it meant never having to watch him run into a burning building again) and everything from the slope of his shoulders to the erratic twitch of his fingers spoke of an exhaustion that threatened to drag him down to the trampled ground. "I did not know if you would come."

"Of course I came. You said Fitz had escaped. I could

never have remained at home, sitting and doing nothing while beset with worries about what was happening." She glanced over her shoulder. Behind them, the core of the crowd had continued on towards the inn, the stragglers falling away to return to their own homes now that the worst of the crisis had dissipated as the ashes drifted upwards and into the night. "But what happened?" She asked the question in a voice meant to convey that she wanted very much to know what had happened but she also did not want anyone within a dozen yards of them to overhear.

"Let us go inside," he told her, in his own version of the same voice, and held out his—bare, soot-smeared—arm. She took it, all manner of decorum flying out the idiomatic window as she tucked her gloved fingers into the crook of his elbow and walked close enough to him that her skirt brushed against the side of his trousers.

It was, admittedly, not the most romantic of situations in which they could find themselves. Not that Mildred was *looking* to find herself in a romantic situation with Mr. Wiggan, though she would not have lodged a complaint if such a situation had thrust itself upon them at that particular moment. However, she had read enough novels during the course of her existence to know that most fictional accounts of evening strolls with gentlemen of at least moderate handsomeness were most often accompanied by the flattering glow of moonlight and the soft hoot of an owl sheltering in a nearby tree. But Mildred had learned a long time before that life did not often resemble how it was represented in novels. For them, the acrid smell of smoke filled the air, while the ground beneath them was rutted and muddy from all of the water and activity around the still-smoldering cottage. And there was the additional detail that they were walking back to check on a young dragon who had —Mildred supposed, as nothing yet had been absolutely verified beyond the description of the arsonist provided by the Misses Primrose and her own paltry gifts of inference—

attempted to burn down a house.

But Mildred still appreciated the moment, brief as a glint of that same fictitious moonlight on the surface of a still puddle. Because the vicarage was only a few more paces away, and Mrs. Babbinton was already waiting for them by the door, as though to lend an air of propriety to Mildred's arrival at the home of a single gentleman at an hour when most of the village's inhabitants—at least when they were not rushing to put out a fire—were settling into their beds for the night. Mildred pulled away to fumble with the strings of her bonnet, and Mr. Wiggan excused himself to "make himself presentable" (his words, muttered quickly before he offered a quick nod to Mildred and darted up the stairs two at a time) while Mrs. Babbinton fussed with her apron and led her guest directly to the kitchen.

"He's just begun to stir," the housekeeper remarked, and pointed towards the basket beside the fire.

Fitz lay sprawled on his back, hind legs and forelegs splayed open with all the grace of a pretentious starfish. His tail twitched in time to the progress of some unknown dream, and when Mildred did little more than sigh and click her tongue against the back of her teeth, his head popped up, his own tongue lolling out of the corner of his mouth while his eyes blinked blearily at her.

It was difficult to connect the two images in Mildred's head, the first of a dangerous creature breaking into someone's kitchen and producing a catalog of mayhem that included setting a house on fire, and the second of the small dragon stretched out in front of her, his stomach bare and vulnerable and shining like a recently buffed boot.

"Oh, you," Mildred said, those two words (or sounds, depending on whether or not one wishes to count the single utterance of "oh" as an official word) working like a command to draw Fitz up and out of the basket. He flopped himself around and onto his legs, then attempted a graceful dismount onto the floor. "Attempted" as it turned out to be more of a plummet that ended with him on his side, struggling to right himself while also extending his wings as though they were panels of a broken umbrella, and all of this set to a melody of intermittent screeches and high-pitched barks while his claws scrabbled at the stones edging the fireplace.

She knelt down beside him, holding out one hand for him to sniff. He rubbed the side of his head against her thumb, then made a clumsy try for climbing onto her arm. Unfortunately, the effects of Mrs. Babbinton's dosing had yet to fully wear off, and so instead Fitz draped himself over her forearm, panting happily as she scratched him behind the joint of his left wing.

No, he did not at all bear the look of a creature intent on burning down buildings while old ladies still puttered around inside of them. But perhaps that was his most inherent danger, that he appeared as innocent as a child's pet and all while harboring the ability to harm people—whether by accident or not—with a handful of sparks from the back of his throat.

Mr. Wiggan's step on the stairs alerted Mildred to his return. She looked back at him as he entered the kitchen, his clothes clean and his cheeks wearing a ruddiness that spoke of a towel having been scrubbed over his skin only a few moments before. He fiddled with the buttons of his waistcoat, only to realize he had made an error in their alignment but he could not be bothered to start over again.

"Tell me what happened," Mildred said. She picked up Fitz, who showed such an inclination to be held that he crawled up her arm as though it was a ladder, settling himself on her shoulder and around the back of her neck like a living stole.

Those of you who are anticipating a harrowing tale from Mr. Wiggan's mouth, I am sorry to disappoint you. Instead, he took a cup of tea from Mrs. Babbinton, raised the rim of it to his lips, then set it down on the table without taking that first sip. "I do not know," he said, and looked at Mildred and Fitz as though he was both seeing them and yet staring straight through them. "Mrs. Babbinton checked on him earlier this evening, making sure he was secure in his pen and had enough straw and blankets to burrow into for the night. An hour or so later, I was in my study when I heard a series of shouts from the direction of the Old Gables. I ran over there, not even considering Fitz could be involved, and..." He picked up the tea again, considering the cup or perhaps wishing there was something stronger than tea contained in its porcelain depths, but still did not take a drink. "I saw the flames through the kitchen window. I made certain the Primrose sisters were already safely out through the front door before I rushed back in and grabbed Fitz. I brought him back here and more than that I cannot tell you, or at least not add much to what you witnessed yourself. But he must have found a way out of his pen and gone over there, slipped in through a window they'd left open for their cat and..." He paused again, unable to push himself beyond that same conjunction. Finally, he took a sip of his tea. And then another, until he had finished the entire cup in three brief swallows.

"I suppose this means he cannot stay here." Mildred said the words to herself more than for the benefit of Mr. Wiggan or Mrs. Babbinton. And yet they had the voice of a gentle scold, as if she were speaking to a small child who had come home with a bedraggled kitten or a toad stuffed in their pocket (two things she had attempted to smuggle home in her younger years). It was absurd, she knew, but a part of her had always held onto a concentrated diamond of belief that she could keep the hatchling. It did not matter that he no longer had the look of those first few days, when he was all wings and tail and neck, or that she had nursed a small worry like a glowing ember that a few more months of eating and growth would imbue him with the strength to snap a grown man's wrist like a dry twig (if he were inclined, which she hoped he never would be). But there he sat, warm and vibrant around her shoulders, and something in her chest ached at imagining him in someone else's care.

"Then what is your advice, Miss Percy?" Mr. Wiggan nodded towards Fitz. "He is, for all intents and purposes, your charge. Whether he knew the egg would hatch or not, it was your Great Uncle who left him in your care."

Mildred shook her head. "You say that, but you and Mrs. Babbinton have taken so much of it upon yourself while I—"

He stopped her before she could continue, one palm held up, the cup he'd recently emptied dangling precariously from his other hand. "We have already discussed this. You are not in a position to keep him."

"And neither are you!" she cried. "We thought we could keep him as though he is some sort of chicken left to roam around the kitchen, but a mere cage will not suffice. I'm beginning to believe—" *To fear*, she wanted to say, but did not, "—that sending letters will not be enough. As you said, weeks... even months could pass before we have any word about what to do with him. And by then..." Images of the fire, the smell of smoke still heavy in the air, the streaks of soot on Mr. Wiggan's features returned to Mildred's thoughts with alarming speed.

"Well, what do you propose?"

Mildred breathed. Everyone breathed, of course. It was a common trait among living things. But this particular breath was needed to give Mildred time to think.

It wasn't often she was faced with such questions as "What is your advice?" and "What do you propose?", words that made it seem as if her opinions were valid and wanted. Any previous time questions along those lines had been posed to her, it was with the asker already knowing the answer they desired, and so Mildred had spent more time aligning her opinions to suit the demands of others rather than voice an individual thought no one had a wish to hear.

Mr. Wiggan still stood with his empty cup, waiting for

her answer.

"I think we should seek out Mr. Gorman," she said, and further warmed to the idea once it was spoken aloud. "He knew my great uncle best, is probably the only living person most familiar with his interests. And perhaps he can even give us some insight into Mr. Hawthorne's arrival here."

"And how do you expect to succeed with this plan? He has yet to respond to my letters. Perhaps he is too busy with the running of your uncle's estate to attend to much of his correspondence, I don't know. But are you simply going to run off to Warwickshire to speak with him in person?"

Was there incredulity in his tone, or was she imagining it? Though whether the former or the latter was correct, she rose up against it regardless. "Perhaps I will. I am old enough that there would be nothing untoward in my travelling alone as a single woman." (A courageous thing to say, but it stemmed more from the foreknowledge that Diana would not release any of their servants to accompany Mildred on a rash jaunt across the countryside if only to shore up the walls of her sister's feminine respectability.) "And I can pay for the journey myself." (A statement made factual by the frugality with which Mildred budgeted her annual fifty pound allowance.) "I can find Mr. Gorman, speak to him, and it should not all take more than a few days, if that." (Those words spoken as if she had plucked them out of the air at random. As someone who was not well-travelled nor carried on regular discourse with people who were, she could be told it would take her a month or an hour to complete her journey to Warwickshire and she would not have the understanding to contradict them.)

"I would feel better about the scheme if you were to have someone to accompany you. I cannot offer myself," he said. An odd thing to say, as his presence with her would do more to harm her reputation than if she went the entire journey alone on horseback. "As much as I would like to be a help to you, but maybe we can ask... Mrs. Babbinton! Would you be willing to go along?"

"Mrs. Babbinton?" Mildred started enough that Fitz shifted restlessly around her neck and took to nibbling gently at her ear. "Surely you could not spare her?"

The fact that he did not immediately rush to contradict her was evidence enough that Mr. Wiggan depended on his housekeeper a great deal. Behind them, Mrs. Babbinton let out a soft harrumph that may or may not have been intended as an accessory to that lack of contradiction.

"If Miss Percy is in need of my help, then I would be more than happy to provide it," the housekeeper said as she chopped up a mixture of lamb and onions that looked as though it would end up serving as Fitz's breakfast in the morning.

"I would be fine for a few days. Well, Fitz and I both, I should say."

"Oh, Fitz." She turned her cheek, the edge of her jaw stroking against his foreleg. One of his wings had opened up as he tangled one of his claws in her hair, draping over her upper arm like a short cloak. She traced her finger along the edge of it. It seemed fragile as parchment. How could something so delicate support a creature of his size and weight in the air? And would it, one day? She could not imagine they were merely attached to him for decorative effect. "I could take him with me."

"What?"

Mildred looked up, her fingers still stroking Fitz's wing. "He is still small, to a degree. He cannot fly away from me." *Yet*, was the word that tacked itself onto the end of her sentence. "And he will lend weight to any discussion I have with Mr. Gorman."

Mr. Wiggan's brow furrowed. "I'm not sure—"

"Right. Imagine, you are a man of business, going about your work. And a plump, aging spinster arrives on your doorstep, raving about winged creatures and large eggs and generally making a great fool of herself. You would be inclined to turn me out immediately, would you not?"

"Well, I–"

"Perhaps not you specifically. No doubt you'd have Mrs. Babbinton stuff me with tea and cakes first before sweeping me towards the door."

He laughed. Not a denial, then.

"But if I have Fitz with me…" She let that hang there, giving him the time needed to paint his own version of the scene.

"And Mrs. Babbinton," he said finally. "If she cannot succeed in convincing Mr. Gorman to listen to you, then it is a lost cause."

She laughed at that, which caused Fitz to shift his position again and try to clamber onto the top of her head like a living hat.

"Miss Percy."

She looked back at Mr. Wiggan. His expression was earnest. She searched for concern there, for any sign that he would attempt to talk her out of going, but instead he only lifted his eyebrows in question and swayed slightly towards her, as if shifted by some subtle turning of the Earth.

"You are certain of this?"

A nod. A single up and down of her head, as final as the slash of a checkmark in red ink. "I need to be doing something. We cannot wait for letters, for others to attend to us. We are not merely sitting here, searching for the owners of a lost puppy. Everything about this is…" She flicked through a dozen words that were not right until she found the one she wanted. "…unprecedented. I think we may be at the beginning of a very important thing. And I do not believe we should wait for the world to get up off its laurels and take notice."

She moved towards the table, realizing that she had been on her feet since Betsy had knocked on her bedroom door several hours before.With one arm, she cradled Fitz against her as if he were an infant (an infant who, if disturbed from his perch, had the potential to screech and claw at her and make its displeasure known in multiple unpleasant ways (not unlike its human counterpart, she had to admit)). Mr. Wiggan pulled out a chair for her, then briefly reached out to brush a bit of debris from her skirt—soot, a bit of lint, she could not tell—before he snatched his hand back as if burned.

He pulled out a chair for himself, but instead of sitting down simply stood there with his hand resting on the back of it, his fingers tightening and relaxing over and again as if the workings of his mind had chosen to manifest themselves in that constant changing of his grip. "And when do you plan to be off?"

"As soon as possible, I suppose. I cannot see why we should wait."

"Very good." Mr. Wiggan gestured towards the doorway, where he had just come through from upstairs a few minutes before. "I will fetch some paper and ink and we can begin on a letter for Mr. Gorman informing him of your impending arrival." He disappeared then, his chair left standing out from the table, his cup still wobbling slightly from when he had hastily set it down.

"So," Mildred said quietly, and reached up to run her fingers along the length of Fitz's tail as it twitched against her collar. "I think we're going on a bit of a journey." He gave no reaction to this news, merely began purring at the back of her neck while the claws of one his back legs flexed and relaxed on her shoulder. "I know, I know. It's exciting, hmm?" She kept her voice down to a whisper, so even Mrs. Babbinton would not hear. "And frightening, too. I cannot think what has gotten into me!"

Fitz was warm against her, still purring, clinging to her with his feet while his wings stretched out above her head before attempting to curl around her. "Oh, dear." She sighed and tipped her head to the side as again tried to shift his weight from one of her shoulders to the other. "How am I ever going to tell my sister about this?"

CHAPTER SIXTEEN

Young dragons show a similarity to their human counterparts in that they have a tendency to grow and acquire new skills in leaps and bounds. A failure to acknowledge such spurts of progress may leave one underestimating the competence of the creature before them, much to their detriment.

-from Chapter Twelve of Miss Percy's Pocket Guide (to the Care and Feeding of British Dragons)

Mildred spent the night at the vicarage. There really wasn't much choice in the matter. Or there was a choice, but it was between walking all the way back to Ashby Lodge (Mr. Wiggan swore that he would accompany her if she was determined, but the warmth and comfort of Mrs. Babbinton's kitchen along with a reluctance to face her sister again crumbled that determination as easily as one of the housekeeper's lemon biscuits) or remaining where she already was, with tea and a fire and a seemingly endless supply of comestibles for her enjoyment. Though it was Fitz who ultimately made the decision for her, as he absolutely refused to descend from his perch on her shoulders for over an hour. By then, Mildred knew her family would have already retired for the night, with the doors locked up and the lights put out until morning. (She might have allowed herself a fleeting fantasy of someone in the household waiting up for her, worrying over her safety and perhaps even teasing with the idea of organizing a search party to—

—no, not even in her imagination could she conjure up such a scenario from her family. Though if Matthew and Nettie were still awake, she did not doubt they would be the first to race off to rescue her—and Fitz, of course—should they believe her to be in any real danger.)

"I can stay up with him first," Mildred said, while Fitz gamboled around the kitchen at her feet, chasing after a frayed end of string she dangled for him. They had already agreed to take turns keeping watch through the night, as the evening's incident (a mild way of describing the young dragon's unintentional arsonist tendencies) had made them aware they could not leave him unattended for any length of time. Even returning him to his pen was out of the question, as he had already proved capable of opening the latch in a matter of only a few seconds. (An experiment of placing him in there again and putting themselves just out of sight had produced the result of his climbing halfway up the door, fiddling with the latch with an alternating process that involved his nose and jaw, and then lolloping onto the ground beyond the confines of the pen with all the brazenness of a creature well aware of the tenuous limits on his captivity.)

"Are you certain?" came Mr. Wiggan's reply. Mr. Wiggan who had begun to noticeably droop twenty minutes before, managing a poor job of stifling his yawns and appearing as rumpled as the bed he no doubt wished desperately to crawl into.

"Go on," Mildred said to both him and Mrs. Babbinton. "My thoughts are too scattered for sleep anyway. I shall wake up one of you in a few hours if I find I finally need some rest."

She thought it would be a pleasant thing to while away a few hours in the quiet of the vicarage kitchen, playing with Fitz and drinking copious amounts of tea. But Fitz soon tired out and retreated to his basket near the fire, and Mildred realized she was left with nothing to do, and a reluctance to stray too far into the various rooms and narrow corridors of a house that was not her own. Of course, she was used to living in a house that did not truly belong to her. Ashby Lodge was far and away the domain of her sister (regardless of Mr. Muncy's name scrawled across any of the relevant paperwork) and Diana had always gone out of her way to make Mildred aware of her status there as a tolerated vagabond. But at least she was familiar with Ashby Lodge, with the sounds it made during the night, with a few spaces set aside where she could feel a little less like an interloper. (That was, until Belinda had invaded one of those few spaces, marking it with her faint scent of lilacs and an air of uprooted privacy.)

Once Fitz was asleep, she began to pace. First, only the length and breadth of the kitchen. Then, further into the hall that led to the other parts of the house. A few more minutes of the same back and forth, back and forth, with the same board creaking beneath her foot every time she stepped on it, and the same wash of warm and cool air as she moved towards the kitchen and away from it, and she found herself hesitating outside of Mr. Wiggan's study.

The door was partially open. Mildred made a note of this in order to relieve herself of any guilt as she took a small step across the threshold and looked inside.

It was dark, of course. The fire was out and the study was situated far enough from the kitchen that only a faint glow reached the edge of the doorway. Mildred moved back, completed two more rounds of pacing, and returned on the third with a candle in her hand and a modicum of daring. Her heart beat faster as she pushed at the door and walked fully into the room. If she had been the easily frightened sort, she might have cringed at the flickering shadows on the walls, or gasped at the sight of her muted reflection on the glass cases perched in various places. She carefully—carefully, as it was clear this was the one portion of the house over which Mrs.

Babbinton did not have complete control, and so death or at least severe injury was a possibility if she did not watch where she put her feet—made her way around the circumference of the room, pausing to study a few of the books crammed (there was no nicer word to use, as Mr. Wiggan had a tendency to shove books and papers into any and every space that proved most convenient in the moment) onto the shelves and to peer into cases filled with jars of shells and stones and shining insects pinned to velvet backing.

It was a strange thing, moving about in a room that felt very much like an exhibit dedicated to the inner workings of Mr. Wiggan's own mind. She feared she was trespassing, and yet she could not bring herself to leave. She had only ever been in here with him, and to be here without the distraction of his presence was as though she was watching him pore over his work when he thought she was not looking. (Not that she would confess to having ever done such a thing, but if she *had* acquired a penchant for stealing glances at Mr. Wiggan from time to time (to time) when he was unaware of her attention, then she supposed this singular situation was close to what it would feel like. That is, if she ever had.)

Her steps brought her around to the desk, where so many of her Great Uncle Forthright's things still took up residence. She ran her fingers over some of the crystals settled there, the stones that in her earlier ignorance she had assumed Fitz's egg to be just another one for the collection, only sized on a grander scale. Many of his notebooks were there as well, some of them tattered and incapable of closing flat, others boasting the clean lines of having been opened maybe once or twice since their binding. She picked up one, its spine creaking as she looked inside. Only a few notes on the front page, followed by a plethora of clean sheets fanning past her fingers with a faint susurration. An idea struck her then, or rather an idea that had tickled at her thoughts for the last several weeks gained sudden clarity.

She gathered up the notebook along with quill and ink, then took everything back to the kitchen and settled herself at the table. Fitz, she noticed, still snoozed in his basket, though his legs twitched beneath him as if he were attempting to run in his dream. The image of him remained in her mind as she smoothed down that first blank page, as she dipped her pen in the ink, as she began to write.

Those unfamiliar with the process of writing will most likely imagine Mildred spending the next several hours adding neat lines of fine lettering to the pages of her Great Uncle's notebook. Perhaps she will pause thoughtfully every few minutes, gazing off into some ill-lit corner of the kitchen before she dips the tip of her quill into the ink again and marks a few more words onto the paper. And all of her work will bear the features of a very clear beginning, middle, and ending, making perfect sense to anyone who might stumble across it and read it for themselves afterwards.

Unfortunately, those familiar with the process of writing will know the scattered nature of her paragraphs, thoughts and ideas leaping from one stepping stone to the next with several tumbles into the raging waters below. Entire pages were crossed out, ink spattered on her fingers and her sleeve while words unbecoming a gently bred woman (and too coarse for repetition on the pages of this book) were muttered heatedly, and a hole was torn through two whole pages due to the vehemence expressed by the scratching of her nib across the evidence of her inability to spell "ephemeral" correctly on the first (or second, or third) try.

"Miss Percy?"

She looked up from the notebook. Mr. Wiggan stood in the doorway of the kitchen, appearing as little more than a blur until Mildred's eyes adjusted from the tiny words on the page to the figure of the vicar watching her. "Oh." She sat up straight. Or she attempted to sit up straight, except that several hours of slumping forward in the chair, her shoulders rounded and her head tilted at an awkward angle had made her feel more like the sort of creature taken to ambling out from under a bridge to harass travellers with a triplicate of questions before they could be permitted to cross rather than someone who could assume proper posture on a whim. "I did not realize how late it had become."

"Or early." He gestured towards the window, where the pale glow of daylight made itself known. "I had expected you to wake me at some point. Are you not tired?"

Mildred blinked rapidly at the thought of shuffling into Mr. Wiggan's room in the middle of the night to stir him from his bed. "Uh, no. Not at all, really. I was just putting down some thoughts I'd had," she added, and dropped the quill back into its pot of ink.

Mr. Wiggan crossed towards the table. "What is it you're writing?" He stopped suddenly, as though he had walked into a wall. "Oh, but I'm not disturbing you from your work, am I? Or is it something personal and you would rather not —"

She waved away his hesitation. "I am writing about Fitz," she confessed. "Since there is nothing out there for us to study, nothing beyond what the realms of mythology and fairy tale have to offer, I thought it might be helpful to keep a record of everything we have learned so far." Those last two words were spoken like a promise, dripping with both hope and fear that there would be many more things to learn about Fitz in the days and weeks ahead. "And then, if there is ever a further need for information on the subject, there will be something for someone to read. Not that I am putting myself forward as any sort of great scholar, but even my meager knowledge could make a difference. Should another hapless individual find themselves with a young dragon left in their care, that is."

He smiled. Mildred had endured an innumerable measure of smiles during her life, smiles meant to placate, to humor her, to show pity. But this smile sparked in his eyes with the brightness of flint and tinder, and she saw something there that filled her up as well as the first breath of fresh air upon opening the window in the morning.

"I think it is utterly brilliant," he said.

"I know," she replied. And her eyes widened when she realized what she had said. "I mean, I hope it will do some good. Because what fools would we be if we did not take the time to document all of this in some way?"

"Like Pliny the Younger, after he had witnessed the eruption of Vesuvius," came Mr. Wiggan's quiet musing as he looked over a few of Mildred's notes.

Mildred was not sure how she felt about Fitz's young life being compared to the catastrophic eruption of a volcano some two millennia before, and yet she could not bring herself to put up an argument against it. "Well, I do believe it to be an important exercise. Not only for ourselves, but in case there are other—"

Fitz chose that moment to twitch awake in his basket and let out a sneeze that sent a tongue of flame from either his nostrils or his mouth (Mildred could not tell which orifice the fire extruded from, though if she was to begin a record of his behavior, she knew she would have to keep herself more aware of such details) before he raised one of his hind feet to his mouth and gnawed at the flesh between his claws.

"—dragons," Mildred finished, and with a click of her tongue against the back of her teeth.

"You should go upstairs for a bit, try to sleep for a few hours," Mr. Wiggan said as he walked towards the fireplace. Fitz watched him as he added more wood to the dying fire, as he stoked up the coals and swung the kettle around to heat for tea. The dragon hopped out of his basket, more sure on his feet than he had been the evening before, especially now that Mrs. Babbinton's dosing had worked its way through his system, and walked over to Mildred. He sniffed at the hem of her dress, then let out a rumble of sound from the back of his throat that might have been a growl or might have been a simple clearing away of morning congestion (which then led to the question of whether or not dragons could suffer from fluctuations in mucus levels throughout the day, a query Mildred set aside to be further explored in her notes).

"I fear I am wide awake now," she said, and reached down to allow Fitz to scrape the top of his head across her knuckles. And she would not be able to sleep while knowing that she still had to return to Ashby Lodge, to speak to her sister about her imminent journey to Warwickshire. A journey she planned to take with or without Diana's permission, though she was certain her sister would not at all see it that way. "I will wait until the sun is fully up and then make my way home."

Mr. Wiggan looked up from his preparation of the tea tray. "Do you wish for me to accompany you home?"

Mildred hesitated over her answer. Because of course she wished for Mr. Wiggan to accompany her home. She nearly leaped from her chair (or tipped herself out of it, as things like leaping were not typically an option after she had been seated in the same seat for several hours straight) in anticipation of an early morning stroll with him. But she was also aware of how it would appear for her to leave the vicarage first thing in the morning in order to embark on said early morning stroll with the vicar. Wouldn't it appear to others as though she had spent the night there? Not that she hadn't spent the night there. As any reader of the previous few pages (and particularly the opening line of this chapter) will attest, Mildred had most certainly spent the entirety of the night at the vicarage. But whiling away the darkest hours before the dawn hunched over a notebook with only a sleeping dragon as a companion was a markedly different circumstance from whiling away those same hours in a manner that would incite gossip among anyone to witness their departure from the vicarage together.

This was when Mildred's existence as a gentleman's daughter made itself stunningly apparent, that in the midst of a crisis concerning such unprecedented players as a mythological beast and elderly sisters displaced from their recently incinerated home, her worries would circle back around to the state of her reputation in the eyes of people with whom she did not take the trouble to regularly associate.

"No," she finally admitted, albeit with a healthy dose of reluctance. "But thank you for the offer. You and Mrs. Babbinton have Fitz to look after, and it will be an easier task with the both of you here rather than one of you on your own." As though aware he had again become the main topic of their discourse (while also not earning the attention from either Mildred or Mr. Wiggan that he so desired) Fitz scuttled over to the corner of the table and began hoisting himself up the table leg, his claws digging into the wood while his mouth opened wide enough to bite at the edge of the top as though he would swing himself up and over with a jerk of his head and neck.

"Oh," Mildred uttered when she realized what he was about. It had taken a moment for the shock to wear off, that he had at some point acquired the skill of climbing up the furniture like an ungainly insect. And then he toppled into a teacup, flicked out a wing that knocked over her inkpot, and squealed gleefully—or at least it sounded like glee, if a dragon could be gleeful—as he tottered through the puddle of ink spreading across the table and left footprints across the open pages of her notebook. "No, stop that. Stop that!" She snatched the notebook out of the way, then took the tea towel Mr. Wiggan tossed to her in order to sop up the worst of the spilled ink. "Fetch him down!" she cried, and Mr. Wiggan scooped an arm beneath Fitz, who showed his aggravation at being so cruelly handled by flapping his wings in Mr. Wiggan's face and screeching loud enough Mildred glanced at the windows for fear they might shatter.

"That is enough!" Mildred took hold of Fitz, holding him at arm's length until he tucked his wings away and ceased trying to nip at her wrists with his gums. Once he was calm, an objective that required five minutes of soothing and a promise of any lamb or mutton Mrs. Babbinton might have stashed away somewhere, Mildred let him climb back onto her shoulders.

"He cannot stay here."

Those were Mr. Wiggan's words, echoing her own from the previous night. And Mildred nodded along to them, as though caught in the rhythm of a melody that would not extricate itself from her head. "The sooner he can be away from Upper Plimpton, the better."

Mr. Wiggan carried the tea tray over to the table and poured out a cup for himself and for Mildred, as well. He fixed it just the way she liked without him finding it necessary to ask or for her to issue a reminder. And she took the cup, and she sipped, and she did not even take the trouble to bat Fitz's inquisitive nose away as he craned his neck around to sniff at the chipped rim of the porcelain.

"I will be all right while you and Mrs. Babbinton are away," he assured her, because he seemed to understand that she needed the assurance. No matter that she would be the one carrying the burden of traveling with a dragon, it was his well-being she would pause to think about.

"I know you will," she said, not even blinking at the slight lie in her own words. "You will have your pupils to keep you occupied, and also making certain the house does not tumble to pieces in our absence."

"Always a possibility," he said with a smile. "Though perhaps my chances of survival will be greater without a certain winged creature under our roof."

Mildred brushed the back of her hand across her brow, unaware that she managed to transfer a smear of ink from her fingers to her forehead in that movement. (Mr. Wiggan was very aware of it, and he found it endearing.) "I am not certain how soon we can leave—"

"I will arrange everything." He fiddled with a few items

on the tray, as though he needed something to do with his hands and his eyes and any other bit that might stray back towards Mildred if he was not careful. "You have enough to worry about. Let me at least do this much."

Mildred helped Fitz down from her shoulder, an endeavor that involved a tremendous amount of claws clinging adamantly to sleeves along with a final tearing sound she knew would mean a bit of mending work when she next changed out of her gown. "I should be off now. The sun is up, and the servants will be awake." The unspoken portion of that sentence implying that with the wakefulness of the servants, she would not be left standing outside, pounding on the door of Ashby Lodge like a madwoman or a midnight messenger attempting to drag the family from the comfort of their beds at an uncivilized hour.

She made her farewells then, all of it exceedingly polite and faintly awkward and laced with a hint of reluctance (on Mildred's part, because she was not looking forward to the prospect of returning home after spending the night at the vicarage and all of the vitriol that would no doubt spill from her sister's mouth like sap tapped from a tree, and on Mr. Wiggan's part because he simply did not want her to leave at all or for any reason) from the both of them. On went her bonnet and her gloves and her shawl, and out the front door she walked, her head held high and her shoulders pressed back as though she had only stopped in for a spot of afternoon tea with Mrs. Babbinton.

The village, she saw, was already well awake. No one paid her much mind as she walked up the main street, though she supposed she would be indebted to the threads of smoke still drifting up from the rear of Old Gables for that convenience. The few people who noticed her were sure to nod in greeting, and she returned the nods with a smile and a wave, yet everything was just tilted far enough away from normalcy that it did not cross anyone's mind to wonder why Miss Mildred Percy was coming out of the vicarage before most households had built up their first fires for the day.

And so Mildred walked all the way back to Ashby Lodge, each step working to create a false belief that the worst of the morning was left behind her, burned away like so much drifting fog beneath the warmth of the summer sun. Because surely a night of fires and dragons was more arduous than anything to be endured once she found herself again ensconced in the bosom of her family.

Surely, she thought. As strains of a dramatic and foreboding nature filled the air.

CHAPTER SEVENTEEN

The mating rituals of dragons are often elaborate and protracted affairs. On first observation, it would appear that the male is the one to initiate the proceedings, choosing the female he desires and presenting himself as a worthy suitor. However, years of detailed study of multiple draconic pairings has shown that it is, in truth, the female who is the first to decide which male she wishes to take on as a mate. And yet the male is still responsible for all of the performative courtship duties, while the female remains unresponsive to his overtures until the moment she chooses to acquiesce to his determined showmanship.

-from Chapter Six of Miss Percy's Pocket Guide (to the Care and Feeding of British Dragons)

"Is this all you found?"

Reginald had gone through the papers twice—no, three times—but there had been nothing stashed in Miss Mildred Percy's room that was of any greater value than the load of utter bollocks she had shown to him at the picnic.

"I searched her entire room," Miss Muncy said, wrapping the string of her bonnet around her finger in what seemed to be a demonstration of unease, but instead drew his attention to her hands and the curve of her neck and... "Of course, it didn't take very long, considering that her bedroom is comparable in size to Mama's closet. But I looked under her bed, in her drawers... everywhere! And it was mostly papers like these." She shrugged, indicating the paltry stack she had provided. "No stones or rocks like you had told me to keep an eye out for. Just rubbish, really."

Reginald rolled up the papers and smacked them against the palm of his hand. He had refrained from telling Miss Muncy everything, though the temptation had been there. Well, he'd told her about the stone, and that it was valuable, and that if they were to get their hands on it, their fortunes would indeed take quite the turn. That had seemed enough for the moment to pique her interest. "Well, I thank you for the effort, at least. And you're sure you were not seen? I would not wish for you to bring trouble upon yourself for this."

"Oh, no." Miss Muncy shook her head, soft curls bouncing around her ears. "A few weeks ago it might have been more difficult, but Aunt Mildred is away so much now, always running off on her little errands."

"Her errands?" Reginald asked, but any answer he would have received was thwarted by the distinct sound of a horse and cart coming up the lane behind them. Miss Muncy took hold of his wrist and dragged him through the shrubbery that edged the path, thorns catching at his coat while he snatched at his hat before an errant branch knocked it off his head.

Once they were through, Miss Muncy turned him around and raised a finger to her lips. He nodded quickly, fully aware that he would do anything she asked of him as long as she continued standing so close that he could count the eyelashes framing her beautiful eyes.

"She goes into Upper Plimpton nearly every day," Miss Muncy said once the horse and cart had rumbled out of hearing. "To the vicarage, I believe. I think she teaches the village children there or helps with their studies. She was even there last night, because of the fire at the Old Gables. Mama was not happy that Aunt Mildred had gone off like she did."

Reginald tried to think, a task made more arduous by Miss Muncy's proximity and the fact that she had him pressed up against a massive shrubbery on the more secluded side of an already—but for the farmer and his cart—deserted lane.

It was Miss Muncy who had told him to meet him here, the note from her arriving at the inn earlier that morning. He had never been the sort to involve himself in clandestine meetings with young ladies whose reputations would suffer greatly should they be discovered tangled up in vegetation in broad daylight, but after today, he thought he might have to make an effort to turn it into a more regular occurrence.

"And this began a few weeks ago?" he asked, once he was able to string together enough words to form a coherent sentence. "These visits to the vicarage?"

"Perhaps a little more than a month?" She tipped her head to one side, eyes closed, the tilt of her features making it clear that things like days and weeks along with her aunt's comings and goings were equally irrelevant.

But Reginald was desperate to press on, and so he held onto his line of questioning like a rope thrown from the deck of a ship, a lifeline to shake him free of Miss Muncy's charms long enough to uncover what Miss Percy was up to. "But would you say that her visits to the vicarage began around the time she received her inheritance from her uncle?"

She screwed up her face in concentration, such a pretty, pert expression that if he had thought less of her, he might have suspected she had taken to practicing it in the mirror to see how it would appear to others. "Well, I remember the first letter, the one mentioning the old man's death. It wasn't long after that, I think. Perhaps a day or so? There was a little to-do—" she waggled her fingers in a way that implied things like 'to-dos' were a welcome staple of her daily life "—between Mama and Aunt Mildred about it, and that's the only reason I can recall it at all."

"The vicarage." Reginald did not have a lot of experience with country vicarages, or churches in general, really. Belief in God and Heaven and all that lot had always seemed to him to be something people followed along with because it was expected of them, like wearing neckcloths or eating dessert after the main part of their meal instead of preceding it. It probably did not help that his father had once been a church-going man, and where had that got him? Drunk and dead after falling into an open grave on consecrated ground. "Who is the vicar here?"

"Oh, that's Mr. Wiggan," Miss Muncy promptly supplied. "He is fairly amiable, I suppose. Nothing about him worth putting in a letter, anyway. Why?" She took a step back from him, yet somehow seemed to lean her upper body towards him. "What is it you are thinking?"

He looked at her. He hoped that without saying a word, she would understand the unspoken theory drawing itself across his features. He was sure they would be of the same mind, that—

"I see," Miss Muncy drawled, fine eyebrows arching upwards. "Mr. Wiggan is a learned man. Well, as much as a gentleman can claim living in a town as small and insignificant as ours. Now, you being from London, I've no doubt you must find us all to be very dull company, very slow and simple in our ways."

It was the right thing to say. How did she always know just the right thing to say? Reginald inhaled deeply, shoulders pushing back, chest expanding with that clear country air that made him feel as if he had taken one step out of London's fog and smoke only to take the next into another world entirely. (To be honest, he missed the fog and the smoke, missed the taste of it—thick and hearty—on his tongue. Living in London was like taking in a meal with every breath, seeing a universe with every sweep of one's gaze across a crowded street. He tried to imagine life in a place like Upper Plimpton, with its cottages sticking out of the ground like mushrooms, its people going about their... whatever it was they did to occupy themselves from day to day. Milk things, he assumed. Or marked their way through the year with a series of village fetes, celebrating such invigorating pastimes as public drunkenness and deciding which farmer's wife made the best jam.)

"Well, not... not all of you," he stammered. "I mean, there is one person I've met whose company I find very..." Intelligent? No. Smart? No, that's not what he wanted to say either. Brilliant? Not quite, but closer. "... exceptional." Yes, that one would do the trick. "But this Mr. Wiggan, if your aunt needed any help with research, with wanting to know something about a peculiar sort of stone, do you think he would be the one she would visit?"

"Most likely. I cannot think of anyone else." Miss Muncy's rosebud mouth twisted with an almost devilish smirk. "Shall I introduce you to him? Perhaps we can pay him a call tomorrow."

Reginald bit the inside of his cheek. Tomorrow seemed like years away. Tomorrow also meant paying for another night at the inn, when his pockets had already put up a notice of being available to let. "What an excellent idea," he said, putting his trust in Miss Muncy. She would see him through this, and then he would be able to repay her with anything—everything—she could ever want.

CHAPTER EIGHTEEN

Conflict within a group* of dragons is not unusual. It is believed that at one time, dragons existed more as solitary hunters, only seeking out one another for the purposes of finding a mate or dying** (when the death was of a natural cause). But it is suspected that an increase of human population in more rural areas, encroaching on the dragons' natural habitats, have forced them to join together for their own survival, a situation that has— unfortunately, yet not surprisingly—created strife among an increasing number of them.

*Group is used here as there is no official word or term for the event of two or more dragons gathering together. Both Flight and Wing have been considered by the scientific community, though this author personally prefers the usage of Clan as found in the writings of one Godwin Aldrich (c. 1057 AD) on the subject of a supposed assemblage of small dragons that had taken up residence behind his sheep pen.

**So far, only seven dragon graveyards have been discovered across England, Ireland, Wales, and Scotland, though it is suspected that many more exist in the higher altitudes that have yet

to be explored and documented.

-from Chapter Three of Miss Percy's Pocket Guide (to the Care and Feeding of British Dragons)

The conversation was not going as well as Mildred had hoped, but at least it was not going worse than she had anticipated.

"Warwickshire?" Diana said it as if she were repeating a word she had never heard before, one from an archaic language left unspoken for a thousand years. "What on earth is there for you in Warwickshire?"

"As I said, I need to speak to Mr. Gorman. He was our great uncle's–"

"Yes, yes." Diana waved away her explanation. "But I do not see why you have to leave your home and travel all the way across the country–"

"It is hardly two counties away," Mildred said.

"–in search of some man who is completely unknown to us, one who was only a servant to our Great Uncle Forthright."

"He was our uncle's assistant in all matters," she countered again. "And from the tone of his notes and other writings, I do believe Great Uncle Forthright counted him as one of his most trustworthy friends.He did leave a vast amount of his property and fortune to him upon his death, if you recall."

Diana picked up her needlework again. She did this whenever she could not yet think of something to say, but did not wish for anyone to assume she was incapable of marshalling her arguments fast enough. "And not even a member of the family," she said, working over the words as though they were chunks of gristle stuck in her teeth. "But one would think you could simply write a letter rather than behave as if the world were ending and you needed to run off in such a state."

"We have tried contacting him already, but there has been no response."

After living with her sister for seventeen years (and another two decades before that with only a brief respite from one another when Diana went off to be married but before Belinda had been born) Mildred should have seen her mistake and made better preparations for the moment when her sister discovered it as well. But Mildred's mind had been so full of other things lately (all of which have been well documented in the previous pages of this book) that she was caught off guard when Diana's fingers paused over her work, the needle dangling in the air as the slender thread untwisted itself between them.

"We?" Diana blinked, that small movement as full of warning as the bristling of a cat's fur. "And who is 'we'?"

"Um," Mildred said, slipping back into her old way of speech as easily as sliding her feet into a comfortable pair of socks. "Mr. Wiggan–"

"Ah, I thought as much." Diana raised her chin, shoulders tilting and posture straightening into a triumphant pose. "You have been spending a large amount of time at the vicarage recently, and now I think I begin to see how things are. Is there some manner of attachment between you and Mr. Wiggan?"

"Attachment?" And now it was Mildred's turn to wrinkle her brow over a word as if it had just been translated to her from wedges marked into an ancient tablet. "No, of course not! He has only been helping me sort through our uncle's things, all of the papers and notes. Tedious stuff, really."

"Of course." And there went Diana's hands again, the needle pushing into the fabric, the thread dragging through, slow and careful, stretching out the silence along with it. "All of the things Great Uncle Forthright sent to you," she said at the beginning of the next stitch, "and that you did not feel the need to tell me about when they arrived."

What was courage? Mildred wondered. What was strength? Was it measured by how well she stood up against her sister, how sharp and biting her barbs? Could it be counted by how long she endured Diana's arch looks and interrogations? Or could one be considered strong simply by their ability to refrain from reaching across a yard of space and wrapping their hands around their sibling's neck?

"I have already apologized for that," Mildred said, her voice vibrating, her entire body thrilling with some pent-up feeling struggling to break free. "But you had seemed so set on my inheritance carrying with it some monetary quality that when it showed a distinct lack of such a thing, I did not have the heart to see you disappointed."

Diana huffed. "As if all I should care about is money." Another stitch. Faster, this one, as if the speed of her sister's hands worked as an indicator of the tumult of her thoughts. "And so you've been spending all of your time at the vicarage—though I still do not understand how a few dusty journals should warrant your being there so very often—and now you tell me you plan to disappear on a whim—"

"It is not a whim, and I am not going to disappear! In fact I cannot see our journey taking more than a few days at the most."

A look of horror sharpened Diana's features. "Surely Mr. Wiggan is not going to accompany you on this journey? The absolute and irrevocable scandal that would create, to have my own sister gallivanting across the countryside with a single man—a man of God!—is too much to contemplate."

Mildred closed her eyes for as long as it took her to draw in one breath and let it out again. It was a peculiar feint, pretending that she could shut out her sister, the room, the entire house with that small movement of skin and muscle on one part of her face, but it achieved the desired effect, and when she opened her eyes again, it was as if some of the seething tension of only a moment ago had been cleared away. Or at least pushed into the corner for a spell. "Then you should consider it a blessing that you will not have to contemplate it at all. My travelling companion will be Mrs. Babbinton, and I cannot imagine my being able to find a more respectable woman in all of Wiltshire."

Diana's mouth flattened, a demonstration of her particular talent at expressing an entire catalogue of emotions with lips bearing neither a smile nor a frown. "Because, of course, *I* cannot go with you, which I'm sure you already considered. For me to leave the children behind, and dear Mr. Muncy… they would be quite desolate without me. So if there is no one else, then I suppose Mrs. Babbinton will have to do. She is respectable, as you say." Though with a tone indicating that not a large amount of weight could be put in anything Mildred had to say when it came to a person's respectability. "Yet how you have contrived to borrow so much of their time, when there really is no reason for you to be travelling anywhere in the first place is beyond my understanding." Her eyes narrowed over her needlework, momentarily abandoned during her speech. "Are you certain you are not entertaining any designs on Mr. Wiggan?"

Mildred was not the sort to splutter, but she thought about giving herself a temporary change in character at that moment. "I am not entertaining designs, as you put it, on Mr. Wiggan or anyone. You of all people should know I have no plans to marry. But I would feel rather less insulted if you could stop alluding to any relationship between us, real or imagined, as if it were a cause of dismay for you."

The needlework went into a basket beside Diana's chair. Her sister stood, taking an immense amount of time—or at least it seemed immense in the moment, as all things do when one's heart is pounding and one's throat is itching with a scream that wants to sound itself into the void—to brush a few loose threads from her skirt, to run a finger over the piping that ran along the high waist of her gown. "What would you expect me to think, Mildred? I dislike being blunt, you know I do, but... Oh, you must realize you are too old to make anyone a proper wife. You've no fortune to speak of, you're beyond the scope of motherhood. And that certain..." she twirled her hand in the air "... bloom of youth that so many men are attracted to deserted you at least a decade ago. I mean, perhaps if you found yourself a widower, already with children of his own. But you must see what I mean. The vicar should have someone younger, someone more prepared for the rigors of married life. And if you insist on spending so much time with him, even in a respectable way," she added, with an edge of unmistakable sarcasm, "it may deter other women—more suitable women —from casting their lures in his direction."

They had never had a great relationship, Mildred and Diana. Despite the short span of years between them, there was never any kind of shared, sisterly bond. No, they had not climbed into each other's beds at night and shared secrets as the fires burned to ash. No, they had not plaited each other's hair or thrown pins into water while holding onto wishes that only the other heart knew. For years, Mildred had never felt the loss of such a relationship, because how could one miss something one never had? But she looked at her sister then, and she felt the insignificance of the blood that flowed between them.

"I am going tomorrow," Mildred said. Unequivocal.

And then Diana reeled back a step as if she'd been struck. "Tomorrow? What can you mean?"

The notes had arrived not long after breakfast, Mr. Wiggan's handwriting assuring her that he had already made arrangements for their travel the very next day. "Squire Manning is taking us as far as Swindon at first light. It is their market day. And then we will travel from there and up to my uncle's—well, Mr. Gorman's home now—outside of

Stratford-upon-Avon. It should not be too arduous a journey," she added, as if her sister could care less about how easy or arduous their trip would be. "And I hope we will be able to locate and speak with Mr. Gorman not long after we arrive. As far as I am aware, he has no plans to sell or give up the property."

Diana took a step backwards, knocked into her chair with the backs of her legs, and put out her hand to steady herself. "I thought you were speaking of something you intended to do some weeks from now, but tomorrow?" She pressed her fingers to her brow. "No doubt you've been planning this for some time and have only now chosen to tell me so that it is too late for me to do anything about it!"

"Why should you have to do anything about it?" Mildred spread her hands before her. "Am I your servant, or a child, that I must win permission from you before leaving?"

"Oh, do not be so dramatic!" Diana cried. "*Am I a servant, am I a child?*" she mimicked. "Of course not! But you are a member of this household, of this family. I took you in when you had no place else to go, and now I am to be treated with such disrespect!"

Mildred let her hands fall. "How am I being disrespectful?" She kept her own voice calm, steady, while her pulse fluttered like a bird's wings in her throat. "And if indeed my behavior is so reprehensible to you, perhaps you should be grateful that I will be away for a few days, and you will not have to suffer from my ill-mannered ingratitude during that time."

She turned to walk away. It frightened her, just that small spin of her heel on the rug and those first few steps towards the door. Why had no one ever told her that sometimes the things that scared one the most were the things one had to leave behind them?

"Mildred."

Well, she made it as far as the door to the drawing room, at least. But for those six steps she had felt as brave (albeit a bit trembly) as Wellington marching across the sodden ground at Waterloo.

"You're not serious, are you?"

Poor Aunt Mildred. Silly Aunt Mildred. This was her loophole, she realized. An escape route offered to her, and all she needed to claim it was to admit that no, of course she wasn't being serious. Silly Aunt Mildred, always in the way and somehow always forgotten. The quiet, unassuming spinster who had given up her dreams of adventure so her sister could marry, so there could be one of them to remain at home with their ailing father.

"I am going tomorrow," she said again, just as before. It was a trick she had learned with the children, to repeat yourself over and again no matter how much they fought against you, until they realized you were not going to be the one to surrender. (Though Mildred wasn't sure how well it would work with her sister when most of its previous applications had involved cajoling the children to eat their turnips or to give their teeth a thorough cleaning before bed.) "There are a few questions about the items I inherited from our uncle and I require Mr. Gorman's assistance to sort them out for me."

"Oh, your bloody inheritance!" Diana snapped, eyes flashing, perspiration beading on her upper lip despite the open window letting in a cool draught of afternoon air from outside. "I wish that letter had never arrived! Such airs you've taken on these last few weeks, and now with your traipsing about everywhere, and dragging the likes of this Mr. Hawthorne up from London to see you."

"To see *me*," Mildred said, pressing her finger to her own chest. (She wasn't going to take this moment to point out that even though Mr. Hawthorne's initial arrival in Upper Plimpton might have been due to her, his interest seemed to have quickly found a new focus in Belinda.) "Not you, but me. And I don't believe you care for that, hmm? That for once, the world has ceased to spin entirely around you."

If one's face could manage to resemble a prune and a mud-swollen toad at the same time, then Diana had taken a fair shot at it. Her next words came out like puttering snaps of gunfire, each one bitten off before the next reloaded. "I… will…not…tolerate…this…insolence–"

"Good night," Mildred said, which would have been a more remarkable finish to the scene if it had not still been late morning and if the children were not scampering around on the upper floors with all the energy of squirrels trapped in an attic. But she had not slept in well over twenty-four hours and so for her, the end of the day could not come soon enough.

"I'm not finished!" came Diana's reply, her voice chasing Mildred as she went up the stairs.

But Mildred was tired. Arguing with her sister was an exhausting exercise, or rather speaking to her sister while Diana argued back at her was exhausting. So she continued up the stairs, ignoring the grumbling still going on behind her. She went to her room, that small space that had lost its feeling of sanctuary only a short while before. She packed. She did not know what she would need for her journey. When was the last time she had taken a journey beyond the boundaries of Upper Plimpton? That brief trip to the shore when Belinda had still been young enough to think that eating sand was the height of childish entertainment? A gown. Two gowns. Stockings? Slippers. No, walking shoes. Her sturdiest pair, the ones Diana hated because she thought they were better suited for a farmer's daughter.

Mrs. Babbinton, she knew, would take care of all the preparations necessary concerning Fitz's comfort and safety for the duration of the journey. Still, she knew she would fret. She would have had even more reason to fret if she had not found herself fretting about it, such was the predictability of her reaction to certain stressful events.

She stood for a moment, her knees against the edge of her bed, a half-folded shawl dangling from her hands. The light from the window had an unusual quality to it, at once both gold and green as it sharpened the edges of every leaf and stone visible from her small window.

There was an entire world out there. A world illuminated by a thousand different rays of sunlight. Her mouth crumpled at the thought that this little journey of hers should so set her life to boiling over, that her previous existence had made it that a short jaunt two counties north would strain the ties of family to a breaking point.

"Ugh, no. Enough of that." Two pairs of stockings, her mind moved forward, after that stumble into maudlin quicksand. And some books. Did one read books while travelling? Of course people read books while travelling. Books had no boundaries, no sense of home or place. They were the entire world, printed in a form one could slip into one's pocket (Well, if the pockets were large enough, which they generally were not. Mildred made a pact with herself then and there to make certain that every future gown and apron she sewed for herself came complete with at least two pockets large enough and sturdy enough to carry most medium-sized volumes.)

And then she sat. There were still two more meals to be got through, but she thought she might skip at least one of them. No doubt her sister would find the meal more agreeable without her presence.

Oh. No. She was becoming emotional again. She rubbed the heel of her hand against her forehead, breathing through the tight burning behind her eyes. Maybe her sister was right. Maybe she was being dramatic. Surely she could have presented the news of her trip to Warwickshire in a less provoking manner. Or perhaps if she went downstairs and she spoke to Diana about—

She opened her eyes. This was how it was done, wasn't it? How it had always been done. Should Mildred attempt to show a spark of independence, Diana would be quick to snuff it out, using all of her words and her guilt to smother that spark into a tiny smut of ash, something to be swept away with a quick flick of a broom. Diana would be waiting for her to come downstairs again, hands clasped before her, head lowered, as chastened as a dog caught relieving itself in its master's shoes. (Not that Mildred had taken to relieving herself in footwear, though if Diana could have found herself a canine capable of teaching the children their lessons, Mildred did not doubt that her sister might have preferred the occasional ruined pair of slippers over living with a sister she placed on the same level of respect and admiration occupied by out-of-date fashions and vegetables suspended in aspic.)

Well, if she could not earn more regard than a boiled carrot, then what use was there in being mopish about it? Two pairs of stockings, books, perhaps an extra pair of gloves if the first were spoiled. Did she have an extra pair of gloves? She would check. And then she would finish packing. And then it would be night, and then morning, and then she would be off. Off and travelling through a different ray of sunlight.

CHAPTER NINETEEN

A dragon can sense a human from nearly three miles away. A human's senses are not nearly so keen.

-from Chapter Ten of Miss Percy's Pocket Guide (to the Care and Feeding of British Dragons)

Mildred did not sleep. Well, she might have slept, but it was that kind of rest where one is still kept fully aware of the passage of time, where the sounds from reality weave into dreams and you're left waking up and wondering if that noise through the night was merely the scratch of branches against the side of the house or the flutter of moth's wings in your nightmare. (Mildred had never confessed to anyone that she suffered recurring dreams in which moths swarmed around her head, tangling in her hair and leaving the dust from their wings all over her face and scrabbling hands. It all stemmed from a childhood incident when she accidentally swallowed a moth, its dry, powdery wings catching in her throat and... Either way, it was not a pleasant experience and went part of the way towards explaining the welcome she gave to all of the industrious and moth-eating spiders tucked into the corners of her room.)

She was up before even the servants, before dawn lit up the eastern edge of the sky. She dressed quickly, quietly, half wondering if her sister was half-awake on her side of the house, listening for her movements so she could rise up and continue on with their argument (because if Diana could not declare herself victorious, then it surely meant their discussion had not reached its natural conclusion). But there were no sounds to greet her as she picked up her bag and tip-toed out of her room, even the floors and that third step on the back staircase keeping their blessed silence as she trod across them.

Outside was cold (of course) and smelled like rain (of course). Because there would be rain, and probably wind and heavy downpours and a broken wheel on the carriage, leaving them to teeter halfway off the rutted road before they —

No, none of that. Mildred closed the door behind her, walked through the garden, out the gate, caught the edge of the lane and followed it around to the front of the property. And there she waited, leaning back against the wall, both of her hands wrapped tight around the handle of her bag. A niggling panic assailed her, that her bag was not large enough, that she had forgotten to include some necessary thing. Weren't people supposed to travel with large trunks and valises, enough to create a mountain of worldly possessions strapped to the top of the coach?

Before she could turn back and race inside to grab another dozen things from her wardrobe that she had already deemed as unwanted the night before, the sound of a horse's steady clopping on the damp lane kept her in place. Another minute, and Squire Manning's cart came into view, with the old Squire himself swaying slightly in time with the slow rocking of his progress.

"Oh, aye! Miss Percy!" He leapt down—or rather tumbled down by slow degrees, the muffled popping of various joints marking the unfolding of his limbs. "Give me that," he said, holding out a thick-fingered hand for her bag. "And I'll see you up onto the seat with me. You'll have some room to stretch your legs, though I can't promise your back won't be complaining before we arrive in Swindon. But I'm not one for soft pillows and cushions under my bottom, forgive me for saying so. You can think me rude and vulgar if you may, and I'll try to curb my tongue once we've picked up that Mrs. Babbinton. She being the vicar's housekeeper and all, she might not take kindly to talk of bottoms and things, but you're a right sensible lady, and I'm not afraid of you claiming the vapors or any of that other nonsense people pretend when something as right and natural as the bodies our Lord and Saviour gave us—made in his own image, you know, so how should it follow there should be shame in them? But, here." He took her bag once the point of his speech had irrevocably lost itself in the tangle of his words. "And up you go!"

Mildred put her foot on the step, hoisting up the hem of her skirt so as not to trip over it and fall gracelessly into the back of the cart. The seat was not uncomfortable, but that seemed akin to saying that boiled, buttered parsnips were a tolerable meal until one was forced to eat them three times a day, every day, for a period not measuring shorter than a month.

The drive into Upper Plimpton was pleasant, especially as Mildred had never seen the town with only the faint glow of impending dawn making its shapes and corners visible. When they arrived at the vicarage it was to see a few low lights already burning in the windows, the faint shadow of smoke curling upwards from the kitchen chimney.

Mrs. Babbinton came out to greet them before Squire Manning had even begun his ungainly descent from the cart. If knitted things were armor, then the housekeeper appeared dressed for battle. Something that resembled a loose cardigan beneath a thick shawl crocheted in a lumpy bobble stitch adorned her body, while thick mittens and a slouchy hat that might have also been a deflated souffle (though Mildred would never tell her as much, seeing as how there had been an undercurrent of scorn in Mrs. Babbinton's voice the one—and only—time French culinary practices had appeared in a discussion) sat on her head.

"And what a fine morning it is!" Mrs. Babbinton's breath puffed out of her mouth in pale clouds as she dove into the conversation as if they were already well into the middle of it.

Behind her, backlit by the fire in the kitchen, Mr. Wiggan stood, still in his dressing gown and cap (it seemed the hours before dawn gave everyone temporary leave to speak of bottoms and wear their dressing gowns in full view of persons not belonging to their immediate household), clutching a cup of something steaming between his hands. He came forward when Mrs. Babbinton started to climb up to the front seat of the cart, helping to steady her until she was safely ensconced beside Mildred, their legs covered by a large blanket the housekeeper had brought along.

"I'll go and fetch Fitz," he said, and turning around, disappeared again into the vicarage.

"Now, don't you worry," Mrs. Babbinton said, patting Mildred's knee with her mittened hand. "Mr. Wiggan and I took care of everything. You shall see."

This small reassurance only served to set Mildred's heart in her throat. For most of the morning she had given herself leave to not think about the details involved in transporting Fitz along with them to Warwickshire. But now they had come to it at last, and Mr. Wiggan walked out of the vicarage bearing a large square basket, the sort farmers used for the containment of chickens or other small, generally winged livestock. Together, Mr. Wiggan and Squire Manning loaded their cargo onto the back of the cart, tucking it in with the other things the Squire was taking to market that morning.

"He's sound asleep," Mr. Wiggan announced as he came back around to the front of the cart, on Mildred's side. "So hopefully you should not have too much trouble with him until you're well on your way."

Mrs. Babbinton leaned towards her on the seat. "I gave him his favorite last night, a large bit of lamb, still with the bones in for him to gnaw on, as he likes to do. And some potatoes, because he does love his potatoes. And"–and here her voice lowered to a rush of air across Mildred's cheek–"just a wee bit of brandy, to help him nod off. Not too much, of course. He should be fine."

Mildred sat very still, for a moment feeling as if she had slipped out of her body and could see the scene as if from the viewpoint of an onlooker. And with such a view as that, she could only be in awe of their situation: Two ladies, neither of them of an age for adventure, heading off together into the light of a brand new day. And with an inebriated dragon loaded onto the cart behind them.

"Miss Percy." Mr. Wiggan held out his hand. Mildred took it. He squeezed her fingers tight, so much she thought she could feel the warmth of him even through her gloves. "Mrs. Babbinton," he said, switching his attention to his housekeeper, yet still keeping hold of Mildred's hand. "I expect to have both of you returned to me in no worse condition then I see you now. Will you promise to look after her?"

At first, Mildred was unsure to whom he posed his question. But then Mrs. Babbinton leaned forward and placed her hand—still encased in its knitted monstrosity—over their clasped fingers. "Don't be a goose," she said, all serious. "If you should worry about anyone, it should be yourself. When was the last time you made your own toast? If you promise not to burn down the vicarage in my absence, then I'll go ahead and give you my word in exchange, though I guarantee we are more than able to take care of ourselves."

"And we'll be off then!" Squire Manning climbed up to his seat, forcing Mildred and Mrs. Babbinton to shift closer against one another. Mr. Wiggan released Mildred's hand, his outstretched fingers hovering in the air for a moment before he finally dropped his arm to his side.

"Goodbye," Mildred said, her voice small and possibly

lost as the Squire took up his reins and started them forward.

Mr. Wiggan raised his hand in farewell. She twisted around in her seat, watching as his outline blurred into the smudges of gray and shadow that made up the vicarage so early in the morning.

"Oh," she said, and set her gaze forward, ahead of them. Beside her, Mrs. Babbinton was digging through a bag she had on her lap, from which she pulled out several blessedly warm rolls that gave off a strong aroma of cheese.

"No worries," Mrs. Babbinton said, giving her side a gentle nudge with her elbow. "Eat as much as you like. I've brought along enough to see us fed halfway around the world and back again. And those buns are best when they're hot, so don't tarry."

***

They had the option of taking a more leisurely journey to Warwickshire, one that would necessitate them spending the night at an inn and finishing up the last few miles after breakfast.

They also had a dragon, so leisure was not a luxury with which they dared to treat themselves. Instead, they purchased seats on a coach that would carry them to their destination with a higher measure of expediency. It also meant they were crushed together with several other people Mildred did not bother to learn the names of—if, indeed, there had even been a moment when names were shared— due to the fact she was encumbered with a basket of groggy dragon wedged onto her lap.

A blanket covered the basket, and the animal inside was described as "the lady's sick cat." This was enough to afford them little interest from their travelling companions, as no one appeared keen on drumming up an intimate association with a housekeeper, a spinster, and the latter's ailing pet.

At each stop (for meals, to change horses, to change

travellers) Mildred and Mrs. Babbinton elected to stay within the confines of the coach rather than risk disturbing Fitz by lugging his basket over all and sundry. (They also didn't wish to risk him waking up at an inopportune moment, like during a meal inside an inn's dining room where there were vexing things like witnesses shambling about.) The most they did was take turns stepping out and walking around the yard to stretch their legs, neither of them daring to leave the basket unaccompanied or to even remove it from the coach at all if it could be avoided until they arrived in Stratford-upon-Avon. There was no worry about feeding themselves, as Mrs. Babbinton had risen to her previous declaration and indeed packed enough food to feed a walking army. Things like smoked ham and hand pies stuffed with potatoes and cheese and chicken were also brought along and slipped through the gaps in the cage once Fitz awoke and showed an inclination towards irritability (an irritability that could only be stymied by sending him back into a digestive stupor).

By the time they arrived in Stratford-upon-Avon, it was already well past sunset. Mildred's legs felt ready to leap from her body and race out of the carriage, so restless were her limbs, and inside his basket, Fitz had taken to shifting his weight from one end to the other, leaving her to deal with something akin to a miniature ocean rocking back and forth across her lap.

"Come along," Mrs. Babbinton helped her down from the carriage, the two of them juggling their bags and Fitz's basket while cramped muscles tingled back to life as they made their way towards the inn. "You have a seat just over there," the housekeeper indicated a small bench near to the fire once they were inside. "I'll find us someone who can take us the rest of the way to…" Her eyes widened and then narrowed as quick as it took Mildred to draw in a breath. "What's the name of the place?"

"Exley Hall. That was my great uncle's home. Mr. Gorman should still be in residence there."

"Right." Mrs. Babbinton nodded once. "Exley Hall. Exley Hall. Now, you should sit. Sit!" She waved her hand. "And I'll take care of everything."

Mildred sat. She did not think she would want to, having been shut up in a cramped coach for more hours than she wished to count, but it seemed that sitting in a moving thing with wheels and sitting on a stationary bench with room enough to stretch out her legs towards a crackling fire were two incredibly disparate things.

She balanced the basket on her lap, turning it so that she could lift a small corner of the blanket and peer inside. Fitz sat curled up in the corner, his head tucked beneath his wing. At the shift of the blanket, however, one eye opened, a gleam of green and gold that blinked at her before he shivered in his place, raised his nose, and let out a terrific squawk.

"No!" She hastily tucked the blanket back in place, wincing as Fitz decided to change his position and scrabble towards the other end of the basket, claws scraping and wings rustling and voice yowling from the moment he had seen her face.

Around her sat all of their bags, Mrs. Babbinton's included. Without worrying about things like permission or the privacy inherent to other people's belongings, she held the basket as still as she was able with one arm while digging into the housekeeper's large valise. There was still some food left ('some' choosing to share its definition with 'vast amount' in this case), the aroma of it striking Mildred in the face as if she had removed the lid from a pot simmering on the stove.

"Here," she said, snatching up something (it smelled like meat and left the fingers of her gloves greasy, so she did not think she could have chosen better) and pushing it through the gaps in the weave of his door. He ate quickly, snapping at the food as if he were a creature left to starve through the majority of the day, then fixed Mildred with a reproachful glare. "Just try to stay quiet," she hissed, as if he were a child she could reprimand. Goodness, another minute of this and she would begin shaking her finger at him.

He crawled towards her, his nose snuffling at the door, at where her fingers had just been. She obliged by returning her fingertips to the largest gap, and his tongue peeked out, licking at the spots on her gloves where the fat from the meat had clung.

"Oh dear," she said, yet not quite sure why she said it. "What am I going to do with you?"

It was a question she did not want to ponder, no matter that those eight words seemed to have woven themselves together into a frame for her current existence. But she was saved from having to ponder them further by Mrs. Babbinton's approach, the housekeeper's expression at once severe and relieved and jolly, as if all of the day's emotions fought across the canvas of her features to be visible to others at the same time.

"Well, and here's where we are." She clasped her hands together—bare now, though her mittens dangled from a strand of yarn affixed to her shawl—and released a long, slow breath. "I've just hired a man who says he will drive us to Exley Hall. He's received a quarter of his payment now, and he'll earn the rest once we've arrived. He says it's only five miles, so it should not take long, but I will be happy not to have to rattle around on an old cart or coach for a long time after all of this."

"I'm sorry." Mildred wanted to stand but also did not want to risk jostling Fitz now that she had him quieted again (and beginning to gnaw a hole in the thumb of her right glove). "I should not have allowed you to accompany me on this trip. If I had known—"

"Nonsense!" And Mrs. Babbinton's mouth broke into a grin. "Did you know this is the most fun I've had in years? Now, I'm not saying I want to make a habit of this, but it is a comfort to know I've not gone completely housebound in my old age."

The man hired to take them the rest of the way to Exley Hall was a Mr. Simonon (nearly rhyming with "cinnamon" as he gregariously pointed out to them) who was tall and long-limbed (or perhaps only appeared more long-limbed than he was as every cuff and hem seemed to end at least two inches before its intended destination) and tolerably sober, which set him apart from most of the other people in the inn.

"So it's Exley Hall you're interested in? I take it you're a relation of old Mr. Forthright? God rest his soul," Mr. Simonon added, with a slight bow of his head and shoulders. "Of course I can see you there. My farm is two miles from here, but it's on the same track, so it won't be too much out of my way." He moved as if he was about to help them with their bags, but Mrs. Babbinton stepped smoothly between him and their luggage.

"Why don't you go ahead and bring your cart around, and we'll be out in another minute."

Mr. Simonon nodded, his fingers raised to the brim of his hat. Once he was gone, the two of them gathered up their things, pushed two more chunks of food into Fitz's cage in the hope it would be enough to keep him quiet for the next five miles, and headed for the door.

Mildred was not well travelled, as has already been established. But unfortunately, Mrs. Babbinton had also never resided far beyond the boundaries of Wiltshire or even Upper Plimpton. Because of this, they did not realize that it was generally unwise to put one's trust in an unknown gentleman they had found socializing with his friends and neighbors in the taproom of the local inn. For them, truly bad people—or rather, people with a greater inclination towards doing bad things—existed only in books and large cities. They had little idea that the man who gave every appearance of being kind and solicitous was, in fact, eyeing them up as a means to fatten his own purse. (Further exceptions must be made for the two ladies, as they were both so weary from the day's exertions that they might have been persuaded to put their trust in someone who displayed a penchant for raving at the moon and brandishing bloody weapons (perhaps even both at the same time) if it would mean a more expeditious arrival at Exley Hall.)

Mr. Simonon helped them up into the cart, an overall shabby contraption that did not allow enough space for them to all sit beside the driver, leaving Mildred and Mrs. Babbinton to hoist themselves into the back with all of their things. Mildred clutched Fitz's basket tight against her while trying to discover a way to sit in the depths of a cart—one that smelled of cabbage and mold and probably moldy cabbages—without having to twist her skirt around herself in something less than a ladylike manner. (Mrs. Babbinton, in contrast, appeared unconcerned with the state of her skirt or whether or not a large portion of calf was on display while she better situated herself.) At one point, Mr. Simonon reached back as if to help steady Fitz's basket for her, but Mildred snatched it back without thinking.

"What d'you have in there?" His question was not at all accusatory. In fact, it was almost too playful for the circumstances, but Mildred would not notice such a thing until she had more time to view all of the exchanges with him in comfortable retrospect.

"My cat." The words were too sharp and too loud. She winced and swallowed and pressed on regardless. "He's sick. And when he's sick he bites. So I would not bother with him, if I were you."

"No worries, no worries, Miss!" He gathered up his reins and clucked his old nag forward, the wheels of the cart creaking as he whistled a tune that floated off into the night.

CHAPTER TWENTY

... and Miss Cynthia Bowlin looked particularly resplendent at the Stokes' dinner party the previous evening. One could not even discern the damage previously dealt to her coiffure at the 'clumsy' hands of Miss Belinda Muncy—and the tipped-over candle—from only a few weeks before. Though I have no wish to speculate how much money must have been spent on a hairpiece to cover that bit of scalp that went up like an effigy on Bonfire Night.

-from the personal correspondence of Mrs. Audrey Haverstick to Mrs. Edith Kunkle, the former a longtime resident of Upper Plimpton and neighbor of the Muncy Family.

Standing outside in a light drizzle was not one of Reginald's favored pastimes. Standing outside of an inn—to which he was now in arrears for precisely one night of his stay—in a light drizzle while waiting for someone who was unequivocally and overwhelmingly late was an experience he hoped to never have to repeat. But standing outside of an inn (arrears, etc.) in a light drizzle while waiting for someone (late, unequivocally and overwhelmingly) when the someone in question happened to be Miss Belinda Muncy... well.

Despite the wet (which had developed into an irregular dripping off the eaves of the inn) and the chill that wrapped around him, the sight of Miss Muncy crossing the road and walking towards him was equivalent to watching the sun rise or a wisp light up the mist on the moors. His gaze tracked her progress until she was at his side, her bonnet carrying drops of rain like jewels. She smiled, and he bowed, and she returned the greeting with a quick curtsey.

"My aunt is gone!" she said, still smiling.

Reginald began to say something and then stopped. "What?" he said instead.

She stepped towards him. It was almost enough to distract him completely from their purpose, but he shook his head and directed all of his energy on her next words. "She and Mama had an argument yesterday. I was upstairs, so I didn't hear. But my aunt did not come to dinner, and when I awoke this morning, she was gone!"

"Gone?" A panic seized him, wrapping around his heart and squeezing tight. "Where has she gone?" And then, "Is she coming back?"

"That's the thing! I don't know! No one will speak to me about it. Well, Mama won't say a word, which most likely means that she did not come out of her fight with Aunt Mildred as a clear victor." She leaned towards him, quite conspiratorially. "If the opposite were true, none of us would hear an end to her crowing!"

He cast his thoughts around in a dozen directions at once, a net trawling through the water for any and all fish gullible enough to become ensnared. "What can be done?"

"We go to the vicarage, of course. Exactly as planned." Miss Muncy tipped her head back, the curls that framed her face somehow withstanding the onslaught of moisture from all around. "If my aunt has been spending so much of her time there, then perhaps the vicar knows something. And it will give us time to think."

"To think," he echoed, just as she hooked her arm through his and drew him out from beneath the inn's dripping corners.

The vicarage wasn't far. (Upper Plimpton being Upper Plimpton meant that nothing was situated very far from anything else. A wonderful feature if one wasn't inclined to walk a fair distance in order to arrive at their destination, but most likely considered a detriment to people who preferred such luxuries as variety or anonymity or occasional marks of civilization.) As Miss Muncy was the one to take on the task of introducing Reginald to the vicar (and thereby treading on conversational opportunities that might lead to more information about Miss Percy and what she might have done with the rest of her inheritance) she rang the bell outside the front door. "It should only be a moment," Miss Muncy said, as the rain began to come down in earnest. "Mrs. Babbinton is very prompt."

But she was not very prompt. Miss Muncy's nose wrinkled. The feather on her bonnet was heavy with rain and clung wetly to a part of her chin where it had drooped down. She rang the bell again.

And again.

"She must be out."

Miss Muncy raised her fist and knocked on the door. "I did not see her in town," she said, and knocked again. "But Mr. Wiggan should be at home. He doesn't have his school this morning."

Finally, a clatter behind the door. It opened an inch, then more, and then a man stood there, mostly dressed (no neck cloth, no coat and his sleeves rolled halfway up his forearms) and staring at them as if he had never encountered visitors on his doorstep before. "Miss Muncy?"

"Mr. Wiggan! Oh, you are home. How wonderful!" She pushed forward, one foot on the threshold. "May we come in?"

They were inside, dripping on the mat before Mr. Wiggan had produced more than a few unintelligible mumbles.

"Oh, what weather!" Miss Muncy removed her bonnet, shook out her curls, and turned her face towards the vicar.

Reginald experienced a pang at the shift in attention, a chill settling on the back of his neck as if the sun had just disappeared behind a cloud. "And here I fear we've come and disrupted your morning. How uncharitable of us! But I bring with me someone who was very eager to meet you. This is Mr. Hawthorne." She placed her hand on his arm, maneuvering him forward in the narrow hall. "He's come up from London to pay a visit to my Aunt Mildred. Apparently they shared an acquaintance with my great-great uncle? Yes, I suppose that is the correct number of 'greats'."

She laughed, tinkling bells and all that. Reginald watched Mr. Wiggan, expecting the vicar's face to reflect his pleasure at having such a gem as Miss Muncy in his home. But the man only looked equal parts befuddled and wary. And slightly bleary, as if he had rolled out of bed a short while before they had arrived.

"Mr. Hawthorne?" A muscle in the vicar's jaw twitched. "Very pleased to make your acquaintance." He held out his hand. Reginald took it, expecting a soft, slightly damp grip from the other man, gathering what he could of this Mr. Wiggan from appearances alone. But the handshake was firm and almost a bit...well, he did not want to admit, but painful. Rather painful. "You're a friend of Miss Percy's, you say?"

Reginald took his hand back, resisting the urge to wince or stretch out his fingers until one of his knuckles should crack. "I wouldn't say 'friend', exactly. But I had come up from London to offer her my condolences following the death of Mr. Charles Forthright. He was a great friend of mine, and he also held his niece in high esteem."

"Ah," Mr. Wiggan said.

They waited for him to say more. Or to move from his current position (he was a tall man, and carried some width on his frame, so while nothing about his character gave off an imposing air, his physical presence alone was enough to hold them in place). But he did not move, and this absence of movement succeeded in blocking them—either intentionally or not—from making further progress into the house.

"Is Mrs. Babbinton here?" Miss Muncy leaned sideways, peering down the hall as if she expected Mrs. Babbinton to pop out of a closet on the end of a spring. "I must say, I would not half mind a selection of some of her delectable cakes! I was only telling Mr. Hawthorne a short while ago that one has not fully experienced all of Upper Plimpton's delights until they have tasted a bite of Mrs. Babbinton's lemon shortcake."

Mr. Wiggan glanced over his shoulder. The hall, the rooms behind him, everything gave off a quiet, almost deserted feel. "I'm afraid my housekeeper is away at the moment. You find me rather unequipped for the entertaining of guests. I think I could manage some tea, but—"

"Do not trouble yourself!" Miss Muncy plowed forward with all the determination of a ship breaking through ice-covered waters. Down the hall, towards the kitchen, and both men were left with little choice but to bob and drift like flotsam in her wake. "And where has Mrs. Babbinton gone off to?" she asked once they had caught up with her in the kitchen. "Will she return later today?"

"Well." Mr. Wiggan glanced towards the fireplace. Reginald noticed a basket there, filled with rumpled, stained linens, but nothing else of interest. "No. I mean, she has gone with a friend. On a trip. To visit some family north of here. Not her own family, but... um. The friend's family." He looked at Mr. Hawthorne, frowned, then settled his attention on Miss Muncy. "You don't have to do that, you know."

Miss Muncy had filled the kettle and was setting it over the fire. "Oh, you two should sit and talk and I will manage everything."

Reginald would have been perfectly content to stand there and watch Miss Muncy as she moved about the kitchen, setting out cups and small plates and searching through little tins and boxes for the tea and sugar and biscuits. Mr. Wiggan showed no immediate desire to sit and talk, but after a minute he gestured towards the table there and the two of them sat down, facing one another.

"I apologize for having to offer you such a paltry welcome," Mr. Wiggan said, and cleared his throat. "I did not anticipate being left to my own devices today, and so the other rooms are not really prepared for visitors."

"When did Mrs. Babbinton leave?" Miss Muncy carried over a tray of biscuits to begin them with, though the water for the tea was still heating over the fire. "And when do you expect her home again? Surely she has not gone and abandoned you for so very long a time, hmm?"

Mr. Wiggan picked up a biscuit and turned it over in his hands. "This morning, in answer to your first. And, uh, I don't really know, to your second. But she's not gone very far, so the hope is she will return in no more than another day or so."

"I hope the roads remain passable with all this rain," Reginald put in, supposing that he needed to add something to the conversation. But the vicar's edginess caught his attention, the way the man's gaze never settled on anyone or anything for more than a second or two, at the most. And, of course, he was not so much of a fool not to notice that this housekeeper, Mrs. Babbinton, had disappeared at the same time as Miss Mildred Percy. "Where did you say she was going?"

"I didn't say." Mr. Wiggan took a bite of his biscuit, his expression lamenting the loss of a few crumbs that broke off and fell to the floor.

"But I thought I heard you mention someplace up north? Yet not so far that it should not prove a lengthy journey? That much is good, at least."

Reginald caught Miss Muncy's gaze as she returned to the table with the things for the tea. *Up north*, her eyes seemed to say to him. Warwickshire was north, or at least north of Wiltshire. And Warwickshire was where Mr. Charles Forthright had lived.

"I hate to be a nuisance, but could I use your....?" Miss Muncy blushed, eyes lowering as she coughed lightly.

Mr. Wiggan stared at her for a moment before realization dawned on him. "Oh. Oh! Yes, there is one outside, in the corner of the garden. Though it's raining so you might prefer to, um... Upstairs, on the right. There is a closet?"

Miss Muncy whispered a delicate 'thank you' beneath her breath and left the room. Mr. Wiggan ate the last bite of his biscuit, then without a word began pouring out the tea for himself and Reginald.

"Miss Muncy tells me you have an interest in local and natural history," Reginald said, and took a sip of tea, immediately scalding the tip of his tongue.

Mr. Wiggan sniffed. "A bit, yes."

"I was fortunate enough to enjoy a great correspondence and friendship with Miss Percy's uncle, Mr. Forthright. He was a very intelligent, curious man. I wonder what Miss Percy has told you of him?"

It was, of course, a leading question, one meant to ignite a detailed and lengthy conversation from which Reginald could glean important pieces of information that would then lead him towards a discovery of the location of the stone. And so he took another sip of tea and he waited for Mr. Wiggan to reply.

"Not much, I'm afraid," came the long-awaited reply.

"But she showed you some of the things left to her? I saw a few of them myself, a very interesting collection of books and papers, so many handwritten things authored by Mr. Forthright himself! I must confess I am rather curious to hear your thoughts, if you have any."

He did not have any. In fact, Mr. Wiggan picked up another biscuit and stuffed the entire thing into his mouth, cheeks bulging slightly as he chewed.

Now, Reginald knew he had two options to consider. The first was that the vicar was so dull-witted that even carrying on a simple dialogue consisting of basic observations and pleasantries was a conversational task of Sisyphean proportions. The second was that the vicar knew something he did not wish Reginald to also know, and so he opted for awkward silence and borderline rudeness to avoid revealing the aforementioned knowledge.

Reginald had very few doubts the latter option was the correct one.

The stilted silences (from Mr. Wiggan) and forced questions (from Reginald) continued for several more minutes (or at least as long as it took for the vicar to eat through an entire plate of biscuits). Miss Muncy returned as Reginald finished the last of his tea, her cheeks unusually pink and her eyes bright. Her bright eyes widened when she looked at him, in that way people widen their eyes when they attempt to communicate something to another person without speaking out loud.

"I am so sorry to have abandoned you, and so suddenly!" Miss Muncy fluttered over the tea tray, picking up cups and stacking things and making a great performance of showing that she and Reginald had every intention of leaving shortly. "But I only just remembered that my mother requested my presence at home this afternoon. We are to have the Boydens over to visit, and without Aunt Mildred there, my mother will be quite put out if she has to shoulder the burden of entertaining all on her own."

As she carried the tray away, Reginald stood. Mr. Wiggan rushed to his feet as well, hurriedly brushing crumbs from his lap and glancing over his shoulder, towards the front door as if he could not see them pushed through it soon enough.

All sorts of comments and apologies and promises were made, the majority of them voiced by Miss Muncy as she swore to bring Mr. Hawthorne again at a more convenient time. And then they were clad again in their outer garments and out the door and walking briskly through Upper Plimpton, the rain battering at them while Miss Muncy held onto his arm and waited until they were far beyond earshot of the vicarage's front door to speak.

"I went into his study."

Reginald stumbled over a stone. "You did what?"

"Oh, you must have known I hadn't gone off in search of the water closet. Here." She tugged a sheaf of papers out from some hidden fold or pocket of her skirts and handed it to him. "I did not have much time, so I took what I could. You might have possessed a better eye, but I nominated myself as being less to be suspected of committing nefarious deeds within the vicar's own home."

They made their way back to the inn, Reginald clutching the papers against his chest until they were inside and safe from where they could be spotted by the rain. They chose a table near the fireplace, Miss Muncy waving away the innkeeper's wife when she came to inquire if there was anything they wanted. Reginald smoothed out the papers with trembling hands, his eyes dancing over the drawings that graced the margins; sketches of half-formed creatures bearing teeth and claws, traceries of wings fading into an old man's handwriting, tails curled round nests of eggs, the pencil strokes with which they were shaped smudged from black to gray to gone.

"There were these as well." Miss Muncy spread several other objects across the tabletop, a mixture of small stones and fragments, a few of them crusted over with crystals varying in shades from indigo to white. "But there was no sign of the stone you described. Nothing that large, at least."

"She must have taken it with her." He traced the drawing of a wing with the edge of his thumbnail, his gaze searching over the things Miss Muncy had taken, as if committing them to memory before even daring to lay a finger on them. "I suspect she's gone to Warwickshire, to Exley Hall."

"Exley Hall?" Miss Muncy had been turning one of the crystals over in her hand, but she paused and stared at him.

"Your uncle's home," he explained. "Your great, great uncle." He sucked at his teeth. "Your dead great, great uncle."

She held the crystal up before her, turning it again slowly, so that it caught the light of the fire and the candles set in their holders across the tables. "And so this is what we're after?" She looked at him, her eyes gleaming as if lit with their own internal illumination. "Like this, but larger?"

Reginald shook his head. He had not lied to her thus far. But he had omitted several truths, and he realized that if they were to go any further with all of this, then he had to take a gamble (a thought that made him slightly nauseated, as things like betting and gambling had always been associated with his father, and he wasn't particularly keen on running a parallel trajectory with anyone who had found their demise in an open grave) and determine how much of her faith Miss Muncy was willing to put in him.

"Miss Muncy?"

She smiled. Her face framed by a damp bonnet, limp feathers wrapped around the thing like wet cobwebs, her cheeks as pink as roses from their walk in the rain and the warmth of the nearby fire, her mouth...

...what had he been about to say?

Ah, right. The truth. Every piece of it.

"Miss Muncy," he repeated. "If I were to tell you something of an absolutely fantastical nature, do you think you would have it within yourself to believe me?"

"Of course." The expression on her face was full of trust, of unerring devotion. She would believe him, those eyes said. She would go with him to the ends of the earth, said the curve of her lips, the soft rise of her cheekbones when she smiled.

He turned the paper around and pushed it towards her. "It is not a stone," he said. "It is something very much more than that."

Lines appeared between her eyes, the corners of her mouth turning down as she studied the paper. And then he tapped his finger near the drawing, and her brow cleared, and her mouth opened as if she would speak before it snapped shut as quick as a trap.

"Once upon a time," he said, his voice lowering, taking on the quality of a storybook read aloud. "There were dragons, here, in England." And there he paused, giving time to his words so they could sink in, so she could turn them over in her mind as well as the stone in her hand. "Where else could the myths have come from, without some truth to spark the stories to life? But I believe they existed, not merely in some form growing with exaggeration as it passed through the ages. And your uncle believed it, too. And when he died, he passed the greatest piece of evidence on to your aunt."

Her lips parted, though her eyes did not leave the page. She reached out and shuffled through them herself, examining the various sketches, the notes accompanying each one. "So it is not a stone," she said, still—still!— studying the papers before her. "But—"

"An egg," he said. Quickly, quickly, forcing the words out before he could turn coward and swallow them back down again. "It's an egg. I mean, it's old. It's a fossil, really. But it could be—no! It *is* one of the great archeological finds of our time. And I've made inquiries." He leaned forward, elbows on the table, fingers curling inward with the urge to sweep up Miss Muncy's hands and clasp them tight within his own. "If I find the right buyer, it could be worth a fortune. It could be the making of us."

And there, she raised her eyes to meet his. "A fortune, you say?"

"Thousands of pounds," he went on. "Tens of thousands, if we go about this properly."

She bit at her bottom lip. Perfect little teeth nipping at

perfect pink lips. "And my Aunt Mildred has it?"

"Yes." He would not allow such pernicious terms as 'maybe' or 'perhaps' or 'I believe' chip away at his narrative now. "Yes, she has it. And we have to get it back."

He held his breath. Or it might have only felt as if he could not breathe, not until he had an assurance from her that she was not going to laugh in his face and leave him sitting there, stuck in an inn in some godforsaken village and with barely enough money left to drag himself back to London.

Miss Muncy closed her eyes. It was more than a blink. He watched as thoughts revealed themselves on her face, her expression shifting like wind turning across the surface of a lake. And then she looked at him again, and her nostrils flared. "Warwickshire?"

"Um. Yes?"

She sat up, straightened the papers into a neat stack and pushed them towards him. "Then what are we waiting for? We're already hours behind."

CHAPTER TWENTY-ONE

I do not believe there is any creature more loyal than a dragon.

-from Miss Mildred Percy's personal journal

If Mildred were to write a guide to travel, one of those little books penned by ladies or gentlemen of middling quality and sold to other ladies or gentlemen of equally middling quality, she would take care to note that travelling in the back of a cart of questionable structure down a muddy, potholed road several hours after the sun had put an end to the day was a mode of transport that should be avoided at all costs.

An hour had passed since they'd left the inn, an hour of creaking, rocking, bracing, and slow plodding. They could have made better time if they had walked, Mildred told herself (and then immediately bit back that thought with the knowledge that if they had indeed chosen to walk, she would most likely now be wishing that any sort of conveyance, no matter how ramshackle or occupied with drivers who chose to pass their time by whistling, would trundle by to pick them up. And then the cycle of wishing for what she could not have would begin again.)

How many miles had slipped away already? One? Five? In the dark, with only a few streaks of clear sky opening and closing above them, she could not tell. Beside her, Mrs. Babbinton's chin dropped down to her chest, her eyes closed and a low snore humming in the back of her throat. Mildred, however, could not sleep. She hurt in more places than she had known she possessed, the cart smelled bad, Mr.

Simonon would not cease his infernal whistling, and she was at once both hungry and yet too anxious to contemplate putting anything in her mouth out of fear it would only add to her current indigestive state.

And then there was Fitz, his basket held on her lap, her arms wrapped tight around it as if she feared some predatory bird would swoop out from the shadows and carry him away. He seemed to vacillate between awake and asleep, occasionally turning around and shifting his weight, or letting out a few pitiful mews before he settled down again. "Not much farther," she said, her mouth near the corner of the basket, her fingers twitching the blanket aside enough that he would hear her voice but hopefully not glimpse enough of her face to agitate him.

However uncomfortable she was at the moment, she knew that Fitz must feel worse. He had not been let out of the basket since he was first put into it that morning. She, at least, had taken a few brief strolls around the yards of the inns they stopped at. So while her entire body ached and her head throbbed and her stomach protested her circumstances with a series of alternating growls and unladylike belches, she was not locked up in a basket, unable to fully stand on her legs or stretch her wings above her.

Well, arms. She knew she did not have wings. But for comparison's sake–

The cart rattled to a stop. Mildred looked up, while Mrs. Babbinton sniffed loudly and cracked open one gimlet eye.

"Have we arrived?" Mildred's voice cracked from disuse. She sat up straight, head turning from side to side as she searched the horizon for any sign of a house or a drive or gate or civilization. But there was nothing but dark and more dark.

Mr. Simonon gave no reply as he climbed down from his perch and walked around to the back of the cart. "You can get out now, I think."

Mildred did not move. Even if she had been inclined to,

she was not certain all of the various pieces that made her—bones, muscles, blood and flesh and other viscera—would willingly comply. "I beg your pardon?"

Mr. Simonon stood with his arms crossed over his chest. She supposed he was attempting to make himself appear menacing, but Mildred found herself too exhausted to do anything more than drop her forehead against the edge of the basket and groan.

"Come along, now! Out, out!" He jerked a thumb over his shoulder, indicating—Mildred assumed—that she and Mrs. Babbinton were expected to follow the path drawn by that gesture. "And you can leave your things in the cart. I'll be having those, if you please."

Mildred still could not cajole any of her limbs into cooperating. Mrs. Babbinton seemed to be suffering under a similar affliction, though hers was associated with a steady repetition of "No, no, no" under her breath while she slowly shook her head.

"But we paid you! You're to take us to Exley Hall!" Mildred cried, still laboring under the belief that someone given money in exchange for a service was expected to provide that service even if the someone in question appeared to have taken a detour into criminal behavior. "You'll receive the rest of your money when we arrive. I don't understand what this is about."

"I'll receive the rest of the money now," Mr. Simonon said, still smiling and jovial, as if this were all a great joke and he could not wait to enjoy the telling of it once he'd taken himself back to the inn and his drunken companions. "Along with everything else you have. Your bags, jewelry, and purses, please. I'll let you keep your cat," he added. "Since I'm a good Christian man and I would not wish to harm one of God's creatures."

She should move. Some alarmed part of her mind knew this. A man was threatening them, and they should obey to avoid the risk of being harmed. Or worse. But weariness and hunger had made her as stubborn as a child, and she dug her heels into the floor of the cart, her shoulders pushing back even as her spine protested such a show of bravery. "You will take us on to Exley Hall, and that is the end of it."

In her imagination, some sort of haggling would follow this declaration. Mr. Simonon would voice more demands and make known the consequences weighing over them if those demands were not met. Mildred would continue to refuse anything that did not culminate with their being driven the rest of the way to Exley Hall, while Mrs. Babbinton would go on with her muttering and inability to drag herself into full wakefulness beside her.

But instead Mr. Simonon chose to circumvent all of that and simply lunged forward to grab Mildred's ankle. She screamed, she thought. Or maybe she grunted as her bottom hit the floor of the cart and she was half-dragged towards the end of it. She kicked, because she did not stop long enough to think about what should be done when someone had her ankle in their hand. She kicked and jerked and did not stop kicking and jerking until Mr. Simonon cried out and the grip on her ankle released and she tumbled off the end of the cart and landed on a—fortunately—soft and wet part of the road.

"Damn bloody females," she thought she heard Mr. Simonon say, and all Mildred could do was squirm in the mud and take offense at her attacker's belief that somehow a man would display a less-violent form of resistance to being forcibly removed from his belongings.

Beside her a screeching sound erupted, and it was then she realized Fitz's basket had gone over when she did, the fall knocking off the blanket and jostling him into such an irate state of wakefulness that he seemed determined to wreak vengeance on the person responsible for disturbing his rest. The basket rocked back and forth and finally tipped onto its side. The door swung open and Fitz, all tottering shadows and flapping anger, burst out and volleyed himself at Mr. Simonon's (who had managed to remain standing through all of this) legs.

Mildred could not react. Not that she would not, but that the sight of an indignant dragonet fluttering and squawking and clawing at the calves of a full-sized man was enough to render her incapable of moving for she did not know how long. Mere seconds? Or was it a full minute before she squelched onto her knees, onto her feet, and made an attempt at herding Fitz away from Mr. Simonon?

"Fitz, no! No!" She rushed in with her body canted forward, her arms spread apart, as if she could scoop him up at the first opportunity. Fitz, however, paid no attention to her and instead managed to hook his claws into Mr. Simonon's left boot and used his new hold to lever himself up the man's leg until he could stretch his neck upwards and bite—

The sound that issued from Mr. Simonon's throat was not something that could easily be transcribed into written English. (German, no doubt, would have a word in its lexicon capable of expressing the particular kind of pain he was experiencing. But as Mr. Simonon was not familiar with that specific branch of Teutonic languages, his unintelligible and agonized warbling would have to suffice.)

"Mrs. Babbinton!" Mildred spun around, hoping for some manner of aid from that quarter, but the housekeeper seemed to have discovered her limits of endurance and so still sat in her place in the cart, holding onto her bags and watching the scene before her (Fitz clinging to Mr. Simonon's nether regions with all of the strength in his miniature jaws, Mildred—caked in mud down her front—circling around them like a goose ready to attack) with impassive interest.

"Oh!" Mildred huffed and returned her full attention to Fitz. She could not have cared less about the extent of Mr. Simonon's suffering at this point, but she did not want to see Fitz injured. And so she forced herself forward just as Mr. Simonon spit out a string of curses and began smacking at the dragon dangling from the part of his body where other bits had a tendency to dangle.

"Stop! You'll hurt him!" She reached out and managed to snag one of Fitz's wings and a leg in her hands. The dragon showed no desire to let go, but a fist (Mr. Simonon's, and certainly not Mildred's) to the side of his small head dazed him enough that his jaws released and both Mildred and the creature staggered backwards into the muddier part of the road.

"What the hell is that thing?" Mr. Simonon stood doubled over, one hand held over his private area, the other stretched out towards them, warding them off. "Don't you... No!"

Fitz had twisted out of Mildred's grip and half-flapped, half-ran back to his victim for a second attack. Mr. Simonon, unwilling to be caught off guard again, kicked out at him (as best as one could kick with one hand still clutching his goods) and caught one of Fitz's wings with the edge of his heel.

Fitz, needless to say, was not pleased.

He spun and scrabbled in the mud, hissing, Mildred realized. And then there was a bright, brief flash of light, a cough of flame from Fitz's mouth. Mr. Simonon, who until that moment had seemed willing—if grudgingly so—to do battle with a creature composed of wings and claws and a snappy mouth, apparently drew the line at creatures fitted out with all of the above along with the ability to produce small blasts of fire.

And so Mr. Simonon turned and ran away.

Mildred watched him go, down the road, back the way they had come. She looked down at herself, streaked in mud, her feet slowly sinking into the wet ground. Fitz had toddled after Mr. Simonon for several yards, but once it seemed clear their erstwhile driver was not going to return, he came back towards the cart, squawking and tripping over the ruts and holes in the road.

It took her a moment to realize something. She was tired, of course, and was still half-distracted by the altercation with

Mr. Simonon, so she supposed that was why her mind was slow at piecing things together. But as the dragon sniffed and gnawed at a corner of his basket, it struck her that not once during the events of the last few minutes had Fitz made a move to attack her. All of his rage had been directed at Mr. Simonon and Mr. Simonon alone.

"Fitz?"

The creature paid her no heed, instead tugging at his blanket and attempting to construct some sort of makeshift nest out of it on the cold, damp ground. Mildred decided she could take her eyes off him (seeing as how they were his only source of food at the moment, she doubted he would run off across the countryside in a sudden and ill-judged bid for freedom) and check on Mrs. Babbinton.

Mrs. Babbinton, throughout all of the chaos of the last— Mildred blew out a breath when it dawned on her that it could not have been more than five minutes since Mr. Simonon stopped the cart—five-ish minutes, had not moved. She still sat in the back of the cart, still with her bags flanking her, still with an expression on her face that appeared distant in the shifting moonlight.

"Mrs. Babbinton?"

The housekeeper shuddered. Or shivered. Mildred couldn't quite tell the difference. So she climbed up and onto the back of the cart, opened one of her own bags, and dragged out the first piece of fabric her hand brushed across. A gown, it was. Plain and muslin, but Mildred draped it around Mrs. Babbinton's shoulders, tucking it in at the front so the older woman was cocooned in white.

"Are you all right?"

Mrs. Babbinton nodded. "I'm sorry," she said. Were there tears in her eyes? "I should have—"

"All is well." Mildred looked away, allowing her some privacy. From behind them came the sounds of Fitz snuffling in his bed. "Mr. Simonon is gone now and we can..." She looked around her. Darkness, and a muddy road, and a cart still tethered to an old horse that seemed content to stamp and twitch quietly in the night. "I think we still have a little ways to go yet."

"I can drive us," Mrs. Babbinton said, but didn't move. "If you'll give me a minute."

"Of course." She smiled even though the housekeeper wasn't looking at her. "I'll fetch Fitz and see him settled with a bit of food."

Mrs. Babbinton chuckled. The sound warmed Mildred's insides as if she had just taken a long sip of hot tea. "The poor thing's earned it, I think."

Mildred scrambled off the back of the cart again, heedless of the bunching of her skirts or the state of... well, any part of her. She was cold and the mud on her dress and face was drying to a crust and there were probably bruises forming in more places than she cared to count. But she wasn't bleeding anywhere—that she had yet noticed—none of their things had been taken, and both Fitz and Mrs. Babbinton appeared, for the most part, unscathed.

And they had a horse and a cart to take them the rest of the way to Exley Hall. So, all in all things were not as desperate as they could have been.

The task of transferring Fitz from the ground and back onto the cart was the next thing to be taken care of. Mildred decided she would not attempt to confine him again. She had no fear he would escape, and after an entire day trapped in a basket only to be knocked off the back of a cart before doing everything in his power to protect them from Mr. Simonon, she thought he deserved all of the space to sprawl that he could desire.

"Easy, now." She crouched down, slipped her arms beneath him—blanket and all—and picked him up from the ground. He did not protest, instead curling tighter as if prepared to snooze comfortably against her chest for the rest of the night. By the time she shifted him onto the back of the cart, Mrs. Babbinton—still wrapped in Mildred's gown—

had moved to the seat at the front and was gathering up the reins.

Mildred constructed a wall around Fitz with their bags and the remains of his basket, then tucked herself in beside him. The cart jostled forward, bumping harshly over the ruts, but settled into a more steady rhythm as Mrs. Babbinton steered them onward.

What time was it? That Mildred could worry over such a common, trivial question seemed to her a good sign. The time, how much farther it was to Exley Hall, whether Mrs. Babbinton had any of her little meat pies still stashed away inside one of her bags...

"I think we are here," Mrs. Babbinton called back over her shoulder. "Is that a gatehouse? Or are my eyes worse than I thought?"

It was a gatehouse, the sort that seemed to continue on with its existence merely for ornamental purposes, as it lacked the necessary items such as a gate (only an empty stone arch curved over the lane that veered off from the road) and a house (there were three out of four walls still standing (or perhaps the fourth was simply so overgrown with vegetation that Mildred could not make it out in the dark) and part of a roof that looked to be partially caved in) to categorize it as functional. But Mrs. Babbinton maneuvered the cart off the road and onto the tidy lane (proof that someone was keeping some part of the property intact) that they hoped would lead them the rest of the way to Exley Hall.

If it had been daylight, there would probably have been lovely copses of trees or streams to look at as they rolled along. Perhaps a folly on the peak of some distant hill or an artificial lake with swans skimming across its surface. But Mildred's eyes squinted for a view of nothing more than lights in windows and the bulk of shadow denoting a house set against the horizon.

The lights came soon enough. Mildred hoped that meant

it wasn't as late as she feared, and also that there would be someone still awake to give them welcome. Mrs. Babbinton drove up to the front entrance and was able to convince their horse to stop only a few yards past it. In the pale moonlight, Mildred saw the lines of a wide staircase, columns, and several other features indicating that this was a rather large estate meant to invoke awe in its guests. The most Mildred could feel was relief, and she sat still for a moment, waiting for the echo of the cart's sway to leave her limbs, for her to trust herself to shimmy down and place her feet on the ground without fear of immediately tripping over them.

Mrs. Babbinton, her former confidence returned to her during their drive, walked up the front steps and knocked—which is another way of saying she pounded the side of her balled-up fist—on the door. It took three rounds of knocking for someone to greet them. The door opened fully, and there stood a man, still dressed for the day—thank heavens!—and holding a single candle before him.

"Are you Mr. Gorman?" Mrs. Babbinton's voice rang out against the stone walls of the house. "I am Mrs. Babbinton of Upper Plimpton, in Wiltshire. I have Miss Percy here and we are two ladies in dire need of assistance."

The volume and strength of Mrs. Babbinton's voice was a bit of a contrast to her claim of their dire need, but then Mildred walked up to the bottom step, and the small circle of candlelight was bright enough to make the state of her appearance known.

"Miss Percy?" The man stepped out from the doorway, holding up his candle so the light would not blind her. "Miss Mildred Percy?"

Mildred spread her arms apart, her palms open. "In the flesh. But we are looking for Mr. Gorman?"

"As you see." He glanced back at Mrs. Babbinton and then again looked at Mildred. "Is there something wrong?" He shook his head. "What happened? Wait, no. This is impolite of me to keep you out here. Come inside and I'll have someone take care of your things."

"No," Mildred said, even as she moved forward onto the bottom step. Closer, and she could make out Mr. Gorman's features more clearly. He was an older gentleman, gray and lined, but still sporting a full head of hair and a trim figure. But what she paid her attention to was his eyes. Were they the kind of eyes that were prepared to see what she was about to show him? "I need you to come here first."

Wariness from him then. Well, she had expected that. "My great uncle," she went on, hoping that if she filled the silence, he would not have time to create any independent scenarios of his own. "Mr. Forthright, left an inheritance to me. You know this, of course?"

"Yes, I helped him put everything together. I was aware of all his last wishes. But what—?"

She turned and walked towards the cart. When he did not immediately follow, she waved her hand for him to join her.

"Just there," she said, motioning for him to stop when he was about two paces away. "I don't want you to startle him. He can be truculent when he's startled."

She climbed onto the back of the cart, unconcerned with how she probably looked from behind with the glow of candlelight illuminating her muddy bottom. She shifted the bags aside, and with that small adjustment Fitz's eyes slitted open, a gleam of gold gazing up at her. Trusting her, she thought.

"A little closer, if you please. And hold up the light. He's rather dark." She wanted to keep her attention on Fitz, to watch for any sign from him that he might become defensive at the approach of an unknown individual. But curiosity won out, and she turned her head and studied Mr. Gorman's face, looking for the precise moment when understanding swept over him.

"Oh, dear Lord. Is that...?" A wide-eyed gaze sought out Mildred. She noticed that his hand holding the candle had begun to tremble.

"I thought it was nothing more than a large rock, at first. Like the geodes, the ones with the crystals inside." She laughed, sounding a little hysterical to her own ears. "We talked about cracking it open for the local schoolchildren, so they could see what was inside. But then it…" She licked her lips. How long had it been since she'd last had something to drink, because her tongue felt like it had taken on a coating of sand. "It hatched," she finished, and knelt down beside Fitz. She laid her hand on him, protectively, and because at that moment she needed to be reminded of the reality of him. That he would not up and drift away like a puff of smoke.

Mr. Gorman took a tentative step forward. Surely there would be more of a reaction from him than this, she thought. More swearing, more utterances of disbelief, more claims that she was playing some manner of trick on him. But instead he set the bottom of the candle holder on the edge of the cart and he slowly shook his head.

"He was right."

Mildred's thumb stroked one of the ridges on Fitz's back. In return, the dragon pushed his warm nose against the underside of her wrist. "Who was?" she asked, when Mr. Gorman fell into silence.

"Charles–" He stopped himself. His voice had thickened, Mildred noticed, and she gave him another moment. "Mr. Forthright, I mean. He was always taken up with such fancies, and I didn't encourage him, but I never took the trouble to restrain him either. What harm could it be, I thought. For him to believe in…" He smiled. His lips trembled. "But in this, Miss Percy, of all things," he paused, and looked up at her. Only for a moment, before his gaze drifted down towards the dragon. "In this, he had the right of it."

CHAPTER TWENTY-TWO

There has been some question as to whether dragons are warm-blooded creatures or cold-blooded, as though they can be neatly stored away into one category or the other. But just because you will find a single dragon dozing on a warm rock in the sun does not mean there are not a dozen others of a different breed sheltering in a cold, damp cave deep among the snow-capped peaks.

In short, there is little about dragons that can be summed up in a few brief words of taxonomy, though I do believe it to be a universal fact that they will seek out good food and comfort whenever it is available to them.

-from Chapter Eighteen of Miss Percy's Pocket Guide (to the Care and Feeding of British Dragons)

Never again would Mildred take for granted the reviving qualities of a hot bath, a warm meal, clean clothes, and a soft bed. She recalled little of the previous night, after Mr. Gorman had brought them inside and she and Mrs. Babbinton had sagged with relief at the realization that finally—finally!—they had reached their destination and the threat of further travel, of mud, of an army of Mr. Simonons was pushed far, far away where it could no longer touch them.

Fitz had been brought in as well. Mildred remembered that, if only because she had been the one to carry him inside herself. They made up a bed for him in her room, a hastily constructed thing consisting of cushions and blankets and a pile of rags for him to burrow into as he wished.

He was the first thing Mildred looked for when she woke up the next morning. Eyes bleary with sleep, mind muddled about where she was and how she had arrived there, she sat up in bed—a large bed, piled with pillows and draped with curtains and so unlike her own bed at home that she wondered how she had managed to find any decent rest in the last seventeen years—and looked towards the mound of blankets and cushions and rags in front of the fire.

An empty mound of blankets and cushions and rags.

Her heart jolted. She threw back the covers, meaning to leap from the bed and search around every corner of the room (also much larger than her room at home, and so would make for a longer search) but stopped when she noticed the weight on her right foot.

She looked at the bed. There, curled up on top of the blankets, his head resting on the ridge of her ankle, was Fitz. The blankets, she saw on closer inspection, bore small tears from his climb up the side of the bed, and a few more where he had obviously turned himself around in a circle and flexed his claws (as he had a tendency to do) before falling asleep.

"Oh, you've…well." She flopped back onto the pillows, a movement she immediately regretted as it brought to life a dozen aches and pains that bloomed through her joints. And her muscles. And her very breath, she thought, if such a thing were possible.

She stayed like that for some time. It was easy enough to do. The bed was soft as a cloud (No, not like a cloud. Clouds were cold and wet and certainly did not give off a faint scent of lavender every time she moved) and the room was lovely, all pale blues and white trim, continuing on with the sky theme Mildred's thoughts wanted to follow along this morning. And there was sunlight coming through the windows. Multiple windows, lined up like soldiers on a wall that had space enough to boast multiple windows.

And then she couldn't stand it anymore. She needed to get up, unless she wished to have an accident in the bed and give the servants additional labor they did not need. A slow wiggle of her foot and she extricated herself from beneath Fitz's chin. She took care of her needs, wrapped a shawl around her shoulders, and crossed to the nearest window.

A beautiful window. Clean, large, and with a wide sill that invited one to sit on it, their feet tucked beneath themselves, a book in their lap and a plate of something (cakes, cheese, cakes with cheese) within arm's reach. She leaned forward and peered out at the grounds—there were grounds, plural, and not merely a garden with a wall and a few trees marking the corners—surrounding the house.

She had no recollection of them from any earlier time in her life. The grounds, that is. She could remember spending brief amounts of time with her Great Uncle Forthright, but had he visited them at her father's home, or had they travelled here? Children's memories, it seemed, were not shaped by the how and why of various events, but rather existed as shards of feelings and sensations, small fragments of a greater picture that would never be fully pieced together again.

She blinked up at the sky, measuring its place above the horizon. Far above the horizon. Behind her, Fitz still snoozed on the end of her bed. But she needed to dress, and find food, and take care of all those little details that foisted themselves upon her as irritatingly necessary things.

Mildred was halfway through dressing when a knock sounded on the door. "Come in," she said, all of her most important parts covered enough that she honestly could not bring herself to care if it was a man or woman who entered while she still struggled with the buttons at the front of her gown.

It was Mrs. Babbinton who entered, her head appearing first, and then the rest of her figure side-stepping into the room like a crab adorned in a cap and lace. "Oh, you're up!" She closed the door quickly behind her, as if there might have been a servant lingering in the hall, waiting for a glimpse of something they were not supposed to see. "But our little friend is still asleep, I notice." She walked up to the end of the bed, her hands clasped tight before her. "I looked in on you earlier," she said, her voice now dropped nearer to a whisper. "And when I saw that he had maneuvered his way up to be with you, I thought it best not to disturb the poor dear. He had as rough a day as any of us yesterday, perhaps even the worst of it."

Mildred came up to stand beside her, her fingers still fussing with the last of her buttons before she clicked her tongue against the back of her teeth and gave up. "I do not believe it an exaggeration to say that he saved us last night. Or at least made quicker work of it than either of us would have on our own."

"Mmm," Mrs. Babbinton said. A thinking sound. Mildred let her think, for she seemed to need it. "Last night," she went on, after taking her moment for thinking. "I am sorry. I should have done more to help you, but when that man came around, when he threatened us, I simply—"

Mildred set her hand on Mrs. Babbinton's arm. She thought of several things to say, words that in her head sounded inspiring and empathetic. But she did not know what comfort Mrs. Babbinton would find from them, or if Mildred's wanting to say them was more as a balm for her own wounds leftover from the previous night.

"But you should have breakfast." Mrs. Babbinton turned to Mildred and reached out to fix her last button. "Mr. Gorman is waiting for you in the dining room. I've already eaten, so I'll stay up here in case Fitz should wake while you're away. I wouldn't wish for him to open his eyes and find himself in a new place and without any familiar faces to greet him."

And so Mildred checked her buttons (all lined up and appropriately fastened) and her hair (brushed and pinned back, which was a feat in itself) and went in search of Mr. Gorman and the dining room. She realized as she made her way downstairs that she should have first asked where the dining room was, as Exley Hall was a large enough house to leave her staring at rows of doors without having any idea what was behind any of them. But it was her nose that turned out to be her rescuer, saving her the embarrassment of searching for a servant to guide her in the right direction, as the smells of bacon and toast and coffee pulled her along as effectively as a ship in chase of the North Star.

Mr. Gorman was waiting for her. He stood when she entered (She never much cared for that piece of etiquette, dictating that a gentleman must stand when a lady entered the room. She understood the mechanics behind it—the man rising so that he might be at the ready to aid her with whatever she should wish—but it always made her think the men in question were contemplating running away at the sight of a new female encroaching upon their space) and inclined his head in greeting.

"Miss Percy, I hope you slept well?"

She took a few steps forward. There was food set out on the table, platters of things under domes and a steaming pot of coffee (she still disliked coffee as much as ever, but she could not argue with the fact that she would greatly be in need of its services today) and she could not take her eyes off them. "I did, thank you. Though I believe I slept quite a while longer than intended."

He waved away her words and pulled out a chair for her. "If you had dealt with only half of what you told me about last night, I would not begrudge you hiding away upstairs for a full week or more to recover."

She sat. He placed a plate in front of her and began filling it at her direction (eggs, yes... sausages, no... bacon, yes... toast, maybe—oh, with honey? Then, yes) and then returned to his own seat once her breakfast was managed.

"So," he said, sitting forward as she ate, his elbows on the remains of his folded newspaper and his hands clasped before him. "How is it that I can be of help to you, Miss Percy?"

She almost choked on her bacon. Not that his question caught her by surprise. In fact, it was the calm delivery of his words, as if they were speaking of nothing more than some local political matter or whether it should be beef or lamb for dinner the next day. Certainly not a tone of voice she would expect of one inquiring as to what could be done about the dragon sleeping at the foot of her bed one floor away.

"I hardly know where to even begin," she said, fiddling with a corner of toast on her plate.

Mr. Gorman placed his hands flat on the tabletop, smoothing out the edges of his abandoned newspaper. It seemed the both of them needed an occupation for their agitated fingers. "Then let's return to the beginning, shall we? Every detail you neglected to tell me last night, allow us to parse through them and see what we can come up with."

And so she did. Everything she had told him when they'd first arrived had been a random selection of facts and events, delivered out of order and from a mind muddled with tiredness and hunger and lingering fright after the attack from Mr. Simonon. So this morning she went through from the very beginning (the arrival of the letter announcing the death of her Great Uncle Forthright) through the arrival of the trunk, Mr. Wiggan's involvement, the discovery of the egg they did not realize was an egg, the hatching (Mr. Gorman especially enjoyed this bit, listening to it with the rapture of an eager child with his eyes wide and his chin resting in his hands), the ensuing growth and care of Fitz—

"You named him Fitz?"

Mildred shrugged. "Well, the children did. Fitzwilliam is his full name, but it just became easier to call him Fitz after... Are you laughing?"

He was laughing, mouth pressed into a straight, straining line, shoulders shaking with mirth. And there was a glistening of moisture in his eyes he wiped away with a brush of his knuckles. "I beg your pardon, and I do not mean to make light of any of your travails of the last several weeks. The stress you must have endured, but I cannot help but imagine what Mr. Forthright would think of all this."

"You believe he would look at it as a great joke?"

Mr. Gorman's face grew serious, though some shimmer remained at the corners of his eyes. "No, not at all. He would be ecstatic, I think, to discover that something he held such a great amount of faith in would prove itself to be real, to be tangible."

"But you did not have as much faith as him?" Mildred ventured, dragging a crumb of bacon through some of the honey still puddled on her plate. (Why someone had not yet developed a breakfast centered around various types of meat and a pot of honey in which to dip them, she could not fathom.)

"I will be honest and admit I did not have any faith in things such as..." He made a brief flapping motion with his hands. "But he was determined to prove that such creatures not only existed at one time—not entirely difficult, as we can dig into the roots of the earth and find the remains of all manner of fantastic beasts—but that they still possessed the capabilities of living among us today."

She mulled over that for a minute, while she licked honey from the corners of her mouth and surreptitiously wiped her sticky fingers with her napkin. Some things seemed easier to be held up as truth if they were merely stories passed down or fragments of bones and teeth dug up from underground. But to be faced with something extraordinary, a living and breathing creature standing as proof that the world around them was not near as small and known as it appeared?

The rest of her story dwindled towards its end, Fitz's penchant for sneezing out sparks at inopportune moments, his ability to escape his pen and set small cottages belonging to elderly sisters on fire duly mentioned. And then she came to the arrival of Mr. Hawthorne in Upper Plimpton, trailing his stories of the wonderful relationship he had shared with Mr. Forthright like flower petals tossed liberally from a little girl's basket.

"I have no idea who Mr. Hawthorne is," Mr. Gorman said, and sipped his coffee.

Mildred leaned forward, peering closely at Mr. Gorman's face as if she could possibly detect some lie written into his features. "Are you certain? Were there no letters, no–"

He shook his head. "I have seen no such correspondence, neither did Mr. Forthright make any mention of this Mr. Hawthorne at any point in his life. If there was any kind of acquaintance there, then it was an imagined one and all on Mr. Hawthorne's side."

"So he lied." It didn't come as shocking of a pronouncement as perhaps it should have. She thought back over everything Mr. Hawthorne had told her, every word and phrase choreographed to elicit as much sympathy from his listeners as could be garnered. At least that was how his stories sounded to her now, framed with the truth that it had all been a clever, charming tapestry of falsehoods. "He wanted the egg. I'm sure of it. But I cannot imagine how he came to even be aware of its existence in the first place."

"Well, Mr. Forthright did not come across it on his own, digging it up in the garden along with the roses. He returned from a trip to London with it, oh… six years ago? Seven? Hmm, perhaps longer than that." Mr. Gorman's gray brows pulled together with the effort of thinking back over too many years. "Said that he won it in a game from a drunkard, though I always doubted the veracity of his story. But he was almost gleeful when he revealed it to me. I think he hoped I would share in his excitement. And I did, in a way, but not because of what he believed the thing to be, but rather because it brought him such joy."

His eyes lost focus then, misting over as he slipped away from her, from the present moment, back towards some scene in which she suspected her great uncle was still alive and the two of them shuffled through the house together, like a king and his steward, revelling in the pleasure of overseeing their little kingdom.

Mildred hesitated. Her next question was one that had plagued her since the beginning of all this, since she had first read her uncle's letter and a small voice had piped up in the back of her mind, one continually asking, "But why give it to me?"

This succeeded in drawing Mr. Gorman from his revery. "Beg your pardon?"

Mildred hated having to ask questions over again, as if she only possessed enough confidence for one recitation and anything beyond that was delving into reserves she did not have. "The egg. Why did he leave it to me? Why not my sister? Or you? Or some fellow in London with whiskers and a beard who belongs to a society of great learned men and scientists? Why... me?"

His expression became what Mildred could best describe as 'perplexed.' And she described it as such because of his creased brow, the narrowing of his eyes indicating a question of his own being formed behind them, and his lips parting as if words were ready and waiting to bound out of his mouth (as soon as they could manage to organize themselves properly before their jaunt into sound). "Why *not* you, Miss Percy?"

"Well." And she imagined her own face contorting to match his. How could he return her question with one of his own, and why did it have to be that one in particular?

Look at me, she wanted to say. Look at the lines on her

face, the gray in her hair. Look at the fact that she was a woman, unmarried and unwanted by so many. Look at her insignificance, and there, she thought, would be the answer he sought.

"I do not presume to know you well," Mr. Gorman said, his words spoken slowly, chosen with care. "But I do know that Mr. Forthright always thought highly of you. He often said you had the spirit of an adventurer, that he saw it in you when you were a child." He took a breath, and he turned his cup between his hands, his fingers long and clean and elegant. "Beyond that, I must add from what I've witnessed myself that I believe you to be a strong, capable woman. You have faced a great deal of adversity, and yet here you are: calm and composed, only hours after facing an ordeal that would have felled any lesser man."

Mildred's own hands had found their way into her lap, her fingers pulling at the edge of her napkin until she feared she might have it unravelled into a skein of thread before the end of the meal. "But I've not accomplished any of it on my own. All through this, there has been Mr. Wiggan, and Mrs. Babbinton, and without them–"

She stopped speaking at the look on his face. Not because he was laughing this time (though there was a spark of something akin to amusement in his eyes) but because her own words sounded small and pathetic when reflected back to her in his expression.

"Mr. Forthright chose wisely, I think." And then he picked up his coffee, and he took a sip.

CHAPTER TWENTY-THREE

There is an instinct in dragons—as with many other animals—that draws them back to certain places over and again, no matter how far they have traveled or for how long they were away. Or is it more than instinct that brings about that longing to return to a place they have been before, an ability to harbor memories that we have yet to apply to them?

-from Chapter Five of Miss Percy's Pocket Guide (to the Care and Feeding of British Dragons)

Mr. Gorman assured Mildred that the servants employed at Exley Hall were loyal to both him and the late Mr. Forthright, a careful way of saying that if she were to take Fitz down to the kitchen and then out onto the grounds—in view of everyone established there—word would not eventually wend its way to the neighbors that there was a winged animal that resembled every medieval depiction of a demon currently in residence at the estate. And so Mildred found herself outdoors after breakfast, her hem hiked up almost to her knees as she stood on the bank of a small stream and watched Fitz splash around in the cold water that burbled over the rocks.

She had not thought a creature with a propensity for spitting out bursts of fire along with the occasional sneeze or cough would take to water with as much excitement as Fitz demonstrated, but as her experience with fire-breathing (or at least spark-coughing) dragons was limited (in other words, she knew of their mythological existence from various fairy tales and the occasional flag, but nothing else) she decided that if he wanted to spend his day frolicking in a chill stream, then she was not about to step in and put a stop to his play.

This was how things were when Mrs. Babbinton found her, bearing a basket over her arm and the ends of her shawl flapping in the considerable breeze. There was a bench beneath one of the trees (some kind of chestnut, as its unmistakable debris was scattered across the ground and had been the cause of two turns of Mildred's ankles and a string of muttered complaints) and so the housekeeper took a seat and began sifting through the contents of the basket as if she had not packed it up herself a few minutes before.

"I've some bacon here for Fitz, if he is interested."

It would have to be tested at a later point in time whether Fitz had already begun to recognize certain words contained in the English language—such as 'meat', 'food', 'pork', 'ham', 'bacon', 'I shall throw this away if no one else will eat it', and 'buttered potatoes'—or if merely the sound and smell of food being unwrapped in his presence was enough to bring him scurrying forward.

He tottered up the small embankment, wings dripping and rivulets of water sparkling on the ridges of his back. He tripped once on a tree root, righted himself with a few quick flaps of his wings—flaps that boosted him several inches up and forward, Mildred noticed with her heart in her throat—then scraped at the base of the bench with his claws until Mrs. Babbinton took pity on him and dropped several pieces of fatty bacon onto the ground.

"I wonder how proficient a flyer he will be," Mrs. Babbinton said, in the same way one would guess at a child's potential height once they were grown. "Will it only be short distances, like a chicken? Or will he be able to soar and fly high like some great bird, an owl or a hawk perhaps?"

It was not a question Mildred wanted to consider. (A slight correction would be that it was something Mildred considered frequently, and even occasionally allowed herself to daydream about. The thought of a full-grown dragon—her imaginings were a bit hazy when it came to details such as size—casting its shadow across the fields as if circled overhead... And then those same thoughts would stumble over the reality of reining in something the size of—possibly!—a small horse with wings that could leap off into the air whenever it pleased and those pesky considerations became a touch less dreamlike in tone.)

"I suppose his wings would have to grow a great deal larger in order to fully lift him off the ground," Mildred said, while pushing away the fascinating mingling of horror and hilarity that came with the image of that same full-grown dragon fluttering madly no more than a few feet above the earth. "Though he is very light for his size, as if he is made for flight."

She sat down on the end of the bench, the basket between her and Mrs. Babbinton. There were sandwiches and fruit—much of the latter out of season, but Exley Hall boasted both a greenhouse and an orangery—and so the two ladies feasted as if the weather were warm enough for strawberries to be plucked directly from the sun-drenched fields.

Fitz soon fell asleep after his meal of bacon and sandwich crusts, curled up in a patch of sunlight that disappeared behind a cloud only seconds after he closed his eyes. Mildred sat as near to the edge of the bench as she could without risking falling off the seat entirely. She envied Fitz, that ability to find rest and relaxation anywhere, similar to the talent many children possessed to fall asleep in the most awkward of positions and then endure being carried to their beds like so much baggage without even catching their breath or fluttering their eyes open.

Now that Mildred was sufficiently fed and rested after

her exhaustion the previous day, her own anxiety took that as a sign that it should make a return, as if it feared she might be lonely without it. Yes, it was a lovely day. Yes, there was delicious food to be had (the strawberries were juicy and so sweet that an accompanying cake might not have been able to overpower them). Yes, the grounds were picturesque enough to be rendered on canvas through the mediocre talents of any unmarried lady with too many pots of watercolors at her disposal. But Exley Hall was not her home (neither was it her Great Uncle Forthright's home any longer, and while Mr. Gorman was incredibly kind to allow her to stay, he was not family, and a stranger to her until only the evening before) and she could not sit on a lovely bench beside a lovely stream on a lovely day and pretend that all of the difficulties that had brought her here had somehow floated away as soon as she set foot on the grounds.

First, there was Fitz. As adorably small and feisty as he was, he was not a kitten or a bird to be treated as a pet. He would grow, eventually to a size Mildred tended not to make an attempt at predicting. The playful nips of his toothless mouth and the small flames that sputtered from his open jaws would no longer be disregarded as interesting characteristics of a rare beast, but rather traits that would elevate him to the level of Monster, the sort that called for a capital 'M' rather than a letter of the paltry lowercase variety.

Something would have to be done with him. Yet Mildred could not train her thoughts to move beyond that first notion. He could not stay in Upper Plimpton, waddling about the garden behind the vicarage waiting for Mrs. Babbinton to toss another batch of scraps in his direction and setting fire to the occasional house. And every time she considered a future for him in London, her mind careened to a halt at thoughts of Great Fires (more capital letters) and rare, exotic animals chained up outside the Tower, left to be gawked at and mocked by bored passersby.

And when they did find a place for him—*if* they found a place for him—what would become of her? Would she return to Ashby Lodge, to her small room at the back of the house with its slanted ceilings and perpetual smell of damp? Could she simply fall back into her previous life, looking after the children, running her sister's errands, letting herself slowly diminish?

She stood up, agitation in all her limbs. To the edge of the stream she went, crouching down to gather a few twigs and small stones to toss into the water. But instead of releasing them into the trickling current, she began pitching them further into the trees, the rocks pinging off trunks and branches, frightening off a few birds and one irate squirrel.

When she was finished, she stood with her arms hanging loosely at her sides, her chest heaving over each successive breath. If there had been a boulder within reach, she might have contemplated hefting it off the ground and throwing it over her shoulder as if the repopulation of the earth depended on it. Rage, frustration... What was it that made her arms twitch as if she wanted nothing more than to punch at the air? Men had such pursuits set aside for themselves, boxing and fencing and all sorts of games women were not supposed to enjoy. But how was one to find release for their agitation through drawing or embroidery? Unless she were to imagine her needle was really a miniature sword and the thread the entrails of her enemies—

But that much was preposterous. She did not have any enemies, at least not in the 'fight and stab or at least deliver a swift kick to the shins' kind of way. Though there was Mr. Hawthorne, who—while not precisely someone she considered an enemy in the truest sense of the word—had come into her sister's house, and had lied about his acquaintance with her Great Uncle Forthright in order to take something that was unequivocally hers.

Well, she still did not have absolute proof that it was

Fitz's egg Mr. Hawthorne wanted, but what else could it have been? Surely handsome—if shabby—young men did not make a habit of dragging themselves up from London in order to offer condolences to an aging spinster (especially aging spinsters who had little connection to the deceased gentleman responsible for the condolences, but for an inherited trunk stuffed with personal items and one large dragon egg).

Mildred put her hands to her brow. She had discarded her bonnet some time before—or rather, as soon as she arrived beneath the shade of the trees and her fingers could undo the drooping bow knotted beneath her chin—and now she squinted at the figure walking towards them from the direction of the house. It was Mr. Gorman, making long strides across the lawn while clutching something—or several somethings—beneath his right arm. He hailed them as he stepped beneath the trees, and Mildred noticed an edge of reservation lending a shadow to the otherwise open gregariousness of his expression.

"Miss Percy, Mrs. Babbinton." He was not wearing a hat, and so the dip of his chin in greeting allowed Mildred a better view of the gray streaked through his dark hair. If she had been possessed of less manners, she might have been tempted to inquire as to his age. He appeared to be at least over sixty years old, though the energy with which he tackled everything belied the lightening of his hair and the slight stoop that had already begun to round his shoulders forward. By all accounts, her Great Uncle Forthright had been the same, a man unaffected by the years accumulating behind him, gifted with good health and a vivacity that many people the same age—that rare group that lived long enough to see the same age—did not share.

Small wonder that the two men had seemed to get on so well together, and at Mr. Gorman's smile she felt a tug of affinity towards him, as if by appreciating his kindness she could somehow posthumously repay her uncle for all the years she had missed with him.

"I come bearing gifts," Mr. Gorman said, retrieving the items—a thick stack of thin books, looped together with a ribbon as if they were indeed a present—from beneath his arm and holding them out to her. "They were Mr. Forthright's," he added as Mildred reached out to take them.

"Oh?" This news alone elicited no great reaction from her. The trunk her uncle had sent to her had been half-filled with so many papers and books that another batch added to the collection seemed more superfluous than anything.

"These are his..." Mr. Gorman closed his mouth, then cleared his throat, then smiled again (one of those strained smiles that was almost a grimace at having swallowed a particularly unpleasant flavor of insect). "His private journals," he finished, lending each word enough weight to scatter them like pebbles at her feet.

"Oh." As she took them, Mr. Gorman seemed to follow along after them, his weight shifting onto the balls of his feet until he suddenly snapped back as if a tether had been severed.

"They were left to me," he went on, his nose twitching with the urge to sneeze or perhaps to fend off some emotion he would rather not express in front of others. "But I believe —I *hope*—they will be in safe hands with you."

She held them to her chest. It was a foreign sensation, to have someone trust her with the care and keeping of something, and not merely because there was no one better to be had at the moment. (Such thoughts had often played through her mind while entertaining—feeding, changing, teaching, raising—her sister's children. At first, there had been a touch of honor to the position, Mildred pleased to believe herself chosen specially by Diana and Mr. Muncy because they wanted the best for their burgeoning family. It did not take long, however (approximately three years, seven months, four days, and eleven hours, give or take) for her to realize that she had only been depended upon because she was the best choice from 1) a pecuniary viewpoint and 2) her availability upon the loss of their father and her home.)

"Thank you?" She hadn't meant it to sound like a question, as if she was unsure of her gratitude or whether any was even owed to him.

He nodded, the lines at the corners of his mouth deepening. "He was not a secretive man, Mr. Forthright. But there were a few things he would not have wanted bandied about publicly." A small lift of his eyebrows, and there was the communication of 'and so it surely is for all of us' written in those twin curves of graying facial hair. "I hope you will not judge him too harshly."

"No, of course not." She glanced down at them, their corners worn, the fine leather of their covers rubbed softer in places by heavy use. "Thank you," she said again, and this time without any hint of question in her voice.

"Now, then." Mr. Gorman clapped his hands together, relief clearing away the shadows from his features. "There was another matter I wished to speak with you about—both of you," he said, turning and making sure to include Mrs. Babbinton in the conversation with that searching glance. "Upon Mr. Forthright's death, I found myself left with the responsibility of keeping charge of this place. Because of that I am taking it upon myself to issue an invitation for you to remain here for as long as either of you should wish. Not only as guests of the late Mr. Forthright, carrying over beyond the time of his passing, but as guests of my own."

"Well, I must say that is very kind of you!" Mrs. Babbinton spoke first, while Mildred still wrapped her thoughts around the invitation. "And if it weren't for Mr. Wiggan, I would happily accept. But I should not like to leave him alone for too long, and I did give my word that I would not stay away for longer than two or three days at the very most." She nodded towards Mildred before speaking again. "Of course, I cannot answer for Miss Percy."

Mildred was not even certain she could answer for

herself. She blinked and stammered and then fell silent. It was the wonder of it that took her words away, that faint almost impossible imagining of being someplace that wasn't Ashby Lodge for an extended period of time.

What would she even do? What *did* people do when they were not living—she almost allowed the word 'withering' to enter her thoughts but did not want to be accused of harboring an inner monologue with a flair for the dramatic—beneath the shadow of a domineering sibling? (And was it so much that her sister was domineering by nature, or that Mildred had been too permissive in allowing herself to be domineered? Could a particular mode of behavior be cultivated beyond the boundaries of one's usual scope of character? And why was she even pondering all of the intricacies of her relationship with Diana when there was a babbling stream and a sleeping dragon and the smell of bacon sandwiches still heavy in the air?)

"Um," Mildred said, in order to fill the silence (or at least the lack of voices overlaying the babbling stream and snoring dragon and digesting sandwiches). Diana would not like it. The staying part, that is. Mildred would, of course, have to write a letter informing her sister that she had no plans to immediately return to Upper Plimpton. It would not be an easy letter to compose. Not necessarily because Mildred felt any sort of heartsickness at the thought of being away from her family for longer than she was usually apart from them (that being about as long as it took her to walk into town for errands and such) but rather because she could not think of a way to phrase a determination to stay in Warwickshire that would not set her sister into the highest of dudgeons.

But then, Mildred would not be there to bear the brunt of Diana's displeasure. She felt sorry for the children and for Mr. Muncy (a man with whom she had shared a home for nearly two decades and yet could not consider her relationship with him as anything closer than 'polite acquaintance') as they would be the ones to catch every volley of her sister's temper. But she could not go on existing as a buffer between Diana and the rest of the family, nor could she remain there forever as a measure of comparison against which her sister could always feel superior.

And with the culmination of that thought, Mildred realized she had almost made her decision. But then she thought of Mr. Wiggan, and her determination to stay at Exley Hall diminished a little. It seemed she had only just found such true friendship with him, her visits to the vicarage and the hours spent with him in his study often becoming the highlight of her days. She would miss him more than anything else, she realized. The deep timber of his voice, the tousled splay of his hair after he had run his fingers through it. Those same fingers brushing across her skirt, and the way his eyes... just his eyes, as they always were.

"I will write to my sister and tell her that I accept your invitation, but I cannot see myself staying for more than a few weeks at the most. But you are certain you would not mind my staying here for a little while?"

Mr. Gorman spread his hands wide. "If it were up to me, I would tell you to stay forever. I had even argued with Mr. Forthright that perhaps he should have left the estate to someone in his family. To you, in fact. But he insisted on leaving Exley Hall to me, I suspect because I have known no other home for the last twenty years. And yet, I would consider it an honor if you would always consider it as a second home to yourself, and as a place boasting a bit more room for your growing friend to enjoy."

Mildred looked at Fitz, still sleeping in his patch of shifting sunlight. Indeed, it was difficult not to look at him more than was needed. The sun played across his scales, bringing out an iridescent gleam beneath the bronze and dark brown, while his tail twitched in his sleep; Mildred hoped the latter was in time with the cadence of his dreams.

"Oh, you are too kind." And she said it without exaggeration, every word sincere.

"You can help sort through the last of your uncle's things, as well," Mr. Gorman added, smiling more broadly now that she had accepted his offer. "That is, if you don't mind spending a few hours looking over decades' worth of... well, I will admit it is mostly rubbish. Mr. Forthright had a tendency to treasure everything and discard nothing. Sometimes I suspect that is the only reason he kept me around for so long." A slight fading of his smile, a crinkling at the corners of his eyes to match the small furrow in his brow. Memories, there. Or grief. Or perhaps, like most matters of human emotion, a complex mixture of the two. "But I'm sure there will be a few gems scattered here and there that one can find if we look close enough."

The journals felt warm in her hands. Like dormant secrets waiting to be read again and resurrected through her attention to them. "I should return to the house, then. Make a start on my letters." More than only the letter to her sister, she realized. She would have to write to Mr. Wiggan as well, and have Mrs. Babbinton carry it home with her. And then she experienced a twinge of regret? Sadness? She was not skilled enough with her own feelings to decipher that pang of *something* that tightened in her abdomen at the renewed thought of not seeing Mr. Wiggan for several weeks. That he would not be witness to Fitz's progress over that time—and considering his precedent for growth, it would not be minimal—and that she would not have her conversations with him...

Mr. Gorman was pleasant, yes. But Mr. Wiggan was...

Well, what was he? An acquaintance? Oh, much more than that. A friend, most assuredly. Perhaps even a confidante, seeing as how he was one of the few people who knew about Fitz, had been there from the first crack in his shell. And perhaps it was because of his chosen vocation—

being a man of God and inclined to focus his attention on others (or perhaps it was a facet of his own character, regardless of whether he stood behind a pulpit or stood laying bricks)—but he had always succeeded in making her feel visible. As if her life, her relationships, her joys and fears were sketched out across her skin as clear as a map for his perusal.

She tucked the books beneath her arm, snapped her bonnet up from the ground and plopped it on her head, and gathered up Fitz's sleeping form into her arms—or at least into the one arm that was completely free. He struggled a bit and nearly opened his eyes, but settled against her chest like a slumbering babe while she readjusted her grip on the books and tucked his head more firmly on her shoulder.

Mr. Gorman and Mrs. Babbinton both returned with her to the house, cutting a path out of the trees and across the wide expanse of lawn that sloped upwards towards Mr. Charles Forthright's former abode. They went their separate ways once inside, Mrs. Babbinton turning in the direction of the kitchen—no doubt to return the remains of their lunch—and Mr. Gorman announcing that he would be spending a few hours going over the estate's accounts, a task that had belonged to him for as long as Exley Hall had been his place of residence. Mildred carried her burdens upstairs and to her room, both the stack of books and the dragon landing on the end of the bed once she arrived (though Fitz was set onto the blankets with greater care than the books, as books generally did not possess a tendency to nip or snort or squawk when released from one's arms).

As soon as she was certain Fitz was not going to stir back to full wakefulness (it took several minutes of Mildred standing completely still whenever he moved or changed position) she sat in a chair near the open window, the books stacked in her lap. There were no dates written in them, no notes or marks that placed them at any particular time. Just pages upon pages of rambling thoughts, most of them highlighting little more than what he ate for breakfast or how sleeping with his window open one night had left him with a sore throat in the morning.

But there were more private writings, as well. Things that made her blush, that made her close the particular book she was reading in order to clear her throat and stare out the window for several minutes before she could bring herself to open it again. These were very much her Great Uncle Forthright's private thoughts and musings: scattered reminisces, wants and complaints and descriptions of his day to day life. She had thought the notebooks and journals left to her in the trunk had been lacking in organization, but these were arranged like select fragments of a jumbled and genius mind. She could see, through these windows of scrawled entries and musings, how well her uncle's personality served as a balance for Mr. Gorman's easy kindness and steadiness of character.

She read until her eyes began to ache—not a remarkable achievement in and of itself, as she had been in denial for several years over the fact that her vision was not what it once was (and there was some measure of vanity counted in her reluctance to begin wearing spectacles)—and when Fitz woke with a snort, she marked her place in her uncle's book and set it aside.

Fitz yawned and stretched, his forelegs pushing out while his toes and claws splayed outward, displaying their sharp points. Mildred thought it a bit overdone on the dragon's part, showing off in such a manner, as the shredded state of the blankets served well enough to highlight just how sharp those claws could be when he chose to utilize them.

"You're probably thirsty," she said to him, as she had taken to speaking to him more and more as he grew.

His response was to raise his head and blink at her drowsily, then to let out an impertinent squeak when she had the audacity to set the dish of water—poured from her pitcher on the dressing table—on an uncarpeted portion of floor near the fire, rather than place it beside him where he could enjoy the prospect of not moving in order to have his drink.

And with that little chore, a vision of what the next few weeks could be played out in her mind. Easy days of taking care of Fitz and watching him grow—while still pretending against the untenable truth that he would soon become too large to treat as a pet with little snacks of cold bacon and saucers of water. Learning more of her uncle's life and studies here at Exley Hall. Enjoying an existence—for a few weeks, at least—that did not contain any member of her family to whom she was expected to feel beholden.

As Fitz continued to drink, Mildred wandered back to her windowside chair and picked up one of the books she had yet to read through. Its thoughts seemed as scattered as all the others, but she thumbed through the pages, her gaze catching on a word here and there, nothing remarkable at first glance, until—this use of the word 'until' should probably be italicized or capitalized or displayed in some way to denote its importance to the whole of the story, but we shall leave it as it is and perhaps let it sit there as a lesson that it is not always the most grand and ostentatious of things that carry the most significance—she saw the map of Wales.

Now, much like the previous use of the word 'until', finding a map of Wales sketched onto the pages of a book should not have been an exceptional occurrence. They were in England, for goodness' sake. The proximity of Wales to their own lands was an incontrovertible fact and always would be (barring a climactic event such as an earthquake or the fountains of the deep opening up and splitting their little island apart like a broken piece of crockery). But this map was sketched with extraordinary detail, a thing her Great Uncle Forthright had not been known for with most of his previous illustrations. Rivers and mountains were marked, as were more than a dozen cities and towns sprinkled like droplets of ink across the land.

And then, there was one spot indicated with a large blot from her uncle's pen. Above it, the words 'Nyth y Ddraig' were written, clear and neat as a child's copywork.

Mildred did not speak Welsh. But she knew it was Welsh, without a moment of doubt. It was a map of Wales drawn on the page and there was an overabundance of consonants in the words scrawled on top of it, so what other language could it be?

"Ddraig," she said. And very likely mispronounced to such a degree that whispers of a Welsh revolt against England and their disrespectful tongues were already sweeping through the Cambrian mountains. "Dragon," she said, feeling tentatively certain about her powers of translation. She looked at Fitz, still nosing at his water bowl but losing interest in favor of a piece of bacon wedged beneath one of his claws.

She swallowed. "Dragon."

Fitz raised his head and looked at her, as if he had been called.

"Ah," she said. And sat down again in the chair with her book.

Fitz came to her, clambering up her leg, up the side of the chair, onto her shoulders where he settled in with a considerable weight. Mildred wondered for how much longer she would be able to carry him thus, if like with Matthew and Nettie there would be a time when she could no longer pick him up with her own meager strength.

But for now, he could sit with her. It wasn't incredibly uncomfortable, though his claws did scratch when he altered his position and he had a tendency to tangle his wings in her hair if he took to gnawing at them when he was tired. But then he would settle around her neck, that soft vibration of sound from his own throat humming against her shoulders. She reached up to still the erratic flick of his tail across her cheek, the dark bronze of his scales shifting in color against her skin as she tilted her hand first one way and then the

Quenby Olson

other.

He was a rather beautiful specimen, she had to admit. She had spent a great deal of her childhood adventuring her way through the countryside, climbing trees and peering beneath old, rotted logs and the slimy rocks decorating the edges of every stream. She had familiarized herself with all sorts of slithery things, things with tails and tongues and throats that croaked or chirped or changed the pace of said chirping according to the temperature. But in all of those wanderings she had never encountered a creature whose skin could change from dun to diamond with a subtle alteration of the light.

"I wonder what the rest of you look like." It was a musing filled with more content than Mildred wished to sort through at that moment. Because it implied there were more out there like him. Perhaps an entire herd (flock? gaggle?) of dragons tucked away on some uncharted peak where it was unlikely for them to accidentally set a house on fire or bite people in places one did not speak of in polite company. "Well, I suppose we may never find out, will we?" Because as often as she reminded herself that the existence of one dragon opened up the possibility of multiple dragons flitting around somewhere, she could not seem to fully wrap her thoughts around such a concept. To her, Fitz was an anomaly, much like finding a new pair of shoes that did not give one a blister upon their first wearing or a planned picnic that did not end because of a sudden and unexpected rain shower.

And so she settled in with her uncle's notebook, along with her own notebook, and a small stub of pencil she thought she might need for jotting down any thoughts or realizations as they popped into her head. It was a quiet, comfortable way to spend the evening, and the only thing she could have wanted to make it perfect was the presence of a certain vicar she tended to miss the most during such cozy and not-quite-perfect moments.

CHAPTER TWENTY-FOUR

It is only in recent years that tales of dragons and mythological beasts have been relegated to the ranks of "mere" children's stories and fairy tales. But it is wise to remember that such stories shaped humankind's love of literature, of all manner of written work. The image of the roaming bard, gracing the ears of his listeners with an account of gods and goddesses, of Cerberus and the Minotaur, of narratives now considered as classics set aside for serious study in their original and ancient languages, is one we would do well to remember. Those tales are the foundation of us, of our very societies. And so perhaps we should not be so quick to dismiss something "fantastical" as being beneath our notice, as it would be akin to dismissing a gleaming facet of human history from our time on this earth.

-from the Prologue to Miss Percy's Pocket Guide (to the Care and Feeding of British Dragons)

It had been surprisingly easy for Mr. Hawthorne to ruin Miss Muncy's reputation, especially considering how little he had to do with the details. She had told him to hire two seats on a coach headed for Warwickshire (or thereabouts), and he had done it. She had told him not to worry about the usual trivialities such as money, and he had not. She had told him that she would pay for everything, and she did.

But it wasn't until they had nearly arrived in Stratford-upon-Avon that Reginald realized the ruination of a young woman's reputation was not a minor thing. (This sudden clarity of thought was not so much an understanding brought on by any of Reginald's own gifts of perspicacity—already scant gifts that were considerably blunted by the presence of his traveling companion—but rather because of Miss Muncy's excited and whispered declaration that this jaunt was 'exceedingly fun' which was immediately followed by another declaration along the lines of 'I can just picture Mama's face when she sees that I am gone! Oh, how vexed she will be, and with only poor Papa and my brother and sister to complain to!' ('Along the lines' in this case meaning 'direct quotation.'))

He had not thought about bringing along some kind of companion for Miss Muncy, to lend an air of respectability to the entire venture. A dowdy maid or elderly relative would have done the trick. It did not escape him that in a different situation it might have been Miss Muncy's aunt, Miss Percy, commissioned to step in and fill such a role. But instead Miss Percy had gone and run off with his inheritance and they'd been crammed into a coach for too many hours while Reginald could do nothing but wonder if he wouldn't come out of all this with Miss Muncy's father challenging him in order to satisfy the damage done to his daughter's honor.

And so Reginald attempted to think on the positive aspects of the situation, one of which being Miss Muncy's assurance that all difficulties pertaining to money would be taken care of by her. While Reginald was not sure how he felt about depending on someone else—and an unmarried young woman, at that—for the funding of this trip, it was a relief not to worry about how he would come by his next meal or if he would have to decide whether an old barn along the side of the road was a viable alternative to a room in an inn.

(To tell the truth, Reginald had absconded from the inn in Upper Plimpton without paying for two nights of his stay or three of his meals. It was an act that should have elicited greater guilt from him, but as the bed had been lumpy, as his lower legs were now covered in tiny red bites, and as the food had given him a bad enough bout of indigestion to make him consider writing out his last will and testament for about seventeen minutes at three o'clock the previous morning, the remorse was in rather short supply.)

And then there was the positive aspect of Miss Muncy herself tucked in beside him. With her smiles and elegant flutters and that one strand of soft, silky hair that continually slipped out from its pins and trailed across the side of her neck as she…

Well. Reginald blinked and cleared his throat. What had he been on about? Right, right. It was Miss Muncy's presence that made the miasma of body odor—and breath and passed gases—from the other occupants of their vehicle into things that no longer had the power to touch him. And when the coach jostled to its halt and the door opened, he unfolded himself from his seat without the expected aches and pains in his joints, held out his hand to Miss Muncy—who alighted from the coach with a slight stumble that knocked her against him—and tucked her hand into the crook of his arm as they crossed to the entrance of the inn.

They were to pretend to be husband and wife, if ever the question arose. "There should be no trouble if we simply put ourselves forward as a married couple," Miss Muncy had said at the beginning of their journey. And so they went into the inn, full of noise and more smells—the latter less to do with horses and bodies confined to close quarters for too many hours, thank goodness, and more to do with crackling fires and tallow and food—and sought out the innkeeper (who looked as all innkeepers should) with his red cheeks and slightly crooked nose, as if a reckless youth had eventually given way to responsibility and occasional bouts of harmless jollity.

"A private parlor, if you please," was Miss Muncy's order when Mr. Hawthorne was asked if they wished to have their meal in the common room with everyone else. "And would it be possible to have a tub brought upstairs to our room while we are eating? I am in dire need of a bath after all that travel."

Reginald nearly choked on his next breath. "Our room?" he stuttered once the innkeeper was out of earshot and they were being led towards the rear of the inn, where the private dining areas were kept separate from the bustle of the main space.

"Well, we cannot take two rooms," Miss Muncy pointed out without sparing a glance for him from around the brim of her bonnet. "How would that appear to others, a man and a wife reserving two separate rooms for themselves? No, no. The easiest thing is to continue on as we have begun. Anything else will draw too much attention to ourselves."

"I thought…" Reginald said. A grand claim, as there was not a single thought clanking around in the vast emptiness of his head at that moment.

Miss Muncy turned around, her eyes still wide before her pert brows pulled downward. "Oh, heavens. Dear Mr. Hawthorne. What a forward creature you must believe me to be, running across the countryside with you, and now spending the night in an inn together." She blushed prettily, as—at least in Mr. Hawthorne's estimation—she did everything prettily. "It will all turn out well. I will take the bed, and we will make certain you have a comfortable place on the floor. We shall request extra blankets and pillows and such, hmm? Build quite a little nest for you!" She patted his hand, then gave it a brief squeeze. "Now, let us eat and let us sleep. I do believe I will fall off my feet if I am not given the opportunity for a proper rest before the day is finished."

Reginald followed, pulled along like a wayward toddler on leading strings. He had not thought that they would stay the night anywhere. In his haste to catch up with Miss Percy, he had not thought much beyond getting back what was his. But sitting down to dinner with Miss Muncy, after a full day of travel, before sharing a room with her...

He gulped. Not a swallow, but a gulp. Loud and slightly painful and leaving him quietly gasping for his next breath.

Oh, and she was to have a bath as well, wasn't she? A bath. In their room. Without clothing, he suspected. As baths often went.

"Hum," he said, and pulled out a chair for Miss Muncy. And then pulled out a chair for himself. And sat. As one did. "Hum."

***

The food was tolerable, or perhaps Reginald was too famished and too distracted to lend his plate the full attention it deserved. After the meal, Miss Muncy declared her intention to retire upstairs for her bath, leaving Reginald to scuff his heels around the common room and down two tankards of ale that tasted rather more like piss than he typically cared for.

An hour, he told himself. That was what he would give her, for her bath and to see herself wrapped up in some kind of clothing again. Tucked into her bed, like a caterpillar in its chrysalis. And then the first hour slipped away, and he told himself that two hours would suffice. Another tankard of piss-adjacent ale while he sat in his chair, hunched forward over the table, watching a tin plate filled with candle stubs as they burned their way down into a puddle of cheap, ill-smelling tallow.

The people at the inn had quieted, for the most part.

Many who had paid for rooms had already disappeared to them, while others—natives of Stratford-upon-Avon and the surrounding area, Reginald assumed—had drifted back to their homes and hearths. A few men (Reginald would not gift them with the title of 'gentlemen' as they carried too much the look of farmers and tradesmen, with their sleeves rolled up on their forearms and the collars of their shirts—no waistcoats, no coats, he noted—yellowed with months of perspiration soaked into the fabric) were louder than the rest, but in a jovial sort of way that indicated they'd imbibed several rounds of ale themselves, but not so much as to lower their behavior to a level that would make anyone else in the room uncomfortable. (Though Reginald doubted the ale was of a fine enough quality to lower—or elevate, depending on the case—anyone to the level of fully inebriated, seeing as how two and a half tankards had given him little more than a vague tingling in his fingers and a rising urge to stumble outside and relieve himself on a shrubbery.)

Reginald took another sip, grimaced as it went down his throat (in a way that made his back teeth clack together) and was beginning to wonder if a third hour would be enough time for Miss Muncy to bathe and dress and fall asleep when a few words from one of the non-gentlemen at the other table caught his attention.

The words were "devil" and "black" and "wings."

Oh, and also, "two old ladies."

"E-Excuse me," he stammered, because even a small amount of drink always made him stammer, and because he was exhausted and there was also an unmarried young woman up in his room who may or may not have been bathing or wearing clothing at that moment. "I hate to interrupt, but what did you say?"

The man who had been speaking (it was Mr. Simonon, as you, the reader, may have guessed, but as Reginald was not yet aware of his identity, I, the writer, will leave you with that and forego any further physical description that would be solely for Reginald's benefit) turned around, the legs of his chair scraping dully on the floor.

Mr. Simonon was the sort of fellow who enjoyed telling a story, and the more people who engaged themselves with the task of listening to the story, the grander Mr. Simonon's performance often became. He did not stand (he would have needed an audience of at least a half dozen for him to feel comfortable delivering his oratory from a higher position) but instead he leaned forward, as if poised and ready to leap from his seat. In turn, his listeners—four, counting Reginald —drew towards him, as if the man were about to impart a secret they might not hear should they fail to give him their undivided attention.

And so he went about telling his story. In spirit, it was not much unlike what had actually occurred. A few details from the beginning bore slight alterations: the women whom he'd so magnanimously offered to drive to Exley Hall—and without payment, too!—gained a sharpness in the retelling (this counted as the sixth recitation of the tale, and with each repetition, the two women gained an untrustworthy sharpness while his own actions were subtly buffed to a shine of the heroic victim) that cast them in the clear light of villains.

Little by little, threaded through the main narrative, he mentioned the basket one of the women carried. Reginald listened for these pieces, attempting to fit them together into a picture that would eventually gain enough clarity to make sense. What did a basket have to do with anything? Was Miss Percy the one with the basket? He assumed she was, as she had been referenced as 'the younger one' (though not by a great measure). Was she carrying the stone—his stone—in the basket? And why was this man alluding to it all in such dramatic tones?

"I don't know what I did to provoke them," Mr. Simonon said, shaking his head. He sat forward, barely clinging to the edge of his seat, elbows on his knees and hands clasped loosely before him. "There I was, carrying out a good, Christian act of charity, and then all of a sudden..." His hands tightened, then came apart, fingers spread, the skin of his calloused palms stretched taut. "Eyes, peering at me through the darkness. I'd never seen red eyes before—and these... ah, they were red as the sun at its setting, red like fire and burning. I saw them looking at me, sizing me up as it were. And then the thing was upon me, flying fast as a demon, wings—" Here, he sat up straight, spreading his arms wide. "—unfurled, beating at the air with all the power of Hell behind him. I could smell it," he went on, forward again, his thumb and fingers rubbing against each other, as if he could draw a particular scent from the air with that gesture. "Sulfur and brimstone. Evil, it was. Those women were handmaidens of the Devil, I would swear my life on it."

A joke then from one of the other listeners, a man who had apparently taken in enough ale to believe his wit was a necessary component of the current conversation. (The "joke" went something along the lines of all women—wives, especially—being handmaidens of the Devil and etcetera and so forth raucous laughter ensued now let's all take another drink.)

But Reginald was not to be deterred by feeble attempts at humor. He scooted his own chair further into the circle of assembled men (*still* not gentlemen, by any means) and cleared his throat in the way persons often clear their throat when the intention is to inject themselves into a dialogue, rather than because the space between their head and their lungs is in actual need of clearing.

"Exley Hall?" It wasn't much, but it was enough to draw the attention of the other men towards him. "Isn't that the home of Mr. Charles Forthright? Or the deceased Mr. Forthright, I should say."

Mr. Simonon (Reginald still did not know his name was Mr. Simonon, nor did he care to learn any identifiable facts about any of the people currently within ten feet of him) deflated a bit at this intrusion on his tale. "Er, yes?" His gaze narrowed, a sudden gleam of interest brightening his eyes, as if Reginald's interference could be used to supply a new embellishment to the story for when it was time to be told again. "Did you know him? Mr. Forthright, that is?"

"In a way," Reginald admitted. "We shared a common interest." There was something in Mr. Simonon's behavior that made Reginald reluctant to construct an entire false history in order to make his interest in Exley Hall and Mr. Forthright and the fate of the two ladies more believable. Perhaps because Mr. Simonon seemed the sort of man who had constructed enough of his own false histories to elevate him as an expert in recognizing the foundational cracks in another person's hastily cobbled-together tale. "But the ladies you mentioned, did they tell you their names?"

Mr. Simonon's expression became jocular, though the mix of too much warmth from the fire and the candles and too much ale from the half-empty tankards all around them warped the edges until his face appeared—at least to Reginald's wary eyes—slightly sinister. "If they did, I can't remember them!"

Ah, another supposed joke. Reginald waited for the guffaws to subside and pressed onward. "One of the ladies was a housekeeper, I understand? She would have appeared..." He drew his hand down through the air from his head to his hip, as if his fingers could sketch a portrait of an elderly woman in cap and apron and with a slight dusting of flour about her figure. "But the other lady, did she have the appearance of a gentlewoman? Um, about forty years of age, or thereabouts? Taller than average, a bit sturdy. Darker hair, unremarkable face?" He thought he might have to continue adding details for another minute, but then Mr. Simonon nodded, a light of recognition widening his eyes.

"Yessss," he said, drawing out the 's' until it became a sort of incantation, dredging up memories from the depths of his mind. "That was her, the one with the basket. She ordered the monster to attack me! Oh, the claws it had, and its teeth! Each one no less than an inch long and—"

"Yes, yes." Reginald dismissed his tangent with a wave of his hand. "Teeth and claws and so on. But you said it had wings? Like some variety of bird?"

Mr. Simonon leaned back, crossing his arms over his chest as he shook his head. "If it were a bird, there would have been feathers, right? But this..." Forward again, and Reginald realized how much of Mr. Simonon's gestures and body movements were a part of his performance. "This creature had no feathers, no fur. Heat radiated from its skin. Harsh, hard scales and spines, like it was fashioned out of heated rock summoned to life by Hell itself. And then..." He swallowed. His gaze darted from one face to the next, his eyes throwing out fishhooks to lead them all in to him. "It breathed fire."

It was not a single, grand "Aha!" moment when Reginald realized the truth. It had grown in small increments, inching ever upwards like a vine creeping towards the sun, from the first moment he had heard Mr. Simonon speak. An animal with wings, dark and scaled, that—supposedly, possibly— could blast flame from its mouth.

And it was then that Reginald had to make a few abrupt changes to his thinking. His stone, he realized, was no longer a thing that existed. His stone, the egg left to him—promised to him—by his drunken lout of a father, the egg that had been a fossil, a relic, proof of a time long gone (but proof enough that his father assured him it would make Reginald's fortune) had twisted all of his carefully laid plans by doing the last thing he would have ever suspected it of doing and hatched.

So with there being no stone to pursue, what was left to him? All of his thoughts had centered around retrieving a lifeless artifact that would sit on a pedestal in a museum to be gawked at and admired by hundreds of visitors. The stone would have returned him to the level of polite, genteel society ('returned' being used here because his father, the former Mr. Hawthorne who had pitched himself into an early grave, had always insisted they were descended from the upper echelons of British society, no matter that their names currently took up no space in the pages of Debrett's). He had dreamed of money and a small portion of celebrity, even of the most fleeting kind. And a wife and children, someone to always be there for him, like an anchor—No! Like a lighthouse, illuminating the way before him to prevent him from crashing into the rocks.

Reginald sat back in his chair and pushed his hands through his hair. There he sat, in Warwickshire, in some godforsaken inn, with a possibly undressed and definitely unmarried woman in one of the rooms above him. And only a few miles away—he guessed Exley Hall was only a few miles away, give or take—there was a living, breathing dragon that had once belonged to him.

Because it did not matter for whom the egg had hatched. This is what he told himself, those words an anthem to the rolling of his shoulders and the renewed rigidity of both his spine and his purpose. In the end, the essentials of the situation had not altered. Miss Percy was still in possession of something that did not rightfully belong to her. And he still wanted it back.

He finished his third tankard of ale, forcing it down while Mr. Simonon went on with the rest of his story—the fight between himself and the monstrous creature (a creature that seemed to subtly increase in size as more details were provided), the decampment of the two ladies along with his cart, leaving him in the middle of a muddy road, miles from anywhere. But Reginald could not focus on the end of the tale. His mind was already awhirl with the new adjustments to his plan (to be honest, a plan that had not developed far beyond: "Find Miss Percy, retrieve stone, go to London with stone, profit.")

He offered a few quick words of goodnight and farewell to the men (even with his faint tingling of inebriation, he still would not refer to them as gentlemen—their lack of neckcloths would not allow it) and went upstairs to his room.

Well, *their* room.

Well.

He knocked lightly before he went in. Actually, he knocked three times lightly, his ear pressed against the wood as he listened for even the faintest proof that Miss Muncy was awake on the other side.

Apart from the sounds of other people interspersed throughout the inn, all was silent. So he went inside.

If he had been asked to describe how he thought someone like Miss Muncy would look as they slept, the true version did not venture far from the one he would have had to conjure up from his imagination. She slept beautifully, because of course she did; on her side, her hands tucked beneath her cheek, lips slightly parted—no drool, because of course—her hair spread out on the pillow behind her, as if the entire scene were a moment caught through wind or water.

For a moment he nearly forgot why he had come upstairs, why they were even in some inn in Warwickshire at all. Instead, he wanted to drag one of the rickety chairs over from the fire—a small fire, and putting out enough smoke that the window had been opened to let in some of the fresh air from outside—and take up a post beside the bed to watch her sleep.

But, no. No. He shook himself and ran his hands over his face, sweeping away the soporific effects of the smoky room and the inferior ale and the tiredness that dragged from his heels with all the dogged persistence of a shadow. He had to remain focused on the important part of all this. And while Miss Muncy was lovely, he could not allow himself to be distracted by her. (An odd thought struck him at that moment, and when he looked again at Miss Muncy, it seemed as if some measure of her loveliness faded. Her cheeks lost their rosy hue. Her lips, instead of soft and glistening in the dim glow from the fireplace, looked thin and dry. And her hair, rather than appearing like a curtain of silk draped over the rough-yet-threadbare sheets, resembled nothing more than a tangle of dry vines or seaweed left to dry on a rock beneath the unforgiving sun.)

A blink of his eyes, an indrawn breath, and there. Her loveliness was returned to its former glory.

"Bloody ale," he murmured, and dropped into one of the chairs by the fire. He drew the other chair towards him with his foot and after debating with himself as to whether or not he wanted to go to all the trouble of removing his boots (he did not remove his boots) he propped his feet up on the seat of the chair, tucked his chin into the crook of his shoulder, and did his best to nab a few hours of sleep before morning returned in all its inevitable glory.

CHAPTER TWENTY-FIVE

Certain breeds of dragon are notorious for their ability to "puff" themselves up in order to appear larger and more fearsome to their enemies.

-from Chapter Eleven of Miss Percy's Pocket Guide (to the Care and Feeding of British Dragons)

Mrs. Babbinton was to leave Exley Hall after breakfast. Her bags—which had hardly reached the status of fully unpacked—were again closed up and sitting in her room, waiting to be carried down and placed on the coach that would take her back to Upper Plimpton. (Mr. Gorman was kind enough to offer one of Mr. Forthright's—and now his —own carriages for her use in conducting her home, and the presence of a manservant to oversee her safety during the journey. Mrs. Babbinton proceeded to accept the offer of the carriage and refuse the offer of the manservant, as she declared she had had enough of men for quite some time—present company included—but would always have to make an exception for Mr. Wiggan who she feared could not get on without her.)

They chose to eat in the kitchen, as Fitz had woken early and no one wished to trouble the servants with the additional task of preparing a room for three people and a dragon (the latter of whom could not be counted upon to keep either himself or the carpets clean).The food was of plain fare, porridge and kippers and some fresh berries brought in from the greenhouse. Extra scones were baked and set aside for Mrs. Babbinton to eat during her trip, the better to spare her from depending on the untrustworthy kitchens of the various inns she might pass along her way.

The kitchen's staff was very good about having a dragon about, and did not seem at all unnerved by his appearance or his antics. The fact that his behavior, as long as he was fed and warm and there was someone nearby to pay attention to him, likened him to something along the lines of a household pet made it all the easier to ingratiate himself into the household routine. (Part of this routine included trotting along behind the cook as she moved around the kitchen, probably waiting for scraps to 'accidentally' fall from her hands so he could scoop them up with a quick dart of his head and jaws. Mildred had to admit that seeing Fitz behave thus brought out a sharp dart of jealousy in herself, and so she began to consider carrying food in her pockets to tempt him back to her side when he seemed inclined to go astray.)

After the meal, Mrs. Babbinton gestured Mildred aside. Mr. Gorman sat at the small breakfast table, still finishing his coffee, while Fitz was curled up in front of the fire, gumming at an apple core the cook had given to him when he would not stop nipping at her heels. Mildred glanced at the window as Mrs. Babbinton led her into one of the narrow corridors that led from the room, distracted by the sight of heavy gray clouds that might prevent her from taking Fitz out for a long walk about the grounds.

"Are you certain you will be fine here on your own?" Mrs. Babbinton asked, leaping directly into the conversation as soon as they were out of earshot of the people in the kitchen.

"On my own?" Mildred glanced around herself as if they were not currently standing in the depths of a large house staffed by at least a dozen servants. But she looked back at Mrs. Babbinton and saw genuine concern in the housekeeper's dark eyes. "I doubt there is any reason to worry."

Mrs. Babbinton licked her lips in the way someone else would touch their tongue to the tip of their pencil before writing. "You will probably think me foolish for even bringing up the matter, but you have no maid with you, no companion of any kind. Of course you are not a young lady fresh out of the nursery," she added hastily at Mildred's confused expression (Mildred knew she bore a confused expression because she could feel it etching deep lines across her forehead and out from the corners of her mouth.) "But you are still unmarried and alone. And Mr. Gorman is also unmarried and alone. And two people who are unmarried and alone should not be—"

Mildred laughed. She hadn't meant to, but the sound burst out of her before she could halt its progress from her throat. "I'm sorry," she said. "I'm sorry," she said again. "It is just… I'm sorry." She put her fingers to her lips and counted to five. "I do not think you need to worry about anything in that, um, particular quarter." She stopped herself then, wondering how much of what she knew—or what she suspected of Mr. Gorman, after spending the previous evening reading through her Great Uncle Forthright's journals—to tell Mrs. Babbinton. "We are quite mature," Mildred decided to say. "And Mr. Gorman is at least another twenty years older than I am. I doubt there will be any danger from him, if that is what concerns you. Nor should there be any talk. The servants have already given their word to keep things quiet as they concern Fitz. And really, what gossip could be squeezed from the rumor of an old spinster and an older bachelor residing beneath the same roof for a few weeks?"

"Oh, I know!" Mrs. Babbinton's hands fluttered as her cheeks took on a rare tinge of pink. "I am being a silly old woman. But at least when you were at the vicarage, closeting yourself away with Mr. Wiggan for hours at a time, I was there to make certain everything remained respectable." She took a step forward and picked up Mildred's right hand, holding it within her own two hands as if it were the most precious of things. "You've become rather dear to me, Miss Percy. All my life, I have taken care of others. I must admit it's a difficult habit to break. If I could tear myself in two and leave one part of myself here and send the other part home to look after Mr. Wiggan, I would not hesitate. But you will be well, hmm?" She patted her hand and released it back to Mildred's keeping. "And you will be back in Upper Plimpton before you know it. And we'll have cakes and tea, and..."

Her voice faltered. It was there, unspoken, in the quiver of Mrs. Babbinton's chin, in the burn of moisture at the corners of Mildred's own eyes. Something was different now. Well, everything was different now. Would there ever be tea and cakes for the both of them at the vicarage again? Would there be another afternoon where they could simply sit with each other—she and Mrs. Babbinton and Mr. Wiggan—and enjoy one another's company, as friends should?

And there was something Mildred had never thought of before, during all of her childhood dreams of thrilling quests and excitement, that in order to have her adventure, she would have to give up the safety and security of the life she had known for so long. And that could be no easy thing. Small wonder then, that she had put off doing it all these years.

"Cakes and tea," Mildred said, and breathed, and held the tears at bay. "As soon as I'm back again."

Mrs. Babbinton hugged her, and kissed her cheek, and fretted over her as if Mildred was the one going off on a journey and not the other way around. "I will write to you as soon as I am home, even before I've fixed Mr. Wiggan something to eat. Poor thing, he's probably wasted down to skin and bones while I've been away!"

The call was made for the coach, and all of Mrs.

Babbinton's bags were loaded onto it while she put on her bonnet and gloves and made certain that her shawl was folded and pinned precisely as she wanted. The basket of scones and other travel-sturdy comestibles was given to her from the cook, and after all of the farewells were traded, Mrs. Babbinton climbed into the coach and settled herself on the cushioned seat. Mildred smiled and waved, and was suddenly torn between wanting to stay where she was and wanting to snatch up Fitz and leap in with Mrs. Babbinton before she could be driven away.

But in the end, all of Mildred's indecision and fear over an unknown future were shunted to the side at the sight of another carriage coming up the drive as Mrs. Babbinton's coach took her away. It certainly wasn't a fine carriage approaching them (and not that Mildred was an expert in the art and science of transportation and its designs, but she could tell the difference between a fine, well-kept private carriage and one most likely hired out to whoever had enough coins in their purse) but it was a few steps above the level of a farmer's cart, and so at least assured her that they were not about to receive a visit from the likes of Mr. Simonon so early in the morning.

Mildred and Mr. Gorman stood at the bottom step, where they had been while watching Mrs. Babbinton leave them, and now where they waited for the new arrival to make its way around to them. "Were you expecting someone?" she asked, needing to break the silence that had fallen over them.

Mr. Gorman shook his head. "No, not at all. But then, I hadn't been expecting you and Mrs. Babbinton either."

Mildred did not know how to receive that, or whether it boded well or ill. Or perhaps she was letting her thoughts spiral away from her again, creating undue anxiety for herself where there was no need for such high spirits.

The carriage came to a halt. The door was opened from the inside and down came a shabby boot, attached to a leg, attached to a body clad in a worn, several-years-out-of-fashion coat and topped with a hat set rather jauntily to one side. And then Mr. Hawthorne turned towards them, the shabby boots crunching on the pale gravel and his mouth tilting into a smile as superficial and frayed as the coat hanging from his shoulders.

"Ah, good morning, Miss Percy!" He raised his hand to the brim of his hat. "Fancy meeting you here, and so far from home, too."

Mildred could not help it. She felt as if she'd fallen into the plot of some terrible novel (quiet, you) in which just as things seemed to have been settling into a more pleasing direction, the author decided to strand her on a bare bit of rock surrounded by leech-infested waters. She stood there, her arms at her sides, straight as ramrods and with her fingers opening and closing if only to prevent their sudden tingling from turning to numbness.

She was thankful she had not chosen to bring Fitz outside with her to partake in the goodbyes, that she had left him slumbering in the kitchen, clutching his apple core as he snored beside the fire. What would Mr. Hawthorne's reaction be to seeing a dragon wrought in miniature clutched in her arms or scraping at the dirt and stones beneath them? She had come here suspecting that he had wanted Fitz's egg for himself, that something about his professed relationship with her Great Uncle Forthright had not rung true. As to the latter, Mr. Gorman had confirmed that Mr. Hawthorne had lied about his close acquaintance with any of the inhabitants of Exley Hall or its surroundings. And if he were willing to lie about that, to create a fictitious friendship to win from her what he wanted, what else would he be willing to do?

Her mouth moved in a way that implied she had words to say, words of forced greeting perhaps, something kind and polite and possibly involving the weather or the state of the roads that had led Mr. Hawthorne all this way. Yet it was impossible for her to even form a sound of surprise at his arrival, because hadn't she been expecting it? Well, not this exact situation, but some part of her had known that it would not, could not, be easy and smooth sailing over calm waters from there forward. Bare bit of rock, leechy waters, Mr. Hawthorne smiling at her before he reached inside the carriage (she had forgotten about the carriage for the moment, and about Mr. Gorman and Mrs. Babbinton and the fact that she was a person with feet on the ground and that the ground was somehow solid and stable throughout all of this) and took the gloved hand of a lady.

Of Belinda. Her niece.

"Belinda?" Mildred said, needing to say the name aloud, as if those three syllables had the power to lend credence to her unexpected arrival, transporting her niece from the realm of visions and tricks of a tired mind to real, corporeal existence.

"Aunt Mildred!" Belinda closed the distance between them, arms outstretched, silk roses bobbing on the brim of her bonnet. "Oh, I did hope we would find you here! Did I not say that I hoped we would catch her before she could dash off again?" The second part was tossed over her shoulder to Mr. Hawthorne, who remained stationed near the carriage, fiddling with the cuffs of his coat like a nervous schoolboy, the only physical sign he gave that the bravado on his face was of the superficial variety."And was that Mrs. Babbinton we just saw leaving? Is she returning to Upper Plimpton, then? And you are to stay behind? How lovely!"

Mildred did not move while Belinda wrapped her arms around her and hugged her. If Mildred had ever felt a kinship with a nut caught in a nutcracker, it was then.

"What are you doing here?" It was a question that could have been asked by either of the women, but Mildred posed it first, and with a full lack of the false sweetness with which her niece would have doused her own words.

Belinda stepped back, hands clasped to her chest, as if shielding herself from threatened wounds. It was a pitiful performance, and a reminder that Belinda had never done well when dramatics or playacting was involved. Mildred almost expected there to be stagehands and perhaps the rustle of a red velvet curtain hovering in her peripheral vision. "This is the welcome I am to receive, after traveling so far and—"

Mildred closed her eyes. She considered plugging her fingers in her ears as well but did not wish to come across as lacking maturity. Instead she sighed, and prayed for patience, along with a continuation of whatever amount of sanity was still left to her. "Does my sister know that you are here? No." She held up a hand before Belinda could speak. "Of course she does not. Never would she have agreed to such a..." She looked at Mr. Hawthorne, her ire towards him flaring anew. "What have you done?" she asked suddenly, directing the question to whichever of them would listen. "Did no one else make the journey with you? Have you been travelling alone with a single gentleman all this way?"

This last question was pointed to Belinda, who, instead of displaying any shame or guilt at having so freely toyed with her reputation, stood taller with a little wiggle of her spine. "I do not see how you can stand there and deliver all these insinuations, when your own behavior is nothing to boast about."

"M-My own behavior?" There should not have been that squeeze of trepidation in her lungs, that thickness in her throat. There, for a few brief moments, she had felt so confident, so unlike the version of herself she thought she had left behind in Wiltshire. Someone who could stand up to another person and speak her thoughts without trembling, without cowing, without choosing silence and invisibility over the need to be acknowledged.

She looked at Belinda, who only a minute before had attempted to win the crowd to her side with a few cheap mannerisms and dramatic flourishes. But her niece's last few words had been delivered with a perfect balance of cunning and mimicry, so that all Mildred heard was Diana's voice

310

carried up from Warwickshire to injure her.

Belinda moved closer. Her smile had not faltered. In the full light of the morning, and with the shadow of her bonnet's brim cutting across her features, Mildred saw the strange dichotomy of her niece's character, of the face she put forward to the world and the face still cast in darkness, smudged and murky, seeming to shift from clarity to blurred and back again beneath her scrutiny.

"There is talk, you know, spreading across Upper Plimpton. Concerning you and the vicar, Mr. Wiggan. What a pall to cast on our family, rumors that will harm our good standing in the county. And you would do this?" Belinda's brow furrowed in concern. "You would risk my future, the future of my dear sister and brother, for what? A fleeting spell of rebellion? Oh, aunt." She shook her head, her lips pursed. It was a look so reminiscent of Diana that Mildred nearly reached out to steady herself. "You cannot make up for a life half lived with these paltry attempts at personal revolution."

That was it. Mildred's breath was gone. She could not fuel her words, she could not even make herself heard in a series of unintelligible squeaks and mumbles.

"And I know what you have," Belinda went on, each syllable like a kick to the ribs as Mildred lay sprawled in the dirt. "I know what you are keeping from Mr. Hawthorne. Well, he would like it back. We both would, actually. And that is what has brought me all this way, against convention and all those silly little dictates of society. To help Mr. Hawthorne, and to help you. Because really, Aunt Mildred. What did you hope to achieve with all of this? Just go home to Upper Plimpton, to Ashby Lodge. It is where you belong. And leave the world to the rest of us, hmm?"

Mildred swallowed. It would be easy, wouldn't it? To gather up her things, to climb into the coach, to let herself be jostled back to her little bedroom with its slanted ceiling and its dust and its spiders. Routine had the draw of comfort on its side, of safety and surety. She could go back and she could always know what each new day would hold for her. It was tempting, that. To listen to Belinda, or rather to listen to her sister's words spoken from Belinda's lips.

Just go home. Do not dream, Miss Percy. Adventure is not for the likes of you.

"No."

One small word. Hardly a word, even. Two letters, one sound, carried off on a breath as unsure of itself as the first steps of a tottering infant.

Belinda's bottom lip quivered until she bit down on it to hold it still.

"You should not be here," Mildred said. Her voice was still weak, but a weak voice was better than no voice at all, she decided. "If anyone has harmed your family with their antics, it is you. And Mr. Hawthorne," She turned slightly to face him. "If you have something you wish to say to me, then say it and be done. But spare me any further falsification of the facts pertaining to my Great Uncle Forthright and your so-called acquaintance with him. If you desire that I should listen to anything you have to say, then you will speak the truth. Otherwise, I wish you a good day."

She thought she might be ill after that. But a fear of heaving up the contents of her stomach onto the steps of Exley Hall was strong enough for her to swallow down her nausea and defer to Mr. Gorman for the final decision on whether or not Mr. Hawthorne and Belinda would find any further welcome there.

Mr. Gorman seemed to understand that and came over to Mildred's side, turning his back towards the newcomers as he dipped his head towards her and spoke in a lowered rumble of a voice. "If it were only Mr. Hawthorne, I would not suffer a moment's compunction over having him banned from the property. But the young lady, she is your niece?"

Mildred responded with a tight nod.

"Then do you feel an obligation to save her? Or is her

character beyond repair?"

As to the first question, Mildred did indeed feel the weight of obligation towards Belinda. She could not simply abandon the girl to Mr. Hawthorne's protection, though looking between the two of them, she wondered if it was not Mr. Hawthorne who was in greater need of preservation against her niece's particular brand of machinations.

But as to the second question...

What did Mildred even know of Belinda's character? She had always been an aloof child, difficult to chastise or correct—not because of any obvious rebellion against the correction, but rather that there had always been something untouchable in her demeanor when any attempt to voice a reproof was made. She had not thought on it so much as Belinda had grown, maturity having drawn her further into her mother's sphere, when prospects such as social calls and the possibility of marriage became less of a little girl's dollhouse realm of play and more of something that deserved the attention and planning of a major military campaign.

Mildred winced. She winced because her own thoughts had taken to pinging around the inside of her head with all the gentleness of rocks shaken inside a tin pot. To protect Belinda, to deal with Mr. Hawthorne, to see that Fitz came through all of this whole and unharmed...

And herself. Did she not have to consider her own well-being at some point? It was not something she was accustomed to doing, as evidenced by nearly every situation that had brought her to this precise moment and all of the repercussions that would ripple outward from it. But if she was to fight for Fitz (and she knew that she would fight for him, like a modern-day Boudicca (only one that perhaps should not have had quite so much cake and did not really know how to wield a sword)) then she needed to be strong for him. And she would not find her strength if she allowed others to pressure her into clinging to her own weaknesses.

Right, then.

So.

Belinda. Mr. Hawthorn. Fitz. Herself. And not necessarily in that order.

She flattened her hands against the front of her skirt. She was perspiring, despite the fact it was not particularly warm outside. "Tea."

The word came out just like that, no comma to imply there would be more conversation to follow, no sharp slash of an exclamation point to imbue those three letters with greater import than they deserved, and certainly nothing like the meandering swoop of a question mark to allow everyone to suppose they might have something resembling a choice in the matter.

In they went: Mr. Gorman first, then Mr. Hawthorne and Belinda, and finally Mildred tacking herself into the rear position, the better to peel away from the others and walk briskly (she would not run, no matter how much her legs vibrated with the need to hurry) to the kitchen and see to Fitz. The dragon still slept, a fact that surprised Mildred at first, until she realized that even though the last few pages had seemed to encompass an hour's length of time or more, it could not have been more than ten minutes since she had left him beside the fire with his rapidly browning apple core.

She scooped him up without ceremony, cradling him in her arms and wincing at the involuntary flexing of his claws in response to the sudden alteration to his comfort as she headed for the back stairs. Quickly, quickly. That was all she could think about, propelled forward on the balls of her feet as if Mr. Hawthorne and Belinda were reaching out at that very moment to tug at the hem of her gown and pull her down to the floor.

"Here we are," she said, all soothing and slightly sing-song, placing him on the end of the bed in her room. (One of the servants had apparently instigated a battle with the bedclothes, determinedly changing out the soiled, scratched up blankets with pristine ones every day—sometimes several times a day—no matter that Mildred had told them repeatedly to leave things as they were and save the expense and effort of attempting to keep the bedroom tidy when she was still attempting to train Fitz to relieve himself on the stack of London newspapers she had stacked in the corner rather than anywhere and everywhere else that proved to be an inconvenience.)

Fitz slitted open one eye and looked at her. He raised his head, or rather tipped up his chin, pushing his jaw forward until Mildred understood what he wanted. She scratched the underside of his jaw, one fingernail dragging along the soft —impossibly soft—part of his skin there. He hummed at the attention, his eye closing again before he lowered his head and settled back into sleep.

"I will return as soon as I can," she whispered, no matter that she did not know if he could hear her, or if he could understand a word she said. "I need you to stay here, and to behave as best you can. Sleep, please, if you will. And if you're good, I'll find a treat for you once all of this…" She halted there, her speech suddenly jangling as if the inadequacy of her statement came out of her mouth with bells hanging from it. "Once I've taken care of a few things," she finished. "Just don't set anything on fire, hmm?" She touched the tip of her finger to the delicate spot between his nostrils, bestowing a quiet blessing on him.

And then she stepped back, watching him until his shape, his color, all of his particulars traced themselves onto her thoughts so that she still saw everything even when she closed her eyes against it.

"This will not be easy," she muttered to herself, her face crumpling as a child's would when given a bowl of something unsavory (… peas, it would always be peas in Mildred's case) for dinner.

But it would have to be done. Which made it infinitely worse than the peas, as childhood had afforded her the mistaken assumption that once she matured into an adult she would be given the freedom to abscond from so many things —eating peas, going to bed early, practicing on the pianoforte—she no longer had a wish to do.

But for Fitz, she reminded herself, and stepped out into the hall, shutting—and locking—the door behind her. She would do this for Fitz, to keep him safe.

And, in some way that she had not quite untangled yet, to keep herself safe as well.

CHAPTER TWENTY-SIX

*A dragon's mood can change in less time than
it takes to unfurl its wings.*

*-from Chapter Three of Miss Percy's Pocket
Guide (to the Care and Feeding of British
Dragons)*

Tea, Mildred realized upon entering the drawing room, would not be a potent enough beverage to see her through this meeting.

It seemed innocent enough at first glance: Mr. Gorman stood near the fireplace, while Mr. Hawthorne and Belinda shared a sofa that allowed the glow from the windows to spill across them, gilding them in such a suffusion of illumination as to make a Renaissance artist scrabble for his brushes and paint before the moment could be lost behind a passing cloud.

She noticed how they sat, far enough apart so that not even a stitch of Mr. Hawthorne's clothing brushed against any part of Belinda's gown, giving them the appearance of mildly chastised schoolchildren waiting for the remainder of their punishment to tumble down around their shoulders.

Such easy complaisance, Mildred thought. So easy that she immediately distrusted their behavior. Like the sudden silence of a young child's play in another room, she doubted it would presage something pleasant. There had to be a kind of trick behind it, the gears turning quietly in their heads while Mr. Gorman made polite conversation and the maid (there was also a maid in the room, a young girl who worked with the efficiency of someone who wanted to be out of the room again before the tea had finished sloshing inside the pot after she had set it down) arranged the plates on the tray.

Mildred stepped aside to give the maid enough space to leave (Mildred heard the rushed exhalation of relief as the girl shuffled into the hall) and then closed the door behind her.

At the sound of it, all three heads turned her way.

So, of course, her mind was immediately stricken clear of any and all helpful things such as words or conscious thought.

"Ah," is what she managed to say, just as one says when there is a need to fill the silence but nothing greater than a monosyllabic utterance is forthcoming. She walked to the tray full of its tea and things, poured herself a cup of tea and filled a plate with things, then realized she had an appetite for neither and turned her attention to Belinda instead.

No, not Belinda. She was not prepared to speak with Belinda again. So her gaze skipped over to Mr. Hawthorne, who appeared slightly less threatening as his expression vacillated between "smug" and "leery" and "attempting to make himself as small as possible" from one shift of his eyebrows to the next.

"Why did you lie about your connections with my Great Uncle Forthright?"

It was much like submerging herself in a tub filled with cold water, best to dunk herself all at once and force her body to adjust to the sudden change in temperature rather than freeze herself one body part at a time.

Mr. Hawthorne winced, or at least his left eye twitched, as if a few drops of that same cold water had splashed onto himself with her question. "I find I must beg your pardon, Miss Percy. I do not make a habit of practicing dishonesty—"

Mildred nearly stopped him here, as she was convinced that anyone who made a point of claiming they did not practice dishonesty was most likely practicing it with that very phrase.

"–but I was worried that I would not be able to gain your trust otherwise."

If the word 'gobsmacked' had been in use in 1816 England, Mildred would not only have treasured it as one of her favorite words, but her current expression would have acted as a perfect representation of its definition. How, she thought, could this man speak the words he was speaking and yet seem to be incapable of also hearing them?

"You," she said, and gestured to him, as if there were any question she was referring to him and no one else, "lied to me in order to show yourself as trustworthy?"

"Oh, Miss Percy." He shifted forward to the edge of his seat, elbows on his knees, hands not quite clasped in supplication but faring well in a vague approximation of mild begging. "What more can I say? I was desperate. My father…" He lowered his head, gaze dropping to the carpet, shoulders heaving with the effort to slather his performance with that droop of his joints and an audible sigh. "It was promised to me, you know. The stone. It was my birthright. And then…well. My father was a good man, I assure you. But too often he made unwise decisions that reflected harshly on our circumstances. He drank, as too many are wont to do. And he was a lover of cards. How your uncle came to know him or that he was in possession of the stone, I suspect I will never know. But there was a game, and a wager, and while my father was suffering under the effects of too much of the drink he loved so well, he lost the stone to Mr. Forthright."

Mildred said nothing to this. Mr. Hawthorne, she knew well enough to suspect, was one of those persons who would continue speaking if no one else stepped up to fill the conversational void. And so she picked up a biscuit from her plate of things, snapped it in half, and popped one of the halves into her mouth, waiting for him while she chewed.

"When my father died," he went on, because of course he went on, "I realized I wanted the stone returned to us, to me.

He had always wished for me to have it, and I will always labor under the belief that my father was not in his right mind when he lost it to your uncle in a simple game of cards. You may disagree with that assessment of my father's cognitive ability while drinking too much gin, but I will beg your pardon for saying that I think your Great Uncle Forthright took unfair advantage of my father's inebriated state in his desire to obtain the stone for himself."

At her side, Mr. Gorman took a hasty step forward. Mildred put out her hand, a gentle touch on his arm to calm him.

"I notice you continually refer to it as a stone, Mr. Hawthorne." Mildred took a deep breath, both regretting having paused long enough to eat a biscuit and wishing she could scoop up the rest of them and shove them all into her mouth at once if it would rescue her from having to push forward with this conversation. "Can you tell me why you and your father ascribed such worth to a mere rock?"

Mr. Hawthorne straightened up. Mildred likened it to watching a fallen tower of blocks right itself again. Gone were the supplicating hands, the rounded shoulders, the look of pleading in every contour of his face. "Very well. You wish for me to speak all in truths, do you? I know it is not a mere rock, as you put it. So do you, I would wager, seeing as how its existence has stirred up all of this discord between us. It makes one feel very possessive, doesn't it?" He smiled a little, one of those grins where only one corner of a person's mouth quirks upwards. "The egg, that is."

This was the moment when tea or even biscuits suddenly proved themselves insufficient. Mildred glanced at Mr. Gorman (jaw set, muscle twitching beside his right eye) and then back again at Mr. Hawthorne. "The egg, yes."

She raised her chin an inch, head tilted in order to listen for any unusual sounds (Fitz rolling off the edge of the bed, Fitz knocking over his water bowl, Fitz sparking a small fire to life and alerting the servants to race to her room hauling buckets of water) the house might choose that moment to provide.

"Well," Mildred said, once she was certain neither house nor dragon were going to make an attempt at shifting the plot in a different direction from the course it was already on. "If you had come to me from the beginning with this version of the truth, instead of inveigling your way into our household with all your stories of admiration for my Great Uncle Forthright, perhaps we would not be in the mess we are now."

None of this meant that Mildred believed a word Mr. Hawthorne said. But it seemed safer for the moment to let him think this other version of events had managed to reach her in some way.

"So, Mr. Hawthorne. Let us suppose I have this egg. And let us suppose I believe it to be mine because it was left to me by my uncle, disregarding whatever means he may have used to acquire it. What will happen if I refuse to give it up to you?"

Beside her, slightly behind her, Mr. Gorman drew in a deep breath, loud enough to reach Mildred's ears like a rush of wind nudging her tattered sails of courage along. A part of her wondered how she would even appear to herself, this unknown version of a woman who could speak with such confidence as if she had been accustomed to doing so for all of her natural life. Perhaps it was as much of a false front as Mr. Hawthorne's pretensions to transparent honesty, but the fact that she could even pretend for a short while made her realize just how much things had altered for her in the last few months.

"You would have me there," Mr. Hawthorne admitted. Easily. Too easily. "I've no legal claim on it, no papers or signed documents as proof it belongs to me over you. Now, I am a man and you are a woman, and perhaps that fact alone would give me greater standing over you if the law were to become involved–"

This time it was Mr. Gorman's hand that found Mildred's elbow, holding her back when she would have started forward.

"–but your familial connection with Mr. Forthright would most likely be enough to ultimately sway matters in your favor."

"I see," is what Mildred wanted to say, in a way that indicated she would take the time to ponder over his words and come up with a fine rebuttal of her own. The words were there, all lined up on her tongue and ready to be spoken. And then Belinda made a short, sharp sound of frustration (which, if written out, would look something like 'pffttch' and is why the phrase "short, sharp sound of frustration" is preferred) and shifted restlessly in her seat on the sofa.

"Really, Aunt Mildred. You must admit how ridiculous this has all become." Pursed lips, a small shake of her head, and suddenly Belinda was the picture of a strict nurse or governess relishing her power over others. "This egg or stone or..." a wave of her fingers to demonstrate how little it mattered to her what the wanted object in question actually was, "Anyway, it cannot mean that much to you. You hardly knew Great Uncle Forthright, so it does not reflect well on you to pretend there is some kind of foolish sentiment attached to the thing."

"Belinda, I–"

"If anyone deserves to have it, why not Mr. Hawthorne? It belonged to his father. It was intended for him, and for quite a while longer than I'm sure Great Uncle Forthright thought about giving it to you. Especially when you consider that there was no great deal made about it, seeing as how it was simply tossed in with all of the other rubbish he sent to you."

"Belinda, you–"

"So let's have it and be finished with all of this absurdity." She clasped her hands and set them on her lap. "Go on, Auntie Mildred. I'm sure you're as eager to have all of this over and done with as everyone else. Especially Mr. Gorman, I would think," she added in an exaggerated attempt at a stage whisper, "as you've gone and made yourself such a nuisance insisting on staying in a home you've no real familial connection to any longer."

Mildred opened her mouth to speak, then realized she was not going to waste another breath on Belinda's name. "Come along," was all she said, before taking her niece's arm, hoisting her off the sofa like a load of old baggage, and leading her ('dragging' would be a nearly accurate replacement, though Belinda had been caught off guard enough to put up little resistance until she was out of the drawing room and halfway towards the stairs) away.

"Enough," Mildred said, turning around and gripping Belinda's arm with enough force to give her a little shake. "Enough of this! I do not know what this Mr. Hawthorne has said to you to make you display such unerring loyalty to his cause, but you will not come into someone else's home—as a guest—and display such utter contempt towards your host and—"

Belinda interrupted with a repetition of her short, sharp sound of frustration.

"What? What is it?" Mildred placed her hands on her hips, a stance she had not performed with Belinda since her niece was still regularly wearing a pinafore over her gown to avoid getting mud streaked on her skirts.

"Mr. Gorman is merely a steward, in case you have forgotten. He is not our host and this matter of his inheriting an entire estate cannot be taken seriously. I am not certain how you were able to talk your way into his permitting you to stay here, but for all of your complaints about my running off with Mr. Hawthorne and without a chaperone, I cannot see how your behavior has been anything less shameful."

It was wrong to strike someone. Mildred knew this. Never once had she raised her hand against another person, not even going so far as to smack the palm of her hand against the children's bottoms when they were inclined to show those bottoms to her as far as their attitudes and behavior went. But her fingers twitched now, and her hand dropped from her hip as if preparing for some brisk, forceful movement outward and away from her.

"You will be going home." Mildred said the words slowly. To someone else, it might have sounded like she spoke in such a way because she did not believe Belinda would hear or understand her should she fail to shape each syllable as if it were a rock being slowly eroded down to the smoothness of a pebble by her throat and tongue and teeth. But she spoke this way only because her voice acted like a lid on a pot about to boil over, the words puffing out as blasts of steam to prevent everything from blowing up and making a mess of the room. "I am sure you are tired, so you can rest here today and tonight, and then tomorrow I will see you returned to Upper Plimpton myself."

Easy enough to say, what with Mr. Hawthorne still in the drawing room and a dragon tucked away in her bedroom upstairs, both of them beyond the reach of her powers of sight and so leaving little impression on her current thoughts. But she would untangle the details of everything as she stumbled over them. As of this moment, she needed to separate Belinda from Mr. Hawthorne, as neither of them seemed to exist as a beneficial influence towards the other.

"Where are you taking me?" Belinda demanded as Mildred took up her niece's arm again.

"To the kitchen." She did not look back, simply tugged her along and hoped Belinda would follow without too much reluctance, though Mildred could not rid herself of the feeling that she was leading a particularly dirty cat towards a long overdue bath. "Cook can prepare something for you to eat and I'll have someone make a room ready for you."

"And what about Mr. Hawthorne. Surely you do not intend to toss him out with so little attempt at charity?"

"Charity?" Mildred spun around at that. Which was most

likely Belinda's intention, for if there was a pot to be stirred then no doubt Belinda would be there brandishing the largest spoon at hand. "You speak of charity when he has told nothing but lies since he first set foot on our doorstep?"

Belinda blinked, apparently unperturbed by this accusation towards her new favorite. "He told *me* the truth of everything."

"And how wonderful for you," Mildred snapped, which was so unlike her to snap at anything that she had to pause for a moment and question if perhaps she had not eaten enough at breakfast or if her stays were laced too tight. But, no. It was merely her frustration bubbling over, and since she could not—and would not—strike or kick or shake Belinda until the pins fell out of her hair, instead she stamped her foot, voiced a very loud and very impolite word that will not be repeated here, and led her niece the rest of the way to the kitchen.

"Now, you will sit here," Mildred indicated a chair, "and you will eat whatever Cook decides to give you," Mildred indicated Cook pounding her fist into a large mound of dough, "and you will not leave," Mildred indicated the door with a final sweep of her hand. She did not wait for Belinda to argue or complain, but turned swiftly away and walked all the way upstairs, peeked into her bedroom, saw Fitz still sleeping on her bed (shifted into a position on his back with his golden belly turned up towards the ceiling and his front claws flexing in his sleep), then returned to the drawing room, where Mr. Gorman and Mr. Hawthorne still assumed their previous poses of awkward and disdainful discomfort.

"So," Mildred said as soon as she walked into the room. She brushed her hands down the front of her gown as if she had just finished a chore that left her fingers with a light coating of dust or other dirt. "Mr. Hawthorne? I believe it will be best for you to return to Stratford-upon-Avon and find a room for yourself there." *Or you can simply go away and never come back*, she wanted to add, but bit the inside of her cheek to prevent the words from spilling out. "For Belinda's sake, for the sake of her reputation, I do not think you should spend another night under the same roof. Perhaps, if we are very lucky, any smudge on her character can be buffed away before anyone has seen it."

Mr. Gorman clasped his hands together. "I will go ahead and call for the carriage to be brought around again for our... guest," he finished, eyeing Mr. Hawthorne with all the regard one would give to something malodorous stuck to the bottom of their shoe.

"No, no, no!" Mr. Hawthorne stood up quickly, knocking against the table that held the tea and things, and nearly setting the entire lot on its side before Mr. Gorman leapt forward to catch it. "This cannot be at an end! What about the stone? It is mine! You've no right to it!"

Mildred stood still while Mr. Hawthorne approached her. She felt no real, physical threat from him. As much as she disliked him, she did not think the man would ever enact any measure of violence against her. And for all of his lies, his poorly devised efforts to see Fitz's egg (which seemed foolish to continue to refer to the egg when there was no longer an egg in existence but instead a small dragon who liked to have his chin scratched) once again in his possession (if it had ever truly been in his possession in the first place, but Mildred was too tired to hold that question up to scrutiny), she suspected that he really believed himself to be on the right side of everything.

There he stood before her, something quite like desperation in his eyes, in all of his features. And he looked at her as if she was the villain, the one who had set out to see all of his plans destroyed, as if she could have that much power over him, over anyone.

"I cannot give it to you," she said. Her words were quiet, soft, measured. And a bit sad, she realized. But why, she did not understand. "I am sorry, but it is impossible."

She did not know what to expect from him. Would he

yell? Would he rage? Would he deliver threats or throw a tantrum or storm out of the house on a wave of slammed doors and stomping feet?

"Very well," he said, as quiet and soft and measured as Mildred's words had been to him. He gave no sign that he was angry or frustrated. Disappointed, yes, but not much more than that. And Mildred was left baffled at this sudden deflation in him. "I am sorry to have caused so much distress to so many." He nodded towards Mr. Gorman and then to Mildred. "You will give my apologies to Miss Muncy? She is deserving of a great deal more than I am in a position to provide."

He strode out of the room, fetching his hat and his gloves and walking towards the front door before the carriage and horses had even made their way around from the stables.

Mildred and Mr. Gorman stood in the hall, watching him depart. *It could not have been as easy as all that,* she thought, because of course she thought it, the words swirling about in her head as if she had just muttered an incantation and brought some dark, otherworldly magic to life. It would not be as easy as all that, because she was Miss Mildred Percy and an old stone in an old trunk was never going to be merely an old stone in an old trunk with her.

"Belinda and I will be leaving first thing tomorrow morning," she said to Mr. Gorman while still watching Mr. Hawthorne through the door.

"What about–" he began to ask, but she wasted no time interrupting him.

"I will see her back to Upper Plimpton and then immediately return. Fitz should be well enough here for as long as it takes me to journey home and come back again. That is…" she looked at him, "… if you are amenable to looking after a dragon for a few days? I would rather not force him to endure so much traveling in such a short amount of time." That, and keeping him from causing a scene in front of strangers was no menial task. The last thing she needed was another bottom-biting incident so soon upon the heels of the previous one.

"It will be a pleasure to see to his care," Mr. Gorman assured her, though it was voiced in the same manner as childless men and women who spoke of looking forward to a visit from a rambunctious nephew or niece without any foreknowledge of what taking care of said rambunctious nephew or niece would fully entail.

"Now we just have to see ourselves through the rest of today and tonight." Mildred held onto her breath for a moment longer than was necessary. Or, judging by the content of her days these last few weeks, perhaps her lungs needed as much air as they could contain for as long as they could keep it.

CHAPTER TWENTY-SEVEN

It is best not to be impatient with a dragon.
They seem to work according to their own
internal clock, their own grasp of time and the
inevitable passing of it. One must not rush a
dragon. The end result will never be of a
pleasant or desirable nature.

-from Chapter Fifteen of Miss Percy's Pocket
Guide (to the Care and Feeding of British
Dragons)

Reginald waited.

He disliked waiting on principle (he wasn't quite sure what 'on principle' meant, but the words seemed to suit how he felt about waiting) but at the moment, he really had no choice in the matter.

Miss Muncy had told him to wait, and so he did. The directive came in her first note ('first' being used here because there were several notes to follow), the one that arrived less than an hour after the carriage from Exley Hall had dropped him off at the inn in Stratford-upon-Avon. He was not certain how she had managed it so quickly, the sending of the note, but a raggedy-looking boy had found him in the main room of the inn, given the note to him—or at least given it to him once the transfer of coinage from one hand to the other had occurred—and disappeared again in a cloud of youthful surliness and disrespect.

Please practice patience, the note had said, among other things. (Most of the 'other things' were brief, scrawled words complaining about Miss Muncy's treatment at Exley Hall, the despair she felt over being separated from him at such a crucial moment and also how the windows of her room faced the side garden and not the roses and the fountain in the back.)

He ran the edge of his thumb over the swoops and slashes of her letters. He imagined he could still feel the warmth from her hand on the surface of the paper (and ignored the nagging truth that it was the warmth of the young boy's sweaty palm that still lingered on the note). At the bottom of the page, his gaze was caught by her signature. Half a signature, really. 'Miss M,' she wrote, as prettily as a schoolgirl with a new pen and ink.

A frisson of want surged through him, to see the 'Miss M' wiped clean away and replaced with 'Mrs. H.' If they could just see this through, this mess with Miss Percy, then an entire world of possibilities would lie open before them.

The other notes arrived—delivered by a different discourteous child each time, as if there was a militia of them stationed outside Exley Hall for the sole purpose of delivering clandestine communications—about once every hour, each one shorter than the one that came before it. The final one came just as twilight settled over everything, darkening the windows of the inn so that all Reginald saw when he looked out was his own face and the reflection of a dozen candles and lamps blinking back at him like inferior stars.

Two o'clock, it said. *Second floor, third window from the left, east side.*

He folded the note, slipped it into his pocket with the others. Two o'clock. Reginald shut his eyes, as if he could also block out the sound of the inn's other patrons, the smell of the piss-ale (a slightly superior variety than what the previous inn had provided) and the cheap candles and the grease from the kitchen along with the momentary obstruction of his vision.

Two o'clock seemed a very long ways away.

CHAPTER TWENTY-EIGHT

A dragon's bones are hollow and thinly
walled, a structural necessity in order for them
to remain in the air once their strong limbs
thrust them up and off the ground.

-from Chapter Six of Miss Percy's Pocket
Guide (to the Care and Feeding of British
Dragons)

Mildred had stayed up too late reading. It was not something that took much effort to do. The house was still crowded with many—so many, too many—of her Great Uncle Forthright's books that she imagined one would have to give up at least a thousand hours of sleep to make any significant headway through the collection.

Books concerning the history and geography and topography and any other '-ys' of Wales were what littered a good portion of her bed. Fitz had nuzzled himself between two rather thick volumes, one of which Mildred had to rescue from him as he had taken to chewing on the corners until they deteriorated to a mushy pulp. The wounded books were added to the ever-growing, ever-tottering stacks that decorated the top of her nightstand, and it was not until one of them toppled over and crashed onto the floor that she looked up at the time and saw how very late—or early, depending on how she chose to view things—it was.

She should have begun packing, she realized. They were set to leave in the morning, she and Belinda, as early as could be managed. Most of the things she had brought with her from Upper Plimpton were strewn about the room, the bag in which she had carried everything deflated and flattened by Fitz's attempts to sleep inside of it. There was probably something to the fact that while she was always able to keep her tiny room in Ashby Lodge so tidy (aside from the cobwebs tucked into its corners) she could not seem to keep any of her belongings in their proper place now that they were given the space to spread.

And now it was one in the morning, and her bed was covered in books, and she had not changed out of the dress she had been wearing all day, and Fitz was buried somewhere under a tattered tome about Owain Glyndwr.

She wanted a snack, she realized, but had no desire to unbury herself from the mess and walk all the way down to the kitchen and search through–

No, even the thought of all that was exhausting and probably not worth any crumbs of cake or cheese she might be able to discover in an unfamiliar kitchen. But still her gaze lingered on the door, and she turned her object of interest towards Belinda, whom she hoped had finally found some rest in her own room at the end of the hall.

It had been a trying day. Mildred turned that phrase over in her head, experiencing a slow, lapping wave of bafflement at how dealing with a seventeen year old girl who 1) had not spoken to her in a civilized manner for the remainder of the day since Mr. Hawthorne had departed, and 2) had chosen to shut her door and respond to any and all knocks or attempts at conversation with the thump of something being thrown across the room and a shouted "GO AWAY!" that reverberated through the walls with all of its bold, capital letters could be as utterly draining as it turned out to be.

"I think one baby dragon is enough for me," Mildred said, and attempted to make a space for herself on the bed without also disturbing Fitz, who had fallen asleep with his legs and tail wrapped around one of her gnawed slippers.

She undressed, blew out the candles that were still lit, and fit herself into the small section of the bed available to her. The coals of the fire still glowed faintly behind their screen, and the windows boasted that faint illumination that only celestial objects shining down from a cloudless night sky could provide.

She should sleep. She was very aware of this. There was still all of the travelling back to Wiltshire and Upper Plimpton to be endured, accompanied by a sullen Belinda and the worry of leaving Fitz in the care of someone else for as long as it would take her to deliver her niece to the bosom of her family and then turn around and immediately return to Warwickshire.

Which meant there was also Diana to be dealt with, unless Mildred succumbed to the inclination to simply boot Belinda out of the carriage as it rolled slowly past her sister's house. And a rather strong inclination, that one was.

Sleep came, eventually. But it was an odd state of sleep, where she seemed to be aware of her surroundings, of all the noises of the house and the passage of time while also entertaining a few glimpses of dreams in her head. So she did not hear the slight click of her doorknob, or the creak of the hinges. The soft footsteps somehow wove themselves in and among the images in her mind, while the shift of weight on her bed was dismissed by some slumbering part of her thoughts as nothing more than Fitz changing position at her feet.

And then there was a hiss, and a shout, and all of that followed by a loud but muffled sound that could best be described as a 'fwump' (this last one finally managing to pull Mildred's head up from her pillow).

"Wherf?" she mumbled, or something very like it, and shouldered a line of drool from her chin.

There was a shadow on the floor. She tried to focus her bleary eyes on it, but it shifted like smoke. Or rather like a person tangled up with a small dragon who was trying desperately not to be heard. Except that the dragon had no compunction against making as much noise as he wanted.

"No. No! Stop!"

That was what Mildred thought she heard, words spoken like they were spat out of a steaming kettle. She sat fully upright, her feet kicking several books to the floor as she dragged her legs out from under the blankets and the warm place where Fitz had been only seconds before. "What is —?" —*happening*, she was going to say, the 'h' of it puffed out of her mouth and hanging in the air just as Fitz grumbled and snorted and then a flicker of flame sparked to life from between his jaws, or where Mildred now realized his jaws were among all the flailing limbs and thrashing shadows.

"No! Oh, no! Oh, bloody hell I'm on fire! I'm on fire!"

Belinda's voice. Of course it would be Belinda's voice.

Mildred leapt up, her gaze focused on the odd smut of orange that crawled its way along the front of Belinda's gown, devouring the lace edging like a meal as it worked its way closer to the ends of her plaited hair. Still on the floor, Belinda tried crawling backwards from the burning, as if she could escape it with the frenetic movements of a mad crab.

"Stop! STOP!" Mildred picked up the nearest thing to hand—a book—and smacked her niece in the chest with it several times in quick succession, enough to sever the fire from its needed air and leave nothing but the smell of burning and the faint aroma of charred hair in the air around them. "There, now. Are you all right?"

Belinda showed her gratitude by shoving Mildred to the floor and lunging for Fitz.

It was a moment that made Mildred curse her age and any general tendencies towards indolence she had acquired in the last decade or so. Drawn from her memories was the image of a turtle she had once found on its back, stumpy limbs pawing at the air without purchase, head and neck straining from the smooth edge of its shell as it sought in vain to find its way right side up again.

Unfortunately, she did not think there would be anyone to

come along and helpfully flip her over. She groaned and rolled and wondered why people were fitted out with hips when they so often failed to function as hips should, and finally managed to totter back onto her knees and then onto her feet and then she looked up and realized that Belinda was halfway towards stuffing Fitz into a sack.

And that would not do.

She thought about asking a question, something like "What are you doing?" or "Why are you forcing that angry dragon into a bag when he so clearly would prefer to set you on fire again?" But as Belinda did not seem to be in the most loquacious of moods, Mildred followed her niece's lead and chose action over words.

She grabbed for Fitz. It was a task beset with difficulties, as the room was still rather dark (the coals from behind the screen were hardly glowing and the windows still only gave off that ghostly silver hue distinct to those few hours between midnight and dawn) and Mildred's eyes had not been given enough time to adjust to the lack of light since waking. Her hand reached for what she thought was Fitz's leg, only it turned out to be his tail instead, and then Belinda —who seemed to have the advantage of seeing better in the dark than her aunt—smacked her hand away and dragged the half-bagged dragon over to one of the windows on the other side of the room.

"Oof!" Not the greatest thing she could have said in the moment, and certainly not a word she would conserve in her memories when it came time to relate the story to others. But the 'oof' came out as she slammed her toe into the foot of the bed, the slamming of the toe slowing her down enough to give Belinda time to throw open the window and shout down to an unseen someone waiting below.

"I've got it! I've got it! Are you ready?" She continued to hiss all of her words in the tea-kettle voice, as if there was still any further need for stealth by that point.

"What are you doing?" Mildred finally managed to say,

while her toe smarted and her hips threatened to rebel and her hands fought to snag a corner of the sack Belinda was pushing ever closer to the edge of the window sill.

She was going to throw it out the window. No, not 'it.' Fitz. Belinda was going to pitch Fitz out of the window while he thrashed and squawked and dangled halfway out of his sack. Mildred could not seem to do more than stand there and watch it happen, as if she were sitting in a box at the theatre waiting for the players to overact their way across the stage.

There was no time to breathe or pluck up her courage or think some grand thought to render the moment more epic and overflowing with drama. She took hold of the sack and pulled as hard as she could. Away from Belinda it came, except without a dragon inside of it.

"Oh," Mildred said.

"Oh!" Belinda said.

Belinda's recitation of the word earned its exclamation point due to the fact that while Mildred was left holding a sack without a dragon, she was standing in front of an open window holding a dragon without a sack. An upside-down dragon without a sack. And he was not pleased.

He demonstrated his displeasure by flapping his way out of Belinda's arms, his tail catching in her singed hair and his claws raking down her arms as he made an ungainly dash for the floor. Belinda turned as if to give chase, but Mildred stopped her, grabbing her arm and holding her there while Fitz fluttered and ran amok through the room.

"No, you will not!" Mildred pushed at Belinda until her niece hit the back of her legs against a nearby chair and was forced to either sit down or take a tumble onto the floor. Around them, Fitz continued to wreak havoc, knocking into furniture and screeching and spitting out little bursts of flame as if he were striking flint and steel to start a fire.

Belinda pulled her arm free of her aunt's grasp, cradling it to her chest like it bore more serious injuries than a few bruises and the run of scratches from Fitz's claws. "It doesn't belong to you!" she cried. "It belongs to Mr. Hawthorne! How dare you try and keep such a thing secret from everyone? What on earth did you think you could gain from it?"

"Nothing!" Mildred said, and loud enough to be heard over another squawk and the crash of something breakable demonstrating its powers of breakability as it shattered into bits on the floor. "I did not think to gain anything from him, anything at all!"

"'Him?'" Belinda stared at her in confusion. "Do you mean Mr. Hawthorne? Or do you mean–"

"Him!" Mildred gestured towards the dragon, or his approximate location as he was still streaking across the room, a flapping, screeching shadow of destructive menace. "I mean Fitz! He has a name."

"But why would you name it?"

Because I'm not the sort of person who would stuff a living creature into a sack and toss it out the bloody window, was what she wanted to say. And then she bit her lip, and she took a deep breath, and she did say it. Including the mild profanity.

"You make it sound so very dire," Belinda huffed. "Mr. Hawthorne is down there, you know. He would've caught the thing."

Mildred stepped over to the open window. There, indeed, down below, stood Mr. Hawthorne on the lawn, quite close to the side of the house. Or at least as close as a row of precisely trimmed hedges would allow him to be.

"Oh, this is exhausting," she said, and stepped back again.

In the time it had taken for her to lean out over the sill and locate Mr. Hawthorne, Belinda had abandoned her chair and gone after Fitz. There was no attempt to shove him into a bag this time. Mildred watched as Belinda reached out with claw-like hands extended, her face turned aside as if she feared the dragon might fight back and deliver some damage to her most prized possession.

"No, no, no," Mildred chanted as she gave chase. (A momentary curiosity sprung to life in her thoughts, a wonder that with all the noise and mayhem they had thus far produced, no one had come to her room to investigate the cause of it. But another second of thought delivered the realization that everything that had already occurred had probably only spanned no more than a minute or two. And it was a large house. And Mr. Gorman's room, if she remembered correctly, was on a completely separate floor. And...)

Belinda went for the door, but Mildred—for once—was quicker. Desperation fueled her now, along with a fear that should Belinda somehow manage to remove Fitz from the room—

Well, she did not want to ponder possible events that far ahead of where they already were. She simply had to focus on stopping Belinda and taking Fitz back into her care.

So she decided to tackle Belinda.

It must be acknowledged that Mildred had never gone so far as to tackle, or lay hold of anyone in such a manner as she was about to attempt. She hoped it would work in her favor to have a more substantial figure than her niece, and at first ('at first' meaning when she threw her weight on top of Belinda—careful not to also crush Fitz in the process—and dragged the girl down to the floor) it seemed to produce a favorable outcome. Belinda squirmed and shouted and tried to smack Mildred in the face (but only managed to swat at her shoulder) and then Fitz let out something like a *'skreeek'* and bit some part of Belinda (her wrist or the side of her hand, Mildred could not be sure amid the chaos of it all) before wriggling out of her arms and bolting across the room.

Surely, Mildred thought with some relief, that would be the end of it. Belinda was trapped beneath her on the floor, and Fitz would be caught and calmed down, and once she called out for help and Mr. Gorman and a few of the servants arrived to lend their—

And that was as far as her relieved thoughts went before Belinda kicked her shin and drove her elbow (slender and bony and a more painful weapon than Mildred would have anticipated) into her abdomen, knocking the potential for any cries for help out of her lungs.

Mildred could make no response to this other than to groan miserably and roll slowly onto her side near the door. Belinda took advantage of the moment—as was one of Belinda's talents—and squirmed away, staggering to her feet as she made another attempt at catching Fitz. Mildred could only watch in unravelling horror as Belinda snatched up a flapping, screaming Fitz, rushed to the still-open window and threw him out of it.

Goodness, she hoped Mr. Hawthorne was skilled at catching things.

Her abdomen throbbing, her shin threatening to up and abandon her for someone who was not regularly kicked in the legs, Mildred hauled herself over to the window as quickly as she could. She stood beside Belinda, both of them transfixed by the sight before them. Or, more accurately, what was not before them.

Mr. Hawthorne stood below, arms up and outstretched. But there was no dragon in his grasp. Mildred searched the ground desperately for any sight of a dark blot of delicate wings and twitching tail sprawled out on the grass. Would Fitz survive such a fall? Perhaps if he flapped his way down like a chicken, the worst possible outcome would be safely commuted. Yet there was no sign of him on the ground, either. Mildred leaned out further, the sill digging into her hips, her balance wavering as she rose onto the balls of her feet and peered directly down the side of the house.

And there sat Fitz, clinging to a ledge only a few feet below the window, his wings curled around him like a gentleman's cloak, his tail flicking in annoyance at having been so thoroughly abused.

"Oh, goodness." Mildred sagged forward, her heart and her stomach and too many other vital organs pushing their way up into her throat.

"Well, now what?" This, from Belinda, who appeared rather deflated at the fact that the dragon was now suspended between herself and Mr. Hawthorne, like a kite caught in the top branches of a tree that no one could reach.

"Please, do shut up." That, from Mildred, who really could not bring herself to give a proverbial fig about anything that had to do with her niece at the moment.

It was then, in an example of perfectly orchestrated dramatic timing, that Mr. Gorman chose to knock on Mildred's bedroom door. She called out for him to come in (which he did, clad in a nightshirt and dressing gown and tasseled cap on his head) and proceeded to join them at the window, only pausing long enough to give Belinda a quick glance (very askance, as was more than Belinda deserved) and ask Mildred what was happening.

"What is happening?" There was the question, quickly followed by: "Is that Mr. Hawthorne down there?"

"They tried to take Fitz," Mildred said, all in a rush. Her abdomen still hurt from the assault of Belinda's elbow, and she suspected most of her joints would refuse to work properly until a hot bath and some kind of liniment was provided for them, but she stood as straight as she could manage and forced herself to breathe evenly. "I believe their plan was to spirit him out the window." She pointed towards the narrow ledge where the dragon had taken up temporary residence. "But I doubt we'll have him down again before he consents to it."

Mr. Gorman sighed, the kind of sigh that went along with a prodigious amount of thought. "Well, perhaps if you could reach your arms down close enough to him, or should we try a large blanket, standing on the lawn with it stretched out between us? And we could coax him to leap down into it?"

Mildred shook her head. She was angry at Belinda, angry at Mr. Hawthorne, exhausted from lack of sleep, hurting from all the tussling of the last few minutes, and now she would have to add worry for Fitz, trapped as he was on the side of the house. "Maybe if I just…" She rose onto the balls of her feet again, then felt her toes leave the floor entirely as she leaned over the sill, one arm extended towards Fitz while the other gripped the edge of the window with the white-knuckled strength of someone who did not care to tip over and fall to a fate of either death or permanent injury.

She could not reach him. He was still several feet below, and she doubted she could convince him to scrabble up the wall into her arms, nor did she want to risk the possible unhappy outcome of such a venture. "Oh, Fitz," she said, or rather ground out between gritted teeth. "I am sorry. If you'll just wait a minute we can come around and—oh!"

The "oh!" was because Fitz shifted on his perch, twisting around enough to unfurl his wings—first the left, then the right—before he let out a timid cry and leapt—or dropped, it really was more of a plummet, Mildred had to admit—off the wall.

"No!" The shout came out of her as his wings flapped, awkwardly at first, leaving him to tilt and rotate and nearly fly into Mr. Hawthorne's face like an off-balance chicken. Instead, only his hat was knocked from his head as Fitz corrected himself and with another flap, along with a screech for accompaniment, soared off across the garden and into the darkness beyond.

"Oh dear," Mildred said, still clinging to the window sill, Mr. Gorman gripping her arm from behind to keep her steady as she dangled halfway out into the night.

Behind her, there came a sound of impatience. Mildred turned, blinking stupidly, amazed that Belinda still stood there by the window and the room was still where it had been and no other part of the scene around her was completely shaken free of its foundations. Mr. Gorman kept his hand on her arm until she had steadied herself, though Mildred worried a full return to steadiness might never happen again.

"Miss Percy?" Mr. Gorman asked, ducking his head low enough to look into her face.

"We have to find him," Mildred said. What other option lay before them? "Or perhaps he'll come back? Should we wait?" Those options, then. Those options were open to them as well, she supposed. "But it's dark, and it's…"

Mr. Gorman gave her arm a brief squeeze before releasing her. "I shall wake a few of the servants. We can make a search of the grounds, see what we can find."

She looked out the window again. Down below, Mr. Hawthorne was retrieving his hat from the ground. She watched as he plunked it onto his head, turned up the collar of his coat against the early morning chill, and dashed off across the lawn in that shuffling, cowardly way people ran when they were being shuffling cowards. "Thank you, Mr. Gorman."

And then she looked at Belinda. Belinda, who seemed to be trying to wear a half dozen faces at once, all guilty and penitent and sullen and smug and too many other emotions for one young woman to express without looking as if she had just bitten down on a worm inside her apple.

"Stay here," Mildred ordered. Her words came out as a rasp. All of her various aches and pains were going to attack her now, but she could not give them the attention they deserved. Not while Fitz was out there, flying about on his wings like some manner of flying creature.

She shut her eyes, pressed the tips of her fingers to her temples and willed her thoughts into some semblance of order.

Dress for the day. Find Fitz. Manage Belinda. There were other things she was sure, but those were the ones vying most vehemently for her immediate attention.

"So." She opened her eyes again and looked at Mr. Gorman, who stood there as a study in patience and slight bewilderment. "I will meet you downstairs in ten minutes? No, five. I should not need more time than that."

"Five minutes." He nodded once, lending a slight disturbance to the tassel on his cap, and turned and walked out of the room, closing the door behind him.

Mildred glanced at the clock, her eyes now finally suited to the darkness of the room. It was only a few minutes after two in the morning, an awful time to be wide awake and preparing to set out with a search party in order to find a young dragon who had just discovered the extent of his powers of flight. At some point in the future, possibly once she had located said dragon and was seated comfortably in front of a warm fire with her feet up on a cushion and a plate of delicious baked edibles balanced on her abdomen, she would make an attempt at determining when, precisely, *was* a good time for preparing to set out on such a task. But for now, she would have to make do with her tired, bruised—possibly broken, considering the pain still throbbing through a rib and one of her toes—body. Convalescence and cake were neither of them an option at the moment.

"What about me?"

Mildred looked up from her search through the myriad garments scattered across the floor. (If she was going to be tramping about outside through grass and dirt and dew, there seemed no point in dragging something clean from her wardrobe.) "And what *about* you?"

Belinda crossed her arms over her chest, the crowning movement in a dance choreographed to the melody of Disagreeable. "Am I supposed to sit here, as if I were some sort of small child enduring a punishment?"

Mildred snatched up a pair of stockings—crinkled, but well enough to do for the day—and shook them out with more force than they deserved. "When you cease to behave like a small child in need of chastisement, then I will no longer treat you as such. Now, sit and wait. And if you're inclined, send up a prayer that we find Fitz quickly and unharmed. Or else ask for mercy for yourself should we not."

Belinda huffed and dropped into a chair. Mildred dressed hurriedly, ignoring things like stays or accessories or anything to do with her hair. She paused at the door, her hand holding tight to the knob as if it might try to slip out of her fingers on its own. And she almost looked back, a quick glance over her shoulder at the mess of the room and the starlight filtering in through the windows and her niece being belligerent against it all.

But she did not look back. Only one of those little decisions she would revisit from time to time in the future, weighted with all of its reminders of how things would not have taken an alternate course had she chosen differently. And yet she would think over it anyway, again and again, as one too often did.

CHAPTER TWENTY-NINE

It is the silence of their flight that makes dragons well-suited for nocturnal bouts of hunting. Their prey will often never know they are in danger until the claws are out and they have been snatched up from the ground and swept away.

-from Chapter Twelve of Miss Percy's Pocket Guide (to the Care and Feeding of British Dragons)

Mildred would have to admit that in all her years of reading and thinking and creating outlandish fantasies from the dregs of her imagination, she had never spared much thought for the amount of skill that might be necessary for the task of hunting down and finding a dragon. If she had considered it, she most likely would have assumed there to be at least a small amount of skill involved, that only brave souls with the ability to tramp through the woods without turning themselves round in a circle or great and mighty fighters wielding swords or spears or other such weapons—as were most prevalent in the annals of storybook fighting—should ever seek to attempt it.

What she would not have described if someone had asked her—oh, six months before—what or who it might take to locate and quell a possibly agitated young dragon was a motley selection of a mere five individuals laden with lamps and rashers and a tattered blanket in case the dragon in question was cold or wet or otherwise muddy and inconvenienced when they found him.

(The five were, in no particular order: Mildred (a spinster) Mr. Gorman (an elderly and kindly steward) Cotton (a groundskeeper with a slight limp and in possession of a tendency to add too many 'r's to his words) Mrs. Frances (an assistant cook with a red nose and clad in boots large and thick enough to probably traverse the channel towards Brittany without soaking her socks) and Tom (a young stableboy who appeared to only be a member of their party because it took him away from his early morning chores. (It will also be noted that Mildred thought he had been introduced as "Tom" but it was the groundskeeper who had introduced him so even with shaving off the superfluous 'r's from each end of the name, she was afraid to say it aloud and discover that she had heard it entirely wrong.))

They began with the gardens. It was still dark when the group set out, all of them stamping their feet and thinking fondly of the warm beds they had left behind. The air carried that odd, damp chill that presaged a fine and warm day ahead, but as it was not fine and warm at that moment, none of them were able to solace themselves with the promise of warm sunshine when it was still so many hours away.

Each person was given a lamp and some bacon—the latter for coaxing Fitz out of a hiding place, should he be reluctant to immediately show himself to any of them—and told to be thorough, or as thorough as they could be at too-early in the morning and with the unspoken strangeness of searching for a dragon across finely manicured grounds cajoling them through their quest.

Mildred, however, did not believe Fitz would be found in the gardens. He did not much care for flowers, as far as she had seen in all of his interactions with the more colorful and scented portions of England's flora, nor had any of the fountains or statuary enticed him to linger near them, dispelling her tendency to categorize him along with the other winged creatures she had witnessed bathing in the water or marking their presence on the sculptures decorating the various gardens. So after a cursory search of the main area beneath her window, Mildred turned her attention to the nearest patch of woods, the one with the stream and the bench and the lovely old tree with all of the nuts beneath it.

"There is a folly out there," Mr. Gorman informed her as they cut across the lawn. "Just on the other side of the stream. If you do not find him beneath or around the trees, perhaps he has taken up residence inside of it. We did have a terrible problem with squirrels out there one year, nesting in the various nooks of the thing."

Mildred stopped at the edge of the trees, the light of her lantern seeming to shudder and weaken in proximity to the daunting foliage.

"Miss Percy?" Mr. Gorman paused beside her, while behind them the other members of their party fanned out in order to cover more ground.

"Fitz?" she called out, her voice wavering more than she would have liked. She waited. There was the steady babbling of the stream, and then the rustle of a few leaves above them. Squirrels? An owl? Belinda perched on a sturdy branch, ready to leap down and be disagreeable to everyone?

She squinted through the darkness, her efforts aided by that pale gray light of an early dawn, and thought she could make out the edge of the foot bridge Mr. Gorman had mentioned to her. "I'll follow the path, towards the folly. Could you follow along the edge of the stream for a bit, see if you can find any footprints of his in the mud?" She did not want to think about him falling into the water, in the dark, and perhaps not being able to crawl out again until he had been washed down a ways.

The bridge was small but sturdy, only a few thick planks set over the water accompanied by a handrail on one side. Mildred winced at the heavy sound of her steps on the wood, like hammers announcing her progress. The path ahead was clearer on this side of the stream, the light from her lamp

348

shining out over a narrow ribbon of packed dirt kept free of brush and smaller trees, and all of it lined with large stones on either side.

There was a bit of a rise, and then down again, and then the folly came into view. She stopped there, and frowned. It seemed too far. Fitz would not have come out all this way, would he? She took a single step forward, paused, then turned on her heel to return towards the stream and the bridge when a small chirrup of sound—not a squawk or a cry, but something that did not match the usual sounds expected from a thoroughly English copse of trees an hour or so before sunrise—broke the ambient sounds of the wood.

"Fitz?"

Did she sound frightened? She hoped she did not sound frightened, more for Fitz's sake than for any other reason.

"Mr. Gorman?"

And, there. Her voice wobbled on the last syllable, a syllable that really wasn't spoken very loudly at all and she wondered how it could be such a demanding thing to raise her voice strong enough to be heard when it was most important to do so.

She turned around again and continued down towards the folly. Another chirrup sounded as she approached, and then something very like a scrabble of claws against stone, and then... silence.

"Fitz!" Her light cast the inside of the folly in golds and bronze and delineated shadows. She looked all around the inside of it, under the roof of the portico and up along the edge, where a series of miniature alcoves served as the foundation for a cupola directly overhead.

"Oh, there you are." It was his eyes that caught her attention, gleaming like gemstones from beneath the shadow of a furled wing. He had tucked himself into one of the alcoves, a feat that seemed impossible at first glance, that he should be able to make himself so small.

There was a bench running along the inside of the folly,

curving along the inner wall. Mildred set down her lamp on the hard stone seat, hoisted up her hem as she stepped up onto said seat, and—while gripping one of the columns that supported the roof with a strength that could tear a tree from the ground, so potent was her fear of standing on something less than two feet above the floor—reached out with her free hand towards Fitz.

"I'm right here," she said, her words carried on a low, sing-song voice. She still had her portion of bacon hidden away in a pocket of her skirt, but she dared not risk shifting her balance in order to reach down and pull it out in order to entice him better.

Fitz shifted a little, claws scraping at the bottom edge of the alcove in which he had sequestered himself, the barbed end of his tail slipping out before he curled it around the base of his legs. He let out a small squawk, then shifted again, then snorted as his gaze switched from Mildred to some point behind her.

Mildred knew without looking that someone else was there. It was not because of a change in the air, as some books she had read preferred to describe it, nor did it signal the hairs on the back of her neck or her forearms to prickle to attention. No, she simply heard a step, and a light cough, and that intake of breath one performs before venturing to speak for the first time after a period of quiet.

"Be careful, Miss Percy. I would not wish for you to fall or harm yourself."

Mr. Hawthorne.

It was an irritating thing, how kind he sounded, as if he really did care for her well-being. And if she turned around to look at him, she knew he would still be possessed of his handsome features, his fine build, and all of it bearing that aura of good nature and affability that those who were blessed with fine looks often managed to carry around with them, like their own personal atmosphere of charm.

So she did not turn around right away. Partly because she

did not want to see Mr. Hawthorne's stupid handsome face, and also because she did not trust herself to change the direction of her sight too drastically in case it altered her balance in a way that could not easily be corrected.

"Come along, Fitz," she said instead, and stretched her fingers until she could just brush the tips of them against the curled edge of his tail. "Please."

Fitz put out one foreleg, his claws splayed.

"Very good, Miss Percy. You fetch him down for me. Foolish thing already tried to bite me once."

Mildred's fingers pulled back into a fist, her nails biting into the soft flesh of her palm.

"Stay," she mouthed, and hoped that in Fitz's scant months of development since popping out of his egg, he had managed to acquire a talent for lip-reading.

And now a choice was before her: To cry out for help? To stay standing on the bench in some kind of protective pose between Mr. Hawthorne and Fitz? To step down where she would be more stable and also in an improved position if she needed to suddenly run away?

"Mr. G—"

She had been about to give a shout for Mr. Gorman, but only managed to make it as far as the "G" when Mr. Hawthorne pulled a bright and shining thing out from the inner pocket of his coat.

It was a knife. Mildred had no need for full daylight to make out that much. All of its requisite pieces were there—a handle, a long blade that curved a bit upwards at the end— and Mr. Hawthorne held it in a way that was meant to not be terribly threatening and yet leave her very, very aware of what he grasped in his hand.

"I will admit," he said, his words clogged with something that might have been a chuckle. "I have never used one of these before. I mean, I have used a knife before for eating and such, but I am not"–a quick, mocking stabbing motion with his hand– "particularly violent. Not at all, really."

And what was that supposed to tell her? That the knife was only for appearances' sake? That he did not intend to use it in any capacity and she should therefore disregard its presence entirely? Or was his little speech meant to set her at ease, to make her sway towards him with the belief that he was not a bad person at all despite the current display of sharpened weaponry dangling from his fingers?

"I will not hurt it," Mr. Hawthorne went on, taking a half step forward. "If that is what you're worried about. It is much too important a discovery for me to even conceive seeing a single scale on his hide come to harm. But you cannot go on in this way, Miss Percy, treating him as if he were no more than a common pet. This creature"–he gestured towards the alcove where Fitz still hid– "is nothing short of a miracle. And the world deserves to know about it."

Mildred reminded herself to breathe. Slowly, three counts in, hold, three counts out again. "And you," she began, then nearly choked on the words from how fast her heart was beating. "And you should be the one to tell everyone about him, I assume?"

He grinned. Even in the low light of the lamp, the soft gray illumination of the sky beyond the confines of the folly, his perfect teeth gleamed. "The egg was my father's. It was to go to me. You are just a bit of an impediment through all of this."

A bit of an impediment. Mildred wondered if there had ever been a better summation of her existence spoken aloud. "So I should, what, exactly? Step aside? Give him over to you as easily as that?"

"Well, yes." Mr. Hawthorne's thumb stroked the handle of his blade. It looked like something he had snagged from the kitchen on a quick jaunt through the house. "It is not very much, really, when you think about it. You will still have your home to return to, your place with your sister's family. You will be taken care of. But I do not have the same luxury as you, of safety, of a constant roof over my head. But with that dragon… oh, it will be the making of me, don't you see? It was what my father intended, I know it. To bring our family back up to its rightful place in society."

"On the back of a baby dragon," she added.

He tipped his head in her direction. "Needs must."

He took another half step forward. She moved back, only to strike the back of her knees on the edge of the stone bench. "What of Belinda?" The question came out of nowhere. To be honest, she had not given a thought to Belinda since stepping out of doors to begin the search for Fitz, but she needed another topic of conversation to distract Mr. Hawthorne while her brain slogged its way towards something resembling rational and coherent thought. "Whether her doing or yours, her reputation has been ruined by abandoning her home and family to travel with you, alone and unaccompanied by any sort of chaperone. How do you intend to remedy this?

He shrugged. "Well, I will just have to marry her, then."

"And you believe she will agree?"

"I hope she will," he admitted, his voice trembling with what almost sounded to Mildred's ears like vulnerability. "Miss Muncy is unlike anyone I have ever met. Do you not notice that when you are with her? How indescribable she is?"

"Indescribable." Mildred nodded. "Yes, that sounds very much like my niece."

"So, you understand, yes?" Mr. Hawthorne's eyebrows rose and disappeared beneath the brim of his hat. "How important all of this is? I am not a villain, Miss Percy," he said, standing there brandishing a rather large knife in her general direction. "I only want what I deserve, what has been owed to me since the very beginning."

Mildred balled up her fists in the fabric of her skirt. She had no one's hand to hold, and yet she felt the need to grip something, to stabilize herself for what she was about to do. "Very well." She moved to step back, remembered the bench, and shuffled a few paces to the side. Beyond Mr. Hawthorne, at the top of the rise, she saw the figure of Mr. Gorman come into view. As he did not appear to be in a hurry to come down to the folly, she guessed that he did not notice Mr. Hawthorne's presence in the folly with her. A good thing, that. Because Mr. Hawthorne still had his knife and no matter his claims against villainhood, the blade pointed towards her did not bode well. "You promise not to hurt him in any way?"

"Of course!" Mr. Hawthorne's face brightened in the way faces did when people realized matters were shifting in their favor. "I give my word. He is worth more alive than dead, I would assume."

A little bit of bile rose up in Mildred's throat at that. "Then you may have him. You and Belinda both. But you must put the knife away and you will have to take him on your own. I will not be a party to it."

Surely, he would not give in as easily as that. She told herself this even as he slipped the knife back into his pocket and gave a little adjustment to his sleeves, as if he were preparing himself for an elegant evening out. She shimmied sideways again, away and away to give him room to approach the part of the folly in which Fitz had stashed himself. Mildred glanced over her shoulder and saw Mr. Gorman finally making his way down to the folly, but she held up her hand in a warning gesture, stalling his progress.

"Here, now." Mr. Hawthorne stepped up to the bench, one hand extended, his fingers twiddling in a way meant to draw Fitz out from his shadowed hiding place. "Do you see? I am not going to hurt you. Just come with me and I shall give you, um…" He looked back at Mildred, his features beseeching. "What does he like?"

"Bacon," she admitted, though without offering up the bits of pork currently stashed in her pocket. "And potatoes, with extra butter."

"Mmm, good taste." He turned back to Fitz. "I shall give

you all the bacon and potatoes you desire, hmm? Just come on out. That's it. There's a good—"

It should be noted here that for a very brief moment, perhaps not lasting more than a second or two, Mildred was forced to question if Fitz would indeed comply with Mr. Hawthorne's request. His tail uncurled, his claws scraped and flexed as he sought to wriggle his way out from the small space, and she thought maybe—just maybe—he would allow Mr. Hawthorne to—

The very brief moment of question ended quite succinctly as Fitz let out a low snort and launched himself at Mr. Hawthorne's face.

It would be a test of Mildred's powers of description to relay the event to others later on. The lantern was knocked over by a swipe of Mr. Hawthorne's boot, the swipe happening as he staggered backwards while Fitz flapped and screeched and clawed at Mr. Hawthorne's arms, now raised upwards to protect his face.

Mildred had no inclination to intervene. She had hoped it would come to something like this, Fitz holding his own against Mr. Hawthorne, though she could not have predicted how remarkably outmatched and outclassed Mr. Hawthorne would be against this particular opponent.

As pleasant a scene as it was to witness, however, it was when Fitz began spitting out small bursts of flame into Mr. Hawthorne's eyes that Mildred finally determined it best for her to step forward. Reaching in to grab at one of Fitz's legs, her arms were pummeled by the beat and snap of his wings, the strength of them much greater than she had assumed.

"That is enough," she said between flaps. "Enough!"

There was blood, she saw, running in rivulets down the side of Mr. Hawthorne's face. His hat was somewhere around, and under her shoes came the crunch of broken glass from the fallen lantern.

"Fitz! You cannot—"

But Fitz was not about to allow Mildred to tell him what

he could or could not do. Sinking his claws deep into Mr. Hawthorne's shoulders, he clamped his toothless jaws onto the man's right ear in a manner that made Mildred suspect not even a force of supernatural proportions would knock him loose again.

"Hold on!" Mr. Gorman arrived at that moment, ducking down behind Mr. Hawthorne and grabbing the man's arms to pull him back, not anticipating that the dragon would simply come along with him. Mildred made another attempt to pry Fitz away, and with one final smack of his wings to her head, she succeeded in dragging him free (though not without a strangled cry from Mr. Hawthorne, the sound no doubt provoked into existence by the last grasp of Fitz's claws in his shoulders and the small notch at the top of his ear that appeared as the dragon's jaws were wrenched away).

"Now, let us just—" Mr. Gorman said, before Mr. Hawthorne spun round—blood in his eyes and streaked down his face, his coat slashed at the shoulders, his ear bleeding profusely and noticeably diminished in size—and punched him soundly in the chin.

It was an unexpected development, in that all of the cold, insidious threat of a sharpened knife had been replaced by the blunt force of fist against jaw. Unfortunately, Mr. Hawthorne's aim was nowhere near the level of expert, so he only managed to graze Mr. Gorman's chin and the edge of his ear. It was enough, however, to leave them startled and slow to react. Mr. Hawthorne, dripping fluids and groaning and cursing all of them, took the opportunity afforded to him by their bewilderment to shoulder his way out of the folly and escape at full speed into the woods.

Mildred gave no thought to chasing him. Fitz was still in high dudgeon, flapping and spitting sparks and refusing to be quieted until Mildred dug into her pocket and retrieved the bacon that had been secreted there long enough to make her entire garment smell of cooked meat.

"It is all right," she cooed, along with an assortment of

other calming words and phrases, repeated over and again until Fitz ceased leaping about from one side of the folly to the other like a caged bird and snapped up one of the bits of bacon offered to him. (Not until he had consumed all of the bacon in Mildred's possession but also everything from Mr. Gorman's pockets would he submit to being picked up, though not without an additional nip at Mildred's knuckles when she attempted to scratch him beneath his chin.)

"I will send another group out to search the grounds for Mr. Hawthorne," Mr. Gorman said, in between odd movements of his jaw to make certain it still functioned properly. "A notice should be sent to the various inns in the area as well, to keep an eye out for him should he pass through."

"He will be more noticeable than he was before," Mildred remarked, thinking of Mr. Hawthorne's ragged ear and the wounds on his face. "I just hope he will not be driven to harm anyone."

Mr. Gorman swept some of the broken glass aside with a scrape of his boot. "If a few scratches and a fair measure of damaged pride is enough to drive someone to harming another person, then I do not believe the wounds are really to blame."

They were words that stayed with Mildred as they returned to the house, calling back the other members of the search party along the way. They went in through the back of the house and the kitchen, Mr. Gorman ordering coffee and sustenance from the sleepy-eyed servants as the first light of dawn struck the leaded windows.

"I think I will just go up to my room," Mildred said when Mr. Gorman attempted to foist some coffee or at least a bit of toast upon her. "Some rest is what I desire more than anything. And once that has been achieved, I will be more than willing to consume as much cake and breaded things as your cook is willing to provide."

Fitz was fully asleep by the time she arrived outside of

her room. It was a bit of a struggle to open the door without dropping him, but she had no wish to knock in case Belinda had fallen asleep while everyone was outside searching for the dragon (or waving pieces of cutlery around in an attempt to steal the dragon, as Mr. Hawthorne had so dramatically demonstrated). But she managed it, kicking the door open the rest of the way with a buss from her shoe, and nearly tripping over a book lying open on the floor (one of many that had been knocked hither and thither during her struggle with Belinda earlier in the morning).

The rest of the room was in a greater tumult than she remembered, though the addition of daylight coming in through the windows was most likely the culprit for this new awareness. Clothes and smaller articles of furniture looked as if they had been picked up in a maelstrom and then suddenly dropped at the peak of the storm, and though Mildred would not claim the greatest housekeeping skills since arriving at Exley Hall, she would hold to the truth that at least she had not left her things to be distributed by terrible weather events.

But it was in the middle of all the chaos that Mildred noticed something important. Or rather the absence of something important. Of someone important.

"Of course she's gone," Mildred said, her eyes fixed on the chair where she had left Belinda. The chair that was now very much lacking in belligerent nieces.

Gone, gone, gone. She said the words in her head, then again out loud as she nestled Fitz into a wadded pile of blankets on her bed. As was Mr. Hawthorne, she reminded herself, absconding through the woods with less blood and less ear than that with which he had arrived. So how long, she wondered—or how very soon—would it be until the two of them found one another once again?

CHAPTER THIRTY

The people of Wales often claim their country to be home of the first dragon. As the location of the first dragon to ever set foot (or claw) on this earth is a fact that has yet to be discovered, the Welsh take this as a clear confirmation of their belief.

-from the prologue of Miss Percy's Travel Guide (to Welsh Moors and Feral Dragons)

Mildred spread more butter on her toast. She was not certain this specific piece of toast was durable enough for the amount of butter she insisted on slathering across its golden surface, but as scooping clumps of butter directly from the dish to her mouth would most likely be considered a sign of poor etiquette in front of others (this is not an admittance that Mildred had scooped butter directly into her mouth before whilst alone, but neither is it a denial), she decided the toast would have to serve as the most polite and socially acceptable mechanism for delivering gobs of half-melted butter to her mouth without instigating a raise of eyebrows from her dining partner.

The exorbitant volume of butter being stuffed into Mildred's mouth was a result of Belinda and Mr. Hawthorne's disappearance. (At least she supposed this was the reason, or preferred to use it as her excuse.) Neither of them had been seen since the previous morning, nor had any report come in from any of the surrounding inns or toll-roads of a young man and woman—either travelling together or apart—that matched their descriptions.

Mildred was torn between a mild relief that they were gone, even if it was only a temporary reprieve—she held no real hope that they would not find a way to work themselves back into her life, like a patch of mildew on a wall or an odd smell from beneath the floorboards—and the desire to know where they were and what new scheme they might even now be cogitating between them.

Because she knew they were together, wherever they were. Neither of them seemed the type capable of fully striking out on their own without someone else prodding them along to further mischief.

"I wish I could convince you to stay a little while longer," Mr. Gorman said, before shovelling a steaming bite of eggs into his mouth.

But Mildred shook her head as she surreptitiously licked a dollop of butter from the side of her thumb. "I need to see my sister. She should know what has become of her eldest daughter, as I doubt Belinda had the courtesy to even write a note, or at least one with any truth in it, before leaving home."

And there were other reasons leading Mildred away from Exley Hall, ones that had already suffered much discussion between Mr. Gorman and herself. There was safety to be considered, for one thing. After the attempted abduction of Fitz—Mildred still shuddered when she thought back to the sight of him being tossed from the window like a sack of unwashed laundry—she did not believe she could stay there any longer. Nor did she believe Upper Plimpton would be safe for him, but there were things that needed to be taken care of before she could see Fitz sent somewhere where there would be less risk of him falling—an unintentional choice of wording—into the wrong hands.

She had made her decision. She would have him sent to London, where Fitz could be raised and cared for by someone with greater scientific knowledge of such things than she could ever lay claim to.

Words scrawled in a letter might not be enough to convince all of the learned men in England that dragons did indeed exist, but the sight of one landing on their doorstep would leave little room for denial. (Mildred entertained this notion as someone who had not endured much interaction with most of the learned men of England. In her mind, they were similar in make and character to her Great Uncle Forthright, men ruled by their own curiosity, a desire to ask questions, to know more. What she did not understand at the moment was that the majority of 'learned' men in England—the use of quotation marks here should be noted, their points curling into each end of the word, siphoning away all sincerity—would not have been swayed to believe something fantastical should the Lady of the Lake herself stride from the water's edge and bonk them over the head with a sword.)

She finished her breakfast—more toast, more butter, a spoonful of black raspberry jam licked straight from the spoon because her ability to care what Mr. Gorman thought of her eating habits was rapidly crumbling as her anxiety about the journey ahead strengthened—and returned to her room long enough to make certain that all of her belongings were packed and accounted for. The larger bags had already been taken downstairs and loaded onto the carriage. And Fitz...

Fitz would be coming with her. He was downstairs, even now, already packed into his basket, overfed on all of his favorite foods and a few sips of brandy—the latter for ease of convincing him to go into his basket—and ready to travel with her back to Upper Plimpton. She could not take him home, of course, so back to the vicarage he would have to go until she could arrange for him to go to London, or possibly Edinburgh, or... well, wherever it was that 'learned' men who might have an interest in a young dragon were most likely to congregate.

Clad and carrying all the various accoutrements of travel —bonnet, gloves, spencer, reticule—she and Fitz made their goodbyes—brief but heartfelt—along with all the promises to return, to write letters, and for Mildred to give Mr. Gorman's regards to Mrs. Babbinton when next she saw her again. Into the carriage they went—Mildred relishing the prospect of an entire seat to herself for the duration of the journey and Fitz, snoring from inside his basket, on the floor at her feet—and then they were off, still with the faint mist of early morning clinging to the lower areas of the land around them.

Many of the details of the journey will not be relayed here, as they are numerous and highly lacking in relevance to the overall arc of the main story. Suffice it to say, the only stops made were to change the horses, all of the food for herself and Fitz coming from a basket packed by the cook (apples were included as a special treat for Fitz), and they did not arrive again in Upper Plimpton until the very middle of the night (or possibly early morning, as Mildred's penchant for dozing in an empty, rumbling carriage had left her unable to keep an accurate check on both their progress and the time).

They went to the vicarage first. There was only a dim light in one of the windows, Mr. Wiggan's study, but as Mildred could not very well take Fitz along with her the rest of the way to Ashby Lodge, she would have to dare waking the household at a most unrespectable time in the morning. (One o'clock, by the driver's watch. Mildred made certain to ask.)

She knocked, briskly and decisively, her actions spurred to further heights of urgency by the fact it was one o'clock in the morning and the sky above her carried that peculiar quality of seeming to have lowered itself near enough to the earth that she had to keep herself from ducking down away from it.

As she knocked the second time, there was the stutter of

uneven footsteps from the other side of the door before it was opened and Mrs. Babbinton peered out at her.

"Goodness," she said, her cap askew atop her gray, flattened-on-one-side-of-her-head curls. She held a single candle, and raised it higher to better see the carriage and horses parked behind Mildred. "Well, come along. I'm awake now, so I shall go ahead and put on the kettle for tea."

Fitz was brought inside and released from his basket the moment Mildred set foot in the kitchen. His original bed was gone, but he waddled towards the fireplace on unsteady legs —unsteady from being crammed inside a basket all day and not due to any latent effects of his morning brandy consumption—and curled up on the floor while Mrs. Babbinton worked to clear out the previous day's coals and prepare a new fire.

"Sit, sit!" The housekeeper waved a long-handled shovel in the direction of the chairs without looking away from her work. "I will leave it up to you if we should wake Mr. Wiggan or—"

"No, I am already up," came his gruff, sleep-thickened voice from the doorway. The vicar had taken the time to dress, Mildred noticed. Or—thinking of the light that had been burning in the window of his study—perhaps he had not yet bothered to retire for the night. Either way, his clothing was rumpled, his tonsure of hair bore the look of having had his fingers pushed through it frequently, and his features appeared drawn in a way that gave the impression he needed more sleep or a meal that hadn't been left to sit and grow cold on his plate. Or a bit of both, most likely. "Good evening, Miss Percy." He bowed, then patted his chest as if he were searching his pockets for something that turned out to be missing. "Or good morning, it would seem."

"I am sure you are exhausted," Mrs. Babbinton said, in between her blowing across a small mound of lit kindling. "And I am sure the best thing for you would be to sleep for the rest of the night and long into tomorrow before you face our barrage of questions."

Mildred leaned forward over the table, her elbows resting on the tabletop, her chin resting on her hands. Sleep was out of the question, as much as the thought of a warm bed should appeal to her stiff muscles. The vicarage kitchen smelled of all the things that shrouded her in feelings of safety and comfort—woodsmoke, yeast, dried herbs and spices—yet the worry she had dragged with her from Warwickshire flicked at her with the sticky fingers of a persistent toddler.

She looked at Fitz, already curled into a ball with his tail shifting leisurely against the edge of Mrs. Babbinton's skirts. "He cannot stay here for long," she admitted. "Nor even at Exley Hall."

That worked well enough as the prologue to her story. She told them everything that had occurred after Mrs. Babbinton had left Warwickshire (she was sure Mr. Wiggan had already been well apprised of everything that had happened *before* Mrs. Babbinton had left Warwickshire, so she did not waste her breath on those details), the tale spilling out like a ball of yarn unravelling as it rolled across the kitchen floor.

Mrs. Babbinton prompted her along with cheese and bread toasted over the fire, along with numerous cups of tea (very welcome, as Mildred could drink with impunity now that she was no longer trapped inside a carriage and worrying about when the next stop would come along) and thin, almond-glazed biscuits. Mildred was onto her fourth biscuit when her story petered out to its conclusion. And then she swallowed, took a sip of tea, and looked across the table at Mr. Wiggan (second biscuit, third cup of tea).

"Well?" she asked when the other two occupants of the kitchen—she did not count Fitz, as he had only woken long enough to gobble up some dropped cheese and gone swiftly back to sleep—said nothing.

"Perhaps..." Mr. Wiggan began, and then paused to finish the last bite of his biscuit. "Perhaps Miss Muncy has anticipated your arrival and has already returned home to Ashby Lodge?"

But Mrs. Babbinton made a sharp sound with her tongue and shook her head. "Oh, you've not heard the gossip then? There are already whispers about town, people talking about Miss Muncy's disappearance. Mrs. Muncy is attempting to cover it all up with some made up thing about her daughter coming down with a fever and unable to leave the house. But Mrs. Dillon claims she saw the girl walking about with an unknown gentleman—who we, of course, know to be Mr. Hawthorne—while Mr. Gallant has already put it about that he saw her round and about Swindon last week, at the same time they would have been making their journey up to Warwickshire."

Mildred blinked at Mrs. Babbinton's powers of gossip acquisition, and all managed in so short a time since her return to Upper Plimpton. "Oh. Well, then. I am sure my sister will be in high spirits when I return home."

She looked around the room for a clock. Mrs. Babbinton, seeming to know her mind, said, "It's past three in the morning already. You may stay here for the rest of the night and head to Ashby Lodge at a less distressing hour, if you would rather. And don't fret over Mr. Gorman's men, I stepped out and sent them on their way to the inn hours ago."

The excitement of the journey had begun to wear off, and with her stomach full of cheese and biscuits and her head full of too many thoughts, she felt the weight of the last few days descend on her like a heavy blanket. "But what about Fitz?" she asked. Because at this moment, even with the cheese and the biscuits and the exhaustion crowding in on her, he remained the most prominent worry in her head.

"You will really send him away?" It was Mr. Wiggan's question, though Mildred had difficulty looking him in the eye after he had asked it, despite the lack of anything the least bit accusatory in his tone.

"I saw him fly," she said. It seemed enough, those four

words. Enough to explain away her intention to see Fitz delivered into a better state of care than anything she believed she or Mr. Wiggan could provide. Enough to thicken her voice, to twist her fingers into knots in her lap. "We cannot keep him here. We knew that before I even left for Warwickshire, after the fire at the Old Gables. And now he has attacked two men. Yes," She held up her hand when Mrs. Babbinton seemed about to interrupt, "I believe they were both more than deserving of their punishment. But what if he harms someone else? Someone innocent? I have let him play with Matthew and Nettie, but what if he should lash out at one of them? What if...?"

She looked at Mr. Wiggan, and she realized she had missed the steadiness of his gaze, the ability he had in his mere silence to make her feel heard. "I know you have written to several people in London and other places, and while we've not found any success in written correspondence, I do believe if we were to just take Fitz to one of these men, or societies, or... Well, they would not be able to deny what he is, how important he is."

Mr. Wiggan leaned forward, his elbows on his knees, his hands clasped before him. Mildred recognized the position as one he often took when he was overwhelmed by too many thoughts and questions, and he would need to release some of them soon or panic would take over. "I do not disagree with you about his staying here." He glanced at Fitz just as the dragon snorted softly in his sleep. "A few more months —"

"A few more weeks," Mildred put in.

"—and he may very well become unmanageable. We have no history of such a creature against which to compare his behavior, or to use as a guide for his future development. However."

The "however" sat there at the end of the sentence, somehow as heavy and final as the period that followed it, despite the implication that more words would follow.

"Here," Mrs. Babbinton said, clearing away the empty cups and plates from the table. "I will go and make up the spare room for you." She patted Mildred's arm. "Allow you a few hours of rest before you have to go home again, hmm?"

After clattering away with the cups, the housekeeper departed from the kitchen, leaving Mildred and Mr. Wiggan to deal with the "however" that still lingered between them.

"I do not think putting him in the hands of someone with a more scientific leaning would be the best choice for him. I've been considering our various options over the last few days, and I fear they might misuse him," he said, speaking the word "misuse" in a tone that made Mildred suspect he had discarded several other words she might not have liked to hear in reference to Fitz. "At best, he will be treated with all the pomp and attention of a starring attraction in a zoo. At worst, they might wish to study him." He blinked. "In ways that might not be beneficial to his overall health." He cleared his throat and raised his eyebrows, translating "beneficial to his overall health" into the phrase "poke him and prod him and possibly gut him like a freshly caught trout in order to see how he functions."

"So." Mildred let her gaze wander towards the table. The tea and the biscuits had been cleared away, and she mourned their absence while her fingers fidgeted with worry. "What do you suggest?"

"Seeing as how you were able to spend some time at your great uncle's home and search through more of his writings, I had hoped you would be able to present us with a well-timed epiphany."

"If my Great Uncle Forthright were still alive..." Mildred began, and then faltered to a stop. Because even a large estate complete with water features and woods and acres upon acres of land roaming with all manner of Warwickshire wildlife would not be able to contain a dragon who could up and fly away with a lift and twitch of his wings. Or set the woods and the Warwickshire wildlife alight with a few snarls of flame from his mouth.

"Wait." She did not know why she said that, as Mr. Wiggan had made no move to shift from his current position. But she made a gesture towards him as if to keep him in place, that push of the hands through the air with the palms flat and turned towards the individual in question, before rushing to the front of the house in search of her bags.

She found them, set just inside the door, still carrying the aroma of travel about them (the 'aroma of travel' in this case being 'horse and dirt'). It was a journal she searched for, one of the personal volumes that had belonged to her Great Uncle Forthright. She had not meant to bring it with her, seeing as how she expected it carried some sentimental value for Mr. Gorman, but in the confusion of Belinda and Mr. Hawthorne's disappearance and a hasty attempt to set her room at Exley Hall to rights in the midst of equally hasty packing for the journey back to Upper Plimpton, it had been bundled up with her things and loaded onto the carriage. It wasn't until they were halfway home and she was in need of something to read for an hour or three that she found the book and made a mental note to see it returned to Mr. Gorman's keeping once she was home again.

She hurried back to the kitchen, her fingers already marking the place that had been marked so frequently during her brief stay in Warwickshire. Like a child showing off a treasure, she plunked the book on the table, the pages falling open as easily as autumn leaves knocked from the branches of a tree. "Look at this." She pointed to the illustration of Wales, done in her great uncle's hand. "It could be nothing, nothing at all. I found no other mention of it in any of his writings. But this, done in such detail, and here—" she tapped her finger under the words written across the top of the page.

"Nyth y Ddraig," Mr. Wiggan read, in an accent that sounded more Welsh to Mildred's ears than her own sorry attempt (though she had never heard a Welsh person speak in her life, so her opinion on how one should sound when speaking a language of which she knew nothing was based more on fancy than anything staking its claim in reality). "What does it mean?"

"I had a moment and looked up the translation," Mildred said, her exhaustion pushed aside and a fresh wind of excitement roaring into its place. "I meant to do more research about it, but then…" She waved her hand. "– Belinda, etc. But! I believe it means something along the lines of 'Nest of Dragons' or 'Dragon's Nest.'"

Mr. Wiggan rubbed his brow with the heel of his hand. "We are talking about Wales. They do have a certain appreciation of dragons over there. It might not mean anything."

"But why is it featured in one of my uncle's journals? And marked with such care? And—" she pressed on when Mr. Wiggan drew in a breath to speak. "—if Wales is already known for its *appreciation of dragons*," she made sure to italicize as she said it, "then why make a note of this at all? What separates it as being remarkable?"

"Well," Mr. Wiggan said.

"And," Mildred said, before he could finish curling his tongue around the first 'l' of his 'well', "I looked at a map of Wales while I was there. Several, actually. And do you know what they all had in common?"

Mr. Wiggan waited for her reply in the way that most people waited for a reply they knew would be as unpreventable as the passage of time or a sock losing itself in the laundry.

"This Nyth y Ddraig? I could not find it on a single map. It was as if it does not even exist!"

Mr. Wiggan scratched at the back of his neck while avoiding Mildred's gaze. "Perhaps that could be because it doesn't exist?"

Mildred sighed, and slumped into her chair, and was torn

between wanting to sleep and wanting to eat and wanting to spend the next seventeen hours talking about mysterious locations hidden away in the Welsh countryside. "A few months ago, I would most likely be in agreement with you. But a few months ago, I did not believe dragons existed. I did not believe that I would be able to stand up to my sister and leave my home and…" She reached for the journal and spun it around so that it faced her. "If we decide against sending him to London or some place on the continent, perhaps he could find a home in Wales. Perhaps this is even why my uncle was interested in this Nyth y Ddraig. Perhaps —"

Mr. Wiggan held up a hand to stop her before she could "perhaps" her way into another dozen musings. "Perhaps," he said carefully. "This could be where the egg came from originally?"

She ran her thumb over the drawing, the miniature triangles sketched in the place of mountains. "Dragon's nest," she said. "And where does one find eggs?"

"In a nest," Mr. Wiggan said.

Mildred looked at him. He was smiling. With the eagerness of a child, she thought. And she realized then just how much she had missed him during her stay at Exley Hall.

"There we are," Mrs. Babbinton said as she returned to the kitchen, her apron bearing a few additional streaks of grime. "There's a fire in your room, and I've turned down the blankets for you already. Your smaller bags I've taken upstairs, as well. Mr. Wiggan can help with anything else you may be in need of. Oh," she added, touching Mildred's wrist as she was about to leave. "And I'll see to Fitz for the night, make certain there's a lovely pile of blankets for him to burrow into."

"Thank you." Mildred snapped up the journal, wished a good night to both Mr. Wiggan and Mrs. Babbinton— despite the faint light of dawn washing the windows in a pale gray hue—and went upstairs to the spare room. There was little to recall after that. She undressed, did her own bit of burrowing into the narrow bed (not as narrow as her bed at Ashby Lodge, but still rather diminished in comparison to her quarters at Exley Hall) and let her eyes drift closed as she watched the flames of the freshly-built fire, letting them guide her into dreams of dragons breathing gouts of flame across the land.

CHAPTER THIRTY-ONE

*When I fall into maudlin thoughts of the years
wasted because of my own cowardice, my own
reticence in making my interest known, I remind
myself of the verse: "To every thing there is a
season, and a time to every purpose under the
heaven... a time to keep silence, and a time to
speak."*

*Now is my time to speak, and I will say that
Miss Mildred Percy is the finest woman-no, the
finest person I have ever been blessed to know.*

-from Mr. Claude Wiggan's personal journal

Mildred did not expect any kind of grand welcome when she returned to Ashby Lodge, her sister's home. *Her sister's home*, she was sure to add. Even in her own thoughts. No matter that it had also been her own place of residence for near seventeen years, never had she come close to forming any sort of permanent attachment to the building. (Ah! There's another clue. *Building.* As if it were nothing more than stoicism rendered in wood and bricks and mortar, incapable of drawing any feelings of affection from its inhabitants.) But in the beginning, her stay had always been referred to as an impermanent thing, and so she had not been able to frame her time there as something meant to last, despite its eventual measurement in years and then decades.

What she did expect upon her return was to be ignored.

Set aside. Perhaps belittled with an additional touch of criticism. In other words, the usual.

What she did not anticipate was stepping into the eye of a storm. And unfortunately, she was the last, lone tree that had yet to be ripped to splinters by the ferocious maelstrom that was Diana.

"This is your fault!" Diana said. It was not the first thing Diana said to Mildred—the first words to come out of her sister's mouth as she stepped through the door had sounded very much like a muttered version of "Oh, bollocks"—but it was the first thing that could be defined as a full sentence and also an attempt at a conversation.

"My...?" was all Mildred was able to say before Diana launched into her next statement.

"You"–this followed by a jab of Diana's finger into Mildred's chest– "set a precedent! Running off across the country! Leaving me here, all alone, to manage an entire household–"

Mildred thought of Mr. Muncy. Matthew and Nettie. The entire household of servants, both indoor and outdoor.

"—and then Belinda takes it into her head to disappear! And with a man! And from whom do you believe she learned such behavior?"

Mildred did not immediately reply. With her sister, one did not always know if the question posed was the type that required an answer. "Um," she said, falling into former habits of speech before she had even managed to remove her bonnet and gloves. "Mrs. Babbinton is not a man," she said lamely.

"But Mr. Wiggan is!" Diana cried, almost in triumph at her ability to tell men and women apart. "And you have spent far too much time in his company these last weeks. It has become most unseemly, and I'm sure has been quite the topic of gossip among the inhabitants of Upper Plimpton."

Mildred doubted the friendship between a middle-aged vicar and a middle-aged woman would elicit much gossip, even in a town as small (or large, depending on the day) as Upper Plimpton. And any talk that had ensued was no doubt already stifled by the disappearance of a seventeen-year-old young woman in the company of a handsome—at the time, seeing as how Mildred could not know how well Mr. Hawthorne's facial wounds would recover from Fitz's attack —young gentleman to whom she was not married.

"Now I have no idea what has become of her," Diana continued, her voice thickening, fingers retrieving a lace-edged handkerchief from some hidden location along the edges of her dress. "I have told Mr. Muncy that he needs to find her, but how can he manage it if I do not know where she has gone?"

Diana had cried her way into the sitting room and dropped into an armchair overdecorated with cushions. Mildred considered leaving her sister to her tears (false or real, she did not take the time to check) but as she was also the only person in the vicinity who had knowledge of Belinda's last known location, she was compelled to follow in Diana's sobbing wake.

"Did she leave any note? Any indication of where she was going?"

Diana shook her head, chin quivering. "Nothing. Not a word. I interrogated the servants, I-I asked the children again and again if they had seen or heard anything, but... No. She simply disappeared. The only reason I knew she had gone intentionally was because several of her favorite gowns and slippers were missing as well. Oh, but she did not take the white muslin with the green piping! And you know how much it always favored her complexion! But she is out there, somewhere, with That Man, and he would never have even set foot in this house had it not been for you!"

It was not an unusual occurrence for her sister to blame her for whatever ill deed had befallen the family. Did someone have a fever? Mildred must have left a window open or let one of the children play outside without a hat or scarf. Was the soup too thick or the roast overdone? Mildred must have distracted one of the servants causing them to neglect their attention to the food. Foul weather on a day when Diana wished it to be fine? Mildred, somehow.

And now a decision lay before Mildred, to tell Diana what she knew of Belinda's activities after leaving Upper Plimpton in Mr. Hawthorne's company, or to pretend ignorance over the entire matter. The former would open up myriad questions about *why* Belinda had followed Mildred to Exley Hall and *why* she had taken it upon herself to disappear again and *why* Mr. Hawthorne would now have to be described as looking like he had come out poorly in a duel that claimed scissors as the weapons of choice.

And it would also push Mildred to the limits of how much she could or would tell her sister about Fitz.

She would not be believed, of course. So she would bear the blame for her niece's disappearance in addition to having the accusation of fashioning outrageous lies lobbed at her.

Mildred ducked her head. "How are the children?" she asked. Because she did care about them, she realized. And hoped they would not be too sad when she told them that Fitz would soon have to go away. Rather far away, more than likely.

"Oh, they are..." Diana's gaze skimmed the ceiling above her, as if she had recently acquired the talent of seeing through walls. "... somewhere around here. It is so hard to keep things in order when there is so much uproar." The weight on that last word. She could have exchanged "uproar" for "Mildred, somehow" and the implication would have remained the same. "And Mr. Muncy will not come out of his study, and Mrs. Haverstick came to call yesterday, supposedly in an effort to be neighborly, but I know she was seeking out information about Belinda. As if that woman could not fuel the gossip fires in this town for an entire year with all of the scandal she has stored away in her thick head..."

Mildred left her then. She did not wait for a lull in the conversation or a clear dismissal from Diana's side of things. She turned and walked away, away from her sister's sputtering into silence, out of the room, up the stairs, and finally into the nursery where Matthew and Nettie were occupied in building a fort from every stick of furniture and every stitch of blanket and sheet dragged from their beds.

"Aunt Mildred!" they cried, and leapt towards her, Matthew catching his heel on a corner of the fort and dragging half of it along with him.

"How is Fitz?" Nettie asked.

"Can we see him?" Matthew asked.

"Will Mrs. Babbinton give us cake?" Nettie asked.

Mildred could have cried. Well, she did cry, a little. That slight burn of tears at the corners of her eyes, quickly blinked away as her smile stretched wide. Ah, but to be a child again, concerned with little else but dragons and cake while their own household fell to pieces around them, pulled apart as easily as their makeshift fort.

"He is well," Mildred replied, addressing the first query tossed at her. "And yes, and more than likely," she added, tackling questions second and third.

"Can we visit today?" Matthew asked.

"But Aunt Mildred has only just returned," Nettie told her brother in a loud whisper. "Mama might not wish for her to —"

"Have you both had your breakfast?" Mildred interrupted, still smiling.

"Yes, Aunt Mildred," Nettie said.

"Warm scones with honey!" Matthew said.

"Then fetch your shoes and your hats," she told them, her words punctuated by her sister shouting at one of the servants downstairs. "We shall go directly!"

***

It was not until Mildred arrived at the vicarage—which she had only left an hour or so before—that she wondered if perhaps she should have stayed away for a little while longer, giving Mrs. Babbinton and Mr. Wiggan a chance to rest after she had kept them both up half the night with her return. But Mrs. Babbinton opened the door with all the alacrity of someone blessed with a full night's sleep, ushering them into the house and leading them directly to the kitchen where the yeasty aroma of freshly baked things was there to greet them.

"Mr. Wiggan is in the garden," Mrs. Babbinton informed Mildred before she could even form the question herself. "I suspect he has not slept at all, and merely retired to his study while you and I slept. Nor do I believe he found any rest before you arrived last night, so I shall warn you that his thoughts are scattered this morning."

If "scattered" could have been presented in tableau form, then Mr. Wiggan would have taken the prize for clarity of display. He sat on the ground—on a blanket, beneath a tree—his legs crossed in front of him, while stacks of papers and books decorated the entire surface of the blanket like apple blossom petals blown about the garden. Behind him, Fitz fretted in his pen, scraping through the layers of straw to the bare ground beneath, plucking up fat worms and grubs from the damp earth in reflection of the chickens doing the same in their own pen on the other side of the property.

Mildred halted halfway across the garden, the joyous cries of the children—Mrs. Babbinton had just presented them with warm buns and jam—echoing behind her. It was a pretty scene before her, the shadows of puffy white clouds drifting across everything, lending greater animation to a picture that would have presented fine fodder for an artist's paints or pencils.

It was a moment she would commit to memory without realizing it. The momentary peace of it, the mundanity, as if it were merely a part of a day that belonged to a long run of days that would play out in the same way, over and over again.

"Mr....?" She began, but stopped. He did not raise his head at first, so engrossed he appeared to be in copying notes from a book laid open in his lap. At that instant, with his hair and his clothing all disheveled from lack of rest, his mouth moving quietly around words he transcribed to a notebook with a short nub of pencil, the voices of the children and Mrs. Babbinton floating through the air around them, while Fitz snuffled in the dirt for a snack...

Well.

She walked the rest of the way to the blanket, her shadow falling across Mr. Wiggan's work. His hand stilled first, in the middle of a word ("border," for those exercising their curiosity), and then he looked up, shielding his eyes with his hand to see Mildred more clearly.

"I take it things did not go well with your sister?"

Mildred twisted her fingers together. She still wore her gloves and her bonnet, as if she could prevent herself from feeling tied to any one place by simply keeping the accessories of travel attached to her person. "I've yet to unpack," she said, and knelt down to join him on the blanket, or at least a small corner of the blanket that was not covered with his work. "But the children were eager to see Fitz again, perhaps even more eager to sample a helping of Mrs. Babbinton's cooking." She did not sigh. She wanted to, the breath was already there, in her lungs and ready to heave its way out of her in a plaintive manner. Instead, she let her gaze roam across the papers spread out around Mr. Wiggan, her attention catching on a rather large, rather detailed map.

"Wales?" She raised her eyes to his face. "Mrs. Babbinton mentioned that you had not slept. What have you been studying?"

"I think..." he said. And he licked his lips, and he set his elbows on his knees, and he pushed his hands slowly through the air in front of him as if he were clearing a path for what he was about to say. "We need to go there, to the place on your uncle's map. It may not even exist, but we won't know until we see for ourselves."

We. Not himself. Not her alone. But '*we.*' Plural. More than one.

"B-But when? When would you leave?" She did not know why she quickly switched the burden of the journey to his shoulders, but it helped to keep her own flutter of anxiety at a reasonable distance.

"I imagine it would have to be as soon as possible." He glanced over his shoulder, at Fitz still snuffling through the straw and stretching out his wings in a thoroughly threatening motion when a cricket had the impertinence to leap at his nose. "He is only going to continue growing larger and larger. And with his ability to fly, and to…"

"Burn things," Mildred added, filling the void left open by Mr. Wiggan's momentary reluctance to mention the dragon's fiery talents.

"… and that," he said, and swallowed. "Well, we have to go before it becomes too difficult to transport him. And at the rate at which he is growing, I am loath to wait more than a week."

"A week?" She thought of her bags sitting in her little room at Ashby Lodge, still packed. "But what of your sermons? Your students?"

He tipped his head from side to side, though Mildred felt certain he had already weighed all of the options and alternatives during his sleepless night. "Mr. Dalton, the curate, can readily step in for as long as is needed. And Mrs. Babbinton will be here, to help things along in her steady way."

Mildred did not say it aloud, but she did not much care for the idea of Mr. Wiggan going anywhere for any length of time without Mrs. Babbinton by his side. Even taking the housekeeper to Warwickshire with her for several days had seemed tantamount to tampering with the laws of nature.

"And you would take Fitz with you?"

Mr. Wiggan reached down and began sorting through some of his papers. Not so much because he was searching for a specific note or page, Mildred realized, but because he was in desperate need of giving his hands a task with which to keep them occupied. "That seems to be the final point giving me the most strife. If he were to remain here, then Mr. Dalton would have to be made aware of his existence. And from what I know of Mr. Dalton, he is not the sort to take kindly to a biting, flapping, incendiary creature cavorting around in the garden beneath his bedroom window. Which would mean he would have to come with us, but that is a long journey, and with no guarantee of success at the end of it. This Dragon's Nest place..." he thumbed through a few of his notes. "We would be taking a considerable chance on its very existence. And then what?"

Mildred shrugged. "Do you mean if it doesn't exist?"

"Or even if it does. Miss Percy," he said, and leaned forward, eating up the distance between them and turning the wide expanse of the garden and great British sky into a cozy little space for only the two of them. "Have you considered what Fitz's existence could mean?"

This would be the moment to confess that she had not, at least not on the scale she supposed Mr. Wiggan was referring to. Beyond how the dragon had affected her own daily life... no, she had not given it much consideration at all.

"What if there are more of them?" Mr. Wiggan's words sounded so simple, as if he were asking after the number of biscuits left or if there was enough raspberry cordial to go around.

"More..." Mildred's mouth scooped the word out of the air, nearly overwhelmed to choking on the size of it, the implication behind those four letters. "... like Fitz?"

"You must admit, the chances of there being one, lone egg are more rare than if there were an entire..." He paused, brow crinkling in thought. "What is the word for a group of eggs? Not a litter, no…"

"A clutch?"

"Yes! A clutch! But imagine, a full hatching of young dragons, roaming about the Welsh mountains."

And so Mildred did imagine it. She had never been to Wales, but it was easy enough to conjure up the picture of dark hills, streaked with fog, streaked with seams of coal (as if it just spilled out of cracks in the ground), rain slashing sideways while a break in the clouds far off on the horizon shot the background through with beams of red and gold. And there, above the peaks of the highest hills, a few dragons circled, their wings spread, riding on the torrent of air pushing the last dregs of the storm through the valley.

It was all suitably dramatic and in need of some grand musical accompaniment (something vaguely German, possibly with horns and loud drums) and Mildred experienced a bit of a shiver, despite the warmth of the sun on her back. "But if there is nothing there? If there is no Dragon's Nest?"

He sighed, visibly deflated. "I do not know. We've been burdened with a rather unprecedented task, I'm afraid."

Mildred picked up the last of his notes, one that was nearly carried away by a light shift in the breeze. "You do not have to take so much of this upon yourself, you know. It was my inheritance, it should be my responsibility. I cannot have you leaving your post here in Upper Plimpton to go gallivanting about the country in search of imagined dragons." She closed her mouth. What she was about to say tasted bitter on her tongue, and yet she knew she would speak the words aloud, as traitorous to her recent stint of independence as they were. "My sister will not want me to leave again, and so soon. She blames me for everything with Belinda, and then there is Matthew and Nettie, and I would hate to make them think I am deserting them."

Mr. Wiggan reached across the short distance between

them and laid his hand on her arm. His fingers were bare, and his touch was warm, even through the sleeve of her gown. She looked at his hand—goodness, his hand was large —and it was a lovely appendage, she had to admit. A strange thing, that something as simple and everyday as a man's hand could catch her attention and hold it, her gaze taking in so many of the details—the soft brown hairs on the back of his hand and disappearing beneath his cuff, the streaks of gray from his pencil smeared across his fingertips, a small cut on one knuckle—before she would let it go and look at his face again.

"Not long ago," he said, and his voice had deepened, scratched and breaking from tiredness. "I was walking home. It was late, completely dark outside, and I ran into a woman who was dragging a trunk out of her house in order to hide it from her sister. I had noticed her before then, I will admit. I saw her in church, always in the shadow of her family, always herding the children about and seeming to cow to the voices of others."

Mildred winced. She did not like to hear him say this. But it hurt because it was true, because she could not interrupt him and demand him to take it back, to accuse him of lying. She had been that person, the one he described. Quiet and subdued, doing as she was told, attempting to be the smallest, smoothest pebble that could drop into the water without producing a single ripple.

Good Lord, she did not want to go back to that.

"Mildred," he said.

Her name. He had never called her by her name before, that name, and now she realized she always wanted him to call her Mildred even though she had always hated every syllable of it up until that very moment.

"I do not think your niece and nephew will want you to suffer on their behalf. I believe they will want you to have a life of your own, one not shaped by their mother's whims." He glanced over her shoulder, at the children in question currently trooping into the garden. "Of course, you could inquire as to their opinion on the matter, though I daresay they will most likely agree with me."

She watched Matthew and Nettie as they went to Fitz's pen, their hands full of treats for him. Mrs. Babbinton watched from behind, wiping her hands on her apron as she issued warnings for them to be careful and to watch their fingers and to give the poor dear some space after all of his time spent locked up inside of a basket, inside of a carriage over the last several days.

"I will speak with them," Mildred said, without looking away as Fitz opened his wings and let out an excited squawk as Nettie pushed a remarkably large piece of cold roasted chicken through the wires of the pen. "But I should let you know that I am only using them as an excuse." She looked at Mr. Wiggan. Could she call him something other than Mr. Wiggan? No, no. It did not feel right to do so yet, no matter that he had already used her name in a way that had felt like a secret shared. "I am frightened, you should know." She looked down again. He still had his hand on her arm, though his fingers had slid down so they were loosely wrapped around her wrist, the relaxed curve of his palm making her wonder if he had forgotten he had even touched her. "If I remain here in Upper Plimpton, in my sister's house, then I shall have a very clear idea of what each day should bring. But if I leave…"

"What do you want, then?"

Did she want safety? Did she want Fitz to be sent away so that she could stay in her little room, occasionally thumping her head on the slanted ceiling and watching as her niece and nephew grew and went away and left her there, an elderly woman who had never lived a day of her life for herself?

Or did she want–

"Aunt Mildred! Aunt Mildred!" Matthew called out from beside the pen. "Come and see! I think Fitz is growing his first tooth!"

Mr. Wiggan removed his hand from Mildred's arm. Mildred sat up, all proper and demure, as if nothing at all had occurred and no one had touched her or said her name— her first name, the name only her sister ever used regularly and in a way that sounded like milk gone sour on a warm summer day—and stood and brushed the grass from her skirt and performed another dozen little movements meant to separate herself from that quiet moment beneath the tree, on the blanket, with Mr. Wiggan.

"I shall let you know what I decide," she said. And she smiled for some reason, though the expression felt false on her cheeks. "Now," she announced in a louder voice, one meant to sound its way to the children. "Let us see this tooth, hmm?"

CHAPTER THIRTY-TWO

I did not set out to do what I have accomplished. I did not believe myself to be an adventuress, at heart. I did not know I possessed a strength greater than what others fooled me into believing I had. But then I think of a simple dragon egg, tucked away in a dark trunk, as still and quiet as any ordinary stone. Unremarkable and underestimated. But inside that stone there rested an exceptional creature, one that had only been lying dormant until the time came for it to burst forth from its shell, and —

Oh, I do not even know what I am going on about. It is late and I should have been in bed hours ago. No doubt I shall rip this page out in the morning once I look back and see what the dire combination of old age, insomnia, and a freshly-sharpened quill can produce.

-from Miss Mildred Percy's personal journal

The letter arrived in the morning, as most letters are wont to do. Mildred was not sure why letters had a tendency to make an appearance at the beginning of one's day rather than at some other point, or why the Royal Mail thought it a better idea to flip the coin of good news or bad news at the general populace before they had finished their eggs and coffee. But the letter came—tucked in with the rest of the newspapers and post—just as the family was sitting down for breakfast. Mr. Muncy slid behind his wall of the news from London, while Diana looked through the various cards and missives until she came upon The Letter (the one this entire paragraph has been shaped around) and everything stopped.

Well, it was the shriek from Diana that put a stop to everything, rather than any power wielded by the letter itself. Matthew and Nettie both ducked down in their seats. Mr. Muncy let a corner of his newspaper droop, the better to peer out from behind it. And Mildred simply held her breath and waited.

Because the letter was from Belinda. Mildred recognized the handwriting. She had taught Belinda that handwriting, and so there was no mistaking the dips and curves and careless slashes of every letter scratched across its front.

It had been four days since Mildred had returned to Upper Plimpton. Six days, then, since she had seen Belinda and Mr. Hawthorne. She had said nothing to her family of encountering them at Exley Hall, nor had she told Diana about Fitz. And she had not breathed a word of Mr. Wiggan's intention to leave for Wales on the morrow (or that she herself had yet to decide whether she would be travelling with him).

Mildred looked at the letter in her sister's hands with the same trepidation of watching the rattling lid of a pot about to boil over. What would be Belinda's news? Would there be any mention of Exley Hall? Of Mildred? Of a small dragon tossed from a window and catching the night air beneath its wings? She held her fork and her knife in her hands, a crumbling bit of sausage falling from the tines of the fork as she waited.

"She is married."

Mildred set down her fork and her knife. Her sister continued to read, but in silence, only doling out little morsels of information at a time.

"To Mr. Hawthorne!"

"In Scotland? No, no, she does not say where they are!"

"We are not to expect her to return to Wiltshire at any point in the foreseeable future?" She turned the page over, but the letter was brief, barely covering one side of the paper. "Oh, how could she do this to us. Ungrateful child!"

And then she burst into tears.

Mildred pushed her plate away, stood up, and quietly beckoned the children to follow her out of the room. It was to be an easy escape, take them out for a walk or into the garden or anywhere that was not the dining room and therefore did not contain their mother holding a letter from her eldest daughter proclaiming the (scant) details of her marriage to someone Diana had already dismissed as a thoroughly unmarriageable man.

But Diana was apparently not inclined to allow them such effortless means of extrication. "Go upstairs," she said to the children, her voice gurgling in her throat. "Both of you. But Mildred," she added, then wiped at her eyes with the corner of her napkin before a fresh flow of tears cascaded from the swollen corners. "I will speak with you, if you please."

If you please was an odd phrase to be put into use. It implied that Mildred should only stay to speak with her sister if she wished it, if the prospect of doing so would bring her pleasure. Mildred, of course, knew she would rather have her teeth drawn by an inebriated man bearing a rusted pair of pliers than remain behind in the dining room to speak with Diana. But she chivvied the children upstairs, and she stood by the door, waiting to see if her sister would speak her piece in front of Mr. Muncy or if she was not inclined to have an audience.

"Come with me," Diana said, still watery.

Ah, so no audience then.

"No," Mildred said, after her sister had pushed past her, striding away without a backwards glance, so strong was her confidence that she would be obeyed.

Diana turned, eyes smudged in the muted light of the hall. "Whatever you wish to say to me, you can say it here. I see no need for secrecy."

"Very well." Diana returned to the dining room. "Mr. Muncy?" she said, and waited for a flicker of life from behind the newspaper to show that her husband had heard. "Perhaps you can give us some privacy?"

"No." Twice in one minute Mildred had spoken that word, and to her sister, no less. Now was most likely the time to brace herself, for surely an apocalyptic horseman was about to trip over their doorstep and beg for a cup of tea.

"No?" Pronounced as if she were utterly unfamiliar with those two letters used in conjunction with one another.

"Mr. Muncy can stay, if he likes." Mildred glanced at the newspaper, shivering slightly at the edges, either because the hands holding it had begun to tremble or the person behind the pages was smothering some desire to laugh or vibrate with fear. "There should be nothing you have to say that you cannot say in front of him."

Her sister seemed prepared to argue that point, but she pulled her lips into a thin line, produced a low "hmm" of sound from behind her truncated mouth, and began to pluck at the corners of her napkin, now bearing darkened streaks of effluence from her eyes and nose. "I gave you a place in my home. Because you were my sister. Because it was my duty to take you in after our father died."

Mildred had heard all of these words before, in an assortment of presentations, though the meaning was always the same.

Diana sniffed, then blew her nose, then made a very indecorous show of wiping her nostrils across the back of her hand. "Now Belinda has gone and done *this!*" She gestured towards the letter, still lying open on the table.

"And I cannot see how our family will recover from the stain on our respectability. For her to run off with some strange man from London, to cast this household in scandal, and all because of you and your silly inheritance and our foolish uncle and you and the vicar and your... " She sputtered to a halt, half in tears, half spitting out her words like poisoned darts flung across the room. "I do not know what to do with you," she finished, and turned away, her arms crossing over her chest.

And that seemed to be the trouble, Mildred realized. She did not know what to do with herself. At the moment she felt a bit like a ship, unanchored, just drifting along and waiting for a good wind to catch up her sails and send her off to the nearest horizon.

"If you are to stay here," Diana said, her voice gaining strength and shedding some of its warbling. "Then I must have your assurance that there will be no more visits to the vicarage. No more guests of indiscriminate origins. No more *travelling*," she added in a tone that elevated (or lowered, depending on one's ecclestiastical leanings) any sort of mobility beyond the borders of Upper Plimpton or Wiltshire to a level accompanying the other deadly sins. "I cannot risk your influence tainting Matthew and Nettie as they grow older. You are already much too free with them. If you wish to stay in my home—"

"No." It was the third repetition that seemed to do the trick. The rule of three apparently even applied to monosyllabic utterances. "I thank you for the time you have given me here, and for taking me in when I was most in need. But I do not think my presence here is as necessary as it once was. As you said, Matthew will be off to school soon, and with Belinda newly married, that will leave you with only Nettie to look after. Surely, you will be able to manage that without my influence."

"What?" Diana spoke the word, then stood there, mouth hanging open as if all the muscles in the lower half of her face had deserted her. "Are you leaving?"

Mildred had never unpacked her bags. She had left them at the end of her bed, only pulling out the few things she needed from day to day, leaving the rest folded and tucked and stored away because...

Oh, she knew this was how it would all end. Didn't she? She had spent the last several days pretending she might stay, that she might quietly slip back into her previous life of caring for her sister's children, enduring her sister's criticisms, watching as her sister's family cowered away from her—hiding behind newspapers, running off to marry the first available gentleman to cross their doorstep—rather than make any move to engage.

Mildred saw the years of a possible life stretched out before her, caring for Nettie—and Matthew, when he was home from school—another decade given away. And then Nettie would be married and Matthew would find a wife and then...

And then?

Diana would glory in being a mother-in-law, a grandmother, in moving on to the next stage in her life. While Mildred would what? Sit in the corner and embroider things? Fade into the background until there was no more notice taken of her than the dust on the windowsill or a forgotten book tucked on an out-of-the-way shelf?

"Yes," Mildred replied, biting off the word before her voice could tremble on it. "I do not think it wise for me to stay here anymore."

Diana shook her head, her face a perfect artist's rendering of the word "aghast." "Where will you go? You don't have anyone."

And that, Mildred understood, was why she had to leave. "I have a dragon," she said, and took a huge amount of pleasure in the confusion that contorted its way across her sister's features. "Now, if you will excuse me, I need to finish packing."

She was halfway up the stairs before Diana shook herself back to attention and followed. "Wait. Wait! You cannot do this! Consider the fresh scandal you will provoke! And leaving me here to suffer it all!

Mildred did not turn around. She continued up the stairs, around the corner, down the hall that narrowed as it went, to her little door that opened to her little room that had never truly felt like her own in all of its seventeen years of use.

"Where will you even go?!" Diana shrieked in her wake, very much like a bird screaming because the worm it wanted to harry had disappeared again underground.

And at that, Mildred turned. She blocked the doorway to her room—not a terrific feat, as the door was not extraordinarily large and Mildred had never made claims to be a slip of a thing—and faced her sister, feeling tall and very much the eldest child of the family for the first time in a very long time. "I am going on an adventure," Mildred said, and shut the door in Diana's face.

***

As fine a place as that would be to end this first volume of Mildred's story, there are—as with most things in life—a few niggling details to be sorted away first.

She did indeed finish packing, taking more of her things with her than had gone along to Exley Hall. She could not bring everything, and as she looked about her room, her blankets and pillows and the accumulated items of her life still scattered here and there, on her bed and shelves and tucked away in drawers, she wondered how many of those things she would ever see again.

She said goodbye to the children. Matthew cried. Nettie sniffed but held her chin higher and said a very solemn farewell along with the extraction of a promise from Mildred that Fitz would be very well taken care of. And also that there would have to be letters. "You must write to us," Nettie announced in a loud whisper. "Or how else will we know how many teeth Fitz has?"

Diana refused to have the carriage brought around for Mildred or her bags. Mr. Muncy, in a rare showing of independent thought, called for the carriage himself and ordered the servants to load her belongings onto it. (Mildred's belongings, that is. Not his wife's. Though there should not be any blame ascribed to the reader for making that mistake.)

Mildred thanked him, wished him well, and made it clear that she would walk into Upper Plimpton while the carriage rumbled on ahead. And that was that, her departure from Ashby Lodge made complete.

She did not know why she chose to walk to the vicarage rather than ride in the carriage, other than that it was a fine day (Wiltshire had been enjoying too many fine days of late, which meant that a surfeit of less than fine days must surely be waiting to sweep in and make the summer a dreary one) and she thought it might be nice to stroll along the streets of the village one final time before leaving for Wales.

For Wales.

The carriage had arrived at the vicarage before her, so there was no surprise in Mr. Wiggan's or Mrs. Babbinton's face as she came up behind it.

"I had hoped," was all Mrs. Babbinton said, before giving Mildred a hug and bustling back inside to make some tea.

Mildred nodded at Mr. Wiggan, who made no great display of shock or happiness at her being there and with all of her things packed into various bags and one large trunk. He simply nodded in return, as if the entire matter of her going to Wales with him had already been well discussed between them so why would there be a need to go over it all again now?

And then there was tea, and Mrs. Babbinton offered some cake, and Mildred remembered that she had not finished her breakfast (the arrival of Belinda's letter had seen to that) and the exertion of packing and walking to the vicarage had left her with a healthier appetite than she normally sported at only ten o'clock in the morning.

So there was tea and there was cake, and along with this was an announcement that Mildred did not find at all surprising despite Mrs. Babbinton's behavior to the contrary.

"I will be going with you!" she said, and clapped her hands together, flour puffing out from the impact as she paused in the middle of tucking a mound of dough into a bread pan. "I thought about it, you know, and I wondered whether the wisest decision would be for me to remain here or to travel along. And then I realized that I could not send the both of you out there—" Another burst of flour as she flicked her hand in a vaguely western direction. "—and without anyone to make certain all of your efforts were seen as respectable. I mean, a single gentleman and a single lady travelling alone together…" she tutted and returned her attention to her dough.

Mildred finished her cake and went out to see Fitz. The dragon was asleep, and Mr. Wiggan informed her that he had been sleeping quite a bit over the last few days.

"I fear another bout of growing may be upon us," he said, as Mildred poked a finger through the wires of the pen and stroked the edge of Fitz's tail, the end of it just within her reach.

He had reached the size of a large housecat, though when he opened his wings, they nearly stretched from one side of the pen to the other.

"We'll have to make good time," Mildred said, and stood up again. "Or else he will outgrow the carriage." It was spoken in jest, but the underlying truth of it made Mildred draw in a quick breath. "So we leave tomorrow?" she asked, changing the subject before anxiety tightened its fingers around her throat.

"Before sunrise, if possible." He moved closer to Mildred. Well, actually he moved nearer to the pen, but the action placed him closer to Mildred as well. "I am glad you're coming," he said, and looked at her. In Mildred's mind, it was always a thing worth mentioning when Mr. Wiggan looked at her. Because he saw her, and she wondered if she would ever become accustomed to it.

"How could I not?" If Mildred had not used up all of her bravery with Diana that morning, perhaps she would have gone so far as to place her hand on Mr. Wiggan's arm, or eat up a bit more of the space left between them herself. But instead she stood where she was, her hands clasped in front of her, her chin ducked down as if she could not decide if she wanted to gaze boldly at him or look away. "We have been together on this from the beginning, since you helped me move my uncle's trunk into a shed late one evening. I cannot abandon you now."

Mildred did not know what might have happened next. Mr. Wiggan seemed to lean in towards her. Or perhaps she shifted towards him? Her breath caught, and her lips moved, and then—

Now, thousands of books before this one have gone into deep and detailed descriptions of the moment when their main characters have their first kiss. Dictionaries and thesauruses have been riffled through, adjectives have been tortured and variations on the word "moist" have been ruined for successive generations. Mildred, herself, had read dozens (possibly hundreds, if she were to go back and make an account of every romantic tale she had read since she was old enough to appreciate them) novels in which kissing (or at least a most unsubtle allusion to kissing) played an integral part to the overall storyline.

This (unless the author has a change of heart during a late-night editing session) will not be one of those novels.

That is not to say that all such suggestive excerpts will be wholly avoided in this narrative. But rather that this kiss— the first between Mildred and Mr. Wiggan, and so elevated in importance due to their respective roles in this story—was not at all remarkable apart from its inaugural nature. Mildred took a step forward. Mr. Wiggan did not take a step forward, but he also did not take a step back, and so his lack of change in position was taken as silent approbation of the unfolding events. Mildred placed one hand on his arm—more for balance than affection—and rose onto the balls of her feet and kissed him.

And that was all.

She stepped back again with such haste the entire incident could have been mistaken for her merely stumbling forward and then correcting herself. "I should..." she said, and gestured vaguely towards the house and Mrs. Babbinton (the latter having failed to witness the unremarkable kiss and so her reaction—or lack thereof—have no further bearing on the scene) before wishing she possessed wings of her own to take herself off in that direction. "I'm sorry." She tried to swallow, nearly choked on the effort, and attempted to cover the choke with a cough. "I should not have assumed that you would... I mean. Well."

Her gaze flicked up towards his. He looked very much as he had before, and yet slightly different, as though a quick windstorm had swept in and given him an appearance of vague disarray.

"A moment ago," she began again, feeling very pleased with her ability to speak full words without a hitch in her breath. "I may have overstepped certain boundaries when I allowed my emotions to overwhelm me. I apologize for having taken liberties with—"

The rest of what she had been planning to say (which was really just more dithering about having kissed him and whether or not he had been offended by her having kissed him) was silenced by the sudden and unforeseen act of Mr. Wiggan closing the distance between them and kissing her.

To save readers from having to endure labored descriptions of affection that may be off-putting to them, we will suffice it to say that the kiss was lovely and everything

Mildred had hoped and imagined a kiss would be. At some point in the future she would question why Mr. Wiggan displayed a higher level of expertise in kissing than she possessed, and she would spend a fair few hours in the middle of the night wondering where he had learned just how to do the things he did. But at the moment, she only concerned herself with the kiss, and his touch, and how everything seemed to have ceased to exist but for the two of them in the garden.

"Mildred," he said. Quietly, reverently, when the kissing bit was over and they simply stood together holding hands. "I may call you Mildred now? It is not too forward of me?"

She touched her forehead to his. All in all, it felt quite nice to have the freedom to do things like kiss him and hold his hands and have her face close enough to his so that the warm rush of his breath teased her cheek. "Does that mean I have to call you Claude?"

Mr. Wiggan (who will continue to be referred to as Mr. Wiggan in most cases, as his appreciation of his Christian name was not to be measured at anything nearing abundant levels) made a face that could be best described as "Discovered a rotted potato in the shadows of the pantry." "As long as I am counted as your friend, you may call me anything you like."

"My friend?" Oh, but wasn't he more than that? Mildred was not certain precisely where the levels of friend and acquaintance and companion lay. But 'friend' did not sound like it was quite enough. At least not anymore.

"Partner in adventure?" he suggested, his eyes gleaming.

"We are going on an adventure, are we not?"

"I suspect we have been journeying through one for some time, only we did not have our eyes open enough to see it."

She leaned forward again, and Mr. Wiggan drifted a bit towards her, and—

Fitz snorted in his sleep, sending out a small burst of flame and a large puff of smoke that drifted upwards before a turn of the air lifted it up and carried it out of the pen.

"Ah." Mr. Wiggan said, just as Mildred said something along the lines of "hmmph" before they both drew apart.

"So, are you ready to continue your adventure?" Mr. Wiggan asked, holding out his arm to her despite the fact neither of them had any inclination to leave the quiet little spot in which they stood.

"As ready as I will ever be," Mildred said, and they both watched as Fitz settled back into his straw, a thin line of smoke still streaming out of his nostrils as he snuffled his way to sleep again.

ACKNOWLEDGEMENTS

I'm not even certain how to begin this, because I'm worried I'll either ramble on for pages and pages about all the people I wish to thank, or I'll try to keep it short and forget someone really important and then lie awake at 3am forever pondering my appreciative shortcomings.

So let's see how this one goes.

I want to thank Kay Villoso, first of all. For always being there. For always listening. For her advice. Her patience. Her encouragement. Her jokes. These past few years have been Rough (capital "R") and she is a rock, an anchor, and whatever other compliments towards her sedentary qualities (yes, I know how that sounds) I could make. Thank you, thank you, thank you.

To the Terrible Ten, for making me laugh and just being awesome. For stepping in to lend a hand when things went absolutely bonkers.

To Bethan, for being such a constant supporter of this story since Day One, when all I had in my head was an idea about Miss Mildred Percy and a dragon egg and something-something about Wales, possibly, at an indiscernible point in the future.

To Mon Macairap. You brought Fitz to life with your amazing art. I still squeal every time I see the picture.

To too many other writers and friends to name individually (because I will forget someone and then there will be wailing and gnashing of teeth) who assured me there would be an audience for this silly little book that was a mixture of everything I loved (which meant I worried no one else would like it). Thank you for being there, floating through the interwebz during this very weird and surreal time of uncertainty.

To my children, because somehow I managed to write this book despite your constant requests for sandwiches (YOU ARE OLD ENOUGH TO MAKE THEM YOURSELF) or to wipe your bottoms (only the younger bottoms, thank goodness).

To my husband, who always gave me a space at his shop for writing when I needed it, when the libraries were closed and the streets were eerily empty and it was nice to simply be in another place with another person, face to face.

Thank you all, so much. Without you there would be no Miss Percy, and I don't even want to think about a world without her.

Printed in Great Britain
by Amazon